YOUNGER

YOUNGER

SUZANNE MUNSHOWER

THOMAS & MERCER

Published by Thomas & Mercer, Seattle
www.apub.com

Amazon, the Amazon logo, and Thomas & Mercer are trademarks of Amazon.com, Inc., or its affiliates.

ISBN-13: 9781477827758
ISBN-10: 1477827757

Cover design by David Drummond

Library of Congress Control Number: 2014952526

Printed in the United States of America

". . . we must be careful about what we pretend to be."

—Kurt Vonnegut

Prologue

Saturday, September 10, 2011

Anna was going over the flat one last time, making sure nothing of her would remain but some makeup, clothes, and a few books, when the bell downstairs rang. Hesitantly, she picked up the security phone by the front door.

"It's Pierre. Please, let me in." Her boss's voice was harsh, and when he arrived at the top of the stairs, he was red faced and fighting for breath, looking very unlike his usual urbane self. His eyes were sunken, his usually impeccably groomed hair hanging lank over his forehead.

"Are you all right?" she asked.

He closed the door behind him and leaned heavily against it, his attaché case clutched to his chest. "Of course. The Bentley's at the body shop, so I had Marina drop me off down the road and walked to make sure nobody was following. Some guy almost knocked me down coming around the corner . . . Just need to get my breath back." Pierre Barton sank down onto the sofa in the living room, his pretense of normality utterly wasted.

Anna wanted to scream, "Where have you been these past few days? Who do you think would follow you?" But she said only, "Would you like coffee? Just instant, I'm afraid. Or tea."

"Some water, thank you. Marina stopped at a Starbucks and got us cappuccinos to drink in the car."

When she came back from the kitchen, he was in the same position as when she'd left, head back, breathing labored. "Pierre?"

He grasped the water and gulped it down. "Sorry. I'm a mess. I'm just . . . I don't know what's going on, Anna, but it's bad. And it's spun out of control now."

"Just relax for a minute." Surreptitiously, she checked her watch. "What's happened?"

He stared at her with haunted eyes. "That couple you said followed you—"

She cut him off. "I saw the paper yesterday. I know they're dead."

"I promise you, I had nothing to do with anything. I know it needs to stop."

"What's 'it,' Pierre? Why are people dying? Are you behind this? Is Martin Kelm?"

"No, of course it's not me." He looked pained. "Not Kelm, either. No, no, my wife—"

"Yes?"

"Marina says Kelm can be trusted."

"And you? What do you say?"

"She—I don't know. I don't know anything anymore. But for your own safety, you should go back to America. The project is dead now. That's one thing I *did* kill."

"And Kelm? Who is Martin Kelm, Pierre?"

"Kelm? Marina . . ." He looked down at his hands, unmoving on his thighs. "Please," he said wearily, sounding parched, "more water. The coffee burnt my tongue." Slowly, as if hypnotized, he raised one hand to his mouth.

She picked up the glass and refilled it in the kitchen. She should stop badgering him until he recovered. He was making no sense, anyhow. The sound of a thud reached her as she turned from the sink. Had he left, slamming the door behind him?

She entered the living room, the glass of water in her hand. She was expecting to find the room empty. She wasn't expecting to find a body in the middle of it, splayed out on the Persian rug in front of the coffee table.

He lay on his back in front of the couch, his face a mottled gray and purple. "Pierre!" She rushed over and shook him, calling his name again.

Somehow, she managed not to drop the glass of water. Her heart pounding, she carefully set it down, then knelt, searching for a pulse. When she failed to find one, she grabbed her handbag from the table and fumbled for her compact. At another time, she might have been amused by her wild thought, *I'm from Los Angeles—I know what to do from the movies.* No mist appeared when she held the mirror up to the parted, blue-tinged lips, and the only sound was her own ragged breath.

"Pierre!"

She was sure he was dead, but she kept trying to find a pulse, first in his wrist again, then in his neck.

Nothing. Nothing.

She reached for the attaché case lying on the couch, then thought better of it. Instead, she rushed first to look out the window to see if anyone was watching the building. On this quiet, tree-lined street in London, a woman walked a corgi, a boy rode past on a bicycle, and a few cars drove by. *Good,* she thought, as if anything in her life could be good at that moment.

Swiftly, she went to the hall stand to grab the leather gloves she'd bought in anticipation of cooler weather. She removed a flash drive from her handbag, then pulled on the gloves before reaching for the attaché case on the couch and gingerly opening it. She removed Pierre's computer and took it back to the chair she'd been sitting on. Waiting for it to start up, she said a silent prayer, envisioning Barton sitting next to her in the Bentley after visiting his mother. She entered "MarieHeloise," his mother's name, in the password box and clicked. No. That wasn't it.

"C'mon, Pierre," she muttered. With trembling fingers, she typed "MarieHeloiseBeaumarchais" then "Marie_Heloise." Then "Marie_Heloise_Beaumarchais." Finally, the welcome screen flashed on.

She inserted the flash drive, avoiding even a glance at what lay on the floor.

It took only a few minutes to copy Barton's Word files and spreadsheets. Then she turned off the computer and slipped it back into the case. She plucked Barton's BlackBerry from his breast pocket, then put it back. Locked. She couldn't waste more time.

A closer inspection of the attaché yielded two current British passports, for Peter and Maria Kelm. The photos of Pierre and Marina Barton in them looked recent. Sick with fear but steely with resolution, she put both in her purse, which already held her American passport and her UK Tanya Avery passport. Only when she had everything in order did she telephone emergency services. "Heart attack!" she gasped, not having to feign the near-hysterical quaver in her voice. "I'm in South Kensington. Please hurry." She gave the dispatcher the address, then took the glass of water into the kitchen, carefully draining and drying it. She averted her eyes from the body as she passed.

It didn't take long for the ambulance to arrive. The look the two EMTs exchanged confirmed that her visitor was beyond help; still, they started CPR and strapped on an oxygen mask as they hustled the stretcher down the stairs.

"What hospital?" she called after them.

A last-minute check, a wipe-down, and she was ready to leave even before the ambulance siren had faded in the distance. She slipped on her jacket, tucked all her hair into her knit cap, then slung her backpack and handbag over her shoulder. She dropped the keys through the mail slot after locking up the apartment that had been her home these past nine weeks.

Downstairs, she steeled herself before opening the front door. She needed to look as if she weren't checking for spying eyes, yet appear worried and rushed. She took a deep breath, then walked out, went down the front steps, and strode quickly to the curb. She let the first black cab pass before flagging the second.

When the taxi stopped, she approached his open window and said loudly, "I need to go to Chelsea and Westminster Hospital, please!" before opening the back door and climbing in.

But once the taxi had turned the corner and traveled a few blocks with no sign of a tail, she told the driver, "I've changed my mind. Mayfair. The Green Park entrance to the Underground, all right?"

Thank God she'd already planned all this—minus the dead body. She knew which Tube train to take and where to get off and backtrack so there'd be less chance she'd be followed. She knew to the minute when she had to board the train at St. Pancras Station.

No one sped up behind as she was exiting the taxi or as she hurried down the stairs to the Underground. She got on the first train going south, then jumped off at the first stop and circled around to get one heading north to St. Pancras, where she paid cash for a ticket to Brussels before hurrying to the platform.

Just as the train was about to leave, she sent a quick text to Marina on her Barton Pharmaceuticals BlackBerry: "Pierre's had some kind of attack and been taken by ambulance to Chelsea and Westminster. I'm on my way." She signed it "Tanya."

On her iPhone, she sent another text. *D. Out of town for a few days' holiday. I'll be in touch. T.*

Then she was in a crowded second-class car on a high-speed train whisking her out of England and into whatever nightmare might be awaiting her.

She had a good idea what they'd do if they caught her. What she didn't know was who "they" were.

———————

While searching online the day before, Anna had decided on the late-morning Eurostar to Brussels. The two-hour trip seemed the fastest and easiest way of getting out of England and into a major transportation hub in order to disappear. She knew she'd have to keep on the move for now.

She'd always longed to see Bruges and Antwerp, but all she got of Belgium was an hour's worth of Brussels-Midi, not even the main station. Then she was on another train to Amsterdam, this time making a passage without border controls.

She'd been there once—decades before, but it seemed unchanged. When she arrived in the afternoon, she headed for the closest hostel offering private rooms. She located it near the red-light district, featuring an attached "coffee shop" where stoners could smoke pot or nibble hash brownies and a clerk she counted on being too laid-back to worry about a guest who said she'd come down with her passport after she dug it out of her bag. She paid cash in advance, plus the half-a-night's key deposit—required when she said she had no credit card—and a rental fee for sheets and towels.

Her room was spartan: a narrow bed and folding chair, partitioned-off sink and toilet, and a footlocker at the end of the bed. The last had a reprogrammable combination lock and was bolted to the floor for security. Into it she put everything important, including her laptop, BarPharm BlackBerry, and all her electronics except her iPhone and the extra SIM cards she kept in her wallet. Her cash, which she'd divided into six small packets wrapped in plastic, stayed where it had been all day—stuck in the socks and boots she was wearing, the world's costliest innersoles. She locked up carefully. Out on the street, she caught a tram to the Leidseplein, where she could blend in with the tourists.

Pea soup in a run-of-the-mill café made for an unexciting but comforting lunch. The canal view was superb, but she might have been looking out at a brick wall, willing her hand not to shake and spill soup, wondering who might be hot on her trail. Thanking her lucky stars that, unlike Americans, not every European possessed a smart phone or iPad, she found an Internet café and checked train times to Berlin. She'd escaped Great Britain; now she was in the Schengen Treaty countries, where no one would ask for her passport to move from one to another. But she needed to get to a big city, where she could be even more anonymous.

On the way back to the hotel, she bought a sandwich and screw-top bottle of wine. She wouldn't be going out again before she left for good.

Back in her room, she topped up the BlackBerry battery while she copied the contents of Barton's computer from the flash drive onto her new laptop. She'd left the old one—BarPharm's property— back in the apartment, the hard disk wiped clean. Going through Pierre's files would have to wait—there were hundreds.

She felt too vulnerable to go down the hall to the shower room, instead washing up at the sink before slipping into her nightgown and between her rented sheets. She was exhausted, and she had a big day coming up.

But sleep didn't come easily. She couldn't stop remembering how this had all started back in the spring—couldn't stop picturing the face she had just seen in the mirror when washing off the day's grime, the face of a woman at least thirty years younger than Anna Wallingham, a woman named Tanya Avery.

Chapter 1

April 14, 2011

The Ivy should have been a giveaway. Anna had been a friend and colleague of Richard Myerson's long enough to know that despite the Gucci loafers and Armani suits, Richard remained a Midwestern boy at heart who saved relentlessly showbizzy places like The Ivy for some kind of occasion. He didn't care that power-lunching was "out" in this year's Hollywood or that The Ivy wasn't what it used to be. "Neither am I, hon," he'd said once when she pointed that out.

She pulled up out front, confident that she looked pulled together in all the right ways. The line of her caramel-and-honey-streaked bob was straight as a knife edge; her makeup was gauzy yet defined. Her clothes epitomized the three Cs: casual, chic, and costly—a cream cashmere Saks Fifth Avenue twinset, stretch Stella McCartney khakis, an old Marc Jacobs bag that could pass as beloved rather than a secondhand "steal" at $750, and the always-in-style SoCal accessory, a pair of Tod's buff suede driving loafers. So what if their nubby rubber "pimple" soles hurt her feet? In Southern California, wearing $450 mocs was as close to pinning hundred-dollar bills to your shirtfront and calling it a tie as you could get. As a longtime maître d' friend once told her, "They look at the shoes, the watch, and the bag. Then they decide where to seat you." Her watch was a Tag Heuer, a splurge a few years back when she'd signed a big account. She looked good. No, she looked *great*. A self-employed image maker in LA had to.

Anna's cream Mercedes CLS looked perfectly in place, too, as she stepped out of it by the valet stand. It was leased, of course, but that was how you got more car than you could otherwise afford.

She scanned the other vehicles awaiting parking—the valets drove them just around the corner, yet no one would dream of parking their own car here—but Richard's red Jaguar convertible was nowhere to be seen, nor was the man himself.

Anna was seated on the terrace, halfway through a glass of Vernaccia, when he bustled in. "Ah, good, my favorite table." He leaned to peck her cheek. "And my favorite girl. Sorry I'm late. One of those days. And the traffic? Don't ask."

"So, my favorite client, is this a business lunch or—"

He raised a hand. "First, we eat. I'm feeling like—"

"Crabcakes, then the chopped salad?" she asked.

"Am I such a creature of habit?" Behind his rimless glasses, pale gray tinted lenses today to match his gray linen suit, his eyes crinkled. "I suppose I am. And a gimlet to drink, I think. Now . . ." He craned around, shaved head gleaming as he scoped out the terrace as though seeking a waiter. "Anyone more glamorous than us here? Oh, look, isn't that Angelina trying to pretend she's hiding beneath that big hat?"

Even though much of their conversation, of their *lives*, revolved around working together and the business of marketing and its publicity and advertising offspring, Anna and Richard always had plenty of other things to talk about, so it was only when the plates had been cleared away and they'd ordered espresso that a silence descended as he seemed to search for the right words. "Oh, no, Richard! Please don't tell me Clive didn't like the scripts for the radio spots."

"No, no, the whole campaign is fine. You've done a fantastic job."

She sighed in relief and leaned back. She'd worked relentlessly on the Madame X "rejuvenating makeup" campaign. She'd been so consumed she hadn't even considered that anyone might change their mind about her ideas, certainly not just weeks before the launch. But Richard's obvious discomfort unnerved her.

"So why do I feel your next word will be *but*?"

"It's Clive," he said abruptly, his voice and face tight. "I'm sorry, Anna, but—"

"Don't tell me I'm losing the account. Please don't. You have that look . . . But that's not possible!"

"You know if it were my decision—"

She blinked rapidly, fixing her gaze on the tablecloth as the waiter set down their cups. She wasn't about to cry on the terrace of The Ivy. Nor would she make it easier for Richard. Even if it weren't his fault, firing someone wasn't supposed to be easy.

"When mergers happen, things get shuffled," he said finally. "If Coscom were still just Coscom, you'd have work for life. But with Barton Pharmaceuticals' acquisition, it's a whole different kettle of fish."

"I appreciate that. But—"

He held up his hand. "When you deal with Barton, it's not like dealing with other health and beauty companies, not even the biggest. This isn't Estée Lauder or Max Factor." He shook his head. "It's Big Pharma—BarPharm—sweetie. Probably worth billions. For the life of me, I can't figure out why they wanted a fifty-million-dollar cosmetics company in the first place."

"Coscom's not just another cosmetics company, Richard. We made it a leader, you and I. We built Gawjus into a top retail brand: it *owns* the eighteen-to-twenty-nine-year-old demographic. Just like Madame X will end up owning the fifty-plus." Her voice quavered. "I did good work."

"And I'm the first person to say that. As far as I'm concerned, you're the best PR and image consultant in the business."

Anna broke the awkward pause. "So?"

"Clive Madden." He sighed. "I fought for you. I promise I did. But he's determined to bring in a young, hungry agency and pay them half of what you've been getting."

"Why didn't he ask if I might be willing to work for less? Why not give me a chance to keep the business?"

"I suppose guys like Clive Madden are ruthless. That's why they're flown in from the UK to run a company after a merger. And he says you're out."

"That's it? 'Thanks for the success, we're looking for a newer model, buh-bye'?"

"Your contract says four months' notice. Madden wants you on board for the New York launch; then you can go, so you'll work a month and get a three-month payoff. That's the best I could do. God, Anna, I'm so sorry. I really am."

"Jesus! He's going to make me work the launch?" Her laughter burned like acid in her throat. "Not too cold-blooded, is he? What do I say to the editors? 'Try our fabulous new cosmetic line for older women. Sadly, I've been judged past it myself, so I'm out the door'?"

"You're not past it. Don't be silly. Look, Pierre Barton himself is coming over from London for the launch. Maybe you can dazzle the chief, get some other work out of all this."

"Does he know I'm being shoved out?"

"Pierre Barton probably doesn't know who either of us is. He's the head of a pharmaceutical company who for whatever reason wants to be in cosmetics, too. Why he's bothering to show for a makeup launch is beyond me. Maybe he thinks the beauty sector is some kind of glamorous whirl."

"And I get to be on hand to pamper his ego. Why not?" She shrugged. "Maybe he'll present me with me a lifetime supply of whatever knockoff of Xanax he churns out . . ." Anna stopped to collect herself. "Ignore me, Richard. I don't mean to drench myself—and you—in self-pity, but I just can't help it."

"Hey, kiddo, you're a survivor." He reached across, squeezed her hand, and then made the "bill, please" gesture in the direction of the waiter. Anna knew the serious talk was over. When Richard called her "kiddo," it signalled he was back in the foppish forties dandy mode he wore like a boutonniere. "And it's not as though you don't have other clients."

Richard didn't know how much Coscom had taken over her client list. Nor was she going to tell him. No reason to make him feel worse.

"Things will be all right," he told her outside as they waited for their cars. "You're a fighter. You're going to land on your feet."

"Maybe." She forced an upbeat lilt. "But I'm fifty-seven years old. I've got more than a few years on these newbies hungry for accounts . . . all these Stacies and Dacies and Tracies. It's scary."

"Look at you: You don't even look *forty*-seven. You're the sharpest advertising and PR pro in health and beauty. And you are, always, the ultimate in cool and a pleasure to be with. You're the best!"

"Aw, Richard, you're my guy." Her smile this time was genuine. "And I know this, too, shall pass. We'll talk strategy next week, 'kay?"

"It's a date. You'll knock 'em dead, Anna."

"And thanks for lunch, darling. Seriously." She held her smile as his car arrived and he slid behind the wheel. But as soon as he'd driven off, she let the tears come. She couldn't have stopped them if she'd wanted. And she didn't give a damn if Angelina saw.

How could Richard have let this happen, she asked herself as she headed toward Laurel Canyon. They'd been close friends since meeting soon after she'd arrived in California. They'd grown together through Coscom. And now?

By the time she'd emerged on the San Fernando Valley side of the canyon, she'd admitted to herself that anyone would have done what Richard had. Being her friend didn't necessitate an "If she goes, I go" meltdown, certainly not at a time when companies were folding faster than bad bluffers at a high-stakes poker game and anyone with a job went to bed thankful.

She should have spoken to Richard about going in-house before the acquisition, when the economy was better. But she hadn't. The Coscom founders—now living in opulent retirement in Palm Springs—were difficult, so she had been thrilled with the company acquisition and the arrival of the seemingly equable Clive Madden.

She clicked her garage door open and pulled in. Just being home in Studio City, in her part of town—the less glamorous, more down-to-earth part of town—would soothe her. She loved the single-story 1930s bungalow she bought fifteen years ago when first starting to earn decent money. With a big office for herself and a smaller one for an assistant in the back, it was her ideal home. Anna moved in and never looked back. Until she started losing clients.

All of them. It was silly lying to Richard, but she feared even he might feel differently about her if he knew the truth. This was Los Angeles. Everyone loved a winner, and she was looking like less of one by the moment.

In the light-filled kitchen with its black vinyl diner booth and black-and-white checked linoleum, she poured herself a glass of pinot grigio, then she moved to the living room, slouching back on the overstuffed couch and staring at the peg-and-groove pine floorboards. She felt numb. And it wasn't just shock. It was fear.

Her car. *Her* house. Like hell. The Mercedes lease was up in just months; the car belonged to the dealership. She'd been trying to decide whether to buy it, paying it off over four years, or to lease a more expensive model. *Yeah, right,* she thought, raking her fingers through her long bangs and pushing the hair off her face. Forget the car; she'd be lucky to find a way to keep the house.

Anna had refinanced whenever the rates tumbled; even so, she had precious little equity in it because she saw refis as a way of giving herself bonuses. Her dwindling bank account wouldn't buy her much time if she didn't get clients. All that hard work—was she going to end up with nothing but a closetful of pricey clothes and some travel photos?

What she needed to do was get word out quickly and quietly that she was "accepting new clients," agencyspeak for "desperate for work." She made her way back to her office to check her email. Her Filofax lay open on the desk. It was one of the accessories that the digital natives had relegated to the 1980s dustbin, but she loved her fat black calfskin Filofax, with appointments scrawled in ink, just as she loved flipping through her old gray steel Rolodex to find phone numbers.

Among the emails, Anna found a much-needed reminder from her college friend Allie that they were meeting Jan for dinner at the Daily Grill at eight. Damn. She took her glass to the kitchen, then curled up on her bed for a brief nap. A nap and a hot shower—that would make her feel more like facing friends. Or so she hoped.

Jan was already pouring herself a glass from the bottle in the bucket stand at the side of the table as Anna walked the last few steps across the Daily Grill's dining room.

"Sit down, have some *vino bianco.* We're celebrating tonight."

"And what's the occasion? Tell me quick, so I can drink."

"Yeah, catch up, A," Allie ordered. "We both got here early, so this is seconds for us."

"Allie is George's new agent," Jan announced. "Sweet, huh?"

Anna raised her glass to her friends. Could any two people be less alike? Jan had been majoring in philosophy when the three of them ended up on the same dorm floor freshman year at Goucher College; she was then, as now, a pudgy, slightly pugnacious flower child with long, flyaway auburn hair. Just after graduation, she'd married George, a junior philosophy instructor far too self-important for his twenty-eight years, and turned into a full-time mother and later a grandmother. Now she worked part-time as a guidance counselor at a private school off Mulholland. Since George had started writing what his publishers promoted as "philosophical tales of those doomed to live forever" some years back, Jan didn't need to worry about earning a real living.

Allie Moyes was a stark contrast, poured into black leather pants and a fitted white shirt, her *maquillage* as perfect as if she'd sprung full-blown from a Serge Lutens photo shoot, her short black hair sleeked with brilliantine à la Joel Grey in *Cabaret*. In college, she'd been a borderline outcast, a "lipstick lesbian" business major at a time when every gay woman was called a "bull dyke" and *all* women were expected to major in education or liberal arts while awaiting their Mrs. degree. She'd confessed to Anna that she couldn't imagine why anyone would choose a women's college other than to meet girls—and she met many. Now an important agent at an important show business agency, she was as tough in her dealings with studios as she was kind to her friends.

"You're handling writers as well as actors now, Allie?" Anna asked, sipping her wine.

"I'm starting to. I think they'll be offering me a partnership in the agency—in preparation for which, I'm now also handling our novelists who sell movie rights. Which includes George."

"That's great! And lucky George, too."

Jan was reaching for one of the menus on the table. "Let's order. Sorry, but I had meetings at school, skipped lunch, and now I'm famished. And then we want to hear all the latest about you."

"Me? Same old, same old." Anna ducked her head and studied the menu. "Let's see. Calories or conscience? Chicken pot pie or chicken Caesar?"

She wouldn't spoil the evening with her news. She worked hard at keeping her mind on the conversation—Jan repeating the laudatory advance buzz for the film adaptation of George's *Die with Me Again*, Allie filling them in on the latest happenings of her girlfriend Shawna, the former Stevie Nicks in a local Fleetwood Mac tribute band who was now starting to see some success as an actress.

After the meal, the subject turned—as it so often did—to looks and the passage of time. "I need some of that Madame X," Jan said mournfully. "I'm starting to look my age, and you know that's a bad thing in these parts."

"I'll give you some products. But Madame X is makeup, hon," Anna reminded her. "You never wear makeup."

"Maybe it's time to start. I want to be like Allie, looking sixteen."

"I take it you've finally stopped telling people your age?" Allie snorted. "Remember, Anna, when I had to tell her she couldn't be my friend if she was going to tell people how old she was *and* that we were at school together? Not all of us have rich husbands to fall back on if the powers that be decide to put us out to pasture."

"I don't have a lifetime guarantee." Jan's lips drooped. "George is at that age, you know? When men start thinking about the trade-in-for-a-younger-model option. You wouldn't believe how many of his friends have armpieces instead of wives."

"Oh, I'd believe it. Just don't ever let him forget he's older than you," Allie said succinctly. "Why not see my doctor? Then let me take you shopping and to the salon and gym. In a month, we'll have a whole new you."

"Oh, I couldn't have a face-lift!" Jan quickly added, "Not that anyone would guess you'd had one, Allie."

"I had a *neck*-lift, Jan, and that's all. And I'm not suggesting you go under the knife. Just some light laser for the sun damage and fine lines, implants to plump out your cheeks, some alpha hydroxy acid creams. A derm can handle that. Just come with me the next time I go. You, too, A?"

Anna jumped. "Me?" she all but shrieked. "You think I look old?"

"Mmmm." Allie leaned in, undressing Anna's face with her eyes. "Hardly old. You have such good bone structure. Still . . . maybe a zap of Botox for the crease between your eyes, laser for those lip lines, and a touch of filler to get rid of the marionette lines."

Anna forced a laugh. *Jesus,* she thought, *just what I need.* "You're making me sound like Grandma Moses! I don't have marionette lines!"

Allie ran her right index finger lightly from the left corner of Anna's mouth toward her chin. "They're not bad, but they do scream 'Fifty-plus!'"

"Gawd, we should have had *two* bottles of wine," Jan said tiredly. "I think I'm depressed now."

"Nothing to be depressed about. Just a fact of life," Allie told her calmly. "Old isn't the new Young, guys. Old is the same old Old. You think they'd be offering me a partnership if the big cheeses at the agency knew my real age? No way, Jay! I need to stay forever nubile."

The waiter raised his eyebrows at Anna and Jan's frantic waving for the check. "Enough. I have work to prepare for school," Jan blurted even as Anna mumbled something about going over some creative briefs before bed.

The drive home was short. Even so, the thoughts kept repeating themselves: *Marionette lines? Botox? Me?*

———————

Those words were still in her head when she woke the next morning. Before she'd even made coffee, she was squinting at her sleep-blurred face in the bathroom mirror. She cursed each tiny crevice creeping upward from her top lip. She plucked at her cheeks, wondering when they'd gone so slack. The lines from her nose down to either side of her mouth weren't so bad—a little highlighter could hide them. Still . . .

After coffee and a bowl of muesli, she dialed Allie's private work number. "Hey, great seeing you last night."

"Yeah, we should work less and do it more often. So what's up, in fifty words or less?"

"I was thinking about what you said last night, about not succeeding because of being too old."

"C'mon, Anna, you don't have to worry. But, yeah, sure I meant it."

"I was thinking, if I decided I wanted to go back to corporate—"

"Why would you want to do that, dopey? You've got what's going to be one of the hottest cosmetics accounts in America, if not the world."

"I've been thinking about in-house benefits," Anna fibbed. "Some days, it just seems like too much hustle for too little reward."

"Then you'd better write a novel I can sell to the movies, because no corporation's going to look at you twice. And even the first time, they won't really be looking *at* you, they'll be looking *through* you. Maybe if you tried a headhunter in New York, something might—emphasis on *might*—happen."

"Oh, come on." Anna set down her cup with a vehemence that surprised her. "It can't be impossible!"

"Look, even most men who snag great corporate jobs come from corporate—or they get a job in-house with a client. So your only hope would be Coscom. Seriously, Anna, it's different for women. And not just in La-La Land."

"So you're resigned to Botox and Restylane and laser and eventually a full face-lift and hiding your birth certificate as though it were the Enigma code?"

Allie laughed. "Do I seem like the kind of person who's ever resigned to things? Eventually, Shawna and I will buy a house in the South of France or someplace, and I'll grow old gracefully. Right now, I do what I have to do to nail down that future. And what I have to do right now is a meeting, even though I'd rather talk to you. Sorry."

"That's okay. Thanks for the input."

"The best thing for you is the status quo. You've got a strong ad campaign, and your client's a winner. Don't risk losing it all on a whim. Got it?"

"Yeah, got it. Thanks."

It was Friday; she had cut her assistant down to just three days a week and was relieved one of them wasn't today. After refilling her coffee cup in the kitchen, she took the *Los Angeles Times* from the front doorstep and got back into bed. Some days, it didn't pay to get up. Certainly not when she'd just been told that her sole job opportunity was with the company that had precipitously decided they'd be absolutely fine without Anna Wallingham.

Chapter 2

Sunday, September 11, 2011

When she woke up, Anna thought she was back in her sweet cottage in Studio City. Then she opened her eyes to the plaster ceiling of a hostel room in Amsterdam, proof this nightmare was really happening. And it was September 11, never a good day.

She didn't go downstairs until half past eight, when the dining room would be busiest. She ate a big Dutch breakfast from the buffet, then, before anyone could remember they'd never seen her passport, she hurried back upstairs for her things. She left the key on the bedside table and slipped out of the hostel.

On the Damrak, the main street running south from Central Station, she found an Internet café already abuzz with impoverished-looking backpackers. With trepidation, she scanned the major UK newspaper sites. Nothing. Googling "Pierre Barton," she found a small item, no byline, that read "Investigation into Death of Pharma CEO?" It stated only that Barton had collapsed "at a friend's" and been pronounced dead on arrival at the hospital yesterday morning, presumably of a heart attack. Almost as an afterthought, it added that there would be a coroner's inquiry.

She read it over twice. DOA. The insinuation that this might be more than a simple myocardial infarction was there, if subtly—the question mark on the headline, for starters. Was it usual to have a coroner's inquiry in the UK, or did the police suspect Pierre might have been murdered? His breathlessness, red face, sweating—she'd hoped to read he had indisputably died of what it had seemed to be: a heart attack. What about the person who'd almost knocked him down as he approached her building? She vaguely recalled the story of someone poisoned years ago by a blade hidden in the assassin's umbrella. If Barton had been murdered, would the police suspect she was the killer? Would *they* be after her, too?

She signed onto her personal email, quickly scanning her in-box. She sent a group note to everyone back in the States, saying only that she was hitting the road again "in search of warm weather in Cape Town." Pretty lame, but anything that might keep someone who was auditing her emails from finding her was worth doing.

Then, unable to avoid it, she went to her Barton Pharmaceuticals mailbox, her Tanya Avery account, where she found three emails dated yesterday afternoon that needed reading.

The first was to the entire staff, sent to both their work and home emails by Pierre's personal assistant, Eleanor, simply and solemnly announcing Barton's death that morning. The office would be closed Monday, with funeral details to be posted later.

The second, from Pierre's wife, Marina, was abrupt. "Call or text ASAP!"

The third was from Becca, a coworker at BarPharm.

Eleanor called to tell me Mr. Barton collapsed at your apartment this morning. Wherever you are, Tanya, I hope you're all right. I thought you should know that a stranger came by the house when my mum was cooking supper, a posh blond type who didn't even introduce himself—just said Mrs. Barton had sent him. He seemed very keen to find you, but he didn't seem like a policeman. Please take care.

Anna typed in Pierre Barton's email address. On the subject line, she filled in "Final Diary Entry." And then she wrote:

This is my last diary entry.

After the ambulance left yesterday, I sent a message telling Marina the hospital name. I knew there was no reason for me to go there.

Whoever reads this—and I know someone will—let this serve as my letter of resignation. I'm not sure what you're up to, but I refuse to be a part of it anymore.

I've left a record of everything that's transpired since April in a safe place. You would be very unwise to come looking for me.

I'm sure you'll try to find me anyway, one of you, whoever you are.

By then, I plan on having figured things out. And it will be too late for you.

Until then, I remain,

Tanya. Lisa. Anna.

There, that should give someone food for thought. She opened a new email account for herself, as TLADesign@gmail.com, her own little sick joke ("The Last Account"). On Craigslist Berlin, she found three "roommate wanted" ads that might do and sent emails from "Lisa" on that account, asking to view the available rooms. "If you can get back to me sometime tonight, I'd like to see your flat tomorrow."

Walking to the station, she was pretty sure that, for the moment, no one knew where she was, which made her feel not *good*, but better at least than she had since she'd come back into her living room with a glass of water in her hand the day before. Could that have been just yesterday?

The Berlin express didn't leave from Central Station, which suited Anna's plan. She bought a ticket from Amsterdam Schiphol Airport Station to Berlin Hauptbahnhof, as well as one for the airport shuttle train. When she reached Schiphol, she found a store that sold prepaid SIM cards and bought one for a standard cell phone. Soon she'd have enough SIM cards for a poker hand.

Next, she picked up a couple of English-language thrillers and a sudoku book, the kind of stuff a tourist might purchase for a trip. She'd already tucked her Berlin *Time Out* guidebook into her shoulder bag.

Twenty-five minutes before departure, she went to the ladies' room near the security lanes leading to the long-haul-flight departure lounges. She turned on her BarPharm BlackBerry, switched it to silent, then climbed onto one of the toilets to wedge it high above and behind the tank where it couldn't be seen. If anyone was tracking it, they'd end up here. With luck, they'd think she'd flown to Cape Town or back to the States. She inserted the new SIM card into her cheap cell phone and sent a single text message, then turned off the phone.

On the way down to the tracks, she bought a sandwich and a bottle of water, reaching her platform with the train already there. The car was half full, not bad for blending in. Toward the door into the car ahead, she spotted a girl with a mass of blond dreadlocked hair sitting alone next to the window in a grouping of four seats with a table in the middle. She didn't mind riding backward, so she sat down across the table, but on the aisle so they'd both have legroom. Now it wouldn't be so obvious that she was on her own.

She settled down, surreptitiously looked around, and saw no one suspicious. With a perfunctory smile at the young woman across from her, she slipped off her coat and pulled her scarf up over her chin and her hat down to her eyes. Closing them, she feigned sleep.

The weeks between that fateful lunch at The Ivy and the Madame X launch had flown by so quickly Anna could almost feel the air rushing past, bringing her closer to no work and too little money. She was busy with the details of the launch party, which she'd booked months ago at Block, the hottest new New York club. Otherwise, life was uneventful; the few things that stood out were notable solely for their awkwardness.

The first was Clive Madden's discomfort when she bumped into him in the lobby at Coscom after Easter. She was arriving to see Richard and he was on his way out. As they came face-to-face, the chubby little Englishman turned bright red and smiled hesitantly.

He's afraid I might make a scene, Anna thought, putting on a fake grin and forcing him to speak first.

"Ah, well, hello there!" he finally blustered. "Here to see Richard?"

Her smile tightened. "Am I still allowed in the building? Hard to finish the launch otherwise, you know."

His color deepened. "Of course you're allowed. You're welcome here any time. And congratulations on the Madame X collaterals. Even Mr. Barton said they were spectacular."

Now it was her turn to be speechless. "No good deed goes unpunished, right?" she finally blurted.

At five foot eight plus heels, Anna towered over him. Looking far from ruthless, he peeked up at her. "Sorry, but it wasn't—it wasn't . . . an easy decision. Naturally, I'll give you the highest recommendation and send any work I can your way. And I deeply appreciate your agreeing to work through the launch."

He held out his hand. Of course, she shook it, a reputation as a poor loser being one of the many things she could now ill afford. "Thank you, Clive." They stood in silence before smiling with jointly false brightness and nodding good-bye.

As she walked down the wide hallway toward Richard's office, Anna couldn't help but think Madden had seemed about to say, "It wasn't my decision."

When she related the encounter to Richard, all she got was a shrug. "C'mon, Richard, if not his decision, whose was it?"

"But he didn't actually say that, did he? And whose decision could it be? You don't think *I'd* suggest letting you go, do you?" He looked horrified.

"Of course I don't. You have to admit it seems odd, ditching me in the midst of a major launch," she mused. "I mean, slashing budgets, et cetera, et cetera. Which other consultants were let go?"

Richard hesitated before shaking his head. "None that I know of."

"Any in-house staff shown the door?"

Another head shake.

"You know, almost twenty years ago, at my last job in New York, the head of the company didn't like me because I wouldn't suck up."

"And?"

"And I was chosen to be part of a general layoff."

Richard peered at her over his glasses, tortoiseshell today to match his brown silk tweed jacket. "And?"

"And the rest of the big 'general layoff' was a guy in accounting with late-stage AIDS." Anna shook her head. "I don't doubt Clive made the decision. But something about the way he spoke gave me a weird feeling."

"Just relax. Don't start getting obsessed with Clive."

"You're right." She did a quick shoulder roll and took a deep breath. "Now, let's decide on these gift bag items and get some of Coscom's excess minions busy."

———

Then there was her lunch with Gregg Hatch, executive director of the Western Cosmetics Council and unofficial go-to guy for anyone looking to switch jobs or accounts. He was also known for being selectively discreet—no single person knew exactly what he knew.

But as soon as Anna said, "I'm in the market for some new accounts," she knew he wasn't going to help.

"Well, good luck to you." His smile was a little too cheerful, his voice a bit too loud. "These are, of course, hard times," he said solemnly, like an anchorman introducing a poor economic forecast.

Liar, Anna thought. "I know there are cutbacks everywhere, but with a product launch like Madame X under my belt—"

"Yes, I hear you've done a fantastic job."

"And the rest of the sentence?"

He looked at her blankly. "I'm not following, I'm afraid."

"The 'but' and the part that comes after it."

"Well, just that . . . just that these are hard times." He waved a hand vaguely, as if hard times were plotting somewhere off to his left.

"So, tell me, do you think these are going to be particularly 'hard times' for me?"

"For you? Of course not." He had the good grace to blush. "You're a thoroughbred, Anna. You want clients, you'll get clients."

"Anyone in mind?" she asked, knowing there wouldn't be.

Gregg motioned for the check, avoiding her gaze. When he turned back, his eyes were flat, the shutters drawn. "I'll let you know if I hear of anything." His smile reasserted itself, sincere as a time-share salesman's. "You can count on me."

Was she getting paranoid? Her assistant handed her only three messages on her return from lunch. Had everyone she knew suddenly decided she was over the hill? *Christ!*

Just three messages, and two were from ad salesmen. "Just blow them off, Kelly," she said. "Then memo Richard asking to whom we should be referring ad reps from now on." The third message was from Jan, inviting her to a barbecue the following Sunday.

"A barbecue? Are you going all Topanga rustic on us now?" she teased when Jan answered the phone. The Bergers had bought a big house in the canyon two years before, in keeping with the piles of money George was making.

"We never had a proper housewarming, and with George's movie opening soon, we thought we'd inaugurate the new screening room, as well."

"Spareribs and bloodsucking nightwalkers? You won't find me passing that up."

Jan didn't sound like a woman worried that her husband had a roving eye, Anna thought as she put down the receiver. Still, even considering how long they'd been friends, Anna doubted she'd be the one on the receiving end of confidences. She and Jan just weren't that close.

Anyhow, she had enough worries of her own. She reached for her Rolodex. There were plenty of people besides that deadbeat Gregg Hatch to remind of her continued existence.

A barbecue that included a screening meant industry big shots and celeb casual dress. Anna wore superstretchy designer jeans, with a fitted white ruffled shirt that had set her back almost $500 at Barney's even on sale, and a pair of black Prada flats. *Over a thousand smackeroos' worth of casual,* she thought as she grabbed a gray pashmina from the coat rack by the door to the garage.

More and more, she saw Jan only at the "girly dinners" with Allie, so she'd been to the Bergers' massive spread only twice. The backyard was walled off, but tonight the double security gate stood open.

Anna made her way toward the sound of voices and muted music beyond. She vaguely recognized a few of Jan's "mom" friends and spotted Allie's boss, a portly, saturnine über-agent almost as well-known as his clients.

Then she spied her hostess perched on a chaise lounge by the pool, chatting with Allie and her girlfriend, Shawna. "Sorry. I guess fashionably late went out of style while I was still doing my makeup," she said as she joined them. "Hey, Shawna."

Shawna smiled warmly, giving her long, curly hair a shake.

"Some barbecue, Jannie." Anna turned and looked at the eight-topper round teak tables sitting under a marquee awning close to the house, next to which a catering team in white jackets and chefs' toques presided over a row of gas grills.

"You think the tables are okay without cloths? George told me that'd make it look too much like a wedding."

"Well, if it isn't the elegant Anna!" She turned to see George bearing down on her. The formerly scruffy, bearded hippie philosophy instructor was now a clean-shaven, balding country squire. All that was missing was the ascot.

Fame had settled on George Berger's spindly shoulders with a vengeance. He'd become embarrassingly pompous, considering that his success sprang from highbrow folderol about vampires that was, nonetheless, utter trash. The new George had handily forgotten the old George's failure to get tenure at a series of Midwestern universities. While the new Jan had retained her down-home style, George had tried remaking himself as a bon vivant, an experiment as fruitless as his tenure attempts.

"Swell party," she murmured, air-kissing a cloud of aftershave.

He gestured expansively. "I think you'll enjoy the food," he promised, his tone insinuating that others rarely got to dine as sumptuously as did the Bergers. To his wife, he said, "Now can you see how gauche white tablecloths would have looked, sweetheart?"

Jan flushed at George's dry chuckle, while Anna mentally cringed as he grasped his spouse's elbow and pulled her to her feet, his smile patronizing. "And now I need to take my lady wife away to greet some of our other guests." Jan followed like a chastened child.

"Whoa! What was that 'lady wife' stuff? And treating Jan like she's twelve?"

Allie shook her head. "I shouldn't say it, especially now that George is my client, but he's become unbearable. You don't see them often, or you wouldn't have been surprised that Jan worries he'll get tired of her. He treats her like the hired help."

"And she just takes it?"

Allie shrugged. "When they're alone, who knows? She'd never cross him in public. And even if she fears being suddenly the *fired* help, she's still in awe of him. Of course, poor Jan's in awe of almost everyone. Don't let her fool you, either. She—Oh, hell, here comes Nadine Metzger." Her voice dropped. "Simply the most boring producer in—Hey, Nadine, how's life? Do you know my friend Anna?"

———

After the most elaborate barbecue Anna had ever been served, everyone filed dutifully into the screening room. In a world where even lowly assistants had monster flat-screen TVs on their walls, the Bergers' setup raised the bar for aspirants. As the guests entered, the back wall slid open to reveal a screen of multiplex proportions; the rest of the room was given over to overstuffed armchairs set in pairs next to small tables. A built-in bar was staffed by a man as handsome as Tapp Blaine, the film's young star, who had suddenly materialized to soak up his share of attention, giving George a brisk man-hug before turning to greet those more pivotal to his career.

To Anna's surprise, the hostess plopped herself down on the chair beside hers. "Aren't you going to sit with George, Jan?"

"Nah." She shrugged. "Hey, lemme get us some wine before he starts yakking. He'll kill me if I interfere with his moment!" Before Anna could say she didn't want more to drink, Jan was on her feet, bumping into a few tables on the way to the bar, having clearly imbibed plenty already.

She came back followed by the bartender, who carried a bottle of white wine in a chiller and two glasses.

"Ah, here goes," Jan murmured as those in front took their seats and the lights faded.

"Have you seen it before?"

"Not seeing it would be grounds for divorce." Jan snorted. "It isn't bad, though."

Anna supposed that, as far as contemporary vampire films went, it would be bearable. George wasn't completely devoid of talent, though Anna had found his last movie more irritating than frightening.

A short way into the night's offering, it, too, irritated. The shallow, gorgeous twenty-five-year-olds pretending they'd lived for two hundred years not only looked adolescent, they behaved like teenagers, too, as though the need for fresh blood came second to tracking trends and getting laid. Then someone on-screen said, "What more could anyone want than to stay young forever?" and she felt the character could have been summing up her own dilemma.

That's what it was all about, and not just in the movie industry. *Especially,* she thought ominously, *when you're fifty-seven and faced with a total lack of income until Social Security kicks in.* She forced her attention back to the screen. She couldn't sob at George's screening. At least not until the sad part. And with this kind of movie, she knew she could count on a sad part before it was over.

By the time the lights went up to applause mixed with whistles and hoots, Anna felt more sleepy than weepy. She turned to Jan, who was pouring herself the dregs of the wine, Anna having left her own glass almost untouched. "That was really"—she wiped the word *interesting* off her lips since everyone knew it was Hollywoodese for *lousy*—"thought-provoking."

"It makes its point. Getting old sucks, doesn't it?" Jan asked, so loudly a few heads turned. She lowered her voice. "I mean, look at old George up there." She nodded toward the front, where her husband was being congratulated. "Older than me yet he's considered in his prime, while I'm past my sell-by date, just an aging woman pampering a buncha spoiled rich brats."

The resentment in her voice shocked Anna. "C'mon, Jan. George loves you. You like your work. You've got a great job, lots of friends."

"Yeah, right." She snorted. "Lucky me. Notice how I'm even wearing makeup? I feel like a fake but, I mean, everyone's a fake, aren't they?"

"Surely not all of us."

"Look in the mirror, honey. You pretend you're happy. But what have you got? No man, no kids, not even a dog. Just clients. And money, of course. One thing about us, huh? No matter what happens, we're set for life. I'll get half of George's pile if he ever dumps me."

Anna tried to look amused, but Jan's remarks, in addition to being mean-spirited, had hit home. "No half of a pile for me. If I didn't have work, I'd just be old and poor."

"Come on. What about that money your grandmother left you? Must now be a nest egg big enough to keep you in omelettes for life. Invested for decades, right?"

"Oh, *that*. I hardly ever think about it. Anyhow, it's not all about money, is it?"

"If I knew what it was all about, do you think I'd still be married to George, sitting in this fucking wannabe hacienda, waiting for him to ditch me?" Jan stood up. "C'mon, I gotta go say buh-bye to these freeloaders."

———————

Out front, chatting with Allie and Shawna in front of her car before leaving, Anna confessed that she was losing Coscom. "Oh, God, that's not good," Allie commiserated. "So that's why you were talking about going in-house?"

"Too late now. And no one wants to know me lately. I'm starting to get scared."

"It's not the end of the world," Allie said crisply. "Why not give up consulting? Write that novel you've been threatening to work on since college. Travel. Or take a little time off and reinvent yourself. Why not put Grandma's money to good use?"

Had no one forgotten about that fucking trust fund? "Maybe." She exhaled deeply. "Anyhow, enough 'woe is me.' It was such fun sitting with you guys at dinner."

Allie nodded. "Nice party. Plus, I managed a relaxing little nap during the movie, and I didn't even snore."

Shawna winked at Anna. "Just one little snuffle, and I nudged her foot just when the guy was going for someone's neck, so no one noticed her jump."

"C'mon, group hug." Allie held out her arms. "And stop worrying, Anna. You'll be fine."

———————

As she headed east on the freeway to Studio City, Anna was shaking her head in amazement. Would people ever stop telling her she'd be fine? And how could she have forgotten that damned inheritance? Did *everyone* know about it? If they did, it might be a blessing, making her seem like not such a colossal loser. But more likely it would be a curse: fewer people would take her plight seriously.

Neither blessing nor curse, in fact, the inheritance was, plainly and simply, invention. Sheer hokum.

Oh, Gram, you must be rolling in your grave.

Her grandmother, Ella Walinski, had come to the United States from Poland before the Second World War with her husband, Lorenz, a plumber, and their son. In Philadelphia, Gram had worked as a laundress; after her husband died, she'd moved in with her child, Walter, his wife, Alice, and their daughter, Anna, in Wayne, a leafy Philly suburb that was part of the social register's Main Line.

Anna's father had changed the family name by deed poll to Wallingham; still, in that neighborhood at that time, the family wasn't recognized as "one of us." Her mother was the unglamorous sort of housewife—one with no country club membership, housekeeper, or bridge club. Her dad was sales manager for a car parts company, closer to the automotive blue book than to society's. They scrimped and borrowed to send Anna to Goucher, a women's college that had social cachet. And they never outgrew being embarrassed by Walter's sturdy peasant mother, with her heavy accent and permanently work-reddened hands.

That shame—the shame of being deemed "NOKD," or "not our kind, dear"—had been an inherited meme. It had turned Anna into a little snob who pretended her Sears school clothes were fresh off the more expensive rack at Wanamaker's. Nor had she stopped there: according to her, her father was president of his company and when she turned thirty, she'd get her hands on the sizable inheritance bequeathed by a grandmother who was, in her version, not only patrician but also conveniently dead.

When her grandmother did die soon after Anna's college graduation, it turned out she had saved up $200 in a bank account with Anna's name on it, money Anna vowed to save forever, then spent immediately on clothes. When her mother died of cancer soon thereafter and her father, within a year, succumbed to a heart attack, she found out that, as the lyric went, all she'd been left was alone. The house had been a rental, and the family was in debt.

Still, the inheritance story lived on, growing even more useful when she was working—it made her appear to be someone who wanted rather than needed this job or that one, someone whose independent streak must be respected. Socially, it swathed her in glamour, made her someone people wanted to know.

She was still shaking her head at her duplicity coming back to haunt her when she pulled into her driveway. She sat in the car in the garage for a minute, savoring the immediate future when she'd walk into her home's comforting embrace, trying to ignore the fact that it was a house of cards on which the bank held a 75 percent mortgage she would soon be unable to pay. *Some madcap heiress you are, Anna Wallingham.*

She was a fake, all right. She led a double life as surely as any of those undead losers on the screen tonight.

Chapter 3

Anna liked to joke that one of her specialties was finding hot launch-party locations epitomizing the kind of place she'd never go to, and New York's Block was no exception. Relentlessly chic, absolutely comfort-free, and obscenely expensive, it was everything the fashion-conscious adored.

At twenty minutes past noon, she told the security man he could unlock the doors that opened onto West 54th Street, then walked back to the dark corner where Richard would stand until he deemed it the proper time to come forward. "Now," she said, "let's just hope *Vogue*, *Bazaar*, and *In Style* show up." She chuckled nervously. "And *Modern Maturity*, of course."

"You say that every time, kiddo. I think it's your lucky rabbit's foot. *Everyone* will show up. They'd better, or Barton won't be so thrilled he flew in for the launch." Anna squeezed his hand. Neither she nor Richard had met the man, and certainly Richard's future depended far more on Pierre Barton's being pleased than hers did now.

"The models look good, don't they?" she asked. They stood in lines by the dining room entrance holding the press kits they'd hand the editors as they entered. All were over forty, dressed in sleek gray raw silk sheath dresses to match their glossy silver hair.

"They're perfect. Very *Mad Men*," Richard assured her. "Which agency?"

"All of them. Did you know every modeling agency now has a 'senior' sector? Wilhelmina calls theirs the 'sophisticated women' division. Others refer to it as their 'classic' category."

"They're fabulous. How many needed their hair stripped to get back to gray?"

"Are you kidding? Every one of them." They both laughed.

"This place is perfect, by the way." Richard coolly surveyed Block's wide-open spaces. Everything was blocky, from the square glasses to the cuboid plates to the uncomfortable boxy black leather chairs. Even the single touch of color—the fat red ranunculi filling the square white ceramic centerpiece vases—had been pruned like box hedges into squares. "Still, Studio 54 it ain't. Where's all the glamour gone? This is just so—"

"Square?" She laughed, then gently nudged him. "Hey, here they come. Gird your loins."

It started as a trickle, then became a stream, as the most influential beauty editors in America arrived.

After everyone had been greeted and seated, Richard dabbed any shine off his bald pate and gave Anna a nod.

She took her place at a podium in the front of the room.

Showtime.

———

After a no-nonsense welcome, Anna said, "We're here to proudly introduce Coscom's exciting new line. And, of course, to enjoy what I promise is a low-carb and gluten-free lunch." She heard some chuckles. "*Entre nous*, this product is so special that Pierre Barton himself has flown over from London and will be here to meet you. And we've got ginormous goody bags for you on the way out. Now, here's Coscom's maestro of marketing, Richard Myerson . . . and the woman he brought to the party: Madame X."

Anna stood far off to the side, watching as Richard quickly went through marketing promotions and technological advances, then wrapped up with the screening of the first TV commercial to what sounded like genuinely enthusiastic applause. "I think it's time to go to the table." Clive Madden had materialized beside her, nodding toward the empty table set up for just four in the front, where Richard was about to sit down.

Fighting the urge to shrug off his hand, Anna let him gently propel her across the room, then smiled wildly at Richard and slid in at his left. Clive took the seat on Richard's right, and Anna realized she must be about to have the great Pierre Barton himself seated next to her. Why in the world would he want to sit next to someone he'd just fired? Maybe Clive just didn't want it to be him.

And then the man himself was walking over. Even if she hadn't recognized him from photos, she'd have known he was Someone. *Some people just have it,* she thought as she watched him stop along the way to introduce himself and shake editors' hands; he was obviously asking how they'd liked the presentation and they nodded enthusiastically, clearly dazzled.

What was it that gave Pierre Barton an almost palpable aura of success and money? His bearing, for one thing, ramrod straight yet relaxed in the shoulders, hinting at what Anna knew he had experienced: a moneyed childhood in England and France and an education at Harrow, Oxford, and the Sorbonne. More than that, it was his air of easy self-confidence, the demeanor of a man who had nothing to prove.

He was undeniably handsome, and he carried his sixty years extremely well. Dark hair graying at the temples, a sort of craggy prettiness reminiscent of Pierce Brosnan. As he came closer, she could see a generous mouth that seemed to smile easily. His gray wool suit, pale blue shirt, and navy-and-gray necktie whispered of fittings on Savile Row, yet he wore his clothes as nonchalantly as if he'd thrown on jeans and a sweatshirt on the way out the door.

"This must be the woman of the moment!" he said as he reached the table, lightly squeezing her shoulder. He nodded to the men. "Clive. And the famous Richard, I believe." His touch glided smoothly from Anna's shoulder to Richard's hand.

"Richard's presentation was quite impressive," Clive said as Barton slid gracefully onto his chair. "Sorry you missed it."

Barton grinned. "It was indeed brilliant, and I didn't miss it. I was hiding behind the bouncer at the door. And now I should toast our editors and thank them for showing up." He reached for the open bottle of Sancerre, one of which had been placed on each table.

Anna was glad Barton spent lunch talking business with Richard and Clive. When the last editor had departed, she thanked the models, then left it to Richard to oversee packing up. This was it, then. Her sole client was now her ex. She had just sat back down when a fresh espresso appeared before her. "Thought you could use this." Pierre Barton set his own cup on the table and reclaimed his seat.

"Thanks. I thought you left with the editors."

"No, just saying good-bye to Clive." He took a breath. "Look, I know what's happened, and I am very, very sorry. If I'd known that you were responsible for all this, I would have insisted Clive cut his budgets elsewhere."

She wondered if he expected an understanding expression, but all she could come up with was a noncommittal shrug.

"You know, I can't go against Clive, can't undermine his authority but . . ."

Well, that woke her up. "But?"

"But I might have something for you. Can you bear another meal with me? Lunch tomorrow?"

"Yes, of course, but—"

"I'll explain tomorrow." He looked at his watch, a Patek Philippe, she noted. "I'll book a table at Seven East. You know it? Seven East 63rd, just off Fifth. I'll see you there at one o'clock. I'm at the Plaza if you need to get in touch with me."

He stood for a moment, smiling down at her. "Superb launch. Truly." Then he moved swiftly to where Richard was supervising his packers, said something that made Richard's face light up, and went straight out the door. The room seemed suddenly dimmer in his absence.

———————

Anna had lied to Richard when she said she was meeting a potential client for dinner at P.J. Clarke's, partly because she didn't want even him knowing she had no prospective clients, but also because he was one of the many who didn't know she had an ex-husband. The image of Anna Wallingham schlepping trays of beer in a Greenwich Village bar while watching her bartender husband slide into alcoholism wasn't the young Anna she wanted to project. It was, as Allie, who knew the story, had once told her, "Not your most marketable self-presentation."

Anna had been twenty-two, a budding actress fresh out of Goucher College and dejected about not having found a job in summer stock, when she visited a former sorority sister who was waitressing in New York for the summer before grad school. When her fellow Pi Phi suggested she move into the bedroom being vacated by a girl about to get married, she quickly said yes. She wanted excitement, not the stuffy Philadelphia Main Line.

She told herself she would waitress only until she found some acting gigs, but life in the West Village turned out to be "sex, drugs, and rock 'n' roll" in all its awesomeness, and she never managed to get to the non-Equity tryouts. Six months after arriving, while waiting tables at a dive on Bleecker Street, she met Mitchell "Monty" Montgomery, the black sheep of a wealthy New England family who, when he wasn't tending bar, concentrated mostly on staying high and/or drunk. Mistaking great sex for love was an easy mistake when rarely fully sober, and so they married. After one great year, two hideous fighting and yelling ones, then three living separately, they divorced and eventually realized they actually liked each other.

The years passed, Monty joined Alcoholics Anonymous, Anna actually started going to open calls to read for off-off-Broadway plays and getting some parts, and they stayed friends. Just friends: Monty had remarried shortly after getting sober and had two kids. Now her ex was standing at the bar talking to the bartender when Anna entered Brasserie Monty, his popular Upper East Side restaurant, and his freckled face split into a big grin. "Hey, Anna!" He hugged her. "Pat, open a bottle of our best Puligny-Montrachet and pour the lady a glass. What's cookin', sweetheart?"

It was probably weird, she thought later, that her two oldest friends—the only ones who knew about Monty—didn't know she was still in contact with him. She'd have been hard-pressed to explain why she didn't tell Allie and Jan. It was no big deal, but Anna had always liked having little secrets. Maybe the white lie about her inheritance had instilled in her a taste for other deceptions. Anyhow, it wasn't as if Monty had been the love of her life. No, that had been David Wainwright, somebody no one in her current life, including Allie and Jan, had ever met or ever would.

Please don't tell me I'll land on my feet, she thought to herself when they were seated with big veal chops on plates in front of them and she told him about losing her only account. But empty platitudes weren't Monty's style.

"That's a bitch. I know from regular customers in the ad game that things are tough right now. Just keep hustling and don't give up."

"Aren't you going to tell me I should start spending my grand-ma's money?" she asked impishly.

"C'mon, honey, this is Uncle Monty you're talking to here, not Mr. Born Yesterday. I know you well enough to know that, if it ever existed, you probably went through it all years ago." He winked. "So, just keep hustling and don't give up."

As Anna approached the white neo-Edwardian façade of Seven East the next day, she tried not to feel either intimidated or excited. For all she knew, Pierre Barton was going to offer her five hundred bucks to write copy for some new jock itch cream.

The doorman's standard dark coat and gold braid belied the calculating eyes of trained security with which he regarded arrivals. His role was undoubtedly to keep the riffraff at more than arm's length from the biggest names in banking, business, and politics. He even had a Secret Service–style earbud and lapel mic to announce Anna, making sure she was expected before opening the heavy iron and glass door. "Take the elevator to the second floor," he said. "Someone will be waiting."

The elevator doors closed noiselessly. *Fancy schmancy.* Anna had been to other members-only places but never one this exclusive. She was glad she'd dressed in her black-and-white Emporio Armani suit with the short skirt that showed off her legs; they probably wouldn't let even Hillary Clinton in here wearing one of her trademark pantsuits.

When the elevator doors opened, a handsome young Indian man in a white jacket and dark trousers was there to lead her to a cocktail table with brown leather club chairs arranged around it and take her drink order. She'd taken just a sip of her spritzer, peering around as casually as possible at the senator, the famed

Internet CEO, and two national news anchors when Pierre Barton appeared.

"Lovely suit," he said appraisingly as the waiter faded noiselessly away to fetch his drink. "I hope you don't mind all this"—his gesture took in the mahogany-paneled room—"but it's as private as it is stuffy, and I prefer places where I can speak comfortably."

"No, no, this is great," Anna assured him as he settled into the chair next to hers. "Seeing the movers and shakers here is a refreshing change from spotting movie stars in Beverly Hills."

The waiter set down a glass of red wine and Barton raised it to her. "To the pleasure of making your acquaintance."

"Likewise." She toasted.

"And now, I have something for you." Barton opened his slim black calfskin attaché case and pulled out a file. Anna half expected some kind of severance check. Instead, she was presented with a four-page document. "Confidentiality statement. It's a serious one, so I suggest you read it carefully. Go ahead. I have some emails to catch up on."

He pulled out a BlackBerry while Anna settled back to peruse the pages. They were boilerplate for the most part, but the "serious" parts were serious indeed. For instance, it stated that should Anna sign, she could—effective immediately—no longer discuss anything relating to her knowledge of, or even her acquaintance with, Pierre Barton and Barton Pharmaceuticals. By signing, she agreed to be legally bound, for the rest of her life, to pay a penalty of $250,000 plus legal fees of up to $200,000 should any breach in the agreement be traced to her unless released from confidentiality.

"Wow. This is pretty heavy," she said when she'd finished.

Barton tucked his phone back into his pocket. "I assure you it's absolutely necessary, and should you decide to hear what the project is, you'll see why. The bottom line is, I'm prepared to offer you work. And to give you $25,000 just to listen to my offer. If you don't want to sign that agreement, we'll have a nice lunch, and that's the end of it. If you decide to sign it, anything, *anything*, between us in the future, from a meeting to an email to a text message, is strictly confidential."

"Well, I—whew."

He smiled understandingly. "Don't rush. Give it a think while we eat. We'll stick to small talk over lunch. I promise."

They moved to the top-floor dining room, where, over a lunch as fine as anything at Le Bernardin, Barton talked easily about himself.

"Nothing dramatic," he said. "My father was a successful pharmaceutical manufacturer. He had factories, first in the British Midlands and later in Switzerland; he had a town house in Chelsea and an apartment in Paris. He was a self-made man—studied chem at uni and decided to go into business."

Anna knew from research materials she'd leafed through when writing the acquisition press release that "uni" had been Oxford and that Jasper Barton's own father had been a well-off land owner. She ventured, "So you were raised in London?"

"Mostly. My mother's Parisian. My father met her on a holiday trip to Paris after he graduated. She was everything he wasn't: a beauty and a social butterfly. He bought the Chelsea house for her, but when I was still a child, she decreed that London was too damp and too drab, deciding her perfect life required an artistic salon in Paris. So she moved back to Paris, and I divided my time between my parents. Maman is quite a character."

"And your father?"

"My father's been dead for years—my parents divorced and he remarried. My stepmother's dead as well. They had no children, so I remain an only child. My mother is still in the Paris apartment. And your family?"

Anna shook her head. "Zero. No siblings, parents died when I was in my twenties."

"No husband or kids in the picture?"

"No. Just the usual series of bad boyfriends or wrong time/ place kind of things. You have children, don't you?"

"Yes, twin boys, terrific lads. Marina and I are very proud of them." He paused. "Now, what can I tell you that you'd like to know and that isn't covered by the agreement you haven't signed?" His challenging smile indicated the chitchat was done for the day.

"What's in it for me in the long run?" she asked. "I don't mind signing confidentiality agreements, but I usually know the reason. And this agreement has industrial-strength strings attached."

"What's in it for you? If, after you hear the job description, you want to give it a shot, you get a one-year contract that will pay you a quarter of a million—that's two hundred and fifty thousand *pounds* not dollars—per quarter. If you say no, you get to keep twenty-five thousand dollars and walk away."

Her stomach tightened at the amount. A million pounds in a year! Even the $25,000 had seemed almost too good to be true, but a *million pounds*? She managed to coolly raise her eyebrows. "Why me? Why someone you just met? I mean, the launch went very well and I shouldn't have been laid off, all that's true, and yet . . . Why me?"

"Tell me, Anna, if you lose other accounts and have to get out there and try to find new clients or a job, what scares you the most? What do you think could stand in your way?"

She lifted her chin. "Nothing. Sure, the economy's bad, but it's been bad before. Maybe—"

"Yes?"

"Maybe being older scares me a little." He had to know she'd feel that way, so she might as well admit it. "It's never easy to start over, and certainly not at my age—not in Los Angeles and probably not anywhere in the world. But I do have a reputation. And a track record. And I . . ." She stopped. She just couldn't lie and say she had plenty of clients. "I guess if I were in that position, my age would scare me."

"Even though the clients wouldn't know and couldn't ask exactly how old you are?"

"Even Madame X can't make me look as young as the competition. That's simply a fact of life."

"And that's why I want you on my team," Barton said cheerfully, as though she'd just passed a test rather than made a difficult confession. "You're talented, you're proven, you're a woman of a certain age, and the Madame X campaign shows you understand how other women your age think. That all works for me."

"And if I sign this"—she tapped the folded agreement next to her espresso cup—"I get briefed on the venture and then can make up my mind, no strings attached except the confidentiality?" He nodded. "And you'll fill me in now?"

"Now? No. In ten days." He reached inside his attaché and pulled out an envelope. "Inside is your plane ticket, hotel information, and check for $25,000."

"Plane ticket? To London?"

"No, to Paris." He smiled boyishly. "I'm going to visit my mother. And now," he added, "may I offer you the use of my pen?"

"I haven't been to Paris in years." She hesitated for just one more instant. "All right, I'll sign. I've got my own pen, thanks. Or do I have to sign in blood?" she added jokingly. Looking up as she signed, she caught him studying her in a way that made her wonder fleetingly if she'd agreed too soon. Then she gave a little laugh and handed the agreement to him. She wasn't Faust, he wasn't the devil, and all she'd agreed to was an expense-paid trip to Paris and a big fat wad of money. Her future was looking up.

Chapter 4

The envelope Pierre Barton had handed her at Seven East contained a business-class ticket to Paris and a travel agent's prepaid voucher for a week's stay at the four-star Westin Place Vendôme near the Tuileries. She hadn't stayed on the Right Bank since splitting up with David decades ago. Sometimes when he had to leave New York for weeks of project meetings in his native London, he would buy Anna a ticket to fly over to rendezvous in Paris. How exciting and romantic those long weekends in a quaint auberge near Les Halles had been! But then it was all over. Since then, Anna had stuck to the Rive Gauche. But this was the start of a new life, a good time to shake off the ghostly traces of that old lost love.

Tomorrow, she'd see Barton. Today, she had decided before the plane's wheels touched down, would require only a brief nap before doing what Paris was perfect for, strolling lazily through the streets.

She'd snatched several hours' sleep in her comfy business-class flat-bed seat, primarily because she hadn't looked at the magazines she'd downloaded onto her iPad until an hour before landing. Articles like "Is Your Skin a Billboard for Your Age?" and "Left Behind: When Your Man Trades You In for a Younger Woman" would have unsettled her. Today, even the ads were insults, with their fourteen-year-old models pouting in garments few grown women could afford.

She hoped Paris would be a breath of fresh air—and that she'd love Barton's offer. While $25,000 was a godsend, it wouldn't keep her afloat for long in Los Angeles.

After checking in, she wheeled her bag to a sleek, if anonymous, chamber with a view of the Eiffel Tower. Her choice would have been something more intimate than this luxury lodge with its hundreds of rooms. Then again, she wasn't complaining about the incredible view, was she?

A long soak in the Roman bathtub followed by a nap left her feeling groggy but fresher when the alarm went off at four p.m. Barton was calling at five, and she wanted to sound alert. She'd already had a cup of tea, put on makeup, and pulled on stretch khakis and a linen shirt before the phone rang.

Five minutes later, she was out the door, having decided the late-May weather was perfect for a stroll along the Seine, an aperitif at a café, and an early dinner at one of the small bistros on rue St. Honoré. Her conversation with Pierre had been perfunctory. After posing one rote question as to how her flight had been, he said his driver Aleksei would pick her up at eleven the next morning. "Are we going somewhere?" she'd asked.

"You are. I'll already be there. You're coming to meet my mother. Enjoy the evening."

His mother? She shook her head as she walked. Was Barton a sentimentalist? Well, it was his dime, and if he wanted her to meet his mother, she would. The rich and powerful felt entitled to indulge their eccentricities, she supposed. And she felt entitled to enjoy her first evening in Paris. A languid look at the river followed by a glass of St. Emilion and a plate of duck *confit* would be an excellent start.

A dark blue Bentley limousine was parked on the street in front of her hotel when she emerged promptly at eleven the next morning. Standing next to it was a tall, well-built man with sandy-blond hair, in his late thirties, wearing a dark single-breasted suit, white shirt, narrow black tie, and dark sunglasses. He tilted his head down as formally as a bow. "Ms. Wallingham?"

"Yes. Aleksei?" She smiled.

She got the head tilt again but no returned smile as he opened the back door and stood at attention. He was no friendlier as she slid onto the smooth, cool leather seat. She noted that it was a British model with right-hand drive; how nice it must be to be driven to Paris in your own car. "We will be there in approximately fifteen minutes," the driver said gutturally—his accent Slavic or Russian—before closing the privacy partition separating the passenger compartment from the front. *Not much for small talk,* Anna thought wryly as the big car moved silently away from the curb.

She'd worn a simple bottle-green silk shantung skirt with matching fitted cheongsam-like tunic and darker green ballet flats, formal enough for meeting Maman yet neither dull nor sexy. This day might be a turning point for her; she wanted to look good for it. Outside, the Champs Elysées slipped past, lined with stately mansions and manicured trees. Finally, Aleksei pulled to a stop in front of an imposing granite edifice—eighteenth century, she thought.

The driver jumped out and opened the door. As he offered a hand to help Anna from the car, he leaned toward her and said flatly, "Mr. Barton said please not to look shocked when you see his mother. And please to take special notice of her hands."

"What—"

Aleksei inclined his head toward the building, where an elderly uniformed doorman was already holding open a massive wood door inlaid with what appeared to be coats of arms in varicolored marble. "Monsieur Couret is waiting." Then, somehow managing to do it without turning his back on her except figuratively, he got back into the car, noiselessly closing the door behind him.

"Madame Wallingham? *S'il vous plaît.*" The old man escorted her across a dark stone floor to an old French cage-style elevator, gesturing her inside. He turned a lock next to a floor button with a key, then slid the metal grill closed between them. "The lift will take you to the fifth floor."

She stepped off the elevator directly into what was clearly the antechamber of a single apartment—one of those rooms designed to keep visitors waiting three centuries ago—with several brocade sofas and chairs along with assorted Louis the Whatever cocktail tables and sideboards, which struck Anna's admittedly unpracticed eye as the real thing.

She stood looking out the waist-to-ceiling windows onto the street just moments before a set of double doors opened to her left, and Pierre Barton motioned her to come into what clearly was Luxeland. Persian rugs gave way like marshmallow beneath her feet; the wall coverings of the rooms they passed through were flocked damask; heavy silver and Lalique crystal filled glass-fronted cabinets and tables. They traversed a smaller anteroom, then a hall with parquet floors and a large circular staircase before entering the salon where Madame Marie Héloise Beaumarchais Barton awaited.

In a room shimmering with sunlight, Madame Barton sat with her back to the door, so Anna's first impression was of a birdlike creature perched on the bergère chair. When she stood and turned into the light, it was all Anna could do not to gasp. She realized why she'd been forewarned.

"Here's our guest, Maman," Pierre said softly. "Anna Wallingham. Marie Héloise Barton."

One look at Madame Barton, and any woman would think twice, then a third time, before committing to plastic surgery. Her eyes were unnaturally wide and round; too much skin had been removed for them to close properly; she must, Anna thought, need to sleep with some kind of pads over them to keep her eyeballs moist. Whatever nose had once sat in the middle of her face had melted into a small, pug-like muzzle, while oversized cheek implants added an almost whimsical touch of chipmunk. Lips too lush for even a twenty-year-old were the finishing touch, ballooning out from her face, turning up at the ends, and making a normal chin look weak and recessive atop a tight, corded neck. *The Joker,* Anna thought. The thick curls of a platinum wig tumbled about this hodgepodge of readjusted features, undoubtedly hiding a hairline a good five inches back from the one with which she had started.

Everything else about Madame Barton was perfectly in keeping with her station in life. She was elegantly attired in a pale blue A-line, its narrow pleats indicating vintage Balenciaga, and matching pumps. Before grasping the small hand Madame held out, Anna looked at it carefully. It was dainty and expertly manicured, the nails short and natural in color, the rings simple but featuring jawbreaker-sized diamonds. The unusual thing about the hand, though, was its skin—its taut, smooth, unmarked skin. It looked almost as if Madame Barton's hand had been transplanted from the arm of a much younger woman.

"What a pleasure to meet you, Madame Barton!" she said brightly, smiling straight into that unforgettable face.

"And a pleasure for me as well. My son has been telling me what a bright girl you are," she said in soft, accented English. "Please, sit down."

Anna sank gingerly onto a high-backed satin bench more comfortable than it looked while Pierre sat on the velvet sofa. She kept her smile in place as the old woman pressed a brass button set into the table next to her and said, "We'll have some tea, shall we?" It had just begun, and already this was turning out to be one of the strangest days of Anna's life.

———————

They stayed less than an hour, almost long enough for Anna to get used to Madame Barton's visage and definitely long enough for her to find the other woman *très sympathique*. She said she never went along when her son was discussing business. "Anyhow, I lunch almost every single day at Chez Jimmy. It is my tradition."

Pierre smiled fondly. "Jimmy's an old Manhattan expat, and Maman has known him for decades. She's his most regular of all regulars."

"I enjoy my own company, *mon petit*. Unlike some."

After they said their good-byes, both Barton and Anna stood silently until the elevator came and Monsieur Couret escorted them to the sidewalk. Once in the car, Anna started to speak, but Barton had already pulled a laptop out of his attaché case. "Sorry, Anna, but I need to take care of some things. Can it wait until lunch? Just another ten minutes or so."

"Sure," she said, then sneaked a peek at his fingers on the keyboard. M-a-r-i-e-H-e-l-o-i-s-e, she saw. Oh, Lord, emailing Maman already? Was this rich, powerful man a mama's boy?

Only when they were ensconced at a table on the wide, awning-covered terrace of a restaurant in the middle of what Anna supposed was the Bois de Boulogne did she manage to say, "Your mother is charming."

Her comment was greeted with a short laugh. "Yes, she truly is. As are you, for saying that. Not the first comment most people have about Maman. Don't look so abashed. I know she could be the poster child for plastic surgery gone wrong."

"What happened?"

"She chose the wrong surgeon and demanded too much. He followed her wishes, then couldn't put Humpty Dumpty together again." A waiter approached, poured two glasses of champagne, then took their food and drink order.

Anna was poised to hear the job offer, but instead Barton began with, "I'll tell you a bit about my mother. Do you know the name Madeleine Castaing? No? A *raffinée* Frenchwoman who, in the 1920s, was wooed and won by an older, very wealthy art dealer. Her dream had always been to host her own salon for artists and intellectuals, and her husband was happy to buy her a big house near Chartres where she could play the *grande dame*—it left him conveniently free to visit his mistresses.

"Madeleine loved being surrounded by artists; she and her husband had scores of paintings by the Expressionist Chaim Soutine, who painted a brilliant portrait of her—it's in the Metropolitan in New York. She wasn't untalented, either. She ended up in Paris as one of the most famous antique dealers and interior designers in the world, with a legendary shop on the Left Bank."

"And she was a friend of your mother's?"

He barked another laugh. "Oh, not at all. She was older than Maman, plus Madame Castaing's tastes were too flamboyant for Marie Héloise—lots of leopard-skin prints and such. The reason I mention her is that as Madeleine Castaing got older, into her seventies and eighties, she started hiding her age in a ludicrous way. She painted big eyelashes directly onto the skin around her eyes and wore a distinctive wig, an auburn bob that she padded inside with tissue paper in order to look taller. It had—get this—a *visible* chin strap, the purpose of which was to pull her sagging neck away from that once-beautiful face." He reached down and pulled a photocopy from his case. "She wasn't shy about the contraption, though she wouldn't discuss it other than to say, 'Oh, yes, my chin strap.' But she never tried to hide it."

The old woman whose picture Anna held was clownish yet Felliniesque, the traces of her former beauty still there. The strap holding her neck where she wanted it to be was dark and stood out starkly. "No surgery?"

He shook his head. "She was almost a hundred when she died in the midnineties." He shrugged. "Even movie stars didn't rush out for plastic surgery in the old days. It was dangerous, for one thing. They relied on clips and ties hidden in their hair to pull their skin taut. They wore lots of scarves. And it was all for the same reason, of course: they couldn't face looking old, neither for their fans nor themselves."

Anna handed the photo back as a waiter arrived with their food. She ate her fish slowly, pondering. While Pierre's mother had none of the feline deformities of Jocelyn Wildenstein, the Manhattan socialite who'd become famous in America for spending $4 million trying to look like a cat, Marie Héloise's face was grotesque as the gargoyles on the buttresses of Notre Dame. She looked up at Barton. "And your mother? Who couldn't she afford to look old for?"

"Herself. My father left her when she was forty and he was sixty-six . . . for a woman of twenty-eight. It did something to my mother's mind, left her a little unhinged. She wanted my father to regret leaving her, even though he was in London and rarely thought about her, much less saw her. I was still living with her when she started. 'You'll see, Pierre,' she'd say, 'you're going to have the most beautiful mother in France.'

"Instead, she became addicted to the knife. Every time she tried to fix something, it got worse. She says she's content to live with her face and others will have to, as well." He chuckled fondly. "She really is a true eccentric." Then he looked up from his plate, his face serious. "Still, no woman should have to go through that, Anna."

"But if girls and women were taught to have more self-respect—"

"Can the world change that quickly? Look at the actors, the tycoons, the politicians, the athletes. Are they choosing women for their sense of self-respect? Look at the real world, Anna—the world where older men remain dignified while older women are scorned. It's not just my mother I'm thinking of. It's every woman who's tried to find work once she's mature or who's felt invisible or devalued after her fortieth birthday. If you ask me, that's even more important."

"Women like me?" she murmured.

"Yes, women like you, Anna. Women who are equal to their male counterparts and their younger competitors in every way. Women who are underpaid, ignored, told, 'Sorry, nothing for you.' We can't quickly change how people think, but we can change how women look."

She stared at the tablecloth, silent, as the waiter removed their plates and Pierre ordered coffee. She took a deep breath, trying to master her emotions. Damn it, it was true. She did feel invisible. Just last night, at a little bistro near the hotel, she'd spotted a man on his own she thought was gazing at her with interest, until she lifted her face into the light. And now the man sitting opposite her—the man whose company had left her high and dry and feeling old and useless in the first place—was the only person tossing her a lifeline.

"That's what Madame X does," she said finally. "Isn't that the whole point of the line, to make older women look and feel more attractive?"

"Yes, of course. But Madame X isn't really all that different from a lot of other lines on the market, is it? The woman underneath the makeup knows her looks are the result of temporary plumping ingredients that swell the skin and light-reflecting minerals that camouflage wrinkles. She knows it can't do more than make her look good *for her age*—and only until she washes her face. What if she looked just as good or even better without makeup?"

"Don't lasers do that?"

Barton shook his head. "Laser is still a quasi-surgical procedure. And it has drawbacks: it's expensive, not successful at rejuvenating the neck, needs to be repeated, and causes thinning or whitening of the skin over time. What if looking thirty years younger was as simple as moisturizing?"

"Retinol?"

He shrugged, very Frenchly, Anna thought. "We've done work with it. We have a line for doctors and we're working on one for consumers. But retinol is what you Americans would call the minor leagues. I'm talking about wiping decades off a woman's skin, not a year or two."

"Thirty years?" He nodded. "Your mother's hands?"

"Beautiful, aren't they? She's been using the formula for six months now. Before that, like Madeleine Castaing, she was never seen without leather gloves, indoors or out, summer or winter." He pulled out a photo. "She pretends she did it as a favor to me, but I know she's pleased. Here are her hands before."

Elderly hands were all alike, Anna thought. Like these. Liver-spotted, with bulging knuckles, ropy veins, and crêpey skin. "Why aren't her knuckles big like this now?"

"The formula—we'll call it Youngskin for now—stimulates elastin and collagen regeneration, as well as the fat-growth layer, at about a hundred-to-one ratio compared to retinol."

"And elastin and collagen, like fat, make skin look young and are depleted with age and sun exposure."

"Good." He nodded, pleased with her knowledge. "Youngskin stimulates growth factors while removing surface cells and increasing overall cell turnover to an unprecedented degree. Maman's knuckles were never really big, not as if she'd had arthritis; she just didn't have any padding, so they stood out. Her hands don't look like a teenager's, but years have fallen away."

"And this is—what?—a skincare product from Coscom or a pharmaceutical from Barton?"

"You know about *cosmeceuticals*, I take it? Skincare meets medicine?" When she nodded, he went on. "Youngskin is the cosmeceutical to end all cosmeceuticals. We're using pharmaceutical-grade ingredients in a cosmetic product meeting FDA approval."

"It's been FDA approved?"

"Pending. But we'll launch the product via BarPharm to dermatologists in the UK and US in about nine months, then about three months later, a less intensive nonprescription version with the Coscom label will hit department stores. We've subjected it to FDA-level tests and standards so it's certain to make the grade. We need a pro on board for at least the next year, someone who can get to know the product inside and out, who can handle all the promotional materials, who can be passionate about it. You'd be ideal."

"Why me?"

"I saw what you did for Madame X, and I was deeply impressed. Not just the launch, Anna, or the research into the billions of dollars spent on anti-aging purchases, but your psychological grasp of the whole look-good-feel-great aspect of it all. I was already convinced months ago no one could do it better than you—then Clive had to spoil it by taking the account away from you without discussing it with me first. I want you back on board."

"I'm very flattered, Mr. Barton—"

"Pierre."

"Yes. Pierre. I'm very flattered, but why not just give me back the Coscom account? I'm not saying I'm not worth it, but why so much money, and why so much secrecy? I understand it's revolutionary, but—"

"It's more than revolutionary, Anna. It's explosive. It will change the world." His eyes gleamed. "We'll discuss the final details over a light dinner, all right? Then you'll either say yes and jump on board or you'll enjoy a couple more days in Paris before heading back to Los Angeles to concentrate on your business there, knowing you need suffer through no more meals with me."

He got to his feet, his abruptness unnerving her. He was making it sound ambiguous with that *or*. "I want to know two things," she said firmly, as she stood. "First, how many other people are being screened for this account?"

"So far, just you. This is too big a deal to hold auditions. As with any important hire, I prefer to consider one candidate at a time, starting at the top."

She nodded. "And how would I coordinate your London team from California?"

"Actually," he said slowly, "you wouldn't be in Los Angeles. You'd work in London for a year. BarPharm would take care of your mortgage as well as providing you with a flat in central London. It's very important that you use the product, you see. Use it and keep a diary of how it makes you feel to be twenty-five again."

She was dumbfounded. Why had he waited until now to tell her this? She was going to be some rich chemist's guinea pig?

As earlier, he was attuned to her thoughts. "It's not dangerous, and it's reversible. But you *must* be able to empathize completely with the customer and be able to use your own experience to tell her how great life is going to be. Don't you think you'd enjoy looking that young again?"

"That's something I need to think about," she said as he took her elbow and steered her gently toward the exit. "Um, mustn't we wait for the lunch check?"

His laughter sounded a little relieved. "It's a private restaurant. Everything is paid for on account. No cash changes hands."

Ah, yes, she mused, *for those not scrambling to stay afloat, how simple life can be.*

She spent the afternoon letting her feet take her where they wished, until they eventually led her over to the Marais. She stood for a long time gazing up at the small hotel she and David used to stay in. Its continued existence, decades after he'd probably forgotten who she was, brought tears to her eyes. But she forced herself to turn away. What was past was past.

Eventually, she took the Metro back to her hotel to rest before changing into more casual clothes and making her way to the Boulevard St. Germain and Café de Flore. Her mind had pretty much made itself up as she walked. A million pounds, her mortgage paid, and a free apartment to boot? She'd never see an offer like this again. But she still had some questions.

Barton was already there, inputting something on his laptop, which he quickly put away when she entered. "Are you always working?" she asked.

"Not at all," he assured her, pouring her a glass of red wine from the bottle on the table. "I was emailing my wife."

"She didn't come with you?"

"No, she's in Moscow—we try to get over there at least three times a year. This time, she's taken Lucas and Leo so they could be with their grandmother for their twelfth birthday."

She should have known a man like Barton would have a trophy wife—a Russian he'd met in Paris, as she recalled from his bio. Again, he knew what she was thinking. "Marina's not as young as your face says you think she is. She was over forty when the boys were born."

"That's not at all what I was thinking," she lied, blushing.

He smiled. "Okay. Have you given more thought to my offer?"

"I have. And I've come up with some questions."

He shook his head at an approaching waiter. "Fire away."

"How do I explain my absence to friends? And what happens at the end of my contract? Am I supposed to just show up in Los Angeles looking like someone else?"

"First, can't you just be traveling, or working on some imaginary project?"

She thought about it. "I suppose. Everyone keeps saying I should take advantage of losing Coscom as an opportunity to hit the road."

"There you go, then. You can do online research on anywhere you say you are. Regarding your reentry, looking like someone in her twenties or forties is up to you. You'll be able to choose an age at the end. We need you to look like someone in her midtwenties for the research, as some women will choose the option to work with a doctor and use the stronger version to look even younger, but we'll cut back gradually before the product launch because we also want to experience how it will actually feel for the retail customer. But you get to choose your end result. We'll supply you with both the weaker over-the-counter formula, and enough of the dermatologist formula for the occasional deeper treatment as well. I'd suggest you go home looking remarkably refreshed from your trip and perhaps fifteen years younger. You'll retain the product account if you like—we'll say you ran into me in London as your final port of call—at a salary to be determined at your contract's end. And, by the way, you'll also receive a salary for working in London, at a lower rate than you're used to and commensurate for someone younger, of course."

"And in London? What if I run into people I know?"

"Ah, that's a bit top secret right now. Until you sign, you see. Let's just say we'll be putting you in place at the office under a different name." He looked serious. "This is a very big project, Anna. We've got some extremely important people on board. Higher-ups, if you know what I mean. And it's important that you enter the Barton Pharmaceuticals workforce as a younger woman. Your diary will be an important marketing tool—it will say in your own words what it feels like to become a new woman, a younger version of yourself. I doubt anyone you might bump into would recognize you."

She had no idea what he meant by "higher-ups" and was sure he wouldn't tell her anyway. The royal family, for all she knew. And here she'd always thought the British took a secret pride in letting themselves go to pot!

"Let's order something, shall we?" He smiled as he discreetly raised an index finger for the waiter. Anna thought of his mother's hands, then of the casual way in which he'd sent the waiter away a few moments before. Beneath the charm and easygoing façade, Pierre Barton was plainly a hard-nosed businessman used to getting what he wanted. She closed her eyes for a moment, picturing herself thirty years younger, looking at a bank balance of over one and a half million dollars. That vision was beatific. For better or worse, she knew she was in.

Chapter 5

Anna spent only three more weeks in Los Angeles before embarking on what she thought of as her "globe-trotting." She closed up the house and put her clothes in mothballs. Deciding what to take was hard at first. A big part of her didn't believe she was going to look like a twenty-five-year-old again, ever. She deemed it more likely the magic formula would take ten years off her looks. If she really did end up looking like someone in her twenties, the sleek clothes in her closet were certainly what a younger woman would dismiss as drab and matronly. All those earth tones! In the end, she took very little, just making sure she had the tights, leotard, and cross-trainers Barton had told her to bring.

She announced the temporary closing of her office with a small release to *Advertising Age* and *Adweek*, as well as to her press contacts, saying she'd be "checking out international trends and developments." The version reserved for personal contacts, as dictated by Barton, was "living my dream and seeing the world while I can."

Richard admitted to envy. "You're so smart, kiddo. This is the perfect time," he said as they lay side by side on lounge chairs next to his pool. "By the time you get back here, the economy will have turned around. And who knows? You might even find clients in the countries you'll be visiting."

"That would be nice, but I'm doing this to clear my head, not scout for work."

"Whatever. You're a lucky girl to be able to afford to do it."

She smirked. "Do thank Clive for me. He made it all possible."

"C'mon, Anna. Clive might not have been the final decider."

"I think he was." She couldn't say Pierre had revealed it was Clive's decision alone. "He wanted to be the new broom that swept clean, and he swept me right out the door." Richard looked so stricken that she reached over and squeezed his hand. "I don't blame him. And I certainly don't blame you. Business is business."

Richard's other half, Max, came out of the house and settled onto the lounge on Anna's other side. "Put more sunblock on your head, Richard," he ordered. "You're red as a stop sign." To Anna, he said, "We might be able to meet up. Maybe in London. If Richard needs to go help with the Madame X launch there, I'd try to come along."

"That would be fun." It wouldn't, of course, because it wouldn't happen; no way would Barton allow Richard in London while she was there.

———

Driving home later, she realized how much she would miss the two of them and Allie and Shawna. Anyone else? Not Jan so much. During a quick phone call a few days before, Jan had been pretty unfriendly. "Nice for some of us to jet-set around the world," Jan had said snidely, as if the Bergers weren't stinking rich.

"I told you, she's having problems with George," Allie said over dinner when Anna mentioned the incident. "I don't know what's going on, but she isn't happy."

"So why take it out on me?"

"Maybe because she's been jealous of you since college?"

"Me?" Anna was flabbergasted. "That's impossible."

"Sometimes you amaze me, A. Even at school, Jan thought you were beautiful in a way she'd never be. 'Anna's Grace Kelly Ice Queen Look,' I remember her calling it. She envied your majoring in theater and starring in school productions. And now—well, you've had a successful career and you've kept in shape. Jan's stuck with George, who takes her for granted when he isn't treating her like an idiot, and yet he's her whole identity. Plus, she's let herself go physically, and her work isn't taken seriously by anyone, including herself.

"She's bitter, and it's made her boring. Not to sound cold-blooded, but if it weren't for George and the agency, I wouldn't see her much, either." The conversation helped Anna feel a little less bad about lying and leaving: one fewer friend to miss.

Not that she was leaving many friends behind. As her departure time approached, she found herself wishing she'd spent less time working and more time getting to know acquaintances better. Maybe next year she would. Having had the rug pulled out from under her was changing her perceptions. She'd always considered herself a loner, but it had never occurred to her she might end up alone.

Then she was on a plane bound for London. This time, she hadn't downloaded magazines filled with articles about aging women. Instead, she waited until she got to Heathrow early the next morning, then, thinking she should learn what was new and hot in Britain, she bought some music and fashion monthlies.

As soon as she walked out to the passenger pickup zone outside the customs exit, she spotted the Bentley at the curb, Barton's dour chauffeur standing ramrod straight next to its open trunk. "How are you, Aleksei?" she asked as he took her two checked bags and her carry-on.

She supposed his unsmiling nod as he held the car door for her meant everything was peachy keen. Once again, the privacy partition was up, isolating her from the front of the car.

Screw you, Anna thought, then settled back and, since she'd slept little, promptly closed her eyes. She woke to see countryside slipping past quickly, Aleksei making good time in the sparse Sunday morning traffic, blurred arrows indicating towns she'd never heard of posted along the divided highway. When they turned off onto a smaller road, she twisted in her seat and noted the signs to London pointed the other way. She leaned forward and tapped lightly on the partition, which inched down minimally. "Excuse me, aren't we going to London?"

"*Nyet*," came the guttural answer. "Another place. Mr. Barton comes to see you tomorrow." *Bzzzzzz,* said the partition as it slid back up. Anna was annoyed, though not so much that she didn't fall asleep again immediately.

She woke again as the car was crunching up a very long gravel drive ending at a sprawling stone mansion. The front door opened, and a burly man in a dark suit, white shirt, and striped vest emerged. He bowed slightly to Anna as Aleksei pulled the bags from the trunk. "I am Mikal. I take your bags." Another Russian. All of Pierre's wife's old family retainers, perhaps.

Before getting back in the car, Aleksei said, "They will call you 'Lisa.' You are Lisa Jones here." Then he turned away and she followed the broad black serge-covered back of Mikal up the wide steps to the open front door.

Inside, a dour Scotswoman introduced herself as Mrs. McCallum. "Come to the kitchen while Mikal takes your bags to your room," she ordered, "and I'll make you a cup of tea. Americans do drink tea, don't they?"

"Yes, thank you. That would be very nice."

In the sparkling clean, large, and modern kitchen, Mrs. McCallum, as befitted her nationality and position, "kept herself to herself." She answered Anna's questions in a miserly manner that showed she wasn't used to giving anything away. "Yes, awhile," she answered when asked if she'd worked for the Bartons for a long time. As to how long, she wasn't saying. "A few years it's been."

Where exactly was this? "Here? This is Gloucestershire. Don't you know the area, then?" When Anna shook her head, she said dismissively, "Well, then you wouldn't know the nearby towns." As if sensing another question being formulated, she whipped out a tray and placed upon it a cup and saucer, spoon, teapot, milk jug, sugar bowl, and plate of oat cookies. As she poured hot water into the pot, she said, "You must be tired," turning it into a statement of fact. "Come along. I'll show you your room and draw a nice bath for you." Anna wouldn't have been surprised if she'd added, "Don't dawdle."

The older woman led the way up the wide, winding staircase leading off the main wood-panelled hall. "No one else is here right now. You're in the Blue Room, and the bath is en suite." She opened the door to a large room with a view over a garden and lawn. There was a four-poster bed, built-in wardrobe, desk, and dresser. When Anna checked the wardrobe, she saw it already held her limited supply of clothing. Did butlers unpack for guests? As best she remembered from *Upstairs, Downstairs*, the old families had employed ladies' maids, but she supposed Mikal did anything that fell outside Mrs. McCallum's areas of cleaning and cooking.

The housekeeper was already running the bath, and she seemed to have every intention of staying in the bathroom until the tub was filled. Anna arranged the items from her carry-on bag on top of the dresser, the bedside tables, and the writing desk by the window. Then she sat to drink her tea.

When the housekeeper emerged, her wire-rimmed glasses were fogged with steam. "That's ready for you, then," she said in her no-frills way. "What time would you like lunch, or would you rather sleep?"

"Oh, no, I'll have lunch. If I nap too much, I'll never get my body clock back to normal."

"I'll bring lunch at one o'clock, then. Dinner will be in the dining room at eight. There are paths in the garden if you want a walk after lunch, though it looks like rain. Behind the panel opposite the bed, you'll find a telly and DVD player as well as one of those iPods and some films. Books over there, next to the desk. Mr. Barton will come for breakfast tomorrow at half past seven." She nodded—curtly, of course—and was gone.

Anna luxuriated in the deep old-fashioned bathtub, letting the tension and airport grime melt away. Then she wrapped herself in the soft robe she'd found hanging from a hook on the door and slipped under the bed's fluffy duvet. She woke on her own an hour later and was already dressed in jeans, sweatshirt, and joggers when the tap came at the door.

Mrs. McCallum, bearing lunch, replaced one tray with another. "If you want to go outside after lunch, close the door behind you and ring when you get back. It's spitting out there but not enough to keep anyone indoors." Her tone implied only the weak shrank from a little rain. "There are wellies and macs in the mudroom off the kitchen. Keep the house in sight and you won't get lost."

Suddenly, Anna was ravenous. God knew what time she'd last eaten a real meal. She couldn't wait to attack the cold plate Mrs. McCallum had brought: cheeses, sliced meats, salad, breads, and a selection of sauces ranging from chutneys to mustard. A little pot held coffee, while another was filled with steamed milk. *I think I'm going to like this hotel,* she joked to herself as she picked up her knife and fork and prepared to dig in.

"Everyone looking after you all right?" Barton asked, as he sat sipping coffee across the table from her the next morning.

"More than all right," she assured him. "I had a meander around the grounds and a great dinner, thank you. You don't live here?"

"Here? No. We live in town and have a country house—just a cottage—not far from here." He gestured vaguely. "This is an investment property we use as a corporate retreat and meeting center. The third floor's all fitted out—well, you'll see it. Now, here's your schedule for the week."

And what a schedule it was. Anna stared at it, flummoxed. The next five days were completely filled with what seemed to be classes: Movement, Speech, Grooming, Attitude, Lifestyle. "You'll spend three weeks here. At the end of it, you'll look thirty years younger and be able to make people think you are. That acting experience of yours will come in handy."

"And these people, these, whatever—teachers?"

"All professionals. Your name for the time being is Lisa Jones. You're an off-Broadway actress from New York who's working on a one-woman show in which you'll need to portray a twenty-five-year-old. You've come here and rented this house to study in preparation for rehearsals, then you'll be taking the show to the Edinburgh Fringe before opening off-Broadway in the fall."

"They fell for that story, that some unknown American actress has all this at her disposal to bone up for a part off-Broadway?"

He shrugged. "They fell for the high fees. Maybe they think you're a wealthy and unrealistic dreamer. It doesn't really matter, does it?" He handed her a folder. "Lisa Jones's fact sheet is in here, as are brief bios of your coaches. You'll have new coaches each week, as your looks change."

"My looks? The results are going to appear that quickly?"

"Actually"—he pulled a paper from his portfolio—"because we're speeding up the process a little, I need you to sign this consent for laser resurfacing. Aleksei will drive you to the facility Saturday. It's low-intensity laser, solely to accelerate the absorption of the ingredients, nothing to be scared about. You'll start using the three products immediately after the treatment: cleanser, moisturizer, and night treatment. Our nurse will explain it all to you. Face, neck, *décolleté*, hands, and arms only, and be sure to use the exfoliating cleanser on all areas first. The products are stronger than what we're producing for everyday use—again, to accelerate the results. You'll be switched to the normal strength after the three weeks." He handed her a white tube. "In the meantime, you need to apply this high-strength retinol morning and evening, starting tonight, avoiding the eye area. Your skin will peel like a sunburn by Saturday, primed for laser. That morning, just rinse your face with water, nothing else. If you go outside any time when it isn't raining, stay out of the sun and use sunblock as well—there's some SPF 50 in your bathroom cupboard."

"Retinol? Laser?" She shook her head. "Why wasn't I told this? And how do I know it's safe?"

"Retinol is given out like lollipops by dermatologists for skin renewal, and laser is done over lunch hour these days. You know that, Anna. As for safe, I can show you the statements from our labs showing that the Youngskin products meet FDA standards. I told you that."

"And besides the classes, what is there to do? We seem to be in the middle of nowhere."

He raised his eyebrows. "Well, yes, we are. You can't just let people see you looking younger every day. Losing ten years a week is going to be pretty noticeable, Anna. Mikal and Mrs. McCallum have been told you're having laser and plastic surgery. No one else except Aleksei knows anything. Have you set up the computer?" At her puzzled look, he said, "Your top desk drawer. The housekeeper should have told you. You'll find your new laptop and your official BarPharm BlackBerry, which will be the *only electronics* you'll use from now on. There's Wi-Fi if you want to go online, but don't order anything or have books downloaded. Don't use your credit cards or anything with your real name on it anywhere from now on. If you want a book or DVD, tell me and I'll make sure you get it.

"Also, you should start your diary on the rejuvenating experience right away. Write about the classes, how you feel, how you see yourself. How does your walk change? What do you think makes your voice sound like that of a woman in her fifties and how can you change it? That sort of thing.

"So you see? You'll have plenty to do, plus homework. All the instructions are in the folder, which you'll return to Aleksei intact when you leave here."

She must have looked like she was freaking out—she certainly felt like it—because he quickly reassured her. "This is all just for confidentiality, Anna. Industrial espionage is always a threat, even more so in pharmaceuticals than in cosmetics. We need to be careful. We're dealing with a very important product. Now"—he pushed his chair back, smiling—"I'll tell Mrs. McCallum to bring your breakfast. I look forward to reading your first diary entry tomorrow."

This is absurd, she thought as she waited for her breakfast to come. *Movement. Grooming. Lifestyle!* Did he really think he could make a fifty-seven-year-old woman pass for twenty-five again? She was a good enough actress not to need these dumb classes, but her age was her age. No one was ever going to buy her as someone in her twenties. And all this cloak-and-dagger silliness about returning files and for-your-eyes-only? She knew companies stole each other's formulas; she was used to some degree of secrecy. Was Barton a nutcase? She pushed that thought out of her mind as Mrs. McCallum arrived bearing a tray. This project was going to make her rich. Surely, that meant she could humor the man paying her and pretend that she, too, thought some skin cream might be a matter of life and death.

Netherlands, September 11, 2011

Anna was roused from her daydreaming as the conductor collected tickets. Her eyes opening was the cue the girl across from her had been waiting for. "Do you go to school in Berlin?"

"Me? Oh, no, I'm just traveling around. I graduated from college in the States. NYU." _Stop overexplaining,_ she told herself sternly.

"Oh, cool! You're American, too." Her seatmate, who wore a holey sweater as long as her miniskirt over ripped tights with clogs, clearly wanted to talk. She said she was taking a year to "hang" in Europe before returning home to Florida to face a master's program. "I was in Amsterdam for a month, long enough. I'm gonna hang in Berlin until who knows when, because it's, like, _the_ place now. Amsterdam has too many old hippies for me."

"It's pretty, though, isn't it?" Anna said, already barely remembering having been there. "I'm Lisa, by the way."

"I'm Chyna. With a _y._" Her grin was open and friendly as a child's. "Hey, we should hang together in Berlin. I don't know, like, a soul. It will be nice that I know somebody now."

That was fine with Anna. "Where are you staying tonight?"

"Thought I'd head over to Prenzlauer Berg where they say the best hostels are. You?"

"I had the same idea. Maybe we can go together, if that's okay?"

"Totally. If it's not crowded, we might even be able to score a whole four-bed dorm to ourselves. You pay by the bed, not by how many people share the room. So we could end up with a deuce for the price of sharing a quad. Cheaper than renting a double."

"Saving money sounds good to me." As did Chyna's being the one to show a passport at check-in.

"Cool, then." Chyna stood and stretched. "I'm gonna walk to the bar car and get a Coke. You want anything?"

"I'm good, thanks. I brought a sandwich. By the way," she added as Chyna turned to go, "what are you getting your master's in?"

"Performance. I'm applying to schools that offer MFA programs." She froze, then did some quick, expert robotic moves. "Please don't hate me for being a mime!"

Then, giggling, she hobbled, bent over in imitation of an elderly woman, to the end of the car, leaving Anna to quickly bend over, too—over one of her books, pretending to read. But she couldn't concentrate. She wondered what Chyna would say if she knew what a great performance artist Anna had learned to be, if she knew "Lisa" was probably older than her own mother.

Chapter 6

"Now, Lisa, put on these shoes and walk across the floor."

Anna slipped into a pair of red stiletto heels, the highest she'd worn for at least two decades, and tentatively made her way across the industrial-carpeted floor of the gym in the old Gloucestershire manor house. Standing, arms akimbo, watching her every move, was a woman her age or older named Gilda, with a dancer's lithe body. She wore, as did Anna, tights and a leotard, leg warmers, and shoes with six-inch heels.

"No, no, no. That simply won't do," Gilda pronounced when Anna had crossed the room and returned. "You look like a female impersonator who's spent his entire life in a pair of motorcycle boots, pet. Do it again, but like this."

Anna watched Gilda as she walked with sexy, sinuous steps, then smaller, faster steps. "You see? No bending forward. You aren't walking into the wind. Lead with the thighs and let your bottom sway behind them."

"May I have a glass of water first, please?"

Gilda shook her head with the firmness of a drill sergeant. "Break's in fifteen minutes. Now, walk." Anna was equally unstable walking, running, even just standing. By the time the lesson had finished, she'd decided she'd just have to insist on being a hot young thing in flats. Plenty of younger women everywhere wore ballet slippers and Doc Martens and UGGs. She'd have to—even if it meant accessorizing with a fake ankle cast as an excuse.

From Movement with Gilda, she moved on to a small meeting room, probably used for Barton Pharmaceuticals' retreat seminars, and Speech with Sam, a fast-talking New Yorker in his forties who specialized in coaching British actors to sound more American. "I'm not used to working with someone who already sounds homegrown but needs to pass for younger, so it should be fun."

By the end of the hour, Anna was speaking faster and dropping more g's at the ends of words, which didn't seem like all that big a deal. She thought she sounded young enough until Sam told her, "Your voice is too low and mellow, Lisa. That comes with maturity. Let's see if we can push it up an octave. Everyone's voice deepens with age, so a younger woman's would have a higher pitch than yours."

She was only slightly offended by being told even her voice was old, but surprised to find it wasn't that easy throwing it higher. At first, she sounded like Tweety Bird, and she snorted with laughter as Sam watched her, smiling. "You have the register. I can tell by your laugh—it's so much higher than your voice."

"You mean my cackle? God, I'd love to change that. I hate my laugh."

"Nah, keep it," he said. "It's cute. It has a lot of personality."

She enjoyed every minute of Speech. Later, sitting at the desk in her room jotting down some reminders for her diary, she realized she'd enjoyed Movement, too, even if those shoes from hell had played their part. It was like being an acting student again or in summer stock. She thought it would be fun playing someone else. *Totally,* she added to herself—youthfully. *Totes.*

Grooming "class" was filled with surprises. Her coach, Fleur, was younger and more blue collar than her name implied. Perhaps

Anna wasn't the only one in the room who'd changed her moniker. The bio in Barton's folder described Fleur as a twenty-seven-year-old who wrote an online hipster fashion blog.

That first day, Fleur asked Anna questions, then told her how wrong she was. "What's your natural hair color?"

Anna shrugged. "I haven't seen it for a long time. I guess kind of dark blond with some gray."

"You gonna have a wig for your performances? No? Well, no one under forty except rich Russians has time for all that blond tortoiseshelling you've got anymore. Unless your director fights it, go red. I'd say medium auburn with flame and yellow stripes."

"Yellow? You mean blond?"

Fleur cracked her gum and looked at Anna as if she'd just stepped out of a spaceship that had landed on the lawn. "Yellow, Lisa. As in, *yellow*. I'll bring some shots on my iPad tomorrow, to give you an idea. 'Cause that style's got to go, too. I'd pick short and spiky if I were you. Your face is kinda long for long hair. Don't wanna look all Celine Dion."

Celine Dion? Before Anna could even express horror at the comparison—she couldn't stand Celine Dion—Fleur was on to the next thing.

"You'll be doing your own makeup? When we meet tomorrow, wear makeup—I mean, wear it all—and I'll critique it for you," she ordered.

"I *am* wearing it all."

That got her an eye roll. "What do you do, go into a store and ask for whatever they have in drab? I can give you some tips to spice it up."

And so it went until, by the end of the hour, Anna felt as if everything about her had been shouting "Old broad coming through!" for years.

Her Attitude teacher, Meredith, described in her bio as a professional acting coach, was a far cry from Fleur. Anna's age, she conformed to the caricature of a typical middle-class Englishwoman. Her appearance was dreary, from her dun-colored hair to her tweedy pantsuit. She went through a list of what she seemed to think were cutting-edge words, but most of them—like *hottie* and *hookup*—were nothing new.

"The thing is, Meredith, I don't need to sound like a rock star, just like a younger woman."

"You should learn the words before deciding you aren't going to use them," was the tart reply. She ordered Anna to go to urban-dictionary.com and to follow young actors' Twitter feeds in order to learn ten new expressions to use every day. "Now, let's go over these words again."

Anna could have used a few BarPharm pick-me-up prescriptions to get through the day. By the time Leo-Nardo showed up for Lifestyle class at five o'clock, she was exhausted, swamped by delayed jet lag.

Leo-Nardo was, in his words, "part Jamaican, part Argentinean, a slap of Chinatown, and a shitload of God Save the Queen." He was small and sleek, with dark olive skin and hair that looked to Anna's professional eye like an old-fashioned Jheri curl. He could have been the runner-up at a Prince look-alike contest.

She was told to call him "just plain Leo," pronounced as "Layo." He worked, she knew from his bio, as a deejay in various clubs around London. He could have passed for eighteen or fifty-eight, being such a mix of styles and tics; it was hard to pin anything down. He dressed "from the 'hood"—in half-laced bulky Nikes, jeans so low-slung the back pockets were almost to his knees, and a tight T-shirt that showed off his muscles and made him look younger than his weary, seen-it-all eyes.

"Imma give you a list of shit to do on the net tonight, and then tomorrow, we do iTunes 'n' all," he said. "But your producer"—Anna wondered if Barton had played that role himself—"says you gotta learn the hot covers, what a girl with her shit together would be into. Yeah? What music do you listen to now? House? Acid? Hip-hop? Rap?"

She shrugged. "You won't be impressed. Sixties and seventies rock. Jazz. Opera. A little pop." Trying not to sound mocking, she added, "*That* shit."

Leo-Nardo burst out laughing. "Man, we got our work cut out for us this week. You probably love that Celine Dion, too, huh?" He collapsed in laughter, so amused that Anna didn't bother to tell him she didn't like Celine Dion. Or that she did *not*—in any way whatsoever—resemble her.

———

Monday, June 20

The "me" that my coaches seem determined to turn out doesn't sound at all like me, the real me, and only slightly like me when I was in my twenties. I wonder if I'll feel like a fraud or if the Youngskin product will make me actually *feel* youthful again?

One thing today's sessions helped me see is that youth is about more than skin, though that is clearly of vital importance and will be to all Youngskin users. But age is a state of mind that runs the gamut from fashion to catchphrases to books and music and movies. The older coaches don't seem all that different from me—I imagine Gilda, Sam, and Meredith spend their free time pretty much as I would. (By the way, Meredith doesn't have a clue how *anyone* of any other age actually speaks; she's useless.) But the younger ones, Fleur and Leo-Nardo, inhabit a different universe.

And in just a few weeks, I'm going to be passing myself off as one of them. Can I do it? Do I even need to? So much of what I'm being taught seems superfluous, behavior that might work in a movie but would seem absurd in real life unless I were a teenager. But I think my own judgment will let me emerge from my lessons with a believable new persona.

So out goes Anna, and in comes Lisa. She'll be a whole new person if she survives this. A *young* one.

———————

Berlin, September 12, 2011

The shared-room-at-the-hostel plan worked fine, and the next day Anna had appointments to look at rooms in three crowded, hipster areas: Friedrichshain, Neukölln, and Kreuzberg. Armed with Chyna's cell number, she went out after locking up whatever she felt secure leaving behind. Those bolted-to-the-floor lockers were making her a hostel fan.

She bought a new German cell SIM at a shop down the street and scrapped the Dutch one she'd used only once. Was she safe? She had no idea. She hoped dyeing her hair a dull brown the other night would be a lifesaver. With a few drab brown hanks poking out from her knit cap and no makeup on, she wouldn't have recognized herself as either Anna Wallingham or Tanya Avery. Then again, she wasn't a killer on her own trail.

She slouched through the streets and on and off the U-Bahn, hiding behind her map like a tourist and trying to call as little attention to herself as possible, refusing to give in to the terror that made her want to check for dangers. The first apartment wasn't a squat but might as well have been, more crash pad than home. One look at the congealed grease in the kitchen and mildewed spots on the walls and Anna shook her head. "Sorry," she told the sullen German girl showing the place, "I'm a clean freak." She got an I-could-care shrug in return.

She'd heard Neukölln was up-and-coming, but the zone the second flat was in was more down-and-going. She negotiated cracked cobblestones between graffiti-spattered buildings with a sinking feeling that proved justified when she was buzzed in only to practically trip over two nodding junkies in the trash-infested courtyard. She went back out front, rang again, and said, "Thanks . . . but no."

Luckily, the third time was the charm. She found Kreuzberg lively and colorful, its streets filled with Turkish women buying produce, up-all-night goths heading home, and others of all types, races, and ages. She lunched on Tibetan noodles in a cute little restaurant, where a two-course meal cost less than a glass of wine in London.

The apartment was a first-floor walk-up off the busy Mehringdamm. Its door was opened by a tall blue-eyed young woman with hair the color of wheat. "I'm Kirsten," she said. "Danish, not German. Come in."

Anna entered, and Kirsten led the way down a long, wide hallway. "Not so pretty, this hall, because the owners covered the original floorboard with laminate," she noted disdainfully. "I think they fear renting to anyone under fifty means their apartment gets wrecked." Anna would have said she'd worry, too, but "Lisa" just smiled and nodded.

The big living room was simply furnished in Ikea modern. "The lease is in Susanne's name. It's her name on the bell, Susanne Francke. She's gone to Turkey for a month with Hana, who's Turkish, so both their rooms are available. There is also Paola, who's Italian. We're like the UN. Come, I'll show you the rooms."

The two bedrooms were tiny, the apartment obviously having been broken up over the years. Each held a bed, chest of drawers, small bedside table, and a wheeled rack for clothes. There were hooks on the wall, with a shelf over them. "Not much space, but this is typical of Berlin," Kirsten noted.

There was a decent-sized bathroom with a tub and a smaller bath with a shower, as well as a long, narrow kitchen.

"I like it," Anna said when the tour ended. "And it's three hundred and fifty euros for a month?" Pretty much the cost of a single week in a hostel or cheap hotel, and no need for a passport.

"*Ja*, either bedroom. Utilities included. And I would need three hundred and fifty euros as a deposit."

"That's perfect! An American I met on the train needs a place, too. Can I call her from your phone and have her come over?"

They waited for Chyna over mint tea in the living room. Kirsten explained that she was studying German for a year before going back to Denmark to teach, then asked "Lisa" what she did. Anna pulled out the old inheritance line. "I thought this might be my only chance to see the world. Not that my grandmother left me much, but since I ditched my awful job, I've been traveling on the cheap: London, Paris, Amsterdam. A month is good—long enough to get to know a place."

Kirsten grinned. "What was the awful job?"

"Supposedly the assistant editor at an interior design magazine. Instead, I was a glorified file clerk. Not so glorified, either. Bumming around Europe was a better option."

When the buzzer sounded, and Kirsten went to let in Chyna, Anna shook her head in bemusement at her own inventiveness. Still, when all this was over, she thought she really *would* try writing a novel. If she survived.

Chyna loved the apartment, so Kirsten went over the house rules. They were simple: no going into one another's bedrooms without asking, no dates brought in without agreement, and no overnight guests ever.

They got to meet Paola before they left. Small, dark, and friendly, she, like Kirsten, spoke impeccable British-accented English. "In Italy, you have the choice of British or American teachers for private English lessons," she explained when Anna commented. "We choose British if we wish to sound classy."

"I'll have you talking unclassy pretty soon," Chyna promised, and with that, the deal was done.

"Come at ten tomorrow and I'll have keys," Kirsten said when they were leaving.

"What's your plan, then?" Chyna asked Anna when they were sitting in a café over big salads that evening. "You're outta here in a month, right?"

"I might leave even sooner if my boyfriend can take a few weeks off and wants to meet someplace else," she said, laying the groundwork for any sudden departure.

"Not going back to the States?"

"No plans yet. Right now, I'm happy to be here." *And to be alive,* she added to herself.

It was only eight o'clock when they got back to the hostel. "What now?" Chyna asked as Anna pushed the button for the elevator. "Want to come check out a club later? I'm having a drink with these Aussies I met earlier, then we're going out. Would you believe some clubs here have happy hour from two to four—in the morning? Mega-awesome, huh?"

"Early to bed for me. I ran all over town today. But have fun."

"Oh, I will. And I'll try not to crash into the furniture when I come in!"

Anna could still hear Chyna's high-pitched laughter as the elevator doors closed behind her. Maybe she'd be glad to get away from so much youthful exuberance at some point, but the girl's enthusiasm was cheering. Chyna also kept her from being easy to spot. That might not make them bosom buddies, but it made her almost as good as a real friend.

Chapter 7

The rest of that first week at the manor house was more of the same, with the addition—starting on Day Two after a prebreakfast piece of fruit and cup of tea at half past six—with a full workout with Joe, a former United States Marine turned exacting personal trainer. Joe's specialty was getting stars in shape for movies, and Anna soon understood how he could turn any quivering blob of jelly into muscle in record time.

She was puzzled that all these coaches were so incurious about her. No one asked any questions. Nor did they say anything about their own lives.

She was nosy. She decided Fleur would be the easiest nut to crack, so in between discussing trends, she tried a little casual pumping.

"Do you coach people like this all the time?"

"No, not really."

"So how did my people get in touch with you?"

"The usual channels. You know."

"Mmmn. And your next job? Is . . . ?"

Finally, Fleur snapped. "Look, Lisa," she said, her voice rising, "I need this gig. And, as I'm sure you know, part of the agreement is that I can't talk about anything except what I'm here for. So please don't do this."

"Oh, God, I'm sorry, Fleur. You must think the whole setup is weird anyhow."

"If your producer has money for all this"—her sweeping gesture encompassed the house, the lessons—"the rest is none of my business. He must know what he's doing."

After that, Anna shut up and submitted to her coaches' supposed expertise, though she was doing little more than humoring them. When the end of the week finally arrived, she thought objectively that she was moving and sounding more like a younger woman, had a bit better grasp of current lingo, and could tell the difference between bands previously unknown to her. But she considered most of the training a waste of her time and Barton Pharmaceuticals' money.

At the end of the week, she celebrated with a festival of old films from back when she actually had been young, movies perhaps no one that age now had even heard of, much less seen, with one common theme: becoming someone else. Watching movies like *Educating Rita* and *Zelig* was her way of not thinking about the next day, when she'd be driven somewhere unknown to meet some mysterious doctor who would begin stripping the years from her face. Who wouldn't be anxious?

———————

Anna didn't sleep well. Her skin was tight and literally cracking; she was comfortable only on her back. When she dozed, she dreamed her face had turned into a chicken's, complete with beak; she pecked futilely and then realized Anna the chicken was pecking at the face of a young Anna, each tap of the beak making that face older.

At six o'clock, she gave up. No workout today, to enable her to stay "relaxed" for her procedure. After showering, she put on the most comfortable of the few clothes she'd brought, sweatpants and a shirt. Then she sat and waited, without even bread and water because she'd be getting light twilight sedation for the procedure.

Aleksei, in his usual chat-free zone, drove along back roads still shrouded in fog. When after about twenty minutes, they reached a road construction barricade and a "Diversion" sign and she saw Aleksei bang his hand on the steering wheel, she almost grinned at his showing human emotion. He pulled off the road to make a call on his cell phone, then turned the car and followed the detour sign. Anna had no idea where they were or how far they'd gone. She saw a signpost saying "Dibden Village, 10k," then just hedgerows and fields skimming by until Aleksei turned sharply into the back driveway of a small, institutional-looking building.

The way the chauffeur stood by the car watching her as she walked to the back door and rang the bell irked Anna. Did he think she was going to run off? A plain, middle-aged woman wearing a nurse's white tunic and pants let her in. "Hello, Lisa," she said. "I'm Marianne. Come with me, please."

Anna followed her down a hospital-green hallway to a small elevator. They went up a floor, then down another hallway, through a miniature operating room, and into a changing cubicle with a metal chair in it. "Take off everything but your knickers and socks, and put on the gown in that plastic wrap along with the paper shower cap and slippers on the counter there. I'll be back in five minutes. Okay?"

Just minutes later, Anna was flat on her back on the surgical table in the other room, an IV needle in her arm. Marianne loomed over her to peer at her skin appraisingly. "The retinol did a good job. I've started the IV drip, so you'll be in dreamland in no time at all. Now you're going to feel a little chill." Anna smelled nail polish remover and felt something cold on her face. "This is just acetone, to remove all the oil from your skin," Marianne explained, swabbing down her face and neck—scrubbing it, really—with gauze pads. "And then all you're going to . . ."

"Lisa, can you hear me? Time to wake up." Marianne was gently shaking her shoulder.

"When's the doctor coming?" she mumbled.

"Oh, he's been and gone. All done! Now, don't touch your face, okay? Just for today, he's put bandages on to make the creams absorb faster, so don't be scared when you see a mummy in the mirror. Don't worry about your hands and arms. No laser there. Just some dermabrasion, and you'll have extra cream on them today but no bandages. I'm coming back with you to your house. In the morning, I'll show you how to use the treatments."

"My house? Oh, oh, yeah, the house. You're going to stay? Maybe we can watch a DVD later . . . Can I have a drink of water now?" Woozily, she tried to move, but Marianne's firm hand stopped her.

"Just relax for a few minutes. I'm going to strap on this oxygen mask, okay? It will clear your head so you'll be able to get up and not feel dizzy or have a headache. Okay?"

Anna nodded, thinking how strange it would be to be a nurse and have to keep adding "okay?" at the end of everything you said. She wondered if she'd ever see the doctor, whoever he or she was. *Secrets,* she thought. *So many secrets, and I don't even know which ones I need to keep.* Then she was asleep.

By the time they got back to the house, she could walk, as long as she held on to Marianne's arm. She was led straight to her bedroom, where no sooner had the nurse helped her put on her pajamas than there was a tap at the door, and Mrs. McCallum entered with a bowl of broth and glass of ginger ale. "We're not eating together?" she asked Marianne, feeling childishly disappointed.

"Oh, no, we can't do that." Marianne grinned, but the smile was impersonal. "After all, you're the patient, and I'm the staff. I'll check on you later." She fluffed up the pillows on the bed. "Sleep only on your back, propped up, okay?"

Marianne's idea of checking on her seemed confined to stopping by before dinner and asking, "Everything okay, Lisa? Want something to help you sleep? No? Let me just put some cream on your arms then, and I'll pop in to see you in the morning."

Alone again, Anna sighed and blinked back tears that might run into the gauze on her face. She should be thrilled—she was going to be a millionaire, look better than she had in years, and have interesting and challenging work—but that didn't make her feel any less lonely. Her physical isolation matched the sense of psychic isolation she felt. She missed her friends and her home. She didn't, she realized, miss her leased Mercedes, her expensive wardrobe, her *things*.

Before going to sleep, Anna watched the latest top-grossing vampire movie that wasn't George's, figuring if she actually were twentywhatever, she would have seen it.

It wasn't bad. Well, other than its premise, which as far as she could tell was that life wasn't worth living after about thirty.

That part really sucked.

Anna was still in her pajamas when Marianne "popped in" the next day after breakfast. The nurse had brought her backpack, from which she took a camera, some jars, and a pair of blunt-edged surgical scissors. "Now, let's have a look at you. Might be a bit pink, so don't be shocked."

As she heard the scissors snip-snip-snipping through gauze and tape, Anna anxiously wondered what was beneath. Would the same old face be staring back at her? Would the changes be minimal? Would she be scabby and burnt? Would it be like a horror film, in which a face like Madame Barton's had replaced her own?

"There we go! Very good. Look straight at me, and we'll get some photos."

Anna let herself be annoyed at how nurses talked to patients as if they were toddlers. But when Marianne coyly asked, "Shall we have a look?" her heart leapt in anticipation.

She hurried into the bathroom. In the mirror over the sink, her face stared back.

Her skin was pink, yes, though no worse than a bad sunburn. There were still lines, and it could be just wishful thinking making them seem fainter. But the texture, the tone! Overnight, her skin seemed to have plumped up. It was dewy. It was radiant.

She saw Marianne's reflection appear behind her. "So? What's the verdict?"

"I think it's good." Anna leaned forward and peered at herself. "My neck feels a little tight."

"That's because you stretch the skin when you move. You want to avoid jerking your head around for a day or two as it heals. It will loosen up. And that puffiness will go down. Now, let me get the products and show you how to use them. You need to do it religiously, Lisa. Just as I say, or the results won't last and won't accelerate. Understand?"

Anna nodded, and Marianne fetched the jars from the other room, then explained in detail how and when to use each one. "No workout today, and it's best if you stay indoors and take it easy. You can resume exercise—but no heavy lifting—and your normal life tomorrow," she said. "Just stay out of the pool and out of the sun, and wear sunblock and a hat outdoors in the daytime even if it's cloudy. Follow the regimen until Friday night, but do nothing Saturday, no breakfast again and just water on your face, and I'll see you at the clinic, okay?"

Alone, Anna stayed in front of the mirror. It was almost as if she were being born again, as if the old Anna Wallingham were being erased, replaced by . . . what? Who would be looking back at her from this mirror next week? Would it be Anna? Or Lisa? Or some new, unknown person younger than both?

———————

Sunday, June 26

Being brainwashed must be like this. I made the transition to Lisa so quickly that I'm not sure I'd respond to Anna's name anymore. Pavlov's dog, that's me.

Can't wait to get out, though, to meet people who aren't being paid to speak to me. Of course, the retail Youngskin client wouldn't be dropping so many years in appearance and having to drop out of real life as I've had to, so she wouldn't feel cut off like this, would she? Will the woman who goes to her doctor for the stronger formula be able to regress this much? (Pierre, this is a question for you. Why thirty years?)

Anyhow, the big news is the face I saw in the mirror this morning. It looked fantastic. Pink and puffy, but I could see the difference. Even without laser, my hands and arms look more youthful, too. I'm actually looking forward to the next treatment, and I'm eager for my reentry as the new, younger Anna . . . or, whoops, Lisa.

I went for a walk outdoors today, and I felt a new spring in my step. Suddenly I felt, oh, I guess I'd say "viable." For the first time in ages, I envisioned a world filled with possibilities for me, as if the IV in that operating room had been dripping in optimism with the sedative.

I think this is the key to promoting the line: bringing not just a new look but a new *outlook*. And now I can see why you wanted me to experience it for myself, rather than just telling potential buyers how great they'd feel.

Tomorrow means new coaches and another new beginning. Bring it on, I say. Bring it on!

Chapter 8

The next days passed quickly. The nights remained long and dull, but Anna filled them with books and movies. One evening, she tried reading aloud the tweets of some women in their twenties, repeating them in her new higher voice, biting the words off as they spilled from her lips. "I look so hawt tonight! Imma rock my jeans and go—" She stopped. Did people really talk like that? Whatever. She wouldn't, and that was all there was to it.

This week's Movement classes were with a young actress named Joy, who thought Anna's walk was fine and flat heels would do most of the time. "The main thing to keep in mind is that the twenties are a transitional age, so you wouldn't be all over the place like an eighteen-year-old, but you still want plenty of movement, more than I can see you have naturally. You probably worked hard to develop poise, but you don't want to be too poised now."

As she felt and saw her movements grow looser under Joy's tutelage, Anna realized the coach was right—she *had* worked very hard to acquire poise—and wondered if she had lost some of her youthful spontaneity along the way. If so, she was prepared to welcome it back.

Speech was replaced by Vocabulary, with a blogger named Rick, who was a veritable trend thesaurus. He taught her all sorts of silly words like *momo*, *cramazing*, and *mega ace* that would never again issue from between her lips. When she got answers right, he'd yell, "Rock star!" Rick was amusing, but Anna pretty much ignored anything he said, deciding her own slang expressions were so old, they might pass for trendily retro.

The most exciting events of the week were her haircut and "wardrobe call" on Tuesday. A multiply pierced guy named Milo came to cut her hair in a short asymmetric crop, which he referred to as "the style you showed your producer," so she figured it had been chosen for her by Fleur. "It's convertible, see?" he said when he was finished. "Go low-key by sticking the longer bits behind your ears and brushing it smooth except to pouf it up a bit on top. When you're ready to rock 'n' roll, piece it out with gel and pomade, then push the sides forward and spike it."

"Gotcha," Anna fired back, astonished at what a difference a hairstyle could make. She looked funky and sassy. The twice-daily applications of Youngskin were paying off, too. In dim light, she could probably pass for late thirties.

Wendi, a photo shoot fashion stylist who looked about twelve and even wore Mary Janes with her minidress, arrived in the afternoon with bags and a rack of clothes. "Your producer says you'll need four to six outfits?" she said, her voice rising at the end questioningly. This, Anna soon discovered, was how she said everything, Valley Girl Meets Brit. "So, I brought, like, pieces you can wear alone or mix up? And I have shoes and bags and all, too?"

Anna wondered if Wendi thought she was weird for taking each outfit into the bathroom to change, but, while she was in great shape for her real age, she worried that the discrepancy between her face and body was growing. She found herself looking at that body below the neckline less often, unwilling to see a mutant. Only the thought of a million pounds, and the prospect of her face returning to a somewhat younger version of her old self in a year, plus her vow to keep working out until her body looked fantastic, kept her calm.

She ended up with a collection of things she wouldn't have looked at twice two months before: a brown-and-red tribal print pencil skirt to wear with the cream fringed crocheted vest (hadn't she bought something similar at Sears in junior high?) and red jersey top; green treggings, a cross between leggings and tights; and the indigo stretchy "skinnies" that were tight as the treggings but heavier and more jeans-ish and seemed also to be called "jeggings." She also picked out an oversized white shirt, cropped jacket, long black cardigan, another skirt, some tops with three-quarter sleeves to cover her jiggly upper arms, and what Wendi termed "the most awesome LBD" (little black dress)—a tight micromini with shawl collar and gauzy sleeves. That would be enough until whenever she could go shopping on her own.

Then there were the shoes. She refused to try on sky-high platforms or multibuckle stilettos that looked like torture chambers, opting instead to totter just slightly in somewhat lower black-and-silver peep-toes that would work all right with the LBD. She lunged at black UGGS and brown low-heeled ankle boots. When she tried on the latter, she did it all wrong, of course, and Wendi looked at her as if she'd fallen off a turnip truck. "But nobody wears ankle boots *laced*, Lisa!" she giggled. She undid them halfway. "This is better."

"I just wanted to make sure they fit right," Anna bluffed.

She also took a pair of red "flatforms" and some standard-issue black Vans. For bags, she chose a big and busy Desigual tote pieced from clashing prints and with all sorts of chains and coin purses and purposeless bits and pieces hanging from it. It was a bag no woman over forty would carry, and that's what she wanted. Its frankly fake pleather trim made her shiver in horror, but it was big enough for a laptop or whatever else she might have to drag around. She also took an oversized black fake-snakeskin clutch and a black backpack.

Wendi meticulously mixed and matched tights and socks for her. At the end, Anna had to ask for a list of what went with what, saying she needed it for the woman who would be her dresser for her show rather than admitting she never would have thought of wearing the lace-cuffed ankle socks with the peep-toes.

"Smalls?" Wendi asked.

"Small whats?"

Wendi giggled. "Sorry. That's what we call undies here, our smalls."

"Really? I've heard *knickers*, but never smalls."

"Well, it's a laundry thing? You know, the smalls are the smaller bits of washing? I guess you won't be stripping down onstage?" She giggled again at her own joke. "I'll make that list for you and then I think we've got it."

She'd need outerwear, too, Anna knew, but it was warm now so the jacket and sweater would do. Still, it was England, where seasons knew no boundaries, rain could go on for days, and it could sleet in the summer. She would shop for a leather jacket and get a heavier coat later. *What I should be buying is a lambskin jacket,* she thought. After all, she was about to become what the British scathingly called older women who didn't dress their age—mutton dressed as lamb. Of course, in her case, no one would know.

After Wendi had left, Anna ate lunch at the desk, wishing the week were almost over rather than just started. She wanted to get on with it. She was bored with reading Twitter and Facebook, sick of scanning gossip columns, weary of watching movies with women in their midtwenties cast as comic-book vixens. The films were never memorable; the gossip was cattier than she remembered from thirty years ago. What happened to actresses as role models? Now, the rage was mocking them for tight pants that showed their "camel toe," exposing their pimples or cellulite as if they were scandals, and rating reality starlets' sex tapes. She was almost relieved this wasn't her first shot at being young.

Still, she had to admit she wouldn't have minded if the treatments literally had been able to turn back the clock. She liked the person she was becoming; she even suspected having to act like someone half her age was going to be the most fun she'd had in years.

———————

Pierre emailed to chide her for not sending enough diary entries. "I don't really have much to write about yet. The people interacting with me are afraid to give away anything so they don't speak unless spoken to," she responded pointedly. "I'll be able to connect more when I can mingle with the real world and not just those you pay to deal with me."

She didn't see much of any of them. Her coaches showed up by appointment only. Mrs. McCallum drifted in and out bearing trays, as unforthcoming as the housekeepers in old horror films. Anna supposed it was Mrs. McCallum who cleaned her bedroom—it was always shipshape when she returned after her morning lessons or a walk.

She wasn't walking much, though. Mikal was more an unseen presence than a butler, and when once she'd walked as far as the front gate, she found it locked. She turned to find him coming up behind her. "Mr. Barton says please stay on the property," he rumbled. She had nodded and scurried off, unsettled and convinced he was more guard than manservant. But was he her protector or her jailer? She pushed the question from her mind. As for Aleksei, she expected to see him only two more times, when he drove her to the clinic for her second procedure and when he took her to where she'd be living in London, and that would be just fine with her.

The solitude was making her think too much, wondering if she should have been more careful before signing any piece of paper Barton waved under her nose. Why hadn't she asked about having to keep her older body covered up or demanded documentation regarding any side effects? But she knew the answer. If she had stayed in California, sold her house to escape the mortgage, and rented a little apartment, she would be at a dead end. *That* wasn't her life. *This* was her life. She'd been given a second chance. She had proof of that: in her folder from Barton she'd found a receipt for the first quarterly deposit from a Swiss bank into her account in LA—£250,000. Almost $400,000! When anxiety pulled her down, she just conjured up the image of her bank balance.

In spite of missing her friends, the time between emails back home was growing longer; she found herself copying and pasting and personalizing the first and last lines. She pasted in photos she found online. So far, she had journeyed to Hong Kong and Tokyo and was thinking about Kuala Lumpur and Bali. She kept everything brief lest anyone guess her adventures were straight out of a travel blog. She didn't go into detail since keeping her stories straight could get complicated, and she couldn't help but feel guilty at Richard's and Allie's enthusiastic responses, at their joy in her supposed freedom.

That evening, Barton emailed to say he would see her after her workout the next day. Was he coming to read her the riot act about not writing her every thought in the damned diary, or did he actually have something to discuss?

As soon as they were seated in the dining room, Barton produced a manila folder. "Here's what we have thus far on the UK launch of Madame X," he said. "I want you to go ahead and start with some ideas for the campaign. You'll find a study done last year on the cosmetics-buying habits of British women over forty, with some variations from the US statistics. The folder also has information on the in-house staff you'll be working with. Becca and Chas are used to dealing with pharmaceuticals, but they're both creative and should work out fine. Becca's a solid copywriter and publicist. Chas is more junior. An ambitious dogsbody and nobody's fool. He'll handle administrative tasks and whatever else you need doing. Nominally, you'll report to our marketing VP, but he's going to let you run with it."

"Terrific. I miss working."

"You're familiar with the Dropbox app to share documents?" When she nodded, he said, "Good. Download it. I've set you up with a new email address. It's tanyaavery@barpharm.co.uk." When she opened her mouth, about to ask who Tanya Avery was, he shook his head. "Later." He handed her a slip of paper with a short line of letters and numbers scrawled on it under the email address. "Log in with this, then change your password so it's yours alone."

She smiled. She had already chosen "FiredByU."

"I'll be sending you a request so we can share a Dropbox folder. From now on, put all your emails and diary entries into the Dropbox where they'll be less susceptible to hacking and we can both check in. Don't keep anything that's just between us or about Youngskin on the computer, only in the Dropbox. The computer is for your regular office files—memos, work on Madame X, and such. Got it?" Anna nodded.

"And, remember, no using your own phone or iPad ever. No purchases, no catching up with BuzzFeed, no downloading, no browsing, no anything."

"I left them in LA."

"Good." He paused. "You look good, Anna. Not at the finish line yet, but very good. From your diary entry, I take it the first procedure went well?"

"Oh, yes. I didn't feel a thing. And I've been slathering on the products day and night."

"Excellent. The doctor will be pleased with the results. Speaking of which, you need to sign these." He handed her several documents, Post-its marking their signature lines. Seeing her narrowed eyes, he explained, "For the injectables. The doctor's going to do more laser, but he'll also give you some minor injections: Juvederm or Restylane to plump up your lips, fill in the fine lines, firm up your jawline. Maybe Botox for the lines around your eyes and on your forehead. Never fear, it won't be so much your forehead goes all white and sweaty like David Cameron's," he added in what Anna supposed was, for him, a quip.

"Shots? Why weren't injectables mentioned before?"

"Simply because the doctor hadn't seen you before last week. The injectables are just fillers, Anna. You know, hyaluronic acid-based; they'll wear off gradually over the course of six months to a year. Otherwise, as your skin grows younger looking, your thinning lips will look strange and the hollows under your cheekbones, which we all have after a certain age, might make people wonder if you're older than you first appear. Why am I telling you this? You know more about these things than I do, I'm sure."

"How can you tell how well the products work if I need all this laser and filler to look younger?" she asked. "It doesn't seem like a fair test. And why do I need to look so much younger if the women who use the product won't?"

"Do you want to stay here for three months?" he asked somewhat peevishly. "That's how long it will take the average woman to see strong changes with the retail version. And the dermatology strength generally requires one month of steady use with a peel first." He sighed, but when he spoke again, his voice was gentler. "You need to trust me, Anna. I understand that you're anxious, but we have a timetable here, and everything is already tested and known to be safe."

She opened her mouth to protest anew the way things kept coming up unexpectedly. Then she thought about her bank balance and the face she was seeing in the mirror these days. Finally, she signed, muttering, "In for a penny, in for a pound. Isn't that the saying here?"

"Just keep in mind you'll have financial security—and a guaranteed supply of Youngskin for the rest of your life."

"You're taking it for granted I'll want to look younger forever?"

"Maybe not thirty years younger, but ten, fifteen, twenty?"

She shook her head slowly. "I suppose it depends on what my life's like as the new me, how I feel when I wake up every day."

He smiled. "Well, how do you feel now?"

"Now? I feel confident and attractive." She laughed. "All the better, I suppose, considering my thinning lips and saggy jowls."

"Please write that down in your diary, then. I want to know how you think and feel every day. Remember, a lot of money is at stake here."

She nodded. Only later did she wonder why, when she was telling him how she felt, she'd hadn't been perfectly honest and added, "I also feel a little scared."

Friday, July 8

I can't believe three weeks of jump-starting my second youth are over already. On the one hand, the time flew by. On the other, I sometimes felt every minute weighing on me. A fifty-seven-year-old with a full-time, often boring course load and personal trainers? It was like being back in college.

Dance training was fun, though. Kenny, the American coach, made a big point of saying at the start, "Remember, Lisa, this isn't *American Bandstand* in the swinging seventies." But dancing's dancing, and other than a few hip-hop moves, he didn't have much he could show me, so we just danced up a storm.

Frankly, I still don't understand why I need to experience appearing thirty years younger when the customer won't. I take it I'm supposed to start off by experiencing the "ultimate result" of looking and feeling younger and communicate that feeling to the target market. I mean, I know the products aren't designed for women to pretend to be someone else, but I think we want to communicate that it's flexibility and openness that make people seem younger, as well as their looks. Youngskin is the key to opening the door to a rejuvenated way of thinking.

The reflection in the mirror when I brush my teeth in the morning gets the day off to a super start. And I admit the injectables were the icing on the cake. I look fantastic. "Rock star!" as my coaches would say. Maybe I look more like thirty than twenty-five in bright daylight, but I can live with that. Let people think I'm a bit older than I pretend to be; they'll still never get close to the truth.

My arms and neck are smooth and resilient, though my upper arms will never have the firmness required to go sleeveless; my face is luminous, poreless, and fresh. The workouts have paid off, so my body has shed at least fifteen years. It doesn't match my face, but I can now absolutely rock my little black dress!

I'm a little nervous about moving into London tomorrow. Saturday in the big city after this isolation will be a change. I'll be ready bright and early for Aleksei (have I mentioned how charmless he is?), and I'm eager to see the apartment, the details of which have not, as usual, been shared with me. (Sorry for the jabs, but I like to be kept more in the loop regarding my own life, more than just knowing I'll be near the Gloucester Road Tube station.) South Kensington is a neighborhood I know a little and like. It might be on the staid side, but I think I'd feel misplaced in trendier areas like Hoxton and

Shoreditch. And, yes, I've drilled myself to remember to tell everyone I'm staying at my aunt's flat.

So much to remember when you become someone else. And now I truly am someone else, someone named Tanya. Are you going to tell me how you managed legally to obtain a new UK passport with a photo taken just the other day, along with the name Tanya Avery and my date of birth approximately twenty-seven years ago? I appreciate your promise that I won't end up in jail. Funny, growing up, I would have loved having an American mother and British father, not to mention growing up in California and studying in New York.

You know, it's great to look this good again, but what really matters to me now is that I'll be working and that as long as I look ageless, I'll have a career—simply because I don't look old. I don't consider this selling out my feminist beliefs, either, which is something we should stress in marketing. It wasn't a woman's idea that women over forty have passed the point of no return in the business world; no female glazier created the glass ceiling. But as long as that's the world's misconception, then all the talented, ambitious women who have no intention of sitting at home turning into invisible grannies deserve a helping hand. A woman has the right to be externally the person she knows she is internally. And if **YOUNGER** is the key to that, I want to be Forever **YOUNG**.

Yes, "**YOUNGER**." I think this should be the brand name, should always be written with the capitals, and should be trademarked that way. We're offering women the chance to remain themselves while looking more youthful. Once I thought about it, the slogo wrote itself:

YOU, only YOUNGER.

Catchy, huh?

Chapter 9

Anna felt as nervous as any new employee on her first day of work as she was ushered into Pierre Barton's office by a woman in her midthirties who introduced herself as Eleanor Hamblett and who managed to look both efficient (tortoiseshell glasses, tweedy suit) and sexy (midlength straight dark hair, skirt short enough and heels high enough to add a note of daring).

"Thank you, Eleanor. And welcome to Barton Pharmaceuticals, Tanya." Barton stood and came around his desk—a half oval of inlaid wood that probably cost a year of Eleanor's salary—to shake Anna's hand formally, then gestured toward the couple seated on the couch against the wall. "Let me present your team: Becca Symonds and Chas Power."

The two couldn't have been more different. Becca was studious looking and shy, her eyes darting like caged finches. From her minimal makeup to her chain-salon haircut and frumpy skirt and twinset, everything about her shouted "workhorse." Becca's bio stated that she was thirty-two, probably younger than the confidence-dripping Eleanor, but she looked older. Anna wondered if Becca was taken advantage of, simply because women like Becca always were.

Everything about Chas, on the other hand, shouted "show dog!" He could have been one of those medium-ish people who pass unnoticed—brown hair, brown eyes, medium height, medium build—but he never would be. He stood out by virtue of the traits that allow up-and-comers to shift into the fast lane, passing lesser mortals like Becca. His haircut was perfect: long in front, short in back, as close to a signature as some top stylist could make with hair. His clothes were simple yet *GQ* chic, stretch corduroys and a Henley of tissue-fine summer-weight wool, with fashionably anti-fashionista suede desert boots. Mostly, though, Chas was all about that feature Anna didn't automatically connect with the UK: an exceptional commitment to dental work. His teeth were the kind of white, straight perfection most commonly associated with movie stars. Bleached, Anna thought, or perhaps veneers. Yes, an ambitious boy.

"Hey, guys, nice to meet you." She flashed her own expensive smile. "I'm really looking forward to us working together."

She stood in make-believe awkwardness until Barton said, "Let's sit over here with Becca and Chas, shall we?" She could tell the wingback chair belonged to the boss; it cut toward the desk-matching coffee table like the prow of a ship. She perched on a small club chair that matched the sofa. A quick look at the surroundings revealed understated luxury, the walls bare except for two framed antique maps, one of London and one of Paris.

Becca and Chas were trying not to stare openly as they assessed this usurper in their midst. Anna had worked long and hard getting her look right, attempting to see herself through alien eyes. Last week, she'd finished with her hair, a new stylist doing the color—going for auburn with some bold yellow streaks (yes, *yellow*), keeping Milo's style but adding what the new hairdresser had called an "in-the-now choppy fringe." She had decided to go with her tribal print skirt and crocheted vest for Day One, with red jersey, red socks, and half-laced ankle boots. She couldn't wear her own jewelry anymore—it didn't fit Tanya's style or price range. So she'd bought a bunch of cheap silver bangles and a red gummy bracelet watch, a look snatched right off the Topshop poster.

"I hear I'm going to work with a couple of real smarty-pants," she said brightly. Becca flushed and Chas worked the teeth.

"We've heard great things about you," Chas managed to get in first. "You were a consultant in New York?"

"Oh, all over." She waved a hand globally. "Did some work in Hong Kong, too. I go wherever the work is."

"Did you work on Madame X's American launch?" Becca clearly knew the answer, so Anna guessed the point of her question was to publicly establish herself as the old pro and Tanya as new girl in town. That was fine.

"Nope. I was working on a numbing product. For tats and bikini waxes, y'know? But I heard from some editor friends the launch party was brilliant. An editor who was at the party talked me up to Mr. Barton, and here I am."

"Hugh, who's VP of marketing on the Coscom accounts, is out of the office until this afternoon," Barton said after a modicum of small talk, "so I'll leave you to Becca and Chas and see you back here at four o'clock."

Becca excused herself—saying she had an analgesic press release to finish—leaving it to Chas to give "Tanya" the tour. He rose to the occasion like a guide at Universal Studios, whisking Anna through the three converted town houses in Cavendish Square that comprised Barton Pharmaceuticals' London headquarters. Even though an elevator had been put in after walls were knocked down, the place still had a homey feeling. "Restoring old houses gave the company two important advantages," Chas noted. "Added security since no other company works here and a comfortable, established atmosphere."

"I'd expected something larger."

"Oh, this is just for Mr. Barton and M&M: marketing and meetings. Wait till you see the conference room. *Off the chain.* The heavy lifting goes on at an industrial estate in Gloucestershire—and, of course, at the Barton Pharmaceutical Research Center in Switzerland."

Anna was struck by how little she knew about BarPharm. To her, the company had never been more than the new owners of Coscom, and while she'd studied up online in the past weeks, she now realized she'd been content to keep her knowledge cursory, concentrating on best-known pharmaceutical products that would add clout to the **YOU**NGER "story." The dull stuff, she had figured she would leave to someone like Becca.

After they'd toured all the floors, Chas escorted Anna to her new office. "We have our own little wing," he said. "I sit here—one-man bullpen. Becca's office is on the right, and"—he opened the door behind his desk on the left—"this one's got your name on it."

Desk. Bookcases. Window. View. Ergonomic chair. Guest chair. Anna nodded. "Super. Could you bring me all the files you have on Madame X and the UK beauty press? After you point me toward the loo, that is." The perfect Chas, she considered, might never need to pee. But she was only human.

In the ladies' room, she reapplied her trendy new brown-red lipstick, wondering if it made her look too hard. Her old one was a creamy pale coral she was sure no woman Tanya's age would look at twice in a shop. She was feeling her own age today, though. She had expected to rest on Saturday and Sunday, but once settled into her new home—a quiet second-floor walk-up in a small older building off Gloucester Road—she felt restless and eager to walk on real streets in a real city.

The flat was fine. The skirted chintz couch with matching chairs in the living room and old mahogany bedstead spoke of what her mother would have respectfully termed "quality." And she even had a closet-sized office. She stayed long enough to check the fridge and note that someone had thoughtfully left some provisions, then she locked the door and clomped downstairs in her UGGs.

She headed for Gloucester Road and the nearest Underground station, bought a rechargeable Oyster card for the Tube, then took the train to Oxford Street. She'd never thought she could have so much fun shopping alone, but being free after virtual imprisonment was exhilarating. She hit just about every midpriced, trendy chain store in London, and emerged laden with bags of clothing and makeup and a black leather motorcycle jacket.

After splurging at an eye-poppingly expensive sushi bar, she stopped at the Waitrose by the Tube station to pick up more food. Back at the flat, she unpacked and hung up her clothes, watched some television as she ate a sandwich and, after she'd anointed herself with **YOUNGER**, slept deeply.

First thing next morning, she caught up with the news online and sent emails ("Hi! Just arrived in Bangkok and am trying to find a cheap pension, but it's just for a few days before I go off to explore and escape the pollution"). When she'd finished, she did everything Pierre had instructed, putting copies in the Dropbox, then deleting both the originals and her browsing history before turning off the computer.

Only after making the bed and tidying the flat did she indulge herself in the guilty pleasure of a real English fry-up breakfast at a café. Sometimes, a girl just had to have eggs, bacon, sausages, mushrooms, grilled tomatoes, and baked beans, right? Then she wandered contentedly around her neighborhood, thrilled to feel concrete under her feet and see throngs of strangers after her lonely weeks at the mansion.

She'd girded herself for Monday, so was pleased with how well it turned out. Becca invited her to lunch, most certainly on Barton's orders, to a brasserie down the street. Over salad Niçoise, Anna tried to draw out the other woman. It was hard work at first. Viewing Anna as a competitor, Becca was on guard, so Anna concentrated on presenting herself as a harmless ally, chattering about her off-and-on boyfriend back home. She made a point of stressing how excited she was about her temporary job with Becca and Chas at BarPharm.

By the end of lunch, Becca had warmed up enough for Anna to learn that she still lived in the suburbs with her parents, liked Chas and had hired him herself three months before, and thought both Pierre's personal assistant and wife were, in her words, "not very friendly." *Crush on the boss*, Anna mentally filed away.

"Pierre's assistant seems like she's got her shit together— oops, sorry, I forgot I'm in London now and not Noo Yawk." She mugged and Becca laughed appreciatively. "I mean, she looks superefficient."

"Oh, she is," Becca said so emphatically it wasn't a compliment. "Efficiency is Eleanor's middle name. As for Marina—Mrs. Barton—she doesn't come to the office often, but when she does, she rarely makes the effort to say hello. Odd, isn't it? I mean, when he's so nice. And gentlemanly."

Anna almost laughed out loud. All that studying and coaching to appear young, and her coworker says "gentlemanly" like a character out of Jane Austen! Still, she returned to the office satisfied that she'd be able to win Becca over, and when they discussed PR and ad strategies for the UK launch, she realized the other had talent. She had come up with some lively lines (like "Unless you're the Queen, you never want to look like it's your Jubilee Year")— enough to convince Anna that, while Becca was no style icon, she would be able to write beauty copy with the best of them. Now that she had the wunderkind Tanya to coach her.

The first week went beautifully.

Hugh, the marketing VP, amicably admitted he was thrilled to have Tanya take a lot of responsibility off his hands, explaining, "You might say I'm a nasal spray and pimple cream sort of chap. The beauty industry is more the wife's area of expertise." She met other employees and especially liked Anezka and Lorrayne, two drug sales reps employed to call on pharmacists and doctors with samples and take orders. They looked around Tanya's age and had a blatantly edgier vibe than Becca. Anezka was a young, statuesque Czech who could have been a high-fashion model, while Lorrayne, a Jamaican with a Cockney accent, punctuated most of her sentences with a good-humored laugh. Anna happily accepted their invite to go out Saturday night.

But she wasn't here to party, she reminded herself. She was here ostensibly to launch Madame X and, in reality, to come up with a marketing scheme for **YOU**NGER. Pierre was demanding diary entries, and she thought she'd better give him what he wanted.

Life was good. So far, younger was better, God was in His Heaven, and all was right with the world.

Then, returning to the office after dashing out at lunchtime on Friday to buy tights because hers had sprung a run, she ran smack into—was almost bowled over by—David Wainwright.

She would look back on that day as a turning point in her life. From then on, it got complicated. Then it got frightening.

Friday, July 15

I want to restate what will be one of the main motivations for buying **YOU**NGER: it makes the user feel so much younger as well as look more youthful. This is not just a secondary benefit. It's as important as the main one. Keep in mind that is the rationale behind most of my criticisms and how I will eventually shape the marketing campaign. We need to make it clear that while other products make the "look better, feel better" promise, they just can't deliver what **YOU**NGER can. And we will want to focus on BarPharm's clinical history to stand out from the rest of the "take years off your age" campaigns.

My **YOU**NGER test products have an excellent feel but a strong artificial scent. I know that masks the odor of the chemicals, but *flowery*? Not only does it put off possible crossover to male users, but if you look at the research data I'm attaching, you'll see that even elderly women prefer fresher scents to cloying florals these days. I'd suggest sniffing around grapefruit and other light fruit scents, such as watermelon or mango. Not almond, which is too sweet, and not coconut, which reeks of cheap suntan lotion. I like lemongrass, too.

Future men's formulations would need to be lighter than women's, not just because men have more oil in their skin but also because of texture preferences. And I think the development of a less oily, lighter consistency spin-off would also be logical for women with oilier skin. In the meantime, let's make the fragrance androgynous. Sorry if I'm straying from my personal **YOU**NGER experience here and telling you something you already know, but this diary will be the basis of our marketing plan, so . . .

To get back to how much younger I feel, part of it comes from being in better shape physically—I'm joining a fitness club to keep that up. But a lot of it's psychological, and this is a big selling point—perhaps even *the* selling point. **YOU**NGER isn't just about having nubile skin or fewer lines; it's about the bigger picture.

If I'd had my hair cut this way when I was Anna, all short and chunky and obviously dyed, it would have been laughed at as garish unless I were an artist. My short skirts would have been a no-no—looked down on with disapproval and even disgust. I feel so much freer now. If the new me dressed like the old me, I might be dismissed as boring, but it wouldn't hurt my career.

Most younger women can't afford expensive clothes, but many who could still prefer to spend less, even if they're badly made, because they know they won't be wearing them in a year or two. Unlike me, younger women were never schooled in "investment dressing," buying simple, costly things that never go out of style. I see now how rarely I bought clothes for fun. I was always motivated by how much my image would help me succeed. So looking younger has caused an internal as well as external change.

The **YOU**NGER woman isn't just gaining a new look and new outlook. She's opening the door to experiencing things anew as well. My job—when the time comes for developing the **YOU**NGER marketing campaign—will be to sell that and to make it clear that no other anti-aging products can live up to that claim.

I'm going out on the town tomorrow night. That should give me more insight into how good my act is, not to mention how much I'll enjoy being a party girl at my age.

Chapter 10

As she moved the entry into the Dropbox and deleted the traces, Anna told herself she was right not to have mentioned an incident in her personal life that had temporarily pushed everything else out of her mind. It wasn't the right time, she rationalized. She didn't even know how she felt about it, other than brain-explodingly freaked out, and there was no reason for Pierre to know she'd encountered someone from her past. Then, too, she did always feel more in control when she held back details about herself, whether it was her family background, her marriage to Monty, or her wild, party-all-night past. *I'm a secrets hoarder,* she told herself. *It's only natural I'd keep this all to myself.*

She pushed away the thought that nibbled around the edges: that she hadn't written about it because she feared for some unknown reason it might not be wise to do so.

If she'd been watching where she was going, it never would have happened. She might have peripherally noted the slim, salt-and-pepper-haired man coming down the front steps of the building, but they'd have blindly passed one another—and that would have been that. But her thoughts were on whether she should have bought the sheer rhinestone-trimmed black tights she'd just seen, since they'd look good with her little black dress on Saturday night.

She'd plowed right into him, almost knocking herself down, and he'd taken her elbow to steady her. "Sorry, I—*Anna*! My God, is it really you?"

She'd looked up, and there he was. David Wainwright. Yes, he had lines around his eyes, deeper grooves from the sides of his nose to the edges of his lips, gray in his black hair, and brushed-aluminum-framed glasses, but he was still the same David.

He was staring at her as if he'd seen a ghost. Then he shook his head as if to clear it. "Of course you're not Anna. Sorry."

"No, it's my fault. I should have been looking where I was going."

"You were going here? To Barton?"

Unthinkingly, she nodded.

"And you're American? Sorry, how rude of me. My name's David Wainwright. I've done work for the company on occasion. And you?"

"Tanya. Tanya Avery," she whispered.

"Well, nice to have bumped into you, Tanya," he said, the same teasing gleam in his blue eyes she'd loved all those years ago. "Sure you're all right?"

"Yes, I'm fine. Um . . . bye."

And she'd run up the stairs and away from him yet again.

She ducked out of the elevator and into the loo, praying no one would spot her. Trembling, she collapsed into a stall, bolted the door, and leaned against it, trying to regulate her breathing. In. Out. In. Out. *David Fucking Wainwright.*

Even though he was British, she hadn't foreseen the possibility of bumping into him in a city of nearly eight million people. She and David had never even been in London at the same time, so it held no memories of him as Paris did. Barton's offer had made her wonder what David was doing—how could it not have?—but she had been sure he was still a television director hanging out in Soho and Battersea, where the TV and media people clustered. For more than twenty years, she'd managed to avoid those areas of London whenever she visited, just as she avoided Googling his name. And she had always been sure he never thought of her at all. Still, while breaking things off with David had made her avoid the remote chance of running into him, it had also motivated her to become the kind of person she thought would impress him more than the struggling actress he'd met soon after he arrived in Manhattan to shoot a BBC crime miniseries based there, the actress who failed not only at her career but at winning his love.

Within two years, she'd changed from a hedonistic and self-doubting thespian into a fit and healthy junior ad exec. The partying she'd once done held no allure. She found it easy to stop after two glasses of wine or turn down a line of blow, and she finally got on track to the success her parents had longed for her to achieve.

She had tried not to think about David over the years, an effort that grew easier after she'd moved to California, away from the New York memories. Her friends Allie and Jan knew about him but had never met him, since neither was in New York at the time, so it was natural never to mention him. She'd had other boyfriends, even been engaged once, but in retrospect, those relationships had seemed like examples of skillful marketing, Anna convincing Anna that "this time" it was the real thing. Her last intense involvement was six months with a guy thirty-four to her fifty, whom she rarely thought of as anything but the Sex God. After that, work kept her too busy for affairs, or so she told herself, so she was thankful he had been an amazing and acrobatic lover, even if all his other good points had turned out to be arrogance in disguise.

And now? Now she was going to have to forget she'd seen David again, no matter how hard that might be.

"Of all the gin joints in all the towns, in all the world . . ." she finally whispered in a shaky voice. Then she splashed cold water on her face and went to her office.

"I need to change my tights," she told Chas, not looking at him but waving the M&S bag as she walked by. "I'll have my door locked for a sec."

Minutes later, totally collected, she strolled out and said casually, "Be right back. Craving a real cappuccino instead of a machine one."

Downstairs, the reception desk was manned by a slightly older, less intelligent version of Chas. "Hey, Brian, I wondered if you know who the guy is who left about fifteen minutes ago, graying hair, glasses?"

"Gray hair? A little old for you, isn't he, Tanya?"

She knew he was teasing, but she still blushed. "Oh, c'mon! I thought I recognized him, and now I'm wondering if it was a friend of my aunt's looking for me. Someone named Bruce or Bryce?"

"Nah, I think you mean David Wainwright, and he didn't ask for you. Was he wearing a light green shirt?"

"I think so. I didn't really notice. He just seemed familiar."

Brian shrugged. "He's a TV director who's done a commercial or two for us. Maybe you saw a red carpet shot that stuck in your mind. Happens to me all the time: I think I know somebody, and it turns out I saw them on TV going into some awards show."

"He's won awards?"

"Not that I know of. He's married to some telly actress or another, I think. Don't remember which. No one really famous, just someone who gets to go to awards shows."

She smiled stiffly. "Not Aunt Marjorie's friend then. Want a cappuccino? I'm going to Starbucks."

"Nah, thanks for asking, though."

As she turned to leave, Anna gave him a blinding smile, hoping that—like the gizmo in *Men in Black*—it would wipe the last two minutes from his memory.

Her smile fell off even as the door closed behind her. *Married.* He was married. Of course he was married. She should have known he'd be married. And to an actress, no less. Obviously someone more talented than she had been. "Forget him, forget him, forget him," she muttered. It didn't matter that he was married since she was never going to see him again.

On the way back from Starbucks, another strange thing occurred. About two blocks from the office, she saw a Bentley, the same deep blue as Pierre Barton's, on the other side of the street. As she got closer, the man himself practically leapt from the back seat of the car. She ducked into the shadow of a doorway without thinking, transfixed by the sight of possibly the most urbane man in London losing his cool. There was no doubt about it. He slammed the door behind him, and Aleksei slid out to gaze at him across the roof of the car.

Barton wasn't yelling, but she could tell he was angry. Aleksei must be in trouble, she thought, shamelessly pleased; then, to her shock, the Russian laughed heartily, almost scornfully. She looked away for an instant—fearing they might feel her eyes on them—and as she looked back, Aleksei said something slowly and calmly to Barton . . . so slowly and calmly that Anna could read his lips. "You should get back in the car." Though he shook his head in apparent frustration, Barton did exactly that. Aleksei, expressionless once again, got back in, too, and drove off.

Curiouser and curiouser. What could that be about? Who was bossing whom here? And exactly which lunatic was in charge of the asylum?

"Curiouser and curiouser" indeed, Anna mused as she sat on the couch that night, picking at her warmed-up kung pao chicken. What did she know about Pierre Barton other than a few press releases and what she'd heard from Pierre's own lips? She brought her laptop over and pushed her food aside.

An hour later, she didn't know much more. Pierre's profile was practically below the horizon. She found a few facts—mostly on the Barton Pharmaceuticals site and in news items regarding the Coscom acquisition—but nothing that told her much. His father, Jasper Barton—later Jasper Barton OBE—had been a chemist who started Barton Pharmaceuticals after developing an arthritis drug while still at university. He built the company into a thriving business, and when he died, his son (who'd already assumed the company presidency when his father moved up to CEO) took over, moving factory and research operations to Switzerland and buying the three adjoining buildings in London for headquarters. The old Midlands factory was sold off and space leased at a nearby industrial estate for some warehousing and support staff.

Barton had studied chemistry and business at both Cambridge and the Sorbonne. He'd met his wife, the former Marina Sybyska, at the Sorbonne, where she was studying French. Her father ran a state-owned chemical factory in the then-USSR, where she worked for years until shortly after running into Pierre Barton at a pharmaceuticals conference years later. By that time the USSR was defunct and the company had been privatized as Sybyska Chemicals. The Bartons had twin boys, but didn't get around to marrying until two years after their birth. That had probably been Pierre's sole brush with nonconformity, Anna thought.

End of story.

Not unusually sparse information on a CEO, really. His father-in-law being a Russian big shot interested her. Could Barton be aiming to take over his supplier? And why the Russian driver . . . if Aleksei was just a driver. Might he be a bodyguard, as well? What had given him the effrontery to laugh at the boss? None of it made sense.

She turned off the computer and went to the kitchen to switch the iced tea she'd been drinking for wine. She would try to unwind by watching a comedy on TV, something to occupy her mind. She didn't want to think. Not about the mysterious Mr. Barton. Not about this bizarre project. And certainly not about the momentary flash of sheer joy on David Wainwright's face when he'd said, "Anna! My God, is it really you?"

The Italian restaurant near Victoria station was full when Anna entered at half past nine Saturday night and walked toward the table where Anezka and Lorrayne sat with two other young women and an empty wine bottle. She'd had a busy first week at work and was ready to relax.

"Hey, Tanya's here! Now we eat." Lorrayne motioned her to one of two empty seats. "Katie got a date, so she's not coming, foul-weather friend that she is. But here's Dawn and Tiffany. This is Tanya, guys, kicking off her first big night out in London!"

Dawn and Tiffany flashed glazed smiles. Drugs? Anna didn't know much about drugs anymore other than that clubbers were big on drugs identified by letters, like E, MDMA, and others even more unfamiliar to her. They all ordered pasta and salads, and Anezka called for more Chianti. "Dawn and Tif sell time-shares," Lorrayne said.

"Oh? That sounds like fun. Where for?"

One of them murmured, "Oh, y'know. Marbella, Ibiza, like that, y'know," then went back to smiling sweetly and head-bopping to music only she could hear. The two looked a lot alike, with short dark hair, although Anna thought Dawn was the one with skunk-like streaks, while Tiffany had one side shaved and the stubble dyed orange. Even with her own yellow-streaked auburn hair choppy and gelled, Anna felt plain by comparison.

"Tif has a mate who used to work at the Pacha in Ibiza," Lorrayne said, raising an eyebrow. "He'll get us into the VIP area."

Anna smiled. Lorrayne had just explained why they were with these sleepwalkers. The evening should be anthropologically enlightening since she hadn't been to any kind of music venue—not even to a concert—in decades.

Thanks to Tiffany's being on the list, they avoided the long waiting line at Pacha and went to the VIP entrance. "It will be supercrowded," Anezka murmured in her ear as they waited to be checked off the list. "Famous deejay tonight. Celebrities in the VIP room, I'll bet."

Tiffany's Pacha friend emphasized the huge gap between Anna and the rest of them. He had a shaved head and was multiply pierced and heavily gauged—his earlobes stretched to hold big steel plugs. She didn't hear his name but supposed it was "Wolf," since tattoos of wolves blanketed his skin, along with lightning bolts, zigzag stripes, and what appeared to be barcodes. He showcased his body art with a muscle T and skateboarder cut-offs.

"Sorry you can't go in the VIP room now, baby," he was shouting at Tiffany as he led them to a staircase. "Crazy-K's got a group there. But I snagged you a table in the other VIP space upstairs."

"Who's Crazy-K?" Anna asked Lorrayne when they were seated on a U-shaped banquette big enough for ten, overlooking the still-uncrowded dance floor below as well as the smaller one on their level.

"You kiddin'? And you from Manhattan? Just the hottest New York rapper and DJ! You gotta start gettin' out more."

Everyone ordered extravagant cocktails, so she compromised with a mojito instead of a Cabernet. "In a tall glass with lots of ice." She'd nurse one along. No way she could risk getting smashed when she was Tanya.

She didn't want to risk *anything*, so she kept her mouth shut and peered from their roost at the dance floors as the club started filling up. It was after midnight, and she was sleepily aware that at Pacha the night had just begun.

I lived like this once, she thought. *All those New York nights at the Limelight and Ones.* How had she ever done it? The noise was ungodly. The bass line of the music came up through the floor into her feet and thumped at a decibel level prohibiting any conversation other than shouting in someone's ear. She was relieved to see most people dancing exactly as her coach Kenny had taught her.

As it got more crowded, it got hotter. Before she knew it, her glass was empty and she was having another. Tiffany had disappeared completely, Lorrayne was over on the dance floor, and Anezka seemed to be having—or trying to have—a bellowed conversation with Dawn. She wondered how long before she could politely say good night.

Then an extremely good-looking young guy was smiling down at her, holding out his hand and gesturing to the dance floor. Why not? She took his hand and stood as he yelled into her ear. "Downstairs. With the big kids."

On the ground floor, it was all lights and music . . . and people, a pulsing wave of dancers, hundreds of them. As he pulled her onto the floor, he leaned down and shouted, "Rob."

"Tanya."

"Let's bust some moves."

She loved it—for two songs. Then, winded, she thankfully allowed Rob to gently pull her off the dance floor, and they snaked their way out of the crowd. He led her through the ground-floor bar to a door that led outside and pulled out a packet of cigarettes. "Fresh air? Fag?"

"Isn't that a contradiction in terms?"

"Okay, Tanya, air for you, fag for me, coming right up."

It was the smallest of small talk, but Rob was bright, witty, and hugely attractive in a Robert Pattinson sort of way. He was, he said, "a nerd extraordinaire" who worked in software. "I started out as a gamer, geeking out developing platforms even before I went to university. As soon as I graduated two years ago—University of Bristol with a degree in computer sciences—I was recruited by Innoscom, big in security and app development. I moved to London to work for them, and now here I am talking to Tanya at Pacha. Your turn."

She shrugged. "American. New in town, job in marketing for an upcoming cosmetic line. Staying in my aunt's apartment while I decide how long to stick around. And *not* Queen of the Clubbers. I came with friends, just to check it out. Now it's almost two o'clock, and I'm about to fall asleep."

"Aw, no, don't tell me you're gonna ditch me," he groaned, but he was grinning. "Don't worry. I'm here with some guys from the office celebrating a promotion, and I'm a Pacha virgin, just like you." He gave her a slow, sexy smile. "Why don't we compare notes at dinner next week?"

She'd forgotten he was flirting with Tanya, not chatting with Anna, and was so startled she just said, "Oh, okay, sure." He reached into an inside pocket of his hoodie. "Here's my card. You got one?"

"Upstairs. I left my bag with my friends."

"C'mon, I'll go with you, then make sure the club calls a minicab. Too late for black cabs now."

When she showed up at the VIP booth with Mr. Hawt Dude and grabbed her bag and jacket, she received knowing smirks. *They figure I'm going home with this guy,* she thought in horror. Then again, that might not be such a bad way of establishing her youthful bona fides. So she smiled at Rob and shouted, "Ready when you are."

As they turned to leave, she looked back and winked. Even over the music, she could hear Lorrayne's raucous laugh.

Chapter 11

No sooner had Anna settled at her desk with a copy of the *Guardian* and a cappuccino on Monday than her phone rang. It was Eleanor, saying Mr. Barton would like to see her.

When would she stop wondering if she was in trouble when Pierre asked to see her? As it turned out, Barton wanted to invite her to dinner Friday. "Marina's been asking to meet you," he said.

"She knows?"

"Of course. She's on the board of the company. Not that the rest of the board knows, but she's also my eminently trustworthy wife." He paused, eyeing her tight mini, neon tights, and UGGs. "I'd suggest something a bit more, um, toned down in the garment department. Marina likes establishment restaurants."

"Got it."

"Also, please leave Wednesday afternoon free. Someone else wants to meet you."

"Aren't I the popular one this week? Anyone special?"

"Anyone who gets to meet you and know your story has to be special. As I've said, with the degree of industrial espionage in our business, we can't be too careful. I won't be here tomorrow, so let's say we'll meet downstairs Wednesday at three, all right?"

"You're the boss," she said smartly. "Anything else?"

"No. Just try to write more in the diary. You aren't sharing enough of your experiences. The 'You, only **YO**UNGER' strap line is terrific, by the way. We're filing to trademark that as well as '**YOU**NGER' with the *you* in boldface. Very clever. And when you next email Richard Myerson, you should ask how much press coverage Madame X is going to get in the States. Remember, he doesn't know you're aware it's a success, so your lack of curiosity might strike him as odd. And please edit Becca's release announcing the upcoming UK launch. It needs your magic."

"Right. And now that you mentioned my magic"—she took a sheet from the small   notepad he always kept on his desk, scrawled on it, then handed it to him—"if you don't have these on hand, could you order them for me? I may not look the average age of a future Madame X buyer anymore, but I still love the cosmetics. And don't worry: I didn't choose any 'old lady colors.' If anyone here wonders how I got Madame X before them, I'll explain that I'm a test case."

As I am, she added to herself. *As indeed I am.*

When she came down to the lobby Wednesday, she'd expected to see the Bentley waiting at the curb, but Barton said, "We'll hail a cab."

"Are we hiding from Aleksei?" she asked, the memory of the chauffeur and his boss squabbling still vivid. Had he been fired?

"He just has other things to do. And," he added portentously, "this meeting is top secret." He put his hand out as a taxi approached. "In city traffic, it's harder to follow a cab than a Bentley." To the driver, he said, "Vauxhall, please, to the station."

"We're catching a train?" she asked, but he just shook his head. She sighed. Okay, there was a lot of industrial espionage, but did it justify this paranoia? Then, reminding herself that **YOUNGER** had erased three decades from her face and that BarPharm stood to make gazillions off it, she said nothing as they drove south to the Thames.

Barton guided her from the station through back streets to an old pub more attractive than the neighborhood surrounding it. It was about half full, its clientele seeming to be those who finished work early—bank tellers, shift workers, salespeople—and those who didn't work at all, retirees and red-nosed career tipplers. Barton chose a small table in the back, which clearly had once been the fancier saloon bar, with cushioned seats and panelled walls.

"I'm having a half of lager. What can I get for you?" he asked.

If he was drinking, so would she. "Half pint of cider, please."

After he returned with the drinks, he surreptitiously checked his watch. When his expression changed to welcoming anticipation, she turned her head to see a man heading for the table. He was very much the British boffin: a posh civil servant type in his forties, with a smooth, pink-cheeked face, sharply pointed nose, and conservatively short pale blond hair. He carried a furled umbrella and old-fashioned brown briefcase and wore wingtip shoes and a dark pin-striped three-piece suit. Yes, as British as the Union Jack; if bowler hats hadn't been passé, he might have sported one.

Barton stood to shake hands. "Tanya, I want to introduce Martin Kelm. Martin, something to drink?"

"Half of bitter would suit me fine, Pierre. Thank you." He sat on the bench next to Anna and across from Barton's seat.

"I've been looking forward to this meeting, Tanya," he said, stressing the name to indicate he knew who she really was, "to meeting you in the flesh."

"In the flesh?"

"I saw photos of your progress earlier on. And might I say, you look fantastic? Well done, indeed!"

Barton returned then with his drink, and Kelm raised the glass. "A toast then? To youth. Always, to youth." He winked. Anna disliked him already.

"I wanted you to meet Martin as much as Martin wanted to meet you, Tanya," Barton said. "We're about to begin a new phase of the project, and you should know why secrecy is vital. Plus, you've raised a lot of questions about the necessity of looking so much younger and the new identity, questions that deserve an answer."

She waited. He seemed uncertain, and the new arrival smoothly took over. "I'm here, Tanya, in an official capacity as a representative of Secret Intelligence Service, SIS—what many still refer to as MI6 although we encompass MI5, as well." He reached into his breast pocket and surreptitiously flashed an official ID card in a leather holder. "You might have guessed that the British government was involved when it was so easy for you to get a UK passport."

She stared at him, stunned. Had she put her brain in cold storage? Why hadn't she been more curious as to how Barton had obtained the Tanya Avery passport? "No," she admitted quietly. "I didn't guess."

"Don't be frightened." Kelm chuckled. "We're not asking you to fly to Afghanistan." He eyed her short skirt. "I doubt you'd be let in anyway, as you're so obviously subversive. My little joke—albeit not a very good one," he added at her stony response.

"Barton Pharmaceuticals has been refining **YOU**NGER as an SIS project. No, Mr. Barton has not been lying to you, although your expression shows you believe otherwise. **YOU**NGER is exactly what it purports to be, a skincare rejuvenation product for women. But it will be available not in two but in three strengths: one for consumers, one for physicians, and one for Her Majesty's Government only."

"Which have I been using?"

Barton answered. "All three. We started you off on Formula One"—Kelm chuckled—"which is Martin's little auto racing joke. It's the formula that will be utilized by SIS exactly as we used it for you, with a laser boost to speed its effectiveness. Then, the week before you came to London, we switched you to the medical grade, the one that will be marketed to physicians—we needed to see if the effects of Formula One would wear off when replaced by the milder Formula Two. We'll soon be switching you to the retail formula to see if the effects are still maintained with that and a quarterly Formula Two application. We'll be providing you with products on a monthly basis, perhaps adjusting the ingredients and ratios. For example, we're adjusting the fragrance based on your comments."

"Now that I've been tricked into helping you and to keep me from walking out, tell me, what's the objective?"

"It's in aid of the security of Great Britain and, I should add, of its ally, the United States," Kelm said stiffly. "The CIA is aware of the work Mr. Barton is doing and will be a beneficiary of it. To cut to the chase, as you Americans say, Formula One will enable us to return nonsecure agents to fieldwork."

"Nonsecure? You mean, spies whose covers have been blown?"

"Ah, a reader of espionage novels, I see." Kelm's chuckle, Anna realized, was not to be taken as an indication of inanity or even good humor. His eyes remained wary. "Yes, people who at one time would have needed to come in from the cold—to keep this conversation in the literary tradition—will be able to return to active status."

"Wouldn't plastic surgery do the trick?"

"Plastic surgery? As someone in the beauty industry, you must realize it leaves much to be desired. It's easy for *women* to cover the signs—scars, discolorations, and such—but impossible for men, who can't count on foundation and eye shadow to hide the traces. Take foreheads, if you like. There's no way to hide a forehead lift on a man with thinning hair other than with a hairpiece or implants, and those are dead giveaways to age as well.

"Nor does everyone want to look young forever. An agent might be fifty years old, needing and wanting to do another job or two before taking his pension while preferring to look like his real self, his 'old self,' if you like, at his daughter's wedding one day. We're speaking of a temporary, long- or short-term physical change that will save lives."

"So that's the reason I've lost thirty years, because agents will do so?"

Kelm nodded, and Barton at last found his voice. "When we first spoke, um, Tanya, I wasn't sure the government was a hundred percent on board. But it's now official, and it's all the more cause for being very careful, for extra security."

"And Aleksei? Is he your bodyguard?" she asked bluntly.

He looked puzzled. "No, he's what he appears to be: my driver. This is still primarily a cosmetic skincare line. I hardly need bodyguards."

"We just want to make sure you're cautious, and that you understand the reason you've been helped to look younger than YOUNGER's customers ever would and realize what an important role you're playing. And that you report any strange activities to Mr. Barton," Kelm interjected.

"Strange activities, like what? Being stalked?"

Again, Kelm chortled. "If you ever get stalked, it will obviously be by an admirer smitten by your youthful good looks." *Smitten?* This guy was as bad as Becca with the antiquated language. "So, strange activities." He steepled his fingers. "People you don't know well who start asking prying questions or know more about you than they should. Anyone overly interested in BarPharm. Anything odd you might hear from your stateside friends. And do be more careful with your emails and so on. Pierre says you sent him a diary entry from your personal account. You mustn't do that. Your personal account is solely for updating your US friends. Use your BarPharm account for all Tanya emails and Dropbox for diary entries and any secure information. Is that understood?"

"I'll be more careful in the future," she said, being serious, not sarcastic. Someone getting hold of the wrong email due to her sloppiness could leave her owing BarPharm a fortune.

Kelm said somberly, "If there is a future."

At Anna's stare, he went on, "What I'm saying is that if you wish to get out now, I can provide an Official Secrets Act document for you to sign and you're free to return to your old looks and old life. Pierre and I have discussed this. You would get to keep the salary you've earned thus far, from both your roles at BarPharm, Tanya's and your own—but no more. You would still be bound by the confidentiality agreement."

"And if I stay?"

"If you stay, it's business as usual. Unless there's a crisis, which I don't expect, you'll never need our protection. You finish your work here, then do and be whomever you choose, wherever you wish."

"But if I left now, I couldn't return to the States looking like this."

"Stop **YOU**NGER, and in just a couple weeks in a discreet location, probably the one where you received your training, you'll go back to looking almost as you did upon first meeting Mr. Barton. A bit younger, thanks to the laser and fillers. Naturally, you'd be completely off the project, which would mean no more **YOU**NGER products for you until the consumer formula hits the shops, when you can buy it like anyone else.

"If you stay, your contract will expire in—let's see—about nine months or so, and you'll receive a lifetime supply of whichever formula of **YOU**NGER you want." He stood. "Pierre will let me know your decision on Monday, so give it serious consideration until then." He nodded to Barton and was gone.

Anna drained the dregs of her cider. "So, Pierre, all this work— the Madame X campaign, the diary, the coaching—no more than a charade the whole time? Helping out the good ol' MI6, Miss Tanya Moneypenny?"

"No. Not at all! Everything I've told you is true. Do you think I hired someone to play my mother? Don't be absurd. If you don't believe me, go to Paris. Visit her!"

"I might do that one weekend." Anna stood up. "Do you need me back at the office? If not, I'll just head home now."

He checked his watch. "You go ahead," he said. "I might have another before I move on."

She knew he'd be on his cell phone to Kelm as soon as she was out the door. But SIS, MI6, or not, she had no desire to stick around and spy on anyone.

———————

Barton had booked Friday's dinner at Gordon Ramsay at Claridge's, and as she entered, Anna understood why he'd said to tone it down. This was what her grandmother would have called "Hoity-Toity Heaven." She arrived wearing newly acquired "grown-up" clothes. Her midnight-blue faille dress wasn't scandalously short or low-cut, and she wore it with a matching long-sleeved shrug. Her hair was brushed back and left unspiked, her makeup simple. Her skin glowed.

A maître d' led her across the elegant Art Deco dining room to where the Bartons were already seated. Pierre stood as she approached, and his wife swiveled around discreetly, then cast a head-to-toe look so appraising that it wouldn't have surprised Anna if she'd been ordered to open her mouth to have her teeth checked. "Hello, Pierre. And you must be Marina."

"I was hoping to meet you sooner, but I had family obliga- tions," Marina said as Anna sat on the chair Pierre held out for her between the two of them. "My mother likes to see the twins frequently, so I am often going to Moscow." She turned to her husband. "Pierre, order an aperitif for Tanya."

She had only a trace of an accent, which to Anna's ears could have been Czech or German as easily as Russian. As with many foreigners who'd spent a lot of time abroad, Marina's English speech retained an odd formality.

She looked extremely good for a woman just a few years younger than Anna and was obviously more than a rich man's bimbo. Her style was the simply elegant kind carried off so beautifully by the rich because, for starters, they flash real jewels. Marina's deep lilac silk sheath had a scoop neck showing just enough cleavage to position her amethyst and diamond necklace to best advantage. On one hand, she wore stacks of amethyst and diamond skinny bands, and on the other, a simple white-gold or platinum wedding band, all the better to set off the engagement ring above it: a diamond as big as the Ritz or, considering present circumstances, a sparkler the size of Claridge's. A man's diamond-faced Rolex seemed a calculatedly quirky maneuver to pile on more diamonds, as well as highlight her delicate bone structure, making her seem even more petite and feminine, while her diamond studs, about two carats each, were neither ostentatious nor modest. Her long hair was professionally upswept, teased to be full, then loosely held with combs, so it came down over the tops of her ears and the back of her neck in a style reminiscent of an old-time Gibson Girl. *Very Anastasia,* Anna thought. Not surprisingly, her hair's shade was Well-Off Bolshevik Blonde.

Anna's flute of champagne arrived, and they opened their menus. The *prix fixe* was seventy pounds, over a hundred bucks a head. Anna had a feeling what mattered most to Mrs. Barton was being in the "right" place—and was proven correct when Marina ordered steamed fish, the simplest dish on the menu. *Screw that,* she thought, opting for the richness of duck preceded by sautéed scallops with Sevruga caviar. Who knew when she might ever eat this well again?

Since Anna had never been to Moscow, it was easy to draw out Marina about the city. "It's not so beautiful as St. Petersburg, but there is something very strong, very firm about Moscow."

"Muscular," Pierre suggested.

Putinesque, Anna thought, but she said only, "You grew up in the city?"

"My family always kept a flat in Moscow and a house in the country. Pierre and I like being in town while my mother prefers the house. When I go on my own with the boys, I stay there. Mama spends time with the boys while I go to the factory."

"The factory?"

"My office is at the factory. I am now—how do you say?—titular head of Sybyska Chemicals, my father's company. I assumed this position on his death. I am a chemist, you know."

"No spoiled housewife here." Pierre chuckled.

So Marina Barton was a chemist *and* head of a chemical factory? How handy for BarPharm.

"I met Pierre at the Sorbonne. But we didn't realize until later that we were connected in this way."

"Marina's father was one of the top chemists in the USSR," Barton explained. "He came to London with Khrushchev on a trade delegation under the Soviets, and one of the factories he visited was Barton Pharmaceuticals, where he met my father."

"After perestroika, Papa took over the company and changed the name to Sybyska. He started supplying raw ingredients to the Bartons." Marina leaned in toward her. "And so Pierre came to our factory and remembered me from the Sorbonne. Fate brought us together. It was my idea for BarPharm to expand into cosmetics to launch **YOUNGER**. Which you so perfectly named. So, you see, fate brought you to us. We were all destined to do this."

Pierre's laugh sounded nervous. "Russians love drama, you see."

"And the Franglais?"

"The French side of me is a romantic. The British side's more pragmatic."

Marina suddenly seemed bored and spoke little after the food arrived. While Anna and Pierre made comments on the excellence of the cuisine, she ate her fish with silent, forensic precision.

When the plates were cleared and their waiter came bearing dessert menus, Marina said abruptly, "We'll have a mix of sorbets. Yes, Tanya?"

She would've liked a peek at the menu, but Marina's tone told her to be happy with what she got. "That's fine."

"Now come with me." Her small, cold hand grasped Anna's wrist. "We'll go to the ladies' room and freshen up."

A woman accustomed to giving orders, Anna thought as she followed meekly. She doubted she and Mrs. Barton would be emerging from the toilets as BFFs.

As they were washing their hands at adjoining sinks, Anna snuck a sideways look down at Marina, who was bent over, scrubbing away with a surgeon's diligence. As her eyes drifted up she saw, running into Mrs. Barton's hairline at the nape of her neck, a Korean-peninsula-shaped port-wine stain like Mikhail Gorbachev's and then, almost hidden in the shadow of an ear— exposed for a moment by the upswept tortoiseshelled hair held in place by real tortoiseshell combs—the telltale sign of a real surgeon, the hairline scar of a face-lift. She looked away.

They stood side by side freshening their makeup, Anna towering over the petite Marina, who, as they turned to leave, again gripped her wrist. "My husband tends to take on too much," she said neutrally, like a doctor discussing a troublesome patient. "I depend on you to move ahead. Even if Pierre doesn't pressure you, please make sure you get him what he needs in a timely fashion."

"Yes, of course." She fought the impulse to pull her arm free.

Marina's grip remained tight, and she leaned in so close Anna was almost overpowered by her cloying gardenia perfume. "A great deal is at stake with **YOUNGER**, Tanya. But I know I can count on you because it's our destiny."

Marina wasn't dramatic, Anna decided. *No,* melodramatic's *a better word.* And why would she say, "I know *I* can count on you" when it was Pierre who Anna worked for? "Do you use it?" she asked, curious to see if the other woman would lie. "I mean, you look so youthful. You look great."

The other woman dropped her wrist, and her eyes narrowed. "Me?" She sounded appalled. "Russians don't need this product. Russians look good because of the genes." Then she turned on her heel and walked off, leaving Anna to trail in her wake once again.

Friday, July 22

Whew, am I glad that week's over.

Too many changes too fast for me to grasp who's on first base here.

So . . . I now work for MI6 and, by virtue of doing so, I'm also aiding the CIA—all of which seems incredibly important to one Marina Barton, a melodramatic Muscovite who lies about her face-lift, has eyes like ice chips, and treats her World's Most Desirable Husband like an irritating child.

I have two more days in which to decide: Do I go or stay?

If I go, I walk away from close to a million dollars and probably the dregs of my career. And I walk away from David forever. Am I strong enough to do that? But I don't plan to see David again anyhow . . . do I? He shouldn't be part of this equation.

Why did I drink all that wine after the champagne? And why the schnapps? So I could pretend I was having a normal dinner with the boss and his wife? So I could pretend I really was a svelte twentywhatever-year-old rather than a world-weary AARP prospect?

Who do I want to be? Anna or Tanya?

I wish I'd fully appreciated the joys of being Lisa when I was.

Fuck, I'm drunk.

Chapter 12

Anna woke up Saturday to a beautiful summer's day. She felt remarkably decent considering the amount of wine she'd put away the evening before, and, after carefully deleting her inebriated diary draft—and thanking the gods she had retained enough sobriety not to have sent it—she left for the fitness club.

So I don't especially like the boss's wife, she thought as she pounded along on the treadmill. *So what?* It was silly to get worked up about things—she should be thrilled she was helping Britain and her own country as well as her bank account. And it shouldn't concern her that she now saw Pierre as a man under the thumb of his wife, MI6, and maybe even his chauffeur. He was still her boss.

If she told Barton to tell Kelm she wanted out, it would be a reverse Cinderella, as she turned back into an unemployed, late-middle-aged woman whose business had, for all intents and purposes, failed. The money she'd earned so far wouldn't last very long once she was back to being Anna "Unemployable" Wallingham. She risked ending up a loser in everyone's eyes, including her own. And David? She shook her head briskly, as if to dislodge him from her decision making.

Back at the apartment, she showered and changed into skinnies, her Vans, and a black T-shirt she'd ordered online that had "NYU" printed on the back and "Property of New York University" on the front. She'd always wished she'd gone to NYU, so why shouldn't Tanya be a grad? Then she grabbed her bag and went off to the Tube and an exhibit of Martin Parr's photographs at a little gallery in Covent Garden. After a quick salad at Pret A Manger, she got back on the Underground to go the Victoria and Albert Museum for another photo show, this one of glamour shots from the 1930s.

The Tube was packed with tourists. Few riders looked noticeably English. Of course, the two women in headscarves and the young blond Slavic couple could have been born in London, as might the tall, ebony-skinned teenaged boy and the older Japanese couple whispering together. No, she thought, not the blonds or the Japanese. The latter looked too anxious, clutching hands and keeping their eyes down, while the blond man had suddenly pulled out his phone and was snapping a photo of his girlfriend or wife. Boring one's friends on Facebook obviously held universal allure.

The V&A was crowded—it was a well-reviewed show that everyone seemed to want to see today—but Anna was glad she'd made the effort. She'd worked too hard back home; she couldn't remember the last time she'd gone to a museum there. That was one thing she'd change when she returned.

The blond man from the Underground was snapping his wife standing by the exhibit's poster of Greta Garbo as she went out. Beauty icons like Garbo, she thought, were famed all over the world. *May Madame X end up among them.*

What next? A walk down to Harvey Nichols, she decided. Most of its stock was priced way out of Tanya's range, but it had been ages since she'd done any upscale browsing. She could also look for jazzy earrings in the cheap accessory shops on Knightsbridge to wear tonight, when she'd be having dinner with Rob, the guy from Pacha. Before entering, she stopped to admire an outrageous

Vivienne Westwood outfit in the window. Off to the side behind her, reflected in the glass, she spied the high-cheekboned blond couple from the Tube again. Was the man taking *her* picture?

As if she had simply changed her mind, Anna turned on her heel and retraced her steps, going back the way she'd come, up a few blocks to Harrods, where she hurried straight to the so-called Egyptian escalators, from which she could look down and see who was behind her. When she saw Mr. and Mrs. Blondie get on and start excusing themselves to pass on the left, she leapt off at the second floor and, heart thudding in her chest, wove a winding path from one department to another, then up two more floors on other escalators before jumping into an express lift to the ground floor just as its doors were closing. Outside, she jumped into a black cab and went straight to South Kensington, looking behind her in fear of seeing two heads of thick blond hair.

At home, she ran upstairs and locked the door. Then, not bothering with the diary format, she sent an email directly to Barton: "I think I was followed today. Please call."

The phone rang soon after. Her employer sounded concerned, but when he asked, "Are you feeling all right?" she realized he was more concerned about her state of mind than any stalkers.

She was fine, she assured him, but she was certain she'd been followed by a couple, Russian or Eastern European, on the Underground and then to the V&A, Harvey Nichols, and Harrods.

"Anna, there are thousands of people on the streets today. You weren't exactly blazing a trail, being on some of the main tourist routes."

"But when they saw me *not* going into Harvey Nichols, they did just what I did—went to Harrods, even though it was in the direction we'd come from!"

"Did you see them follow you from the museum?"

"No," she admitted.

"So for all you know, they took a taxi to Harvey Nichols, then realized they'd meant to go to Harrods instead and had to walk back that way."

The explanation was so logical, his voice so patient, Anna felt foolish.

"You mustn't let the meeting with Kelm lead you to imagining things that aren't there," he warned.

He was right. When they'd hung up, she felt annoyed at herself for not having bought those earrings she'd had in mind.

When Rob had called her midweek to ask about dinner, she had jumped at the chance to socialize, already suspecting her dinner with Marina and Pierre wasn't going to be one of the best times she'd had in any of her lives.

He said he shared a place with "some fellow nerds" in Fulham, so he wasn't far from her neighborhood. "Have you ever eaten in a Tootsie's?" he asked. "In case you're craving an American burger, there's one near you." When she said that sounded great, they agreed to meet there at eight.

Only after she had hung up did it sink in that this wasn't getting together with some friend's kid for a bite. This was, in Rob's mind, probably a date. Anna had forgotten how to dress for *any* date, much less one with a man who could be her son.

She settled on her black treggings with the big white shirt and her Vans, aiming to look neither sexy nor boring. "I am hot, hip, young, and at the top of my game," she told her reflection in the mirror as she went out the door. "I am woman. I am invincible." She winked, as much to check her deep violet–shadowed, kohl-rimmed eyes as to affirm her self-confidence.

Rob was waiting for her in front of Tootsie's. "Just stealing a last fag," he said, inhaling deeply. "I know it's a filthy habit, and I plan to stop. Not an addict, I see?"

"Not me. Smoked. But it was a long time ago."

"What's a long time ago? When you were twelve?" He laughed.

"Not much older." She covered up her blunder. "I quit before high school graduation."

"Around the time I started. You look great, by the way."

In spite of herself, she blushed with pleasure.

When they were seated waiting for their drinks, he asked about her life in the States and she regurgitated her porridge of truth and lies, sugared with tales of the aunt who'd loaned her the flat and her on-again, off-again boyfriend back home.

Her cheeseburger hit the spot, and Anna found it easier than she'd expected to talk to Rob—maybe because his specialty was security, and she'd recently acquired a serious interest in aspects of it. "So, how can you keep someone from hacking your phone or your computer?" she asked.

"Some bloke bothering you?"

"No. Not really, but"—she had practiced this—"let's just say some guy I'm not interested in has become a little overamorous. Not a stalker or anything. But I should know what to do if he turns into one."

"First, call me, and the Nerd Squad will beat the shite out of him. No, seriously, there are a few things you can do now."

He suggested some free computer virus and malware programs with good firewalls, as well as a couple books and websites that would help her make her computer more secure. What about cell phones, she asked. Could a computer track her from hers?

"I hope you don't want to get away from me yet," he teased, then went on to suggest she buy a couple of cheap cell phones and SIM cards she could use to escape detection. "And, in the meantime, turn off location apps or services so your phone won't show anyone where you are. I'd get an iPhone or BlackBerry because they're harder to hack into than a regular cell. Don't use voice mail as it's not always secure, and erase all texts immediately after you read them. The easiest way to protect yourself anywhere is to be sure to have a different password for every single account you have—phone, computer, email, banks, everything."

"Sounds like a lot to remember."

"Nah, it's easier than most people make it. See, first they screw up by creating blindingly obvious passwords begging to be hacked: birthdates, phone numbers, even their own passport or pension fund numbers. Or they go the other way and make up complicated stuff they can't remember. Then they do the worst thing anyone could do: store password lists in obvious places or on their mobiles. Mobile gets stolen when it's not locked. Boom—some gangsta gets it all."

"How do you come up with good passwords you can memorize, then?"

"Well, I use stuff no one else would ever guess. For instance, dates with the numbers and letters scrambled, the name and birth date of my girlfriend when I was fourteen—hey, don't laugh, I was in love." He thought a second. "Simple phrases or movies but using letters for numbers, numbers for letters, and varying letter cases. I used to use 'EyeH8Werk,' written like this." He scrawled it on a napkin. "And I once used 'DwanOtheDead.' Just be creative. And use symbols, too—like the hash mark or the 'at' sign."

"Got it."

"You sure nothing's wrong, Tanya?"

"No, I'm just interested in all this stuff." She shrugged. "It's nothing."

Most men her own age would have insisted on paying, but Rob blithely accepted money for Anna's share of the bill. She found it cute when he insisted, "Now we're going to go have a drink at a secret place I like a lot. Just two things: you can't tell anyone I go there, and it's my treat."

"How can I refuse? You know how to get a girl's attention."

He led her through a few side streets to Harrington Gardens and the Bentley Hotel. "Here?" She laughed. "Isn't this like one of the most expensive hotels in town?"

"Eight hundred quid a night. Yeah, it's pretty piss-elegant, which is why my mates don't know about it. Come on, I'll show you the bar."

Anna didn't have to fake Tanya's awe. Gleaming wood, over-stuffed sofas and chairs in rich malachite green and deep ruby velvet—every American's fantasy of what a prewar English gentle-man's club should be. "I can see why you like it."

They sat down, and Rob ordered two cognacs with the élan of a connoisseur. "How do you know the hotel?" Anna asked.

"My uncle stays here when he's in town."

"Your uncle must be seriously rich."

"Yeah, he's an earl, actually. Why are you grinning?"

"Because I had an Uncle Earl, too. Only, mine drove a truck."

He grinned. "Well, my uncle *the* earl got the money, mansion, and title, while my father—aka the Younger Son—got the gate-keeper's house. He's no pauper, but he doesn't stay in places like this when he travels."

"And you?"

"Hostels all the way. Not that I travel much these days, what with work and all. Prague, when I have the time."

"You like Prague? I've never been."

"You should go. Real old-world Europe. And there's a girl—I mean, not a real serious thing at this point, but I go there to see her." He shrugged. "That's my story."

"Sounds good." She hoped she didn't sound too relieved. She'd been flattered that Rob was attracted to her, but she couldn't be jumping into bed with a guy in his twenties.

Still, when he walked her to her door an hour later, he seemed to have forgotten that girl in Prague. "I had fun," she said. "Thanks for asking me—and for showing me the bar."

He grinned. "You could consider returning the favor by showing me your apartment." And then he reached for her, pulling her against him as his lips found hers.

It was nice. Too nice. *Maybe this,* she thought as she returned his kiss, *is what I need to wipe all memories of David Wainwright out of my mind.* Then she remembered the mutton's body beneath the lamb's clothes and gently but firmly pushed him away. And what was Anna doing, thinking of David Wainwright when another man was kissing Tanya Avery?

As she got ready for bed, she studied her body in the bathroom mirror, wondering how much **YOUNGER** it would take for her to look twenty-five all over. Her body was pretty firm for her age and the workouts had her looking good, so it wasn't like the contrast between Madame Barton's face and hands. Yet she couldn't deny that she looked as if a young woman's head had been grafted onto a middle-aged woman's body. She sighed and turned away. She shouldn't be worrying about taking off her clothes in front of anyone. That just wasn't going to happen, certainly not now that MI6 was involved and the stakes even higher. Even in the dark, that wasn't going to happen. She went to bed leaving her diary blank. She wasn't sure how much better she wanted Pierre Barton to know her.

———

Sunday brought rain and a good day to stay in and sort out her thoughts. Monday dawned steamy. Anna went straight to Barton's office before Eleanor had even arrived and entered immediately after knocking, a little steamed herself. "Clearly I was too shell-shocked from having lost the Coscom account to notice there's a lot more to **YOU**NGER than meets the eye."

"In some situations, the less you know, the less you have to worry about," he responded evenly.

"That sounds suspiciously close to 'Don't you worry your pretty little head,'" she retorted. "Mightn't it have been a good idea to tell me about MI6 prior to my signing your contract? Or that your chemist wife now runs her father's company?"

He looked at her steadily. "Telling you about Kelm was his decision to make, Anna, not mine. As for Marina, so what? I'd have thought you'd approve of a man marrying someone with a career."

"That has nothing to do with this, and you know it. I deserve to know more about what's going on. And I'm not convinced those people I first spotted on the Tube weren't following me. They seemed . . . Oh, I don't know, so focused on not seeming focused on me, if that makes any sense."

"To be honest, I don't think it does. Look, I *am* trying to keep you as informed as possible. I really am. And I immediately passed on the information about that couple to Kelm, because while I'm sure it's nothing, I'm naturally concerned. And I'm not humoring you when I say I would be nervous if I saw the same couple popping up all over the place. Let Kelm check them out. He has the resources."

"Why only my face and hands and neck?" she blurted. "Why isn't **YOU**NGER for all of me? Surely you can mix bigger batches. Don't you realize you've turned me into a freak?"

"You're hardly a freak. My mother and other women who've gone too far with surgery, they're the freaks. You're a beautiful woman."

"With an old body that doesn't match."

"With an *older* body," he reminded her. "*Your* body, Anna, which looked very good before. And I'm sure, with your workouts, it looks pretty damned great now. Please don't let this experience make you doubt yourself." He paused. "Look, we don't want to use the product comprehensively until the entire testing phase has been completed."

"What does that mean? I'm going to end up with cancer?"

"It would help if you didn't keep putting words in my mouth," he said patiently. "You're not going to get cancer. It's simply that the proper time to push the limits on this product isn't while we're looking for Food and Drug Administration approval in America. We're hoping we'll have everything in place soon, Anna. We do have a lab-testing program, remember, and the products have been tested for off-the-face use as well as for long-term effects."

"Long-term effects? How long is long-term in this case?"

"We have people who have been using the product for almost two years now. During that time, the formula has been changed and improved. And the good news is, it's perfectly safe. We mix small batches in the lab rather than big batches on an assembly line because we're fine-tuning, which means there isn't enough of any single batch for you to use all over even if I was willing to give it to you. In any case, if you stick with us, you'll eventually have a lifetime supply of **YOU**NGER for your face *and* your body, if that's what you want."

"Tell me again," she asked sarcastically, "just what am I here for?"

He sighed before answering. "You're here for exactly what I told you you're here for: to help us with the **YOU**NGER marketing as you oversee the launch of Madame X. I know you find some of the work, such as the diary, boring—"

"Not just boring. *Unnecessary*. Seriously, Pierre, who notices if a twenty-seven-year-old isn't up-to-date on trending jargon or dance steps? Okay, maybe for some out-to-pasture spy looking to come back in that might be important, but isn't that what they call 'tradecraft'? Doesn't SIS have experts to handle that? What are they going to learn from me?"

"Your diary is important for various reasons, one of which remains the consumer campaign. You're bored? Then go ahead and concentrate more on ideas for promoting **YOUNGER**. Come up with a marketing plan. But keep up with the diary as well. In the meantime, I want you and your team to have a launch plan for Madame X ready to look at within two weeks. And you need to get Becca to put more pizzazz into her press releases. She's too dry and pharmaceutical. All right?"

"Okay," she agreed reluctantly, feeling as if she'd lost the argument here.

"Excellent." He stood, making it clear the meeting was over. "You should get out more. Didn't you say you were having dinner with some guy? How was that?"

She didn't recall saying she was having dinner with anyone. But all that wine and champagne at dinner had been unwise. If her loose lips were going to sink any ships, she'd be the one going under. "It was what it was," she said flatly. "It's hard work making conversation with a guy in his twenties."

They traded facile smiles as she headed for the door.

"One moment," he said as she reached for the doorknob. "I think you're forgetting something."

She turned. "My answer to you and Martin Kelm? I thought that was obvious. I'm staying on until my contract is up."

Chapter 13

She didn't care if she was being paranoid. At lunchtime, she bought a cheap pay-as-you-go cell, then went down the road to a different service provider and bought another. She also paid cash for an iPhone. That one required a contract, but she used her real name, US address, and American credit card and paid a year in advance, hoping that would keep anyone from knowing she had it.

Back at the office, she summoned Chas and Becca to a meeting on the Madame X UK press launch and collateral materials. Chas got a list of possible venues to check out and was encouraged to scout new sites as well.

When she was alone with Becca, she gave her a pep talk on creating sassier beauty copy. "You have bullet-point lists of features and benefits; use those. Focus on these being cosmetics for the woman who's not trying to pass herself off as a kid but wants to look terrific."

Not trying to pass herself off as a kid? *Yeah, right,* she thought later as she gathered her things to go home. *That leaves me out.*

When she got out front, David Wainwright was leaning against the building next door, waiting. For her.

"Hi." He smiled warmly. "Remember me? I decided I owe you an explanation."

When she found her voice, she muttered, "You don't, really. I bumped into you, after all."

"But I was the one who acted like an idiot."

"Okay, sure, you can explain. But not here, huh?" she said quickly. "Give me a minute, then meet me around the corner." She smiled, then hurried off. Did he really want to explain? Or had he come because he wanted to see her again? Why was her heart pounding?

"What's with the cloak-and-dagger routine?" he asked when he joined her out of sight of BarPharm.

"Just some nosy people at the office. C'mon, I know a little wine bar on one of the back streets."

"Maurizio's?"

Her eyebrows went up in surprise.

"When I had meetings at BarPharm, I'd sometimes make a detour for a nice glass of wine. Not often. I did some commercials for Barton—I'm a director—so I was in the studio or edit bay more than around here."

"Maurizio's has good wines by the glass. Let's go there." It struck her that she wasn't supposed to know anything about this man. "You direct commercials?"

"Mostly episodic television. Mystery and crime. Comedy at times."

She nodded as they entered the small, cool wine bar. "I write: copy, press releases, stuff like that."

"In the States?"

"Usually. Working here for a year, then going back to real life."

"And if *this* were real life, what would I be getting you from the bar?" he asked, nodding toward a table.

"A Vermentino would be nice, thanks."

She sank back against the banquette, trying to look relaxed. She knew he'd come back with a glass of a red for himself. And he did.

"*Cin cin.*"

"Mmmn. The perfect wine for a hot day," she said after tasting. "What are you drinking?"

He held up his glass so the light from a wall sconce made the contents gleam like rubies. "Rosso di Montefalco. You know it?"

"Basically a young Sagrantino, isn't it?"

He smiled. "For someone so young, you know your wines. Lighter than Sagrantino, so good for summer. And half the price, to boot."

"I like the light reds better. I guess that makes me a cheap date." She blushed. "That came out wrong—sorry, I've forgotten your name."

"David. David Wainwright."

"Right. What did you want to explain, David?"

"I didn't mean to lurk like a stalker, but I know I behaved oddly the other week and you might even think it's weirder that I came back to apologize. But it occurred to me I should explain. And to be honest, I wanted to see you again."

"You wanted to see me again? I mean—"

"I'm old enough to be your father?" He laughed. "It's not like that, honestly. I wanted to see what you looked like again. I guess I should start at the beginning."

He peered down at his wine before going on. When he looked up, he stared at her as he had that first day, as if a ghost sat opposite him. "Years ago, before you were born or when you were a child, I knew a woman who looked exactly like you. Different hair and makeup, sure. But . . . Her left eye was even a little smaller than the right, just like yours. It's just uncanny. I was just gobstruck."

"I didn't even know my eyes weren't the same size."

"It's a tiny thing, but I looked right into your eyes when you bumped into me, and it just blew me away."

"That's why you thought I was this Anna, why you called me by her name?"

He looked away, as if still stunned by the sight of her. "You must have thought I was mad. And I suppose I was for moment, to have looked at you and thought for even an instant you might be a woman who'd be in her fifties now. It was as if I'd gone through the looking glass and back in time. That's why I babbled like an idiot. I was massively confused, because it just didn't compute."

"What happened to her, to Anna?"

He shrugged. "Dunno. I met her when I was in New York working on a British series set there and she was a struggling actress. We had a long-distance transcontinental affair—when I wasn't in New York, we'd meet in Paris, all very romantic. And then—well, after two years, it ended, as those things do. We didn't have friends in common so . . ." His voice trailed off. "One loses track over the years."

"And you? What happened to you?"

"Well, here I am. Let's see, since that time, I've worked on TV series here and flown to Los Angeles to direct episodes of some American ones."

Oh, my God, she thought, *he was in and out of LA when I was there.*

"I had a fallow period two years ago when many production budgets were cut, so I fell back on making commercials and corporate videos. I didn't do much for Barton and not for some time now, but I needed to return a reel to them the other day. I'm done with commercials now, I'm happy to say."

"And you forgot about Anna?"

"Part of me did. I got married not long after I returned to London. It was a stupid thing to do and lasted all of six months. Then I married an actress, a moderately successful one, at least in England, and we did the house-in-the-suburbs and kid thing."

"You have kids?"

"Just one, a son." He smiled. "Don't worry, I won't do the whole 'Let me show you my boy's photos' bit. Nick's fifteen, a day boy at Westminster. Sorry, that means he lives at home and doesn't board."

"He lives at home?" She was practically holding her breath now.

"In Wimbledon Village," he answered. "Technically still London, but surburban-ish."

"Where the tennis is."

"That's in Wimbledon Centre. The Village is beyond that; it's the posh bit. A friend once described it as the sort of area where pop stars' ex-wives open exorbitant boutiques selling pillows handmade by Buddhist monks." He grinned. "Another round?"

"Yes, but"—she fumbled in her handbag as he got up, then waved a twenty-pound note at him—"my round this time." He started to refuse, then understood she meant it and took the money.

"So what's Wimbledon like?" she asked brightly when he returned.

"Good place for a teenager, I think. And Nick and his mum are happy there. Me, the only really good part about getting divorced was moving back into town."

And with that, her whole body suddenly let go, as if she were sinking into a pool of warm water. She actually grasped the table, then looked up to see his concerned face.

"Are you all right, Tanya?"

"Yes, sorry. Must be the heat today. I felt all woozy for a second. I'll just run to the ladies' room."

She made her way to the back hallway on weak legs. *He isn't married. He isn't married.* Was that good or bad?

In the mirror, Tanya's youthful face peered pallidly out at her. She splashed cold water on it, then freshened her makeup. The more she had on, the less she resembled Anna. She had to get out of here. This was madness.

Yet back at the table, his still-familiar face and concerned expression melted her resolve, and she sank back down onto the banquette. "I really need to go after this," she murmured.

"No problem. And I'm glad you came for a drink instead of yelling for a policeman."

"Oh, don't be silly," she said, but she was smiling. "It's been nice. I don't know many people here. Hardly anyone, in fact."

"Well, if you'd like, we could get together for a film and dinner. I know I'm not exactly date material for you, so I promise it would be nothing like that. Nick's with me for the next couple of weeks, but the Saturday after he goes back to his mum would be fine."

Her brain screeched, "Say no!" but the words off her lips were, "I'd like that, David. Thank you." She wrote her new iPhone number on the back of a Barton Pharmaceuticals card, turning away as she did it so he wouldn't see her hand tremble. "It's best to call or text me on this number."

"Will do. Can I walk you to the Tube?"

She shook her head as she got to her feet. "Thanks, no. Call me uptight, but I really don't like people from work knowing my business."

He laughed ruefully. "You like secrets? You know, you may be like Anna in more ways than looks."

Her look of puzzlement wasn't wholly feigned. Then she chirped a bright "See you" and headed for the door. All the way to the Underground, she refused to think about what he'd meant by that remark.

———

Anna spent the next few days fretting over all of her recent decisions. Had it been a mistake to tell Barton she'd stay? Was she nuts, agreeing to see David again? As she tended to do more and more lately, she pushed aside her doubts and concentrated on the job at hand.

She was genuinely enjoying working on Madame X and developing a marketing plan for **YOUNGER**. She no longer deemed Chas's eagerness annoying and now found Becca's solemn frumpiness and dedication to hard work comforting. Their little team made genuine progress that week. Thursday, Becca delivered her revised UK press releases and said almost sassily, "I did what I could to Brit things up. Hope you like them."

"Thanks. Have a minute to talk?"

Becca nodded and sat down.

"I worry that some of the US copy might be a bit too sexy for older British women. Do you know what I mean?"

Becca thought it over, finally saying, "Well, I do think British women don't want a whole new you and all that, just to look a bit better."

"And younger, yes? Younger is always better, right?"

"Is it? My mum's fifty-five, and when I told her I could get her Madame X products to try, she laughed and said, 'I am who I am. Some of us are content with that, young lady!' She's a bit of a straight talker, my mum. But I do think British women aren't as looks obsessed."

"I see. But what we're selling is still that younger is better, isn't it?"

"Now you sound like Olga."

"Olga?"

"Oh, just someone who was here last year." Becca looked suddenly uncomfortable. "She had this office."

"What did she do?"

"She worked on an advanced retinol anti-aging line that was in development. And she hinted that something incredibly important was coming up. She was over-the-top about everything, so once the Coscom acquisition was announced, I figured she'd known about Madame X. She was always saying things like, 'What if you could decide every day how young you wanted to be?' Which isn't a bad tagline for Madame X, I suppose."

"Except it would be promising a lot more than poor Madame X could deliver. Is she British, this Olga?"

"Oh, no, Olga Novrosky. Russian. She worked on a single account, like you. Only hers was the retinol."

"And she left after the acquisition?"

"Before the acquisition." Now Becca looked downright miserable. "She didn't exactly leave, though, Tanya. She—" She blew out a puff of air.

"She . . . ?" Anna prompted.

"She died."

"She *what*?"

"Died. She was acting oddly. Jumpy and nervous. Kind of obsessive. She accused Chas of listening in on her calls, but his line didn't even connect to hers. It's the way it is now: you need to go to intercom and ring through. She was rushing off to Mr. Barton's office all the time, and I could see he was trying to avoid her." She shrugged. "Obviously, he has more important things to do than deal with a copywriter's personal problems or whatever."

"So she was let go?"

Becca shook her head. "No. She fell or jumped under a train at the Oxford Circus Tube station one day after work. You know, at rush hour, one needs to be careful not to go too close to—" She blinked. "I still feel as if I'd let her down in some way. She wasn't an especially likable person, but I feel terrible that she'd do something like that!"

"How awful! When did this happen?"

"Last winter, just before the acquisition. I guess Mr. Barton decided to scrap that retinol line afterward because he didn't replace her and the line just went away. Then, after the launch in New York, he told us about your joining us. 'Top drawer,' he said, which is one of his highest compliments." She sighed. "I wish I'd done something to help her."

Anna aimed for a consoling smile. "You mustn't blame yourself, Becca. We can't save everyone. She could have just fallen, and you weren't close. Anyhow, give the campaign some more thought and we'll touch base again Monday."

"Will do. And, thank you, Tanya. It's very generous of you to give me more responsibility."

"It's nothing. You'll be here long after I've gone." *Good thing I'm not superstitious,* she thought as Becca left. *I could be tempting fate saying something like that.*

———————

As soon as the door closed, Anna took out her iPhone and typed "Olga Novrosky" on its memo pad. She ignored the inclination to run to Pierre Barton demanding, "Why didn't you tell me about Olga?" Instead, since it was past five, she grabbed her things and left.

She ran down the steps of the Oxford Circus Underground station and swiped her Oyster card at the turnstile; once on the platform, she stood back by the wall, far from the edge and the drop to the tracks. When a standing-room-only car arrived, she slipped on and held tightly to the pole as she was borne through the dark tunnels.

She didn't go straight home. Instead she headed to a café with free Wi-Fi and took out her iPhone. She connected to the café's Wi-Fi and then switched to the untraceable Virtual Privacy Network (VPN) connection Rob, whom she now considered her personal security expert, had recommended if she went online with her own electronics.

Then she Googled "Olga Novrosky." News reports were perfunctory. Olga Novrosky, twenty-three, a Russian national who had recently moved to London, died after falling or jumping in front of a train as it entered Oxford Circus station. A coroner's hearing was scheduled, blah, blah, blah.

The only paper that had anything more was one of the down-market tabloids. On half a page, eight pages in, it strayed from the official line, asking "How Did Olga Die?"

She read:

A mysterious young Russian woman, recently arrived in London, died when she plunged into the path of an incoming train at Oxford Circus Underground station yesterday at approximately 6:00 p.m. Witnesses said the woman, Olga Novrosky, had pushed ahead of those waiting in front on the crowded platform just as the train was on its approach. "Then she just shot forward and was gone," said a witness.

Novrosky had been employed at nearby Barton Pharmaceuticals for two months and was on her way home from work.

"It was too crowded to tell much from the CCTV footage," said a police source. "We see her arrive and move through the crowd. Several people move forward behind her, but that's to be expected of anyone waiting to board a rush-hour train. Further investigation will depend upon the coroner's verdict."

Police have thus far been unable to trace friends or family. Service on the Victoria line was halted for two hours due to the incident.

Swell, Anna thought, *the Victoria line.* Did Olga usually take it to Piccadilly and change, as she herself did, to get to Gloucester Road? Had Olga had a handy "aunt" in South Kensington? The journalist's name was Nelson Dwyer. She checked the time. Past six-thirty, but newsmen probably worked longer hours than beauty editors did. She might as well see what she could learn, especially why he'd used the word *mysterious*. An online search supplied the number, then she dug out one of her new cell phones to call.

She was nonplussed by how easy it was. Dwyer sounded pleased to speak to Lisa Jones, an American reporter investigating press coverage of unexplained violent deaths in the post-terror-attack world.

"See, none of these hacks bothered to do anything but take the police statement. Me, I spoke to witnesses at the scene. One woman was hanging around with that 'I-want-to-be-interviewed' look on her grill, so I was happy to oblige. She said this Olga had barreled past her on the stairs down to the trains, looking behind her as if someone was chasing her."

"Worried about being late, maybe," Anna suggested.

"Yeah, well, you see, luv, that might fit with the slipped-and-fell theory, but no one's in that big a rush if what they plan to do is off themselves. You know what I'm saying? I mean, there's always another train, ain't there? Also, the way she fell was a bit queer. Fractures on both wrists. Means she put her arms out to try to stop or break her fall. Not common suicidal behavior. Yeah, I know, means nothing. But after that bit you read was printed, this Ukrainian bird got in touch. Said she'd met Olga a couple nights before in a pub off Queensway where the Russkies gather; Olga was knocking back the tattie wine—vodka, luv—and told her she needed to scarper out of England real soon because of a bad situation. Said Olga from the Volga seemed scared—even terrified."

"And the coroner's verdict?"

"It would have been death by misadventure, I think—recognizing the possibility of a big fat shove—but her boss testified, told the coroner's jury how strangely Olga had been acting lately. So it came in as a suicide. Case closed. That was the end of it as far as my editor was concerned."

"Her boss?" She held some paper next to the mouthpiece and audibly leafed through it in a notebooky way. "Would that be Pierre Barton?"

"Nah, that's not the name. It was . . . Manning? Martin? Nope. Madden. That's it, Clive Madden."

August 4
Email sent as a blind copy to Anna's "Friends" list:

Hey, sorry I've been out of touch, but I've been on the move again! I came and went from London, too expensive in the long run for a thrifty traveler like me. Or almost anyone! Yeah, should have done the big European jaunt when I was young and less fussy about bathrooms down the hall.

So I headed to Belgium. And it's not at all boring. How did it get that reputation? Bruges was breathtaking. Brussels was all right, but hard for me to warm to, so I went to Antwerp and am loving it. Most Flemish speak excellent English, and the city's very cosmopolitan, with not just all the diamonds but also designers like Ann Demeulemeester and Dries Van Noten making great clothes featuring clever bias cutting and asymmetric lines. Even the nondesigner knockoffs at half the price are fabulous creations!

I miss you all but have to say I'm having the time of my life. Mwah!

A

Thursday, August 4

I've been giving more thought to **YOU**NGER, and now that I do "seem young," I don't think it matters at all other than for your Formula One agents. Your forty- and fiftysomething women, while certainly looking much more youthful, will never truly look twenty-five again, so why act as if they can?

In case my imposture wasn't strictly for Mr. Kelm's research, I must, in all honesty say, it wasn't 100 percent necessary. Young people are not this, that, and the other. A twenty-seven-year-old woman dressing like Anna used to and wearing Anna's old makeup might appear a bit staid but she would never be mistaken for a dowager. Look at Becca. Not every girl on the street is in stilettos or even UGGs. Not everyone under forty, or even thirty, hangs out in clubs. Plenty are shy, subdued, conservative, eccentric.

Tanya is a far cry from the **YOU**NGER poster girl. The **YOU**NGER woman doesn't want to be a hot young babe. She doesn't want to be someone *else*; as our tagline states, she wants to be herself but younger. And since she can't *be* younger, she's content to *look* younger. Most women my age don't feel middle-aged or older. They feel ageless. It's society that labels them. They'd like to have others see them as they themselves do in their mind's eye. And they want others—especially potential employers—not to be able to take one look before pigeonholing them by age. It's that simple.

Chapter 14

The next day was Friday, and Anna supposedly had the morning off for her "doctor's" visit, as she would on a monthly basis. Wearing no makeup, she was conveyed by Aleksei, in his habitual tomb-like silence, to the huge Strand Palace Hotel, where Marianne was waiting in an anonymous room. The nurse took photographs, then lightly scraped a scalpel along the skin of Anna's cheek and neck, using the scrapings to prepare two slides, which she put in a seal-able bag with a cool pack for the laboratory.

Then Marianne applied a light non-**YOUNGER** moisturizer and Anna put on makeup. "Good to see you again, Lisa" was the only phrase to escape Marianne's lips before "See you next month." Downstairs, Aleksei waited at the curb. When she got in the back, she noticed a bag filled with her next four-week supply of **YOUNGER** products on the back seat. She was at her desk by ten o'clock.

Becca had a doctor's appointment at lunchtime, most certainly a genuine one in her case, presenting the perfect chance for Anna to pick Chas's brain. Over moo shu pork and kung pao chicken, she was relieved to hear he had no interest in Becca's job. He was working on a novel set in the ad world, and he considered his job at BarPharm a "pretty stress-free" research opportunity.

"What about when that Olga woman died, though?" she prodded. "That must have been stressful."

"Bad news, yeah. Stressful? Not really," he said with the insouciance of the genuinely young. "Olga never had much to do with me. Or with Becca, for that matter. She spent a lot of her time holed up in her office or in with Pierre. Uh, Mr. Barton."

"Pierre will do." She smiled. "She didn't report to this whatsisname, Mr. Madden?"

"Clive?" he laughed. "No way! We called Clive 'Mr. Yes, Your Majesty.' He's a marketing expert, but he let Pierre act like everything was his own idea. Now, it's really Pierre and you, isn't it? Hugh's the first person to admit he's still really just sales VP. Clive's a great guy, but too leery of making the wrong move. Maybe because he really needs the job. Sick kid, some kind of genetic disorder."

"Oh, that's awful. Is that all he has, the one child?"

"Nah, that's his son and he's got a girl who's older. Small children. And I heard he foots the bill for a private-care home for a mother with Alzheimer's, too. If I were him, I guess I'd worry about finding myself on the street, too."

"I thought Olga was working with Clive on a makeup line like Madame X that got dropped after the Coscom acquisition." She hoped he wouldn't ask who'd told her that since she had just made it up.

He didn't, but he had nothing to offer, either. "Above my pay grade, ma'am." He grinned cheerfully. "That was great moo shu. First time I've eaten here. Anyhow, as soon as Olga died, whatever she did stopped being done, as far as I know. She didn't seem to be working hard on the retinol thingy. Or on friendliness. She barely acknowledged my existence."

"You must not have been thrilled when you heard I was coming."

"Well, we didn't know much, did we? But no worries, Tanya. To speak ill of the dead for a sec, she was a prize bitch. You treat us with respect, give us responsibility, and even ask the lowly office boy to join you for Chinese. Who could ask for more?"

"Thanks, Chas, that means a lot. And lunch is on me." When he weakly protested, she interrupted. "I say, 'On me,' but I mean this one's on Madame X."

The night before, something had suddenly struck her, and she'd called the journalist Dwyer again to ask about the CCTV tapes from the platform the day Olga died. Did he have copies? "Negative, I'm afraid. You'll need to go to the rozzers for that. But I might have some stills from the tapes. That help you?"

She couldn't let this go without seeing them, nor could she go to the police, so she asked him to take a look. "I'll call after lunch tomorrow and see if you found them."

Now, telling Chas she had a few things to pick up before going back to the office, she walked him back, then kept going, ducking into a tobacco shop to buy a phone card and ask where she could find a pay phone. She called Dwyer and arranged to meet him at a pub in Soho at seven.

She was uneasy. Something strange was going on, and she feared she'd waded into a mess that could be dangerous, even deadly. Still, she also felt exhilarated. Shuffling Madame X copy she'd already written once for the US launch, guiding Chas and Becca, and scribbling increasingly mediocre fiction for her diary and emails just wasn't enough. And now that she was growing more certain she was a pawn in someone's game, she was both pissed off and determined to figure out who was moving the chess pieces.

After work, she went to the big Waterstones in Piccadilly Circus and picked up one of the books Rob had recommended on computer security. Then she moved on to Tottenham Court Road to a discount electronics shop, where she bought a small, inexpensive laptop, some flash drives, and universal electrical adapters. Then she picked up the mousiest light brown hair color she could find. She hoped she would never need any of these things, but for only a few hundred pounds' cash outlay, she now had whatever might be required should she suddenly need to disappear.

The Wardour Street pub Dwyer had suggested was an old place, reeking of stale cigarette butts. Either regulars smoked illegally during off-hours or the stained velour of the seats was as old as it looked and had absorbed more tar and nicotine than a four-pack-a-day addict's lungs. Nelson himself fit in with the surroundings: fiftyish and seedy around the edges, wearing a shiny suit and stubble, and with cigarette-stained teeth like walrus tusks. The gleam of sly intelligence in his eyes completed the tabloid stereotype.

He got himself a second pint after draining the one he'd been nursing when she walked in, bringing back a half of cider for her. "So, Lisa Jones, tell me," he said as he sat back down again, "why hasn't your newspaper in New York heard of you and why the fuck did you think an old hack like me might believe some cock-and-bull story about suicide in a time of terrorists?"

His tone was light, but she sagged into herself, diminished by her stupidity. "Don't be glum, luv. Not a bad cover story, but nobody in the world would have any interest in Olga from the Volga's final Tube journey unless they had a better reason. I'm not refusing to help you, but you need to level with me." He paused. "And sweeten the deal."

"Sweeten the deal?" *God, did this tabloid hack want a king's ransom for the photos?*

He tapped his red-veined nose. "I have a feeling, Lisa Jones, that you're investigating a hot trail gone cold. Eh? And hoping

Olga's tragic 'passenger action,' as they call it, might lead to some-thing on the real story, eh? Getting warm? Needless to say, if there's a story there, I want it first for the UK, with a shared byline, if you please."

"Well—" In the dead silence that followed, she was surprised Dwyer couldn't hear the gears of her brain racing around like a hamster in its wheel. She needed to pass for the savvy journalist he thought she was. "Shared byline for the UK, I take it? Not for the US, too?"

"Well, it's a necessity to have both, innit? Otherwise, it will look like your mate Nelson gave you the good stuff only to be fobbed off with just a wee British byline, won't it?"

She sighed as if in reluctant agreement, then said a silent prayer that the new lie she'd just worked up was slicker than her last. "A source told me that some names that must not be named—*serious* higher-ups—are involved in subsidizing and protecting a Russian and Eastern European call girl ring, the clients of which comprise a roll call of celebrities, city wheeler-dealers, and peers straight out of Debrett's—a list harder to get into than the Royal Box at Ascot."

He laughed. "Depends which royal's box you're thinking of, pet. If you mean the Royal Enclosure on Royal Ascot Day, it holds so many people you could be there all day without setting eyes on a bloody royal. But I get your drift. And I've heard whispers, too," he bluffed. "You were told this Olga was involved?"

She nodded. "Attractive Russian girl, working in some half-assed marketing job, unfriendly to her coworkers and out of the office on 'appointments' a lot. Could be nothing. But your write-up grabbed my attention."

"The other papers dropped the ball. Looked at the statistics and shrugged it off. See, about eighty people end up under a Tube train each year, more than ninety percent of them jumpers. Most of the others are written off as slip-and-falls, what with folks shov-ing to get in front at rush hour. If, at a coroner's hearing, some muckety-muck from the office says, 'Yeah, Olga wasn't herself lately, acted weird and depressed,' then Bob's your uncle, the verdict's going to be a jumper. So by that point, it doesn't strike anyone as odd that, for all intents and purposes, Olga Novrosky didn't exist. Police never managed to trace a family; no one ever reported her missing."

"I'm going to do some more digging," she said. "If I need to call you, I'll just say it's Lisa from Wardour Street, all right?"

He chuckled. "You'll be having the lads thinkin' I've got some bimbo in a knocking shop. This part of Soho was all brothels once upon a time," he explained. "Still not exactly Pall Mall." He reached under the table and pulled up a manila envelope. "Here. Typical crap CCTV quality, I'm afraid."

They bent their heads together over the copies of the photos. "See, this is her. Now, look here: in this sequence either of these two blokes could be following her on purpose." He pointed to two indistinct blobs.

"Dark hair, both of them?"

"Nah, black caps, I think. Like watch caps. That's clearer in the other photos. Here, this is immediately after she went under." The two men's heads were now closer, and the figure that had been Olga was no longer to be seen. "So, siren's going off now, announcement being made to clear the platform." He leafed through a few more photos and then spread out three. "And here they start to leave."

The faces beneath the dark caps were indistinct, but the two were moving separately and didn't seem to be together. It was hard to make out any one person moving toward the cameras; all were partly blocked by others or out of focus. And then, staring at those last three, flipping through them to see one after another quickly like CCTV footage, Anna caught something that almost made her gasp.

Walking toward the camera—not 100 percent clear but in sharp enough detail to be recognized, not with the dark-cap men at all—was Martin Kelm.

———————

She didn't tell Dwyer she'd recognized anyone; she just tucked the photocopies into her bag, paid for the next round, and made inconsequential small talk as best she could about her imaginary journalism work in America. She felt a little skeevy lying to him; on the other hand, there was an actual chance of his one day getting his scoop.

It was easy to find a Pakistani-run call center and Internet café near Leicester Square. There, she fed Olga Novrosky's name into every search engine she could find. Dwyer was right: she'd existed no more than Tanya Avery did.

She went onto the BarPharm website, vaguely remembering seeing photos of staff parties in the newsletter archives she'd skimmed while seeking background on Pierre. There were plenty of photos, most with the subjects identified—but no Russian names.

She did find something, though: a feature on BarPharm's spring retreat in March. Photographs showed a sprawling estate. But it wasn't the one she'd stayed at, the one in which Barton had told her all retreats were held. Even the exterior was of a different color stone. "Our spring retreat for department heads and managers brought together key players from throughout Britain and Switzerland. Held at the company's exclusive sea-view villa in Cornwall . . ." *Sea view? Cornwall?* If this was the BarPharm estate, then where had she been taken for training?

Maybe the company had two estates, but that seemed unlikely. She was going to have to find the answer to that question for herself.

As long as she was online, she checked her BarPharm and personal emails, responding in the affirmative to one from Rob asking if she wanted to have brunch Sunday. Daytime was good; perhaps his way of saying he wouldn't be putting the moves on her again.

Richard's email said Madame X was doing well, "but it's not the same without you."

Allie's message brought the happy news that Shawna was up for a TV sitcom, but with a disturbing note at the end.

Have you heard from Jan? She and George are going to London for the film's British premiere, and she might want to meet up, even though she knows you've gone to Belgium. The movie's a hit here, so George has become even harder to bear, and Jan's drinking a helluva lot more than she should. She quit her job at the school—said it wasn't 'challenging'—and is working out with a trainer and secretly (she hasn't said a word) getting Botox and bad filler from some quackatologist, judging how her face is now both puffy and unmoving. Think: 'taxidermied squirrel hiding nuts.' And her bitterness level is through the ceiling! Sad, but I feel something close to dread when I know I'm going to see her. So get bored with the rest of the world soon, Ms. A, 'cause we need you! xoxo, Allie Oop.

Anna sighed. She missed Richard and Allie and hated deceiving them. And, even though she didn't miss Jan, she wished she could see her in London instead of lying. It sounded as if poor Jan could use a friend.

It didn't take long for Anna to get a feel for the Ford Focus she rented when she showed up at the Luton Airport car rental counter the next morning, although she suspected she'd still be automatically starting to get in via the passenger-side door by the time she returned it. After circling the airport twice for practice driving on the "wrong" side of both the car and the road, she followed signs toward Northampton.

Last night, poring over a road atlas she picked up at a news dealer's on the way home, she'd found a Dibden, Dibdin Village, and Dibden Village. She remembered only seeing "Dibden" or "Dibdin" when Aleksei had run into detour signs en route from the house to the clinic that one day. Dibden Village turned out to be the only one within two hours of London, in the area between Leicester and Northampton. How she might find the house or clinic, she didn't know, but even if she passed her time driving in circles for nothing, it was a crisp, clear August day and she had nothing to lose.

Dibden Village turned out to be a quaint hamlet of brick and ochre stone buildings, but nothing Anna saw within a ten-mile radius looked familiar. Back in the village, she ate a pub lunch, then, while returning to the lot where she'd parked, she crossed the street for a closer look at a jacket in a boutique window. It was nothing special, but what she saw two doors along in the window of an estate agent's office was. On a small easel stood a photo of the stately pile she sought, a placard at the side bearing directions to the house, the decorous murmur, "Price on request," and the added note that today's afternoon open house was from two to four.

As she sped out of the parking lot, Anna was close enough to an oncoming Range Rover to see the frightened face of the woman behind the wheel. *That* woman was, of course, driving on the left side of the road. Anna swerved to where she belonged, then slowed down, determined to solve the Mystery of the Mansion while still in one piece.

Soon, the surroundings became familiar. Small details she'd forgotten—an antique mailbox here, a brightly colored shed there—now stood out. Even without the estate agency sign, she would have turned left into the long drive. She was home.

When he came to the door, the real estate agent offered a disdainful glance, dismissing Anna as yet another looky-loo. Well, screw him.

"Hello, my name's Lisa Harcourt Jones. I'd like to see the house." Putting on her best Long Island lockjaw drawl, she delivered something between a request and an order.

He made no move to invite her in. "Something this large?"

"Not for me. For my employer." Now it was her turn to smile patronizingly. "Silicon Valley? Software? He's looking for a place in the English countryside. Exactly like this, I believe."

She had his interest now, and the door and smile opened wider. "Please."

Paul Timmons supplied his name like a coin doled out to a beggar, as if he were an old codger with a stick up his ass rather than someone under forty. As he steered her through the ground floor, he pointed out a feature she'd never noticed: a sliding pass-through disguised as bookcases. "Lord Haddon had it installed in the 1920s to turn two rooms into one large salon for entertaining."

"Lord Haddon?"

His look implied puzzlement at her ignorance. "The family built this dwelling at the end of the nineteenth century as a residence for the soon-to-be fifth Lord Haddon and his bride. The fourth lord and his lady remained at Haddon Hall, and this was christened Haddon House. Your employer plans to live in England?"

"I believe he wishes to spend more time here." *God, we're vying to out-pompous each other now.* "His wife is British."

"And he's in computers?"

"We reserve 'in computers' for people who sell them." She chuckled condescendingly. "I'm afraid I'm not authorized to tell you which at this point. What I *can* say is that he'd like to buy something he'd consider 'top drawer.'"

He smirked. "Well, a lord's house would fit the bill. Let me show you the rest."

By the time they'd reached the upstairs hallway, she and Paul were frigidly chummy enough for her to ask casually, "Who's selling and why?"

"Our client is the town of Dibden Village. The sixth lord left it to the council, which can no longer afford either to pay the upkeep or to donate it to the National Trust and lose the income. They want a private buyer rather than an institution, so the rooms would remain intact. And there's no question of selling to a commercial concern." He pronounced the words *commercial concern* as if he were saying "toxic waste dump."

She had thought she was past surprise, but it turned out she wasn't. "It's owned by the council?"

He nodded.

"Strange. Because a friend told me about the house. She visited here a few months ago."

"Hmmm, possible. It was rented to an acting school for a short time, I believe. Before that, a family had it. Australians," he said acidly. "It had already been listed before the school took it, but we arranged an occasional showing through them. Perhaps your friend knew someone with the school." His narrowed eyes indicated that bohemians were as unacceptable as those from Down Under.

They had arrived at Anna's old bedroom. How naïve she'd been when she'd slept there! Had it really been just a month ago? "And corporate retreats? I thought she'd been to some kind of corporate retreat here."

"Definitely not," he said emphatically, with both an eye roll and a moue. "The will forbade renting or selling to commercial interests. Even the acting school was a stretch, but the council needed the income." Back downstairs, he handed her a glossy color brochure for her nonexistent boss.

"Are you from around here?" she asked.

"Norfolk. My wife's from here. But I can assure you, your employer would find Dibden idyllic."

"Speaking of finding, I think my family's former housekeeper lives nearby. A Mrs. McCallum?"

He shook his head. "I wouldn't know. The name's familiar . . . Ah, yes, I know. The discount auto supply shop near the motorway. But it's a chain, not local, so no help there, I'm afraid."

He was familiar with no clinic nearby where the supposed family retainer might now be working, either. His farewell was almost warm as he asked her to contact him to arrange a showing for her employer.

As she swerved her steps from the passenger's side of the car to the driver's, she congratulated herself on having retained at least a modicum of her acting skills. The fool didn't have a clue her boss didn't exist, no more than she'd suspected that neither the BarPharm retreat story nor Mrs. McCallum was real.

She wondered how the actress who'd played the housekeeper felt about being named after a place selling cheap tires and wiper blades. Bloody annoyed, no doubt.

Chapter 15

She'd just climbed out of the shower Sunday when her phone rang. To her surprise, it was Marina Barton.

"Please join us for dinner Friday. My younger brother will visit for two nights on his way back to Moscow from New York. You are available?"

"Well, I—" Did she really want to sit through another dinner with the Bartons? Or would this be a chance to see their house?

"Good, you can come. My brother knows only that you are Tanya and work for Pierre. Dmitri is very entertaining. I think you will have a nice time," she said in her stilted way. She wouldn't get to see the house, since dinner was to be at The Ivy. No relation to the California Ivy, the London one was even more impressive, the number one showbiz restaurant in the world, and reputedly harder to get into than five-year-old jeans.

She walked the mile to the Chelsea café where she was meeting Rob, who was, not surprisingly, smoking out front and looking very Eurocool and handsome. *Too bad I'm not really his age,* she thought as he held the door, *or I'd be giving that Prague babe a run for her money.* They ate waffles, drank cappuccino, and chatted until Rob said it was time for him to meet a friend at the gym.

She took the Tube to the East End and enjoyed her own company, mingling with the young and the carefree, window-shopping, stopping for a cider at a pub with tables outside. The mystery of Barton Pharmaceuticals nagged at her, but she pushed it away. For the moment, she wanted to enjoy pretending to be young again. She feared it might not be for much longer.

Later, after installing security apps and copying her files to her new laptop, Anna started a secret file, in which she put, in chronological order, everything that she'd learned or that had happened to her in relation to **YOUNGER**, hoping it would help her sort things out as well as create a record. It didn't clear up anything, but it did astound her. How could she have been so malleable, so unquestioning? Why hadn't she poked around Haddon House instead of just playing at being an acting student? And her coaches? Who the hell were they?

She chose the ones with unusual names first: Fleur and Leo-Nardo. Online, she switched to the untrackable VPN, then Googled "Fleur fashion blog" and stared in amazement at the ton of listings. Fleur was real! She clicked onto the link to Fleur's Flares.

And then she sighed. Yes, Fleur was real. She was also chubby and fortyish. She moved on to "Leo-Nardo Deejay," and, as she expected, no one could have mistaken the real thing for the Leo she'd known.

Imposters. No doubt they all were. Actors and actresses, who'd been told—what?—that she was an eccentric American pretending she was an actress in a charade her wealthy husband set up to humor her? A harmless nutcase? An MI6 agent learning to impersonate an actress?

Was Marianne really a nurse? Had there ever been a doctor?

She had no answers. Only the question: Why had she been lied to over and over again?

No use asking Pierre Barton, whose easy charm had been woven from a tissue of lies. She couldn't trust anyone at BarPharm; she wasn't sure she could trust anyone at all.

Anna made Chas and Becca jump through hoops Monday morning. As long as she was here and they were working hard for her, she owed it to them to help them be better at their craft. She was in her element. She didn't have Richard Myerson behind her or his hive of worker bees in front of her, but she didn't need them now that the heavy lifting was done. She was content with her team of two, who'd turned out to be both sharper and nicer than she'd first thought.

In the afternoon, she met with Pierre and Hugh, the nominal VP of marketing, to go over the Madame X rollout, scheduled for March in high-end department stores as well as upscale chains like Space NK. She had detailed memos: lists of store publicists and press, packaging deadlines, ad deadlines, possible October dates for the press launch.

She hung around after Hugh left to thank Barton for inviting her to The Ivy. "Believe it or not, I've never been there."

"You'll like it, I think. Very good food and a comfortably unstuffy atmosphere."

"I'm looking forward to it." She started for the door, then turned around. "Oh, and I was wondering if the woman who was here before me who died—Olga?—might have filed any materials regarding the UK market for Madame X."

Barton's mouth hung open for a moment before he said, "Olga Novrosky? No, she had nothing to do with Coscom. If anything was filed, it would have been your own materials for the US."

"Maybe there's something," she persisted. "I'm really trying to get a handle on the UK marketplace, and—"

"Do your own research. I'm paying you enough," he said sharply.

"Sorry, I didn't realize it was a sensitive subject, Mr. Barton."

"Pierre," he corrected her automatically. "And it's not sensitive. It's just always disturbing when a young woman takes her own life."

"And she was young? *Genuinely* young?"

She could practically see the icicles hanging off his words. "Yes. She was. A tragedy."

"Of course," she agreed soberly.

He nodded dismissively. "If I don't see you before, the booking is for eight o'clock Friday. Dress as you like, but not down. Got it?"

She nodded meekly and let herself out.

She went through anything in her office that wasn't part of the furnishings, from drugstore magazines to old binders of press clips. She found nothing of Olga Novrosky. It was as if she'd never existed. Or had existed only for a brief period of employment at Barton Pharmaceuticals.

Wednesday, David texted her iPhone to suggest meeting in Soho at four Saturday afternoon. *Drink, decide on film, dinner after?* She replied in the affirmative, though the thrill she felt seeing his name on a text warned her she was entering a high-risk zone.

That night, she stood naked in front of the mirror. Even if she was in good shape physically, her reflection made her think of a funhouse mirror, Tanya's glowing skin and firm facial contours stuck together with someone else's slightly sagging belly, gently drooping breasts, loose thighs. She collapsed in sobs after she pulled on her nightgown, no longer able to hide the truth from herself. How had she imagined in her wildest dreams that Tanya would end up with David? Even if he didn't look upon her now as someone who might be his daughter, she couldn't let him see what an outlandish mutant she was! *No more mirrors,* she vowed when her tears had stopped. If she kept this up, she'd soon be carving "freak" on her midriff with a razor blade. As for David Wainwright, she needed to give up, however tenuous, the fantasy that they could be together. Or give him up altogether.

———————

Though she had never dined at The Ivy, Anna knew a lot about the venerable theater district restaurant because Richard made sure he and his partner, Max, ate there whenever they visited London and always returned with tales of stars spotted in the dining room.

To banish the memory of that full-length mirror, she needed to feel young and sexy. So she wiggled into her little black dress with sheer stockings and the peep-toe shoes that were really too high for her, praying she'd make it to the table without a pratfall.

With her hair pomaded like Allie's and eyes smoky with kohl, she was very Sally Bowles. She'd hammily blown herself a kiss in the hall mirror before going out the door. "You're money, and you know it!"

Now she was seated at one of the coveted—she knew from Richard—banquettes in The Ivy's main room, trying not to stare at Hugh Grant here and Stephen Fry there and one of the stars from *Absolutely Fabulous* arriving. In front of her was her third glass of a heady Bordeaux and the remains of what had to be the world's most elegant shepherd's pie—a freestanding stack of wine-rich meat and mashed potatoes.

Not only was she sated, she was enjoying herself. Marina had thawed slightly, and turned out to be, like Anna, a John le Carré fan. "But only the good ones, the older ones with Karla," she'd said severely. Anna had suppressed a laugh; even when it came to secret agents, Marina preferred the Russians. Her brother Dmitri was her antithesis, charming and chatty, more international than Marina, openly gay.

"Moscow is an exciting city, and it is seeing a rebirth. But it is not cosmopolitan. It is cold and in many ways behind the time, isolated by weather, geography, and provincialism. My friend and I have a small property in Ponza, near Naples. You know this island? Very hot in summer. We are beach boys. Well, we are older, so perhaps more *Death in Venice* than *Blue Hawaii*."

Dmitri laughed. Anna laughed. She couldn't have said why his comment struck her funny bone so hard. Perhaps it was Marina's lips tightening as if she were considering rapping her younger brother across the knuckles with the cutlery. Maybe just those three glasses of wine. But Anna and Dmitri dissolved in laughter.

And then it happened.

She felt someone materialize next to her. She looked up, and there was Jan Berger, swaying and red faced. "Anna! My God, what have you done to yourself?"

Her laughter died on her lips. She managed to smile apologetically. "Sorry, I think you have me mixed up with—"

"I have you mixed up with nobody, so don't lie to me, you stuck-up bitch. After almost forty years, I'd recognize that laugh anywhere. And I want to know what you've done to yourself. Sitting here like a fucking princess looking twenty years old and acting too good for your real friends. You fraud!"

"Lady, if you're someone's real friend, I'd hate to see their enemies, but I don't know you."

"We'll have her removed, Tanya." Pierre was on his feet now, signaling to the waiter. Then George was there, his face purple with embarrassment, apologizing, dragging Jan away even as she turned to yell back, "You always thought you were better than me! Just wait. You can change your looks but not your karma."

Then they were gone. People at the surrounding tables started speaking again. The maître d' appeared. He, too, apologized profusely as he handed Pierre an envelope. "From the gentleman, sir."

Anna watched in stunned silence while Barton opened it as gingerly as if the small, flat Ivy envelope might contain a letter bomb. Then he laughed wryly. "Man's a writer. He apologizes for his *quote* 'jet-lagged wife' *unquote* and invites us to the premiere of his film next Saturday night. If we call him at The Savoy, he'll put us on the VIP list."

"As if we are peons?" Marina snorted at the idea that anyone might consider a VIP list a big deal for the Bartons.

"The film?" Dmitri asked.

Pierre shrugged. "Something called *Die with Me Again*."

"Oh yes, of this I've heard . . ." Marina sneered. "Vampire rubbish."

"Fitting, since he seems to have married something out of a horror film," Barton quipped, refolding the note and slipping it into his pocket. "I think we'll pass on it, shall we? And now, perhaps an after-dinner drink to cleanse that scene from our palates, if not from our minds."

When Anna asked for more coffee instead, Dmitri reached over and patted her hand. "You're not going to let that crazy drunk upset you, I hope," he said.

Across the table, she felt Pierre and Marina's eyes boring into her. "No, of course she won't," Marina said firmly. "Nothing to do with Tanya, thank goodness. What a shrew!"

———————

Anna was still distressed when she got home. Her first thoughts when she'd calmed down weren't kind. First, how typical it was of George to apologize to one of the *men* at the table for Jan's having attacked *her*. Second, her old school friend's filler was more disastrous than Allie had implied. She looked like a lumpy dried-apple doll. But even more shocking was Jan's venom. Did she deserve the loathing Jan felt?

Sitting over a cup of herbal tea in the living room, cold sober now, she thought back to college when she and Jan first became friends. She'd tried so hard to be sophisticated, to be someone other than the granddaughter of a Polish laundress. Had it been at the cost of her humanity? She didn't think so. Maybe she had been a snob, but she hadn't been unkind to Jan.

And in later years? She and Jan didn't see each other for at least a decade before Anna relocated to California. Jan had trodden a different path—marrying George, becoming a mother, hanging out with other moms.

She'd always thought of herself and Jan as having grown apart, as happens with some college pals. It was different with Allie. She and Allie connected on many levels, intellectually, politically, career-wise, as feminists. The only thing she and Jan shared on their "girls' nights out" were long rounds of "remember when?" Still, it had never occurred to her that Jan might hate her.

No, she wasn't responsible. The problem was Jan's opinion of Jan, not her opinion of Anna. If George wanted to dump her, she'd be better off without him. Whatever happened, it wasn't Anna's problem—and after tonight's display, Jan was never again going to be Anna's friend, either.

Before going to bed, she texted David to request going to a cinema in Kensington instead of Leicester Square. As long as the Bergers were in the West End, she would go elsewhere. The last thing she needed was David watching some hyaluronic acid-engorged harpy screeching through her pumped-up trout mouth that Tanya Avery was Anna Wallingham.

And she needed to suppress her all-too-distinctive laugh in the future. It could lead to having nothing whatsoever to laugh about.

———————

"I hope you don't mind my asking to meet here instead," she told David after they'd found a table at the pub he'd suggested, The

Builder's Arms, which was bustling with Saturday shoppers taking a break.

"Not at all. Now, what would you like to drink? My shout."

"A half of cider would be super, thank you."

"Sounds good. *Moi, aussi.*"

She grinned. So he still did that! They used to do it with each other all the time, adding a stupid little ironic tag in French. She watched him walk to the bar. He was still much the same: tall and slim, with a long upper lip quick to lift in a smile and little frown lines, deeper now, between his eyebrows. He was the same age as she was and looked good for it—other than some gray hairs and glasses, he hadn't changed.

Just like me, she thought wryly.

They spoke about episodes David had directed for a current series, the storyboarding he'd be doing for a new one, about how London had changed. In the last instance, Anna sat back and pretended she hadn't been coming here for longer than Tanya would have been alive; it was easy, because she loved watching and listening to him talk.

He'd brought a newspaper, and the film they decided on was just what she'd hoped for, funny and not especially romantic. Afterward, he led her to Kensington Church Street, saying, "I've booked us at one of my favorite restaurants. Traditional English food and modern French wines. Good combo."

At the table, she quickly looked up from the menu. "Fish and chips for me. Yummy."

"And I'll have the fish cakes." He scanned the wines on a blackboard. "How about the Whispering Angel rosé from Provence?"

"Divine. But *ooh la la*, not cheap."

"We're saving by choosing comfort food over haute cuisine. And it's still my treat. You get to choose the place and pay for our next dinner. Deal?"

"Ah, *monsieur*, you like ze, how you say, Big Mac?"

It was like the old days. They spoke about inconsequential things, from books recently read to favorite cities. It was as if a quarter of a century had been weeks, except now Anna had to be careful not to reach across the table and take David's hand. Or to laugh, of course.

She was relaxed being with him as Tanya in a way she hadn't been as Anna, at least not at the end. She wasn't fretting that he didn't consider her talented enough or connected enough or interesting enough. Suddenly, she was no longer so sure about what she had assumed for so long: that David had been the one responsible for making her feel unimportant.

They were drinking coffee when he suddenly stared off into space, then shook his head and turned back to her. "This is so weird. I keep forgetting you're not Anna, the woman I thought you were when I first bumped into you."

"Because I look like her?"

He studied her. "It's not just that. It's as if she's been reincarnated. The way you hold your head. The way you pick up your glass. It's haunting."

"What happened between you, all those years ago?"

He laughed ruefully. "Beats me. I knew she was unhappy. But I thought it was something she had to sort out on her own. I mean, we all do. We all have disappointments and failures and . . ." He shrugged. "I flew back here for some meetings, and when I returned to New York two weeks later, she'd not only taken the things she kept at my apartment and left her key on the table, she'd also moved out of her own flat."

"And that was it? Wham, bam, thank you, ma'am?"

"That was pretty much it. I got a letter that week saying she couldn't do it anymore, that my lack of respect for her was devastating. I didn't even recognize the man she was describing." He shrugged. "She was right to some degree. I *was* too caught up in my own career; I *hadn't* been thinking about the future, when my work in New York was over. But I'd never realized it had been eating away at her.

"She asked that I not try to find her or get in touch, so I didn't. I wanted to, but I felt I had to respect her decision."

"And then all this time . . . ?"

He sipped his coffee and shrugged. "All this time? Well, I haven't been Mr. True Romance pining away. I carried on, as one does. I finished the job in the States, came back to London, worked, met women, got married, got divorced, got married, had a kid, got divorced again. I can't even say I thought about Anna a lot. When I did, it was intense, but months—even years—went by without a thought. People fade in your memory when you haven't seen them for so long; they grow to be more like fictional characters than flesh-and-blood people.

"And then I bumped into you on a street in the middle of London, and Anna became real to me again, as if she'd been there all along. And I'm—" He stopped, then smiled. "I'm boring even myself. I think that means it's time to go."

Outside, he hustled her into a taxi. "I'm in the mood for a bit of a walk," he said. "And since I'll be strolling through the past, I should do it on my own." She leaned toward him, part of her desperately hoping he'd take her in his arms. But he just smiled down at her. "Don't forget to let me know where you're taking me for dinner. I'll text you next week."

Then he was gone, and she wasn't Tanya Avery anymore. She was Anna Wallingham, heading south in a black cab. Alone. Very much alone.

Chapter 16

Sunday dawned cold and blustery, a phlegmy North Sea kind of day that made umbrellas useless against its windborne mists. Still, Anna forced herself to get out of the house, having no desire to stay home alone with her thoughts. She'd called Lorrayne on the off chance she was free, but the voice at the other end of the phone sounded more like someone who'd been taking recreational drugs than selling pharmaceuticals. "Can't move, Tanya. Got a headache big as a Routemaster bus and a drunken hulk sleeping next to me." Then she giggled. "Uh-oh. I woke the sleeping tiger. Gotta go."

She'd forgotten what it had been like being in her twenties, separated from Monty, out with a different guy every night, dancing in Village clubs, drinking screwdrivers until her stomach burned, rarely turning down the occasional line of cocaine. If she had a breakup, she simply partied harder.

After she'd split from David, she'd been older and too depressed for debauchery. It was as if she'd had to exact a penance for lacking a thriving career, verifiable talent, a man who loved her. Through a roommate agency, she found a dreary woman who worked as an editorial assistant and pined for a married, unavailable boss. Weekends, the roommate either went to stay with her religious mother in the Bronx for endless rounds of mass or camped out in the bedroom of the small apartment without changing out of the filmy peignoir set she'd undoubtedly bought with hopes of luring the editor into her bed. Anna, who slept on a studio couch in the living room, would wander the streets of Manhattan, yearning for David, alternately thinking she'd been a fool and raging silently at him for having let her down.

She didn't envy Lorrayne her youth or the young man in her bed now, but she would have then. She'd longed to feel interest in another man, but she was so shrouded in her unrequited love for David, she felt no sparks for several years. Her New York life was all work, and then she had dedicated her LA life to pursuing even more success. Had this been a sort of revenge, becoming the kind of woman David might want? Yet, the feelings he showed when discussing the Anna he had known didn't seem connected to her being a success or failure, just her essence, and this belated knowledge made her feel a stab of remorse. She had misjudged him and, thinking she was salvaging her self-respect, had destroyed everything they shared.

Checking online, she found an early twentieth-century exhibit at the National Portrait Gallery. That would do for a Sunday outing. It meant going to the West End, but the risk of running into George and Jan at a museum was small. Once cultured, their artistic interests were now limited to hot buttons. *Picasso! Monet! Hockney!* Only artists who'd be billed above the title as if they were A-list actors counted.

At least she had accomplished what she had set out to do after calling it quits with David, she told herself as she headed out. She'd created a career out of nothing, channeled her dramatic flair into her advertising work. Still . . . for what? To end up in this sick charade? *C'est à rire.* It was laughable indeed.

The exhibit, crowded on a wet Sunday, was reassuring, like visiting old friends: the Woolfs, the Sitwells, Roger Fry. Anna wandered on afterward, through permanent collections of Victorians and Georgians, the posers and the poseurs.

She was making her way toward the exit when she paused for a second look at Lucian Freud's searing self-portrait from the '60s, unaware that someone had slipped up behind her until she heard a voice close to her ear. "He stripped a face down, didn't he? Even his own. Down to its sinews, I'd say."

"Mr. Kelm." She flushed as if caught spraying graffiti. "You're a portrait fan?"

"Of course. People are infinitely more interesting than fields or dead pheasants, aren't they? And I'm a great fan of Freud's—Lucian only, not his grandfather Sigmund. He's the master of depicting how we're betrayed by our flesh. And the aging of it," he added, with a bright smile. He took Anna's elbow. "Allow me to buy you a drink." It wasn't a question.

They took the lift up to the restaurant in silence with three other people.

At the bar, she ordered a glass of pricey Sancerre. Hang the expense; let MI6 spring for something from the top shelf. Spy Boy had a mineral water.

Today the meticulous Mr. Kelm sported a blue shirt, discreetly patterned tie, and clubby-looking blazer. He made a show of raising his glass of water. "In Italy, one isn't allowed to clink glasses that don't hold alcohol," he noted.

"One more reason to drink, then. Ah, very nice wine, thank you."

"Everything going all right?"

She nodded.

"Mr. Barton is pleased with your work," he noted.

"Oh?" She wondered what details Barton reported but knew asking was of no use.

"As you probably figured out, much of what he asks is as a favor to us—how the age change affects you, your confidence in being accepted for whom you appear to be."

She nodded. "I worked that out."

"I appreciate your agreeing to stay on the project. I understand that you're bored with the diary and perhaps even the impersonation you consider unnecessary. There's a possibility we can cut your contract short by several months, so you could concentrate on the **YOU**NGER campaign and then go home sometime in the winter. Would that please you? You'd receive the same remuneration. Barton's assured me of that."

"Would it please me?" She was sure he had his own reasons for asking, which made her obstinate about giving him nothing. "It's hard to think about the future. Right now, I am who I am, doing what I do today and tomorrow."

"Yes, of course," he said brusquely. "That's the right attitude. And keep in mind that Barton Pharmaceuticals will ensure life-long delivery of **YOU**NGER products to you. If you so desire, of course."

"If I so desire?"

"Right now it behooves us that you continue to be Tanya, of course. But after this, you can be Anna at any age you choose. As long as you complete your work satisfactorily. You understand this?"

She stared at him. She had no doubt he was here because of her last diary entry. Somehow what he was saying sounded like a veiled threat, but she wasn't sure why. Sitting here, having this conversation, made her feel threatened enough in itself. "I think so."

They both gazed out the window, at the gray sky, almost palpable with unshed rain. He gestured. "Why I don't like landscapes. Too bleak, so many of them." Turning back to her, he said, "Mr. Barton worries you're a bit obsessed with a woman who worked for him last year named Olga Novrosky."

Ah, the other reason for this meeting. "Hardly obsessed. Wouldn't you be curious if the person who had your office before you had died mysteriously?" She laughed dryly. "Well, I suppose *you* wouldn't be, but you know what I mean."

He ignored her joke. "We checked her out. No, no, not because she was involved in our product's development—she wasn't—but because we feared there might have been a relationship between her and Barton, something messy."

"Messy relationship? You mean an affair?"

"It's been known to happen. This Olga turned out to be exactly what she'd appeared to be: a young woman who wanted work experience in England and had been recommended by a friend of Mrs. Barton's. No affair, no conspiracy, just a foreigner on her own. This can be a cold city. Not just the sky."

"Yes, I know."

"And you? You've made friends here? You aren't lonely and depressed?"

"And likely to hurl myself under a train?" She snorted. "Look, I see this as a temporary work assignment. I could be introducing an American breakfast cereal in Slovakia or a shampoo brand in Spain. I like what I do, I like the people I'm working with, and I get out enough to not feel isolated. Just the other night, I had dinner with the Bartons, for instance."

"Ah, yes? And how was that?"

She was sure Kelm already knew about Jan. "Fine," she said firmly. "I can now attest to The Ivy's shepherd's pie being beyond any ordinary shepherd's wildest dream." She finished her wine.

Throwing a bill and some coins on top of the check, he stood. "Come, I'll see you to the front door."

"You're staying?"

"I'd only just arrived when I noticed you. I have some time to kill before a meeting." He pointed to himself with both hands. "This is not my usual weekend attire."

As they exited the elevator, he smiled blandly. "Enjoy the rest of your Sunday, Miss Avery. And don't worry so much." His smile widened but still didn't reach his eyes. "That's an order."

The sky opened up as she speed-walked to the Underground. By the time she'd reached her apartment, water was running down her neck and squelching in her shoes. Shivering, she stripped down, then took a hot shower. It was only mid-August and turning chilly already. She missed the LA weather. How did the British survive?

She'd left her iPhone at home—she often did, carrying only her "official" BarPharm BlackBerry in her bag. Now, swaddled in the thick terry robe that had come with the apartment, she checked it and saw that a text had come in from David: *I had a great time yesterday,* she read. *Still tied up, but hope we're still on for September 2. Your treat!*

Her heart soared as she texted back, *Details soon!* Obviously, this couldn't go on, but she wasn't prepared to give him up yet. *Just one more time,* she thought, *then I'll cool it.*

The following week was like the best days of working on accounts in California, knee-deep in Madame X launch prep, busy but exhilarating. Barton wasn't in the office, so she couldn't ask him about her "chance" encounter with Kelm.

After work one day, she had a curry with Anezka and Lorrayne, feigning interest in their chatter about clubs and guys, going along with their teasing about Rob. Better they should think there might be a romance there so they wouldn't expect her to go out dancing with them again. It had been fun once, but for a fifty-seven-year-old, once was precisely enough.

Barton remained out of the office so she didn't see him until the following Tuesday; she'd been told by Eleanor the day before that Mr. Barton couldn't see her until three, and she made sure she arrived on the dot, closing the door behind her.

"Nice work on the new materials," he said. "I approved them all this morning and told Eleanor to coordinate with Becca on release dates."

"Good." She sat down across from the desk. "Hey, you'll never guess who I bumped into last Sunday."

He raised his eyebrows questioningly.

"Your friend Martin Kelm."

"Martin Kelm?" His voice rose in surprise.

"At the National Portrait Gallery, of all places."

"At the National Portrait Gallery?"

"You told him I'd asked you about Olga," she said, which snapped him out of echo mode.

"Did I? I may have, but I certainly—well, it never occurred to me he'd speak to you about it. I might have mentioned that you had seemed a trifle worried."

"I'm 'a trifle worried' that you're taking the time to speak to Kelm about me on a weekend and that I'm being followed by MI6 when I go to a museum, Pierre." The heat rose in her face. "I signed on to work on a skincare account, if you recall, not to be Mata-fucking-Hari." Only as she bit off the words did she realize how angry she was.

He exhaled loudly, plainly flustered. "I'm sorry. I'll ask him not to bother you again."

"What else does he know about me? Does he have people following me all the time? Was that couple pretending to be Russian tourists or whatever actually just his British agents on my tail? Do they trail me to the movies, to Marks and Spencer to buy knickers, to The Ivy?"

"Please don't get upset. What makes you so sure he actually followed you to the museum?"

"He made it quite clear he knew I was ready to leave rather than just arriving. And I'm not upset, so I'd appreciate your not telling Martin Kelm I'm upset, all right? In fact, I'd prefer if you don't even mention to him that I said anything. And if, in the future, you don't pass along any comments I might make that aren't directly related to **YOU**NGER. Is that asking too much?"

"No. Not at all. I certainly don't want Kelm invading your privacy." His look of concern seemed genuine. In fact, for the normally unruffled Pierre Barton, he appeared disturbed.

"And what's all this about being able to get out of my contract sooner than expected, with full pay?"

"What?" His surprise struck her as both genuine and dismayed, but he quickly recovered. "Well, yes, there's a chance." He cleared his throat and avoided her eyes. "We should know in a month or so."

She nodded and stood up. She wasn't going to push her luck by asking anything else. She remembered what Becca had said about Olga bugging Barton.

You're just being paranoid, she told herself. But she no longer believed anything she said.

———

She had to admit she'd be thrilled if this whole **YOU**NGER charade wrapped up ahead of schedule. She often had a hard time concentrating on her work and feared that after the US Madame X launch, the UK one would be anticlimactic. She didn't miss her real age, but she did miss her real life. Except for David, and that was another one of those things she didn't want to think about.

The incidents with Jan and Kelm left her deeply unsettled and anxious. By the time Friday rolled around, she wasn't up for more than grabbing a takeout chicken baguette on the way home, then tugging off her jacket and plopping herself down at the living room coffee table to eat. Only when the sandwich was gone did she go to the kitchen and pour herself wine, wondering if this was how Olga Novrosky had spent her evenings, alone and self-pitying. She felt irrationally annoyed with David for being busy this weekend.

She took her glass of Vermentino and computer into the little office. *What to write in the stupid, useless diary tonight,* she wondered. Certainly not what was on her mind: that mounting evidence indicated she was being used, that she didn't buy the official line about just another lugubrious Russian hurling herself under a speeding subway train. What would happen if she admitted that she was afraid of—in no particular order—her boss, her boss's wife, her boss's chauffeur, and MI6? Or that she was fast approaching the point where what had driven her to take this damned job—the threat of losing her house, her car, and her reputation—was starting to seem like a day at the beach compared to this bullshit?

Enough sulking, she chided herself. Then she logged on to her personal email, and her heart sank.

The first name was Allie's and the subject line said, "Sad News." Praying that the news wasn't about Shawna or Allie herself, she clicked.

I hate to be the bearer of bad tidings, but Jan died last week in London, after the premiere of George's movie. I would have told you sooner, but it's been so upsetting for me dealing with George and the funeral that I couldn't dredge up the energy. You know I told you Jan had been drinking a lot? It seems she got drunk at the after-party for the movie. George couldn't leave the party, so he walked her outside to get a taxi to take her back to the hotel. But she stormed off on foot and he says he figured the walk might sober her up. When he got to The

Savoy about an hour or so later, the police were in the lobby waiting for him.

It looks like a garden-variety hit-and-run. Her blood alcohol was stratospheric, so she might have walked in front of a car—confused by people driving on the other side of the road in England. George says the police say it could have been an accident but that the driver was speeding, so panicked and kept going. No witnesses. Two kids on their way to a club tripped over what they thought was a wino until they saw all the blood.

Anyhow, terrible all around. I'm so sorry to have to be telling you this. Jan wasn't a pleasure to be around anymore, but we were hoping she'd get better. Do try to remember the best, funny side of her, as I'm determined to. You two were my oldest friends, and I'm missing you more than I can say right now. Wish you were here. When are you coming home?

Love, The Other A.

Anna sat back in the chair, taking a deep breath as the room spun before her eyes. How terrible! Could it be connected to her? Could Jan have been drinking even more than usual because she'd been so sure it was Anna at The Ivy? Worse, much worse, could Jan have been run down because she'd recognized Anna?

She considered calling Nelson Dwyer to see what he knew, but she didn't trust Mr. Tabloid any more than she did anyone else. What she needed to think about now was protecting herself, and she knew who might be able to give her some advice without her revealing what was going on. She texted him on her BarPharm phone. No reason to hide meeting Rob—if anything, he was convenient for hiding David's presence in her life. *Are you free for lunch Wednesday, my treat?* she asked. *Fab curry place between our offices.*

She didn't know much of anything, but the news about Jan convinced her of one thing: she needed a solid plan, not just a bottle of hair dye, in case she had to get out of London quickly. She peered into her empty glass. Either that, or end up an alcoholic . . . or like Olga.

In the bedroom, she decided against the suitcases she'd brought from LA, now stacked on top of the armoire. If she had to flee and was being watched, a large bag was too obvious. From the hall, she fetched the backpack she normally used for the gym. Into it, she put jeans, her Vans, a T-shirt, and a sweater, as well as two changes of socks and underwear and a nightie. In the bathroom, she prepared a small waterproof bag with toiletries. She'd just have to add her **YOU**NGER products, makeup, and assorted electronics if and when the time came. For all she knew, someone might be coming in to check the apartment when she was at work. This bag could pass for something she'd put together to change clothes at the gym. She knew she'd have to keep the phones and laptop hidden until the last minute.

Finally, exhausted, she crawled into bed, hoping "the last minute" wasn't coming closer, but fearing the clock was already ticking.

Chapter 17

The following Friday, looking at David's ordinary if attractive face across the table at a homey restaurant in Soho, she wondered why any man would want to spend money on plastic surgery to look younger. The lines on his face added depth to what had been pretty standard good looks. Now his face reflected character and experience. And hers? What had hers reflected before **YOUNGER**?

His voice interrupted her musings. "Not to be a walking cliché, but a penny for 'em."

She blushed in spite of herself. "Honest? I was thinking how handsome you are."

It was his turn to redden. "In that case, you must consider Bob Hoskins a hunk of burnin' love."

She laughed, just a little, then stopped as she saw the look in his eyes.

"Your laugh is so like hers, like Anna's. You're sure you aren't a ghost?" He sounded only half-kidding.

She almost told him then. *Almost.* Instead, after a pause, she said lightly, "Oh, God, I hate my laugh! And I refuse to believe another person could have it. Or that you'd remember her laugh after all these years."

"You're probably right. Meeting you has opened the floodgates of memory, I suppose. It's been a rather emotional time for me."

Without thinking, she reached over and took his hand. He looked at her hand on his, patted it, then slowly pulled away, his face serious. "I wish I weren't so much older than you, Tanya, but I am. And, you know, there are three of us here: you, me, and Anna. I was stupid not to have resolved that relationship. I did what she did: walked away and never looked back. You know what I've decided? Once I finish work on this pilot I'll be doing at the start of December, I might go to the States and look for her. Or hire a detective in New York. I want to know what happened."

"Look for her? For *Anna*?"

His face was grim. "I want the truth. Maybe when I see her, I'll feel the same happiness I felt that moment I bumped into you and thought it was her. Maybe I'll realize it ended at the right time." He shrugged. "At least I'll find out why she did what she did, what she was hiding from me."

For the first time since she'd reencountered David, she was annoyed. "Do you seriously have no idea? A woman was so unhappy she just disappeared, and you haven't a clue? If she was hiding something, what about you? Were you so open with her?"

Caught off base, he looked defiant. "Well, I wasn't, was I? I mean, no one's open and honest all the time. I was juggling a lot of things, a lot of commitments." He sighed. "I did have someone else here in London, which is why the only times we met outside New York were in Paris. You know that trip when I returned to New York and got the letter from Anna saying she didn't want to see me again? The joke was on me because I had finally broken off with the woman here. What messes we humans make of our lives, eh?"

"Was that the one you ended up marrying? The one you broke up with?"

"No. That one ended up marrying a French journalist. I guess what I'm saying is maybe Anna and I can meet up and find the truth. Or at least compare lies."

After a pause, he asked, "And you, Tanya? How's life treating you?"

She shrugged. "It's okay. My work here might be finished before I'd expected."

"Then back to New York?"

"Yeah, I guess." She took a deep breath. "Listen, would you promise me something? If I ever contact you and ask you to call me from a pay phone or to be at one at a certain time, will you do everything in your power to do that?"

"What? Why?"

She took out a card on which she'd written just an email address, studiocitygirl@hotmail.com, and the password "2Gud24Get" and handed it to him. "Keep this in a safe place. It's important. In case of an emergency—only in case we absolutely can't get in touch with each other—log into this account and look in the Drafts folder. And if you need to communicate with me, do the same thing: write an email from that account, not to me, to any fake name, and put it in that folder. Do *not* send it. Do *not* email me. We can both read the drafts without sending emails. And don't use your own computer. Go to an Internet café, all right? I'm sure this is all for nothing, but it could happen. I could decide to leave London in a hurry, and if I do—"

"Whoa! Hang on a minute. Are you in trouble?"

"It's nothing like that."

"Nothing like that? You're talking about calls to pay phones, not using my own computer, strange email accounts, and it's 'nothing like that'? What's wrong, Tanya? Tell me?"

The look of concern on his face made her want to confess everything. Only the knowledge that he'd hate her if she did made her say evenly, "Really, it's no big deal. It's just that I think there might be something funny going on, like maybe some industrial espionage or whatever. Seriously, no biggie." She paused. "So I might have to leave suddenly, and I want you to know I'd never leave again without saying good-bye."

"*Again?*"

The blood rushed to her cheeks. "No, I didn't say 'again,'" she lied. "I said 'London.' I'd never leave London without saying good-bye. That's all. I don't mean to be a drama queen."

"So you're not serious about the pay phone?"

"No, I am serious." She waved to the waitress to bring a check. "Listen, it's complicated. It probably won't happen. But if it does, I'll explain it all, I promise."

Outside, she told him she'd walk to Shaftesbury Avenue and grab a taxi.

"You're sure you aren't in trouble? Okay, we'll talk soon then," he said. "Thank you for dinner and for listening to me natter on about a bygone romance."

"I like listening to you natter, David. Honest." She kissed him lightly on the cheek, but her lips lingered because it was just so damned hard to turn away, and then, before she could, he did what she'd been longing for all along—pulled her abruptly into his arms and kissed her. Deeply, passionately kissed her. She didn't even try to stop him. She responded, melting against him, the contours of his body fitting familiarly into hers, his taste on her tongue, her lips. Then, just as abruptly, he pulled away.

"I must be mad." He stared at her, then reached out and touched her cheek. "We'll talk." Then he turned and walked away.

She walked past Shaftesbury Avenue and on to Piccadilly, needing fresh air and a few minutes to sort out her thoughts. One more glass of wine and she might have begged David to come home with her. And then what? She couldn't go to bed with him. How could she even see him again?

She wished she'd been able to tell David, if not the whole truth, at least that a friend of hers had been killed. How crazy would that have been? But she hadn't been able to stop thinking about Jan. She kept seeing Pierre at The Ivy, folding the note from George and slipping it into his pocket. Why hadn't he crumpled it up and tossed it on the table? Had Jan died because of knowing Tanya was Anna? Was Barton involved?

Kelm or no Kelm, she had to end her contract. Not just to get away from Barton Pharmaceuticals and whatever was going on there, but to escape from the mess she was making with David as well. Neither situation, she was sure, could end well for her.

It had been a busy week that had led up to this serious scheming and her instructions to David. Monday morning, she'd stopped by Barton's office on the way to her own desk. "He's decided to take a few days off again," Eleanor told her, sounding exasperated. "He said he might not be back until next week."

"Anything wrong?"

"Who knows?" Eleanor said testily. "I didn't bother inquiring why he called at the last minute to tell me to cancel all his appointments, then snapped at me when I asked when he'll be back." She got control of herself. "Ignore me. I'm just busy enough without having to deal with making excuses when I cancel meetings for an entire week."

"I don't want to put you to any more trouble, so do you mind if I check his Rolodex or whatever for a phone number?" she'd asked.

Eleanor gave her a you-must-be-kidding smile. "Has anyone used a Rolodex since Margaret Thatcher was in office? Mr. Barton keeps his numbers on his BlackBerry, Tanya, and he keeps that with him."

"There's no place else he might store numbers? You must keep a list of calls you place for him, no?"

Peering up over her glasses, Eleanor looked doubtful. "If you give me the name, I can see if I have a number. But he places most calls himself, not through me."

Anna took a deep breath, knowing that, morally, she was about to break confidentiality—but legally, it was a gray area of her restrictive agreement. "The name's Martin Kelm. K-e-l-m."

She watched as Eleanor's fingers moved over her keyboard. "Nothing. And the name isn't familiar. A supplier?"

"No. Just a contact. I'll check my office again. Otherwise, it can wait."

She waited for fifteen minutes before ringing Eleanor. "I found that number, thanks. Silly me, I'd stuck the paper under the telephone." She hoped that was enough to make Barton's efficient assistant forget she had asked.

Wednesday, she'd met Rob for curry, and, toting out her would-be stalker for what she hoped was the last time, picked his brain about the relative security of landlines, mobiles, text messages, and emails. He asked a lot of questions, and at first she wondered if he was one of "them," someone in Kelm's pocket, though that seemed far-fetched. Only at the end of the meal did he provide the reason for his anxiety. "So, this Romeo with his eye on you, you don't think he's going to come after *me*, do you?" His relief when she said that if the guy was going to follow anyone, it would be Neil, the nonexistent man she was dating, convinced her that if some vast conspiracy existed, Rob wasn't part of it.

Over lunch, he'd supplied the helpful information she would give David about using the Drafts folder in Hotmail to communicate without sending emails that might be intercepted. Before they'd parted, Rob made her promise to call him if anything frightened her.

At lunchtime Thursday, Anna had stealthily made her way to the Tube and headed for Vauxhall Cross. Looking up while entering the forbidding-looking SIS building, she was surprised by the airiness of an atrium going up through all the floors, flooding it with light. But once fully inside, the security desk, metal detectors, and guards erased any resemblance to a Marriott.

The middle-aged man behind the desk looked up without expression.

She'd decided stupidity was her best approach. "I'm trying to contact someone who works here. Is there a house phone so I can be put through?"

Her silly question did manage to make the man look more human, though he didn't hide a snicker. "This isn't The Ritz, miss," he said. "We don't ring through. If you give me the name, I'll check on the department and number for you, but you'll have to go call on your mobile or from a pay phone. The name?"

"Kelm. Martin Kelm."

He worked a minute on his computer, muttered something, then pulled out a big directory and flipped through pages. "No such person here."

"Might he be in a different building?"

"If you're looking for the Intelligence Service, this is the one. What department would Mr. Kelm be in?"

She frowned, aiming for awkward, embarrassed, and lovesick. "I don't know. He never said."

"Well, if his name's Martin Kelm, you won't find him here." At her stricken expression, he leaned forward and said softly, "It's not all that unusual, you see, blokes telling the ladies they're MI6. All very dashing and James Bond, I suppose. But if he worked here, his name would be on the lists." He nodded. "Sorry I can't help."

"But—" His pitying yet cool stare said louder than words, *Don't waste my time, girly.* "Thank you." That was that.

Outside, she walked to Vauxhall station, then retraced her steps to the pub she'd been to with Barton. Taking a stool at the bar, she ordered a half of cider from the barmaid, a stout older woman with badly dyed copper hair. "Quiet today," she noted as the woman set her glass down on the bar.

"Because we don't do set lunch during the week, luv. So we don't get the crowds in until later, just the punters who place bets at the bookie's down the street. You from the States, then?" She set down the cider, and Anna spied a roadmap of broken capillaries under her veneer of powder.

"Something for yourself as well?" she invited.

"Ta, I'll take a Bell's." She poured herself a measure of whiskey, toasting in a ladylike way before saying, "Down the 'atch then," and knocking it back.

Anna put a ten-pound note on the bar. "I'm from New York. Just here for a few weeks. Friend of mine brought me here and I liked it. Comfy but nicely maintained."

"Yeah, it changed owners last year, and the new fella put a bit of dosh into fixin' it up." She leaned in conspiratorially. "You know, the secret service people are right up the road, posher types, and 'e went after their custom. Smart man. Come the rush hour, this place is filled with three-piece suits and brollies."

"Suit and umbrella sounds like my friend. He comes in often, I think. And that's where he works, too."

"Yeah? What's 'is name then?"

"Martin," she said. "Martin Kelm." And when the woman shook her head, Anna added, in what she hoped sounded like adoration, "Older than me, not too tall, blond hair, kind of pointed nose. I guess he's not handsome to everyone, but . . ."

"What counts is that 'e lights your fire, eh? Nah, don't know 'im. But then, we get a lot of that type in 'ere."

By the time Anna had finished her cider and a bag of potato chips, some of what the barmaid called the "lunchtime non-eating regulars"—a few badly shaven old men in worn clothing—had arrived and taken up posts at various tables with racing forms and *Daily Mails*. She shouldn't have had that drink; she felt a headache coming on.

When she was walking up the street across from the office with yet another Pret A Manger sandwich for a hurried desk lunch, she saw Barton's Bentley at the curb, Aleksei at the wheel. She tapped at the window, and it slid slowly down two inches.

"Is Mr. Barton in the office?"

"No, Mr. Barton is in the countryside. I came to give you this." He slid the window down the rest of the way and reached over; his hand emerged, holding a small tote bag. "He says these are products for you. No nurse visit tomorrow." As soon as she took the bag, the window slid back up. She started to cross the street, then turned back so she was facing the driver's side of the car, then turned around and tapped on Aleksei's window. With a venomous look, he slid it halfway down. *"Da?"*

"Your fender. What happened?"

"Hit-and-run." He shrugged. "Someone hit the car in a parking garage. I park, come back, and it's like this. Nothing you should worry about."

"But—" The window slid up, cutting off her words, as Aleksei turned the key in the ignition. Without another glance at her, he drove away, leaving her staring after the car, a knot in her stomach.

———————

Aside from her dinner with David, Anna spent most of the weekend at the gym trying to work off her anxiety or curled up with the books she bought for cash on Saturday morning: *Time Out*'s latest guides to Prague, Berlin, Rome, and Amsterdam.

Of course, Aleksei hadn't killed Jan, Olga had tripped, there was no plot, and MI6 agents couldn't be expected to go around using their real names all the time. She'd probably have a good laugh at herself when this was all over. She would tell Pierre she wanted out and hope that would be that. In the meantime, she needed to make that plan and be prepared to put it into practice.

After a restless weekend, she called the office Monday morning and asked Eleanor if Pierre was back. "Not coming in today," Eleanor said succinctly. "Now he says he might not be back until Thursday or Friday, if then. Anything you need? I thought you found that number you'd lost."

"Oh, that. Yes, I did. No, I was just checking 'cause I'm not feeling so hot, but I was going to drag myself in if Mr. Barton wanted me."

"No. You may as well stay home. I'll let Becca know. I'm thinking of bunking off early myself. Like a morgue here today."

Bad choice of words, Eleanor, Anna thought as she hung up. She turned on her computer, stuck in one of the flash drives she'd bought, and carefully copied all her files. She'd opened a safe-deposit box at the bank the week before; she'd take this there now, first getting more money from a cash point or two. She'd been withdrawing her Tanya salary in bits and pieces on a regular basis, storing it up in the envelope, almost £2000 of it already converted to euros, that she'd left in the box with all her real ID. If she ever had to flee London, she couldn't risk leaving a trail of bank card transactions.

She spent the next days moping around the flat, calling in sick and checking to see if Pierre had turned up, going out only to buy groceries. She was just killing time now, but she couldn't leave without speaking to Barton. She owed him that, and she should try to salvage as much of that other £750,000 as she could. She went to the office Thursday in the hopes of finding out more, but it was pretty much a wasted day. Eleanor said she hadn't heard anything, Chas was on vacation, and BarPharm was indeed like a morgue.

At the end of the day, she knocked on Becca's door to tell her she was going to work from home the next few days and to say

Becca could, too, if she liked. "I think I'd best be here in case any calls come in, Tanya," she said. "Besides, my father's taken this week and next off to refurbish the kitchen, so it's pleasanter here."

Anna couldn't imagine finding BarPharm pleasant ever again.

Friday she woke feeling jumpy and unsettled and decided to treat herself to a comforting traditional breakfast at Bailey's Hotel down the road. Outside the Gloucester Road Tube station, she picked up both the *Guardian* and the *Mail*, then she let a plate heaped with bacon, sausage, and eggs in quiet, dignified surroundings soothe her jangled nerves. When she'd eaten the last grilled mushroom on her plate, she ordered coffee and opened the papers. She expected the news would be the same as usual. Trouble or smooth sailing in the Eurozone, depending on which paper one read. Prime Minister applauded or heckled, ditto. Too much spending or too much taxation, ditto.

No sooner had she thought, *Slow news day*, than she saw a photograph of people who struck her as vaguely familiar. The headline made her sit up straight: "Russian Couple Found Dead in Luxury Hotel." It was breaking news, and the story hadn't really been fleshed out yet: a couple who had been staying at the five-star Park Lane Lodge for the past two months had died in a probable suicide pact or murder-suicide. Galina and Pavel Rusakov had registered as representatives of the Russia UK Business Association (RUKBA), but that organization said the Rusakovs were unaffiliated and unknown to them. The police were asking anyone with information to come forward.

Quickly, she paged through the more sensationalistic *Daily Mail*. Instead of just the passport photos released by the police, the *Guardian*'s only images, the *Mail* had others. Most could have been of any young Russians, but one caught Anna's eye like a fishhook:

the last known photo taken by Mr. Rusakov—of his wife in front of Harvey Nichols. Not only did Anna recognize the woman's blue jacket with white piping, she also knew her own NYU T-shirt when she saw it. There, behind the corona of Galina's wheat-blond hair, was the back of Ms. Tanya Avery, who was busy pretending to study the Vivienne Westwood outfit in the store window. She finished her coffee as if she didn't have a care in the world, but her mind was running fast and furious. She needed to go to several cash points to make more withdrawals from her UK account and then visit her safe-deposit box—not to put anything in but to take everything *out*. In the nearby Earl's Court area, she could go online in an anonymous Internet café instead of at the apartment. Her Virtual Private Network wasn't enough to make her feel secure about her new computer today. Deep down inside, she'd known for some time that people were dying for a reason. She was determined to find out why.

Anna arrived back at the flat with a list of times for Eurostar trains from St. Pancras to Brussels. She still wanted to try to speak with Pierre before she left; she didn't think he was a killer, and if she could get answers from him, she might know who was and be protected. Even if Barton still insisted everything was hunky-dory, now he'd undoubtedly agree to her contract being cut short. Considering what she already knew, he wouldn't dare try to renege on their deal, especially not if she threatened to sic Nelson Dwyer and his tabloid on him.

She texted Barton from her BarPharm BlackBerry, saying she needed to speak to him as soon as possible, that it couldn't wait until Monday. Hooking up all her electronics to charge overnight, she switched handbags, from the smaller one she'd been using to the big Desigual bag. She put her new **YOUNGER** products into

Boots containers she'd bought for the purpose, first flushing the original Boots creams down the toilet and wiping out the jars with alcohol. She put them in a Ziploc bag and added that to her backpack.

She went to bed with no response from Barton and with her backpack, ready to go, under the bed. Was she really going to go through with this? She slept for what seemed to be only a few minutes at a time, waking always to the sound of her own gasps.

As soon as the alarm went off early Saturday morning, Anna colored her hair, then showered. She dressed in skinnies, a shirt, and her black cardigan. It had already turned cool enough that she wouldn't look strange with her leather jacket and UGGs. She tied her long black scarf around one of the pack's straps, the better to partially cover her face if need be. After combing her hair, she let it dry lank and frizzy, then applied the lightest touch of makeup. She looked as dull as she wished her life were.

There was a train leaving around eleven. By half past eight, she was almost ready to go. She was going from room to room, methodically wiping down surfaces and making sure few traces of Anna Wallingham remained, when the bell rang, and there was Pierre's voice, harsh and breathless, asking to be let in.

Chapter 18

In celebration of finding a good apartment in Berlin, Chyna went out with her Aussie friends, so Anna, hat pulled down low, went off on her own to get her bearings in Berlin. At Alexanderplatz, she boarded a Berlin-by-Night double-decker hop-on hop-off tour bus. Not that she hopped off. Being alone made her a sitting duck, and she was content to stay in her seat.

The next morning was moving day. Kirsten gave Anna and Chyna keys, then left. They decided who'd get which almost identical room, then Chyna said, "Come talk to me while I put on my makeup."

In the bathroom, it took Anna a second to realize the white stuff Chyna was putting on her face wasn't cleanser. The truth sunk in: "You're dressed in black and putting on white makeup? Omigod, you really are a mime!"

"Well, duh!" was the answer, not spoken but conveyed in pantomime.

"So you're going out as a busker? How do you know the best place to go?"

"Busker, that's English, isn't it? But, yeah, street artiste extraordinaire. Met these dudes last night who break-dance by the Europa

Center. Great spot—like, the heart of West Berlin shopping. They said to come on by and try out their turf. It's territorial, see? You can't stand on just any corner. If these guys dig what I do, they'll be like my pimps. I'll work during their breaks and pay them fifteen percent of the haul. Come by. I'll be there all day."

"Maybe tomorrow. Today, I need to do some stuff. And work on a memoir about my trip." *Ding!* Chalk up another InstaLie. She must be up to five dings a day now.

She watched Chyna apply black liquid liner around her eyes, turn her mouth into a tiny vermillion cupid's bow, then flatten her dreadlocks into a piece of cut-off stocking and pull on a black bob wig. "Chyna gone now. New girl here. *Sehr* Louise Brooks. I haf Dietrich-look *Haar*, too, zee blund *Haar*, so I can lipzync 'Lili Marlene.'" She looked almost like that Madeleine Castaing, to whom Pierre had compared his mother.

Anna added "wig" to "suitcase" on her mental list. "I'll see you back here later, then. Good luck."

After jamming as much as she could into her backpack, Anna walked to the U-Bahn that would take her to Adenauerplatz in the western part of Berlin. There, she was walking toward an Internet café and call center she'd spied from the tour bus the night before, when she came upon an inexpensive chain salon with wigs in the window. Inside, she pointed to a rich honey blond on a color wheel and told the stylist, "This will do. I want single process color. No highlights. And I want to try on wigs first."

She knew the black wig she chose would look real only if properly trimmed, so she told the hairdresser, "While my own hair color processes, thin out the wig a little all over, then cut into the front so some pieces hang down in a feathery fringe. I want a curly bob that looks real, okay?"

She was amazed at the two new people who emerged. With her hair lighter, she looked older than Tanya—more like a younger version of the original Lisa, the character she'd played during the

YOUNGER process. When she tried on the wig, she looked like a stranger, hard and invulnerable.

The Internet café was also a convenience shop in the front, so she bought a bottle of water, noting with satisfaction the many computer stations as well as a long row of phone cabinets in the back. That would suit her fine the next day. Before leaving Holland, she'd texted David:

> *Had to leave. You'll soon know why if you don't already. Remember dinner convo? Need number of pay phone where I can reach you Wednesday at 1 p.m. London time. Put it where I told you to. TELL NO ONE. ERASE THIS TEXT.*

Even if the text had been intercepted, it could lead no one anywhere but Amsterdam. All the pointers Rob had provided were going to come in handy now. She just hoped David trusted her enough not to volunteer anything to the police.

She quickly checked the UK and US news. When she saw nothing on Pierre Barton's death, she breathed easier—until she looked at her personal account.

There was a message from Richard Myerson telling her about Pierre's death and adding,

> You should know that someone from Scotland Yard called and said they were looking for you. He wouldn't say why, but it was obviously about Barton because he asked if I knew if you knew him. I said you'd met him just once, at the New York launch. Then he asked if I knew where you were. I hope it's all right that I said you'd mentioned maybe going to South Africa. I'll write more when things calm down here. Needless to say, it's madness.

Madness, yes. She didn't look at her BarPharm account; she logged off and paid at the counter, then left. From a street vendor she bought a black knit cap and put it on, wishing she'd worn the wig instead of stuffing the bag in her purse. Someone was definitely on her trail. She didn't know who, but she doubted it was Scotland Yard. And if it *was*, it could only mean they knew she was Tanya Avery and suspected she was involved in Pierre's death.

Stopping at a discount store, she bought a cheap rolling suitcase with built-in lock to keep in the apartment. Her backpack, loaded with charged-up electronics, she toted to Südkreuz Bahnhof, which she'd learned was a main station for trains heading south, and deposited the backpack in a locker, keeping only her laptop and her iPhone in her purse.

She felt vulnerable on the S-Bahn heading east from the station. She rushed through the streets, arriving at the apartment breathless and sweating. "Hallooo?" she called, then collapsed back against the door when no response came. She was alone.

Is that what people think? she wondered. *That I killed Pierre?*

She sat tensely on the edge of her bed with a cup of tea a few minutes later, trying to think it through. Could Scotland Yard help her? But why would they believe anything she told them? Under any of her identities, she had nothing to back up her extraordinarily fishy story.

But it had to be someone besides Scotland Yard. After all, there was nothing to connect Anna Wallingham to Pierre Barton other than a brief encounter at the launch, and she was sure now he'd planned it that way. Plane tickets from travel agents, probably paid for in cash. A room in a large, anonymous chain hotel in Paris. Contracts she'd signed with no proof they'd been drawn up by him. Lies to friends regarding her whereabouts. She hadn't a clue whose name was on the lease to the flat she'd been living in. A British passport bearing her photo and someone else's name. As for Tanya Avery, she had never even existed.

But there *were* people who knew that Tanya Avery couldn't exist without Anna Wallingham, and those were the people she needed to beware of until she could get to the bottom of this. At least one of them was looking for her now. When they found her, they'd kill her. Even if it turned out Pierre Barton had died of a heart attack, the corpses of the Russian couple, Olga, and Jan assured Anna she could be next. On the one hand, she knew nothing; on the other, she knew too much.

That afternoon, she pored over the contents of Pierre Barton's hard drive once more. Did he keep nothing there that might help her? She found file after file of chemists' reports and market analyses, but not the words *Youngskin*, **YOUNGER**, or *Coscom*. A search for her own name yielded nothing, while a search for "Tanya" brought up only copies of regular interoffice mail from Pierre to Ms. Avery. Neither her diary pages nor copies of her emails to the United States were here—they were in the Dropbox.

Seeing in-house emails addressed to her made her wonder if Pierre had filed copies of others he wrote. That might at least give her a clue as to where he might hide another email account. Her search for "Richard" and "Myerson" and "RM" yielded nothing. Then, upon trying the same routine for Clive Madden, she found a file named "CM_Notes."

That file spat out pure gold.

Copies of emails from Pierre Barton to Clive Madden.

The emails dated only from after Madden had left London and come to run Coscom in California. Perhaps Barton had kept all his Coscom-related messages on another drive or in his Dropbox and overlooked this file. The first few missives were simple, thanking Clive for a report or asking for various status updates on Madame X. Then came one saying he might fly in for the launch. Since she couldn't see Madden's emails, Anna had to rely on guesswork, but the first one concerning herself was cuttingly clear.

You need to get rid of the outside ad/PR consultant. I want
her off the account without my name used. Say that it's a bud-
get-based layoff and request a review of new agencies with
younger owners. She must be informed six weeks before the
NY launch, with the paying out of her contract contingent
upon her attendance there. Please confirm you understand
this. As for the materials you sent me, they're fine. I'll sign off
on each and have Eleanor scan and send . . .

There was another email a week later, seemingly in response
to a protest by Clive.

I don't care how happy you are with her, Madden. She's off the
account. Who's that association chap who took you to lunch
and pumped you, the one you say discreetly gossips madly?
Take him out. Slip in the news that she's losing the account.
Make it a very *entre nous* kind of thing, you know, the 'I didn't
say this but . . .' bit of bait. You've decided she's 'a bit past it and
no longer effective.' You know what I mean?

Then another, a threat. Why? Because it seemed Clive had
argued for keeping Anna on.

The gist of it is, you don't always have to agree with my decisions, but one reason we work well together is that I can
depend upon you to act upon them. This doesn't mean they
can't be carried out without you, but I'd hate having to explain
to people you would be going your own way.

And the final one, reassuring.

Glad you've had a think, Clive. And don't worry about your precious consultant. I'll speak to her in New York and make sure she's well taken care of.

She was Clive's "precious consultant"? She remembered how awkward he'd been, bumping into her in the Coscom lobby after she'd gotten the boot, and how cold she'd been. And Pierre had been behind it all! He'd wrecked her career, ruined her reputation, and then picked her up again. That sleazy, lying . . . Then she remembered Barton gasping for breath on her living room couch, eyes wild, and the anger drained out of her.

So why had he done it? *Because he'd needed me feeling old and desperate for work,* she thought. She'd been a more reliable, more capable substitute for Olga. Now she was certain he'd lied when he said Olga hadn't been there for **YOUNGER**. How old had she really been? Whoever did the autopsy report must have thought she had a prematurely aged body—or was what was left too messed up to tell?

She remembered how strangely Gregg Hatch had acted at lunch. Of course he wasn't going to recommend people sign with some loser he'd been told was a has-been.

What else had Pierre Barton lied about? She'd been the fly, and Barton had spun her a lovely web. She'd been put into play by a master. Then she envisioned Marina's chilly smile, Kelm's robotic chumminess, Aleksei's hostility, Eleanor's curtness. More masters than one? Anyone else could be involved, and Pierre was certainly afraid of someone when he died, and Anna couldn't imagine him summoning up this kind of ruthlessness on his own.

There was a tap at her door, and Paola asked if she'd like to join the others for a light supper. "I thought I'd make some pasta and a salad."

"Super. I bought some wine. Let me turn off the computer, and I'll come right out."

She'd learned enough about Pierre Barton's duplicity for
one day.

———————

Anna felt better just being with the others, feasting on Paola's tagli-
atelle with lemon-cream sauce and an arugula salad. These young
people—college graduates who planned to go on to advanced study
but also liked a good time—were different from material girls like
Anezka and Lorrayne or shy, introverted types like Becca. Only
Chyna was at all like the slice of hottie hipness Anna's coaches had
been convinced "Lisa" needed to become.

Though she'd taken the name on again only for disguise, Anna
realized she felt more comfortable being Lisa, even though she was
a different Lisa now, a sort of Lisa Jr., the person she would have
been with **YOU**NGER but without all the Tanya baggage.

Still, she went to bed feeling lonely. She was concerned about
calling the next day. Much as she hated dragging David into this,
she had no one else. He was the only non-BarPharm person she
knew with access to the company. Her personal feelings and the
memory of his passionate kiss made her wary. Still, he was the only
person she could trust.

The next morning, searching for more old news on BarPharm
over coffee in an Internet café, she found two things of note. From
a *Financial Times* archive item—dating back to the time of the
Bartons' marriage—she learned that Barton wasn't the private
corporation's sole stockholder and that Pierre had bought out the
other partners except for his mother and sold those shares at a
nominal price, to Marina. *Nice wedding gift.* No wonder Marie
Héloise might not be Marina's biggest fan. And no wonder Marina
sometimes acted as if BarPharm were *her* company.

A link to a more recent pharmaceutical trade magazine
provided the second nugget. About a year before the Coscom

acquisition, for an amount unstated but reported to be grossly inflated, Barton had acquired a small Taiwanese manufacturer of dermatology products, absorbing the company into BarPharm. This, Anna thought, was a more likely source of the original YOUNGER formula than BarPharm's own research.

She logged off. After grabbing an old-fashioned Berlin currywurst lunch, she still had time to kill before calling David, so she headed for the Europa Center piazza to see Chyna in action. In spite of her preoccupations, she was soon clapping as appreciatively as the rest of the audience.

The girl was a born mime, eschewing the corny posing-as-a-statue stuff or the mechanical-man routine for something harder: as people walked past, she quickly positioned herself behind them, mimicking their every gesture, expression, and move, creating *Doppelgängerin* that had even the surprised victims joining the laughter. *Chyna would be a good Movement teacher,* Anna thought as a young woman trudged wearily past, pushing a stroller with one hand and dragging a toddler with the other, and the mime became that mother to such a degree that Anna could almost see a stroller and tot, when in reality, of course, Chyna was pushing air with one hand and tugging it along with the other. She applauded even more enthusiastically, and her friend, spotting her, beamed before putting her head down low to copy the posture of a man striding purposefully against nonexistent gusts of wind.

She's the one who should have been working for MI6, not me, Anna thought as she walked to the bus stop. Then again, *had* she herself ever been working for them?

At the call center in Adenauerplatz, she asked for a computer slot and booked a call booth for a half hour later. Online, she logged into the "studiocitygirl" Hotmail account and breathed a sigh of relief when she opened the Drafts folder.

"Whatever is going on?" David wrote. "Barton dies & U disappear? I'm worried. Found pay phone & will be there as directed.

Number's below." She carefully copied the number onto a piece of paper, then deleted the draft. That's what made the Drafts folder secure, Rob had told her: unlike an email, once a draft was deleted, it was gone forever, leaving no traces of its existence.

She entered the booth, picked up the phone, then counted the seconds until the connection went through, and she heard David's voice, sounding exasperated. "I don't mean to sound like somebody's father, but I hope you have a good explanation for this," he said. "It's not just strange behavior. Considering that Barton's dead, it's disturbing." Then his voice softened. "Sorry, but I've been worried sick. Where are you? And are you all right?"

"I'm fine, but it's better you don't know where I am. It's too complicated to explain now. You can say no if you want. But I can't think of anyone else I trust and I really, really need someone to help me right now." She wiped away the tears that had started flowing.

"Hey, c'mon, don't cry. Of course I'll help you."

"It's not that easy," she said. "I'm in danger. Not because of anything I've done, but because of what I know, about BarPharm. But I don't know enough to protect myself. Does that make any sense?"

"To be honest, no. I mean, you're in marketing, Tanya. Since when is marketing high risk?"

"It's not about marketing," she said. "It's a product, an experiment I was tricked into taking part in. Pierre lied to me about everything, so I don't even know who all's involved: MI6, Russia maybe, assassins—"

"Whoa, hold on. Are you kidding me?"

"Do you have any idea how vicious Big Pharma is? Industrial espionage is a game played at the highest levels—and for the highest stakes. Please believe me."

After a thoughtful pause, he asked, "What do you want me to do?"

"A small favor. No one knows that you know me, so I thought you could find an excuse to drop by BarPharm. Stop and pay condolences to Eleanor. See Becca. Ask what happened. See if anyone mentions me. If they do, just play dumb and ask questions. Remember, you don't know me. Can you do that?"

When he told her he would, she said, "Good. When you've done it, stick another message to me in the Drafts folder, and I'll get in touch."

"I'm in back-to-back meetings on the new series, but I can stop by BarPharm Monday."

No! she wanted to scream. *Monday isn't soon enough.* But she didn't want David deciding the situation was so urgent he might call the police. What were a few more days? So she said, "Monday's all right. Whichever day you contact me, give me a time and a new pay phone number to call you at the following late afternoon or evening."

"Got it. Are you sure you're all right?"

"I'm sure. And, remember, don't use your own computer. I'll speak to you soon. I'm fine. Honest. And I appreciate your help more than I can say. You're special, David."

"So are you. Or I wouldn't be doing this."

She paid for the Internet and phone call, wondering how special he'd think she was if he knew the truth. She went down the stairs on the corner of the street to the U-Bahn. A little later, as she walked from the Mehringdamm station to the apartment, she channeled Chyna and tried walking like different people she passed on the street—a businesswoman hurrying home, a middle-aged woman stomping along mad at the world, an older woman with a limp. Her Movement classes at Haddon House had taught her how to move like someone younger, but they hadn't taught her what was much more important now: how to move like someone else.

———

The next day, she shopped.

It dawned on her that anyone looking for Tanya Avery might be familiar with her extremely limited current wardrobe. Plus, she knew her supply of **YOUNGER** would one day run out and she'd need more "Lisa" clothes. On Kirsten's advice, she hit the mall at Alexanderplatz.

Not only were the clothes she ended up with more "her," they were even more her than clothes in her closet back in Studio City, in that they were more fun, less dressed-to-impress. It was as if being Tanya had led her to who she really wanted to be. In the mall's chain shops, she bought a lightweight long black duffel coat with a drawstring hood, high black boots with flat lug soles, and some stylishly hip yet unobtrusive black jodhpur-style pants that laced all the way up the sides. She bought mix-and-match clothes that could add up to ten outfits. No little black dresses, either—she wasn't dressing to kill but to avoid *being* killed.

A plain black canvas messenger bag would replace the flashy Desigual bag she had habitually carried as Tanya, and, remembering how a darker lipstick had made Tanya look too hard, she picked up some dark, unflattering cosmetics. With her black wig, she could become a whole new person if she had to. And maybe she could feel as tough as she looked.

Her goal was to convince David to meet her so she could give him a flash drive containing the report on which she was now working, her diary pages, and the files she'd copied from Barton to give to Nelson Dwyer should anything happen to her. But she needed to hand it to him in person to know the information was safe. Was she fooling herself in the hopes of seeing David again? No, she decided. As much as she yearned to be with him, this was about life and death and not romance.

As to whom David might be meeting, she looked less like Tanya every day, and everything she'd been doing since she fled London had been leading up to ditching that identity completely. Ruefully, she admitted that the end of Tanya Avery would also eliminate the romance aspect. His kiss that last night meant he was physically attracted to twentysomething Tanya and not fiftysomething Anna. Now if she could just accept that!

She had enough **YOUNGER** left for just a few weeks. Tomorrow, she would start cutting back to every two or three days. Eventually, Anna would look more like her old self, a younger-looking old self until the fillers and Botox wore off, but no one anybody would mistake for a twenty-five-year-old. In the meantime, the changes should be subtle enough not to be noticed by her roommates. At a drugstore, she bought skin products to use on the "off" days.

While still continuing to go out by day to scour the Internet for anything about Barton and hurrying to pick up her electronics from the Südkreuz locker and return them charged the next day, she did what she could to act normal. Chyna was glad to take off a half day from busking to visit the Checkpoint Charlie Museum, with Anna pretending that, like Chyna, she'd been too young to remember the Wall coming down. With Paola and Kirsten, she saw a moving, if stark, production of La Traviata at the Staatsoper ("So very German, so very un-Italian the bare stage," murmured Paola when the curtain went up), mascara running down their faces by the end. She cried as much from emotional exhaustion as from Verdi's music.

Berlin had plenty of Internet cafés, so she went to different ones to check for a draft from David. She didn't get one until a week after they'd spoken; it had been sent the night before. He'd said he'd dropped by BarPharm that day, asking Chas if he could scout up a copy of the commercial reel he had returned.

When I mentioned my shock at Pierre's death, he murmured all was hush-hush, but think that was to keep me from thinking him a gossip. Also eager to show me he was in the loop. He asked if I knew U; when I said, 'Who's Tanya?' he explained—praised U, btw—and told me a private det. working for Marina

B. kept asking about U because U'd supposedly been on the way to hospital where they took Pierre but U never showed. He said this guy asked if U'd ever mentioned friends in Amsterdam.

Uh-oh, Anna thought, *more mysterious detectives looking for me.* Hurriedly, she read on. Eleanor, David said, looked terrible.

Venomous about Marina. Says Mrs. Barton took off for Moscow at earliest possible convenience after memorial service. Implied it was just to dump the boys at her mother's.

Why didn't U tell me your predecessor killed herself? Eleanor said people whispering that Ur office is jinxed. Figured I could throw in 1 more bit of nosiness so said I heard Marina had hired a private eye. It was odd, Eleanor said, because U'd been asking for the same guy's phone # not long ago. some1 named Kelm.

I hope this helps U. It certainly worries me. I'll wait for Ur call 2moro. Hope U can do 1 pm London time again cuz it's hard for me to get away. If not, I'll go back again at 8 pm. New phone booth, # below. Hope U're all right & that everything will soon be cleared up. D.

Anna deleted the draft and then logged off, her mind racing. If Kelm had managed to trace her to Holland—through her BarPharm BlackBerry, obviously—he, or someone else, might soon know she was here. She almost groaned out loud. Once again, she needed to be prepared to leave at a moment's notice. Back at the flat, she packed up most of her things, just in case. Then she got dressed and headed off to Adenauerplatz to make her phone call to London. She put the too-recognizable Desigual bag into a supermarket tote as she left and stuffed it into a collection box for the needy down the street.

She and David spoke only briefly. She thanked him for playing detective, then asked him to do one more thing. "Could you find out when Marina's coming back from Moscow if she's not back already, then call to express condolences and casually ask what her plans are for the company? You can say you're interested in doing more work for them, whatever. Put a new phone number in the Drafts folder, and I'll call you after that and try to explain more, I promise."

"Are you sure all this is really necessary? Is there no chance Pierre died of a heart attack, end of story?" He sounded more as if he wanted reassurance than that he believed his own words, but Anna wouldn't lie.

She sighed in exasperation, then realized David didn't know Scotland Yard was supposedly involved, so he could be forgiven for thinking she was overreacting. "I can promise it isn't the end of the story. Even if you think it is, it would mean a lot if you'd humor me."

A few days later, there was a draft in the email folder saying only, "Marina back yesterday. U can reach me at # below Monday. 1 pm my time again."

That was Sunday; Monday, she took pains to look as unlike Anna, Tanya, or Lisa as she could. She felt uneasy. She knew she was pushing her luck using the same call center yet another time. After today, she'd have to switch. She wore dark clothes and, even though it was mild rather than chilly, the duffel coat. At the last minute, she stuck on the black wig. With darker lips and cheeks, she became a stranger once again.

In her nervousness, she got to Adenauerplatz early. Not wanting to hang around the call center, she grabbed a cappuccino from the underground bakery at the U-Bahn station. But she could drink only half before she dumped it and rode the escalator up to the street. She usually took the stairs, not just for the exercise but because the escalator led to the opposite side of the broad

Kurfürstendamm from the call center. But today she had time to waste, knew her disguise was good, and was more alert than ever.

Out of all the empty seconds and minutes spent and misspent in Anna Wallingham's life, these were probably the most important of all, because if she'd gone up right away, she'd already be in the call center. Because if she'd finished her cappuccino and then taken the stairs, Martin Kelm would have been right behind her—or by her side.

She saw him on the other side of the street before she'd even cleared the top of the moving stairway. They must have just missed each other among the multiple exits underground. He'd just come up the stairs from the U7, by the stairs that were her usual route. The other side of the Ku'damm was about two hundred feet away, but in profile Kelm was unmistakable, his distinctive pointy nose giving him away.

Anna stepped off the escalator as briskly as she could on legs like jelly, being sure to turn fully away from the street as she did so, then walking straight to the window of a drugstore and gazing at Kelm in its reflection until he was out of the frame.

Then, slowly, slightly, she moved to watch him almost straight on. He didn't look like either MI6 or a private eye today. In overalls and an ill-fitting denim jacket, his blond hair uncombed, he could have been just another Croatian or Polish workman going to call his family back home. Because, of course, he halted in front of the call center, his hand on the door. Anna quickly turned again and took a left into Wilmersdorferstrasse, walking away quickly but a little bent over and favoring her right side like someone with a bad knee. As soon as she was around the corner, she ducked down a side street, then doubled back to the main thoroughfare farther toward the east, hailing the first taxi that came by.

It took the whole of the fifteen-minute cab ride for Anna's pulse rate to slow to normal, then just minutes to get her things together and leave her keys with a note to her roommates, some hogwash about that boyfriend of hers asking her to meet him in Barcelona. She'd pulled off her wig before entering in case anyone was home, but she carefully re-donned it before leaving, pulling her rolling suitcase behind.

In the taxi heading to Südkreuz, she texted David on her cheap cell: *Sorry. Can't talk today. In touch soon.* Then she opened the phone, removed the German SIM card, and tossed it out the window as the driver tsk-tsked in the mirror. "Mein chewing gum," she said apologetically, shrugging. He tsk-tsked again.

The station's departures board listed a train leaving for Prague in just minutes. Anna bought a ticket for cash from the self-service machine, grabbed her backpack from the locker, and rushed to the track, just beating the train's arrival. Her luck was holding: she found a second-class window seat with no one seated next to it or across the aisle, without a reserved sign, and close to the toilet, so she could bolt herself in and pull the emergency cord if anyone came after her. She pushed the large case into the space behind the seats, keeping her backpack on the empty seat next to her. The train, being German and in Germany, left precisely on time, which meant that less than an hour after spying the pointy nose of Martin Kelm poking its way back into her life, Anna was back on the run.

When the food cart came around, she bought a sandwich, chips, water, and coffee. Then she sat back and tried to unwind. Anna would be on this train more than four hours, and there was no way anyone in the entire world could know where she was headed.

She'd been halfway hoping she was wrong about Kelm, since his being in MI6 would mean he was her ally. But today's sighting put the kibosh on the creep's credibility. He could have been MI6 pretending he was a detective or some slick shamus masquerading as SIS—but an Eastern European laborer, he was not.

About an hour out of Berlin, her food and drinks still untouched on the tray table, Anna grabbed her bags and rolled her suitcase into the cramped lavatory compartment. She divided things between her handbag, backpack, and the case. The **YOU**NGER she had left, she unhesitatingly dumped in the metal toilet bowl. Then she pushed the flush button and watched as, she thought sardonically, her youth literally went down the toilet. The product may have been proven safe and effective, but it was toxic through and through. She had expected the product to bring her not only financial security but also happiness. Instead, it had brought her terror and perhaps fresh heartache if she lived to see David again. To others, it had brought death.

She wasn't looking forward to being fifty-seven again. Not really. But she was looking forward to staying alive. Besides, she *was* fifty-seven and she *was* Anna Wallingham. If Anna Wallingham was unemployable, she would find a way to survive without working for other people. Hadn't her whole life been about surviving? Wasn't everyone's? If she had been in a more humorous mood, she would have found her beloved slogo, "YOU, only **YOU**NGER," laughable. All she wanted now was to be "YOU, still alive."

Chapter 19

Shortly after the train pulled into Prague, Anna checked into a budget hotel near the station. It was shabby, and the bathroom's fetid smell made keeping both the toilet lid and bathroom door closed at all times a necessity. But it was just for the night, and the room was clean even if the bed was harder than a park bench. She pulled the old I-need-to-unpack-my-passport trick on a desk clerk who cared only about getting back to computer solitaire. Since he'd never be seeing any ID, she filled out the registration card as "Lisa Smith," paid in cash for the room plus the extra night's deposit that would be sacrificed, and then, carrying anything of value and with her cash in her boots as always, she locked her suitcase and went in search of an Internet café.

She found one with a call center attached and checked room rentals online. One in Vinohrady sounded fine, just three Metro stops from the old center, in what her *Time Out* guide called a good area. She made an appointment with a man named Adam to come by first thing in the morning. Then she wandered down to the famed Old Town Square with its Astronomical Clock. The pastel-painted gabled buildings lining the huge square lent it the air of a medieval fantasyland. Prague might be the most beautiful city she'd ever visited. She hoped it wouldn't be the last.

The winding streets surrounding the square led her to the Vltava River. Prague Castle towering over everything made her think of Franz Kafka, whose books she'd loved in college. Now, here she was in his hometown, where, like Josef K. and Gregor Samsa, she was no longer sure who she really was and couldn't figure out what was going on. *Kafkaesque for sure,* she thought wryly.

She'd read about Kafka's old haunt, Café Louvre, and walked in that direction. Up two flights of stairs in the warm and noisy café, she snagged a table by one of the wide windows overlooking the street—the better to see who entered.

She gave in to thoughts of how pleasurable it would have been to be here with David. That would never happen, of course. She couldn't stay long enough for him to join her, and, much as she hated thinking about it, she couldn't count on his sticking with her after he found out who she really was. As for Kelm's sudden appearance, not for a moment did she think David might have given her up. If she couldn't trust him, she could trust no one.

By the time she left, a chilly drizzle was making the cobblestones slippery. She walked in Kafka's footsteps, taking care not to fall.

Adam was a gangling, bearded, thirtyish Czech PhD candidate. "What you call poli-sci, yes? Political science." The apartment, which he said had been his grandfather's, was a sprawling four-bedroom space on the third floor of a classic mint-green stucco Liberty building close to the Náměstí Míru Metro station, from which reaching both the main train station and Old Town would be quick and easy.

The place was opulent compared to the apartment in Berlin, with some of Adam's grandparents' antiques still in place. The other rooms were let to Tadeusz, an economist for a banking consultancy, and Heather, described by Adam as an "older, retired" Englishwoman. "She's here until next week," he said. "She came to study our medieval art."

The room that would be hers was charming, with a view over downward-sloping streets. "*Vinohrady* means 'the king's vineyards,' which this land was originally. When you're up high like this, you can see it's slightly raised."

"This is perfect," Anna said, "and the stairs will keep me in shape. I expect to stay a week or two, maybe longer, so I can pay you for two weeks now and whatever I don't use, you can keep. How's that?"

"That's excellent," he said cheerfully. "You and Heather share one bathroom and Tadeusz and I another. We all share the refrigerator. I make sure there is coffee, fruit, and other food on the counter before I leave for class at seven-thirty. There's a jar to put money in for what you use. Then we all take care of our own lunch and dinner. You can cook for yourself if you like. But there are inexpensive cafés all over this area."

Before he could ask for the dreaded passport, she fumbled in her bag for her wallet. "Let me pay you now." She held up a two thousand Czech crown note, a lovely shade of lavender. "Your currency is so beautiful. I especially love this one."

"The euro is not so pretty, no? Nor the dollar: all one color, all one size. Strange for a country that celebrates diversity."

"American diversity rarely applies to money and success."

Adam nodded thoughtfully. "Funny. The land of freedom, America. Here, in the Czech Republic, we give thanks every day for our freedom. Because we lost it for so long, we value it more than riches."

A blush crept up from his beard to infuse his cheeks. "Sorry. I get too passionate sometimes. We Czechs can be very sentimental in our unsentimental way. Lugubrious rationalists, if you will. So, you can move in now, if you like."

"That sounds good. Do I need to fill out anything?"

"Just write down your cell phone number and name, and I'll give you a receipt and a key. Then you can relax, and I must be off to school. I have classes to teach."

"Oh, you teach, too?"

"Just a remedial course today. Yah, I teach, I study, I work on my dissertation, and on weekends I drink too much and stay at my girlfriend's place." He grinned. "That's my life. So, welcome to Prague. There's a supermarket up on Slezská and a good pizzeria in Náměstí Míru. I'll see you tomorrow."

Once the all-too-trusting Adam was gone, Anna—rather than stealing the valuable heirlooms—fixed herself a cup of tea, dropping change in the collection pot on the kitchen counter. After that, she collected her suitcase from the hotel and lugged it up the stairs to the apartment, then went only as far as the pizzeria for lunch. With Kelm closing in, she felt even more vulnerable on her own. She took off the black wig, then stretched out on the bed for a nap, too weary to plan her next move. She couldn't contact David without a plan, but she couldn't unmuddle her thoughts, and she wasn't steeled to check the Drafts folder at her "studiocitygirl" account yet. She hoped she hadn't put David in any danger. She didn't know how she could live with herself if she had.

———

Anna woke feeling less shaky and went into the living room to find Heather, the "older" woman, seated on the couch reading a guidebook to Milan. She'd called, "Hello?" before taking any steps down the hallway, and a slim woman with gray hair in a long braid smiled up as Anna entered the room. "You must be Lisa. Adam told me you were here."

"Hello, Heather." She took a seat in a worn leather club chair.

"Nice, isn't he, Adam? So's Tadeusz. Handsome young devil, too, that one. My second husband was a Pole, so I've a soft spot. And what brings you to Prague?"

The fiction about being a budding novelist seeing Europe that rolled off her tongue seemed less like fiction than ever. Perhaps she really would write a novel when she got back to the States. She'd certainly developed a sense of plot and drama in the past months. Meanwhile, she tried to figure out just how old Heather was. About her own age, she supposed.

"I took early retirement in March at age fifty-nine," the other woman said as if reading Anna's mind. "I'm a fiend for medieval and Renaissance art, and perhaps on my way to being a writer, too—which is to say I'm thinking of scribbling a book about contrasts in European religious art during the two periods." She laughed. "It's easy to be overly ambitious when one's just thinking, rather than writing."

"Are you going to Italy?" Anna nodded at the book.

"I started there, so I'm a bit Rococo'd out. Those churches in Naples and Rome! Like walking into overdecorated wedding cakes. I have to make my way back down south again, to Bulgaria to see their icons, but in the meantime"—she held up the book—"I missed Milan, and da Vinci's *Last Supper* is calling me there."

The word *supper* did it. Anna suddenly noticed the time on an ornate antique wall clock. "Is it really six? Oh, dear, I'll be up all night, napping like that during the day. Sorry, but I've got to run to the market to pick up some food. Need anything?"

"I'll come along, if you don't mind. I can show you the way. Plus, I've figured out what some of the Czech words mean. The language makes grocery shopping an obstacle course."

After the supermarket, they stopped at a nearby café Heather liked, ostensibly for coffee, but once they sat down, for an early dinner of duck and red cabbage instead.

What a pleasure to speak with someone her own age! Heather had been in Prague almost three weeks and knew it well. Anna, who'd run out of reading material—she was down to just her Czech and Italian guidebooks—was pleased to learn that Heather knew a good secondhand English bookshop. "It's across the river, near the Kafka Museum. If you're a fan, you could plan a whole day's trip over there. See the Castle, too. Just take the tram in the square near the flat. I'd come along, but I was just there."

"I've gotten used to sightseeing alone. It's not that easy meeting people when you're on the move."

"Yes, and now that summer's over, it's mostly school groups and slackers in their twenties, isn't it? Hard to find older people— well, very hard to find them my age unless they're retired couples or Elderhostel groups, but even hard to find at thirty or forty, I'd imagine."

That conversation had Anna standing in front of the mirror when she got back to the apartment, where her eyes confirmed what Heather's words implied. Cutting back on **YOU**NGER and then stopping it completely had already left its mark. She was definitely in the "Lisa" phase now—and going in reverse. She looked about thirty-five already, she thought, not forty yet. Still, at this rate, she'd be looking close to her real age within two weeks. What would she tell her roommates then? That she'd had a peel that was wearing off and was a fortyfivishsomething? She wondered how women with plastic surgery kept track of the lies about their age. It was work.

Tadeusz—short, ponytailed, built like a dancer—was just leaving the apartment when they got back. His regal good looks were balanced by a charmingly goofy gap-toothed grin. "We'll have a chat this week, Lisa. I want to hear all about you and your

American life. Now I'm off to meet Tibor. It's Blond Night at the Barbie Club, all drinks for us blonds half price, Lisa. You should come, too." He wrinkled his nose. "But why did Adam tell me you had dark hair?"

"Oh, my hair was a mess from traveling so I put on this wig I have. Incognito, you know," she joked. "And right now I'm too tired to go anywhere but to sleep. Have fun!"

"I'll be sorry to leave," Heather said a few minutes later as she and Anna were sipping a last glass of wine in the living room. "These boys have been terrific. Czech men are so elegant, and the younger ones are all ravishing. Girls, too. The Czech Republic is the supermodel capital of the world, you know.

"Anyhow, speaking of leaving, if you decide not to stay here long, you might think of coming with me. I'm renting a car and dropping it off in Milan—a little splurge so I can drive through the Austrian countryside. I'd be happy for the company, and you wouldn't even have to share the driving. So, if you want to head that way, just let me know. I leave in a week."

"Can I let you know in the next day or so?" Anna said.

"Not headed anywhere special?"

"I think I'm going to try to hook up with an old boyfriend, maybe in Italy."

"Not Italian, is he? My third husband was Italian, and he was nothing but trouble."

"If it's not prying, can I ask how many times you've been married?"

"Oh, just four times, fewer than the old Hollywood stars. Gerald was the first; he's a solicitor and the father of my grown-up twins, both of whom live in Norfolk, where I am most of the time. The second was the Czech dreamboat, exciting but easily depressed and sulky. The third was Francesco, the Italian, until his idea of fidelity turned out to be not sleeping with more than two of my friends in the same week. And the fourth is Stephen, who's also a solicitor, but an easygoing one who's happy to let me do my own thing."

"You're married now?" Anna asked, bemused.

"Oh, my, yes. Thirteen years. Stephen's an angel, but he's what my Italian husband would have called a 'slipper man,' happiest at home by the fire. This is a nice break for him—he gets to garden without someone telling him, 'Plant that there.' I tell him he's my last husband, the keeper. You've never married?"

"Once, but it was a long time ago."

Heather winked. "Never too late to do it again. Trust me, when you finally find the right one, it's magic."

"Oh, I like my life the way it is," Anna said quickly, at the moment as big a lie as any of the whoppers she had already told.

The next day, Anna donned her wig and caught the tram at Náměstí Míru. It crossed the river, then zigzagged its way up the steep hill to Prague Castle. There, she stood gazing at the roofs below, then ambled down the tourist-clogged Old Castle Stairs, stopping to admire the views while checking for possible followers, relieved at seeing none.

Down below, she picked up a couple of secondhand novels, then lunched at a small riverbank restaurant next to the Kafka Museum before going on to be inspired by the life of someone who'd faced much greater challenges than her own. Compared to growing up a Jewish outsider, laboring joylessly in an insurance company, then dying of tuberculosis when only forty, Anna's life had been charmed. Yet Kafka had left behind a legacy of novels and short stories universally hailed as masterpieces. If Anna didn't write a book soon, what would she be leaving? Marketing memos and PR plans?

She felt almost serene when she left the museum, though increasingly aware that the possibility of being found grew stronger with each passing day. She found an Internet café next door to a shop, where she bought a Czech SIM card for the cheap cell phone in her purse.

Online, she found nothing in the Hotmail account Drafts folder. Checking her BarPharm account seemed risky no matter how she did it, but she had to do it. She stayed in the café but pulled out her iPhone. Surely, the VPN was safer in keeping her location untraceable? She would have given anything to call Rob to find out, but she didn't even trust him anymore. She was afraid to stay connected for more than a minute or two, so she ignored emails from Becca and Chas. But one couldn't be ignored: from Marina.

What she saw made her shiver.

Anna, you must call me so I can help you. I will say only that some people, people you know, are not what they have seemed to be and do not have your welfare at heart. I think they killed a woman who worked for us. And that they will kill you if they can. Call me, and I will come to you. Trust no one. Pierre came to warn you, didn't he? And he paid the ultimate price. I don't want that to happen to you. Marina.

Quickly, she bundled up as much as she could to hide her face. Then she all but ran out, with no thought but getting back to the sanctuary of the apartment. *Yes, I'll go with Heather*, she decided on the Metro as she made her way back to Vinohrady. She'd be crazy not to. Free transport to Italy—and with another woman, looking like friends traveling together. Anna felt safer in transit, and she didn't feel safe now. She didn't know what freaked her out more: Marina's saying someone was planning to kill her, or being called "Anna" and reminded that some people knew who she really was.

She would make her way to Rome. Even if she couldn't get to the bottom of the **YOUNGER** conspiracy by then, she'd be in a place with a US embassy, a city she'd visited several times and knew well, a chaotic madhouse in which hiding would be easier than within the sedate environs of Prague. Yes, she could throw herself upon the mercy of the embassy in Prague, but she had things she had to do first. There was no way she'd contact Marina, nor did she feel ready yet to speak to David. She knew that reluctance stemmed from fear: he was all she had now. What if he turned her down?

She had just a few days to get through before leaving, and she left the apartment alone only when necessary, telling the others she'd been out in their absence. She checked the news online on Adam's computer, which was set up on the living room desk and which, Adam being Adam, wasn't password protected. Still, she didn't dare log on to her email from there.

One day, summoning her courage, she took the Metro to a big mall in the Smíchov neighborhood, said by her guidebook to be well off the tourist path and boasting a Marks and Spencer. She wore the dark, hard-looking makeup, her blond hair tucked up under her black hat. She was going stir-crazy but also she would need more conservative clothes than what she'd bought in Berlin if she was going to pass herself off as an older, well-off tourist in Italy, and that was what she'd have to be, because, as the mirror in the brightly lit M&S changing booth told her, "Anna" was rapidly overtaking "Lisa" in the looks department.

She ended up settling on a beige twinset, a lot like the one she'd worn to lunch with Richard at The Ivy, except this was some kind of manmade "cashmerevelous" or whatever, costing a fraction of what the other had set her back and chosen mainly for its innocuousness.

Recalling that day, she sank onto the booth's bench, shaking her head. What a fool she'd been, gliding up to the valet in a car she couldn't afford, with her designer mocs and $400 hair color and cashmere sweaters, worrying only about how she looked. Who had that frivolous person been? Never again. She would never go back to that. What she *was* going back to—being a woman pushing sixty—scared her. Not as much as being stalked did, but it still scared her. As she was hurrying back through the mall, she heard someone calling her—actually, calling, "Lisa! Lisa!" She turned, expecting to see Heather, and came face-to-face with someone she couldn't immediately place.

"Hey, it's me, Fleur? Forget me already? I mean, I'm not Fleur, of course. I'm Chloe. Don't worry. It took me a minute to place you, too. I didn't expect to see you here, of all places! Maybe now you can tell me why I didn't get the part?"

"The part?" She realized with a start who this girl was, but she still didn't understand.

"The part in the film! I did everything the producer told me. I even refused to drop out of character when you pretended to pump me for information, remember? I thought I was pretty good, y'know?"

"Oh . . . Yeah, you were, Fleur. I mean, Chloe. Excellent. But I . . . I don't know what happened. The whole project got cancelled."

"No! Bummer! And here I thought the producer was your rich boyfriend. Not that you aren't a good actress or anything. But what are you doing in Prague?"

"Just passing through on my way back to the States. And you?"

"I got a place with this English-language acting troupe. We're dark right now, but in two weeks we open with a new comedy. Will you still be here?"

"Nope. My flight leaves tomorrow," she lied.

"What about your chauffeur?"

"Chauffeur?"

"That guy who picked me up to take me to meet the producer in London. I thought I passed him yesterday on the Charles Bridge. He didn't see me, though."

"Oh—not my chauffeur. The producer's." She forced a careless shrug. "Look, good luck to you, but I've got to run!"

And run she did, making a mad dash for the doors. Could Aleksei be in Prague looking for her? Was he hunting her down for Kelm? And what about Fleur or whomever? No, that had been what it seemed, a chance encounter. If the girl had been following Anna, she never would have mentioned Aleksei. Outside, Anna hurried to the taxi stand, too scared to take the Metro.

Alone in her room that night, she gave up on one of the used books she had bought. She wasn't in the mood for rereading *The Picture of Dorian Gray*. Oscar Wilde's tale of eternal youth wasn't amusing her the way she'd expected. Instead, she found Gray's lust for youth pathetic, and she tossed the book aside when he was carrying on about being willing to give anything if his portrait, rather than he himself, would age.

Oh, no, you wouldn't, Dorian, she thought. *Trust me.* Sure, it had felt fantastic to be Tanya, to look in the mirror and see the person she considered herself to be on the inside, just like in her **YOUNGER** marketing notes. But it wasn't real, it never had been, and it was a hard truth with which to be slapped in the face. *In the end,* she thought, *we are who we are. And stuck with it.* And the more she thought about it, the less she thought that might be such a bad thing.

At long last, it was the day before departure. Adam had insisted on returning Anna's deposit, which was good, since she was getting low on cash. She'd now made notes of all her experiences, then copied them and everything else to do with **YOUNGER** onto yet another flash drive, which she wrapped well in paper and sealed in an envelope, on which she wrote, "To be opened only in case of my death or an emergency and given only to the proper authorities. Anna." She stuck that in another sealed envelope, writing on the front of it: "Allie, I wanted someone to have a copy of my will and you're It. No need to open now." She put on her wig, then stealthily hurried around the corner to buy a padded mailer and send it to the United States.

She stayed in the rest of the day, packing and charging her equipment. Then, when it was dark and her roommates were all out, she put the wig back on and went out.

She avoided the central areas, taking a tram to student-filled Žižkov and finding an Internet café, where she checked her personal account emails. There was one from Richard telling her Clive Madden was being recalled to London. "But he's here for another month and is trying to raise money to buy Coscom in the hopes BarPharm will want it off their hands." A brief note from Allie said only that George, taking Jan's death hard, had remained holed up at home since the funeral. The "studiocitygirl" Drafts folder was empty.

Outside, on her cheap cell phone with the Czech SIM card, she rang David's home number, willing him to answer. When he did, she said nothing, overwhelmed by hearing his voice, biting back the temptation to tell him to call her back. She hung up. At least now she knew he was alive. In a grotty student hangout café, over a much-needed glass of wine, she cleared the phone's memory and SIM card. She wouldn't be calling David again. And she'd leave no new notice in the Drafts folder until she was sure of the plan forming in her mind.

As she got off the Metro in Vinohrady a short time later, she surreptitiously left the phone, turned on, on her empty seat. With luck, someone would find it, see there was still three hundred crowns' worth of credit left, and carry it around Prague for the next week or so.

Chapter 20

On hearing that Anna would be going straight to Milan's Central Station, Heather insisted on depositing her there, saying succinctly, "I drove in Naples. I'll never be afraid of traffic again."

Anna was sad to see the rental car drive into the setting sun and kept waving until it was out of sight. She had enjoyed both Heather's cheery chatter and the feeling of being safely ensconced in an anonymous vehicle without having to worry about madmen speeding up behind it.

Still, she wasn't sad enough at parting from Heather to have been honest when she'd said she was catching a train to Florence. Inside the massive train station, she bought a different ticket for the following night. Outside again, she went quickly to a large, bustling tourist hotel across the street, not to register but to copy down the number of a pay phone off the hotel lobby. Then she rolled her suitcase in the direction of a street Heather's guidebook had assured her was lined with inexpensive hotels. Along the way she stopped at the first Internet café she came to, where she wrote a two-line email to David and put it into the Drafts folder. The vision of Kelm in Berlin, Marina's email, and the fake Fleur's sighting of

Aleksei had spurred her to work out the rudiments of a plan as Heather drove them to Italy; she was itching to take action.

Anna had, she knew, reached the end of the avoid-the-passport-issue road. Italians were strict about documents; any hotel would demand her passport. She was running out of time and options and would soon have to get to Rome and beg for help at the embassy. But first, she had a few things to take care of.

So, promising herself it would be her final assumed identity, she walked into a down-at-heel pension just a few blocks from the station and handed the desk clerk the fake passport she'd found in Pierre's attaché case. She checked in as Maria Kelm, her accent Benny Hill British. She looked the right age now to be the woman in the photo of Marina Barton. Not that it mattered, the desk clerk being of an age that considered anyone over thirty elderly.

The next day, she checked her big suitcase at the train station's luggage deposit, then took the Metropolitana to the chic shopping area near the Duomo, having found the name of a good hair salon online and decided to take her chances by just showing up. When she emerged three hours later, she could have passed for Marina's taller, more robust sister. She was lucky, the salon receptionist had said: there'd been a last-minute cancellation. A stranger implying that fortune was on her side was enough to help her ignore her own restlessness and sit patiently for the intricate balayage highlighting of layered tones. When she caught sight of her reflection in a mirror on the way out, she smirked. *Totally Russian hair.* Still, she looked more like the California Anna than she had in months. Her old look, she decided, was her best look.

She was going to be Anna again. It was impossible to go back completely; the procedures and residual effects of **YOUNGER** had left her with fewer lines and more youthful, glowing skin. *This I can live with,* she thought. She knew the time had come to reclaim her lost identity; she was more reluctant to admit that she wanted to look good for David, if he agreed to meet her. She left the salon feeling almost optimistic.

The weather had turned cool since yesterday, the sky threatening rain and a haze hanging over the crowded Piazza del Duomo. In spite of the chill, waiters at the cafés shuttled among crowded outdoor tables. Trusting that she wouldn't be noticed in the crowd, Anna sat and ordered a late lunch of mixed antipasti and a glass of Barolo.

All around her, people were laughing, shopping, using their phones to take photos of the city's imposing main church. Surely, she was the only person there wondering how she might tell someone that not only was she thirty years older than she'd been pretending to be but was also his former lover—and that she'd been letting him air his feelings about her all this time without setting him straight.

She didn't dawdle. As soon as her plate and glass were empty, she settled up and backtracked to an Internet café she'd passed earlier. She logged in to the Hotmail account, which now showed a new saved draft. *David!*

If anything bad has happened, I'm to blame. Early on, I thought Ur imagination was working overtime so failed to take pay phone biz seriously. The # I gave U for that 1st call was my 2nd phone line at home. Beyond stupid of me! I promise I've never gone to this acc't except on public computers.

Some odd things going on. Barton's autopsy report still not released, & some newspapers are asking why. For another, 4 days after U were supposed to ring me, I had a visit at home from that 'private detective' of Marina's.

According to him, police r 'pressuring' Marina about Ur relationship w/ Pierre, saying they suspect U were his mistress & refusal to leave wife left U unhinged. Yes, implication was cops think U killed Pierre. Except that I didn't want him to know I was on to him, I'd have laughed in his face.

Kelm! Had he tapped David's home telephone? Could a slime-ball like him be telling the truth? Did she have cops as well as killers coming after her? But if he was the killer, why should she believe in the cops?

The draft went on,

> When I rang Bartons' house, told Marina not in London now. Don't believe any of them and worried about Ur safety, Tanya. I will call as U asked, every day at the same time if needed. Plus, have a new phone & new SIM cards now, all just for you. In case of emergency U can reach me any time at # below. Pls forgive me. I miss our dinners. D.

By the time she finished reading, Anna had already made two important decisions: she was going to tell David the truth, and she was going to stop being such an escapist scaredy-cat and take control, play offense rather than defense. Her life might depend on both.

She copied out the cell number David had given her, then deleted the saved draft. Before going off-line, she checked the British tabloids but found only one small item on Barton, stating that the coroner's jury had not announced its findings pending toxicological test results and that the police had no comment. Barton's widow, according to the ever-persistent Nelson Dwyer, released a statement saying only, "My grief is overwhelming, but for the sake of my sons, I must put this behind me." *Bullshit,* Anna thought. The Marina she'd known wasn't someone likely to be "overwhelmed" by anything other than being seated at a top restaurant's worst table.

The night before, she had lain awake thinking about Marina, Martin Kelm, and Aleksei, the three people who knew her secrets. Marina seemed to have been a, if not *the*, driving force behind **YOU**NGER and the acquisition of Coscom. What had Pierre been about to tell Anna in his final minutes? How would the sentence "My wife . . ." have ended? And how did Martin Kelm fit into the picture? Pierre had looked genuinely shocked when she told him about Kelm showing up at the National Portrait Gallery that day, but why would Pierre be out of the loop—unless the real loop was elsewhere? And Aleksei? She no longer believed he was, as Pierre had put it, "what he appears to be." But what was he? And which of them was her enemy?

Anna paid for her coffee, then, queasy with anxiety, took the subway back to the bustling hotel near the Stazione Centrale and stood by the pay phone. She picked up on the first ring.

"David? I got your message," she said. "I think the Drafts folder is secure, even if someone manages to intercept emails."

"I'm sorry. I shouldn't have doubted you."

"That's all right. I can't blame you. The situation's insane. I spent week after week in London thinking I was just paranoid. Now I know I'm not."

"What can I do to help?"

"You can meet me in Italy." She hurried on before he could say no. "I've got some important docs on a flash drive, and I need someone I trust to put it in a safe place in case anything happens to me. I mailed one to a US friend, but I want to put this one in someone's hand so I know it can't go astray. I don't know from one minute to the next who's watching or what's being monitored."

After a long pause, he said slowly, "I'm not sure I'm the right person to help you. I mean, don't you have someone you're closer to, a relative, a friend?"

"I don't," she said. "I can't ask someone to fly from America."

After another pause he asked, "So why don't you come back to England?"

"I don't know who's waiting for me there or what they plan to do. When you hear the whole story, you'll understand why. I'm sure now Pierre was murdered, David. And other people, too."

"But why not fly back and go to the police, Tanya?"

She took a deep breath. "There is no Tanya, David. I'm Anna."

She heard his sharp intake of breath. "But—*Anna*? Jesus, this is a hell of a time to make jokes!"

"Listen to me, please. Barton set me up so I'd accept his offer to work on a product that takes thirty years off anyone's appearance. At least three people have already died over this."

"You really expect me to believe—"

"Anna always loved the song *I'm a Believer*, and you used to sing it to her. You'd go to the Elgin Theater on Eighth Avenue to see movies together at the midnight show." The words poured out. "Whenever you ate at Joe Allen's, she had a cheeseburger and you had a plain burger with grilled onions. Your favorite sushi is sea eel; hers is yellowtail. You gave her a copy of *Lucky Jim*, and she gave you *Steppenwolf* to pretend she was an intellectual. And that flash drive I just said I mailed? I sent it to Allie—remember I used to talk about her, my old college friend?—but I have no idea if it will arrive."

"My God—I can't—Anna, what the hell? Is it really you?"

She didn't speak, couldn't speak, and after a moment, he said, sounding grimly resigned, "Okay, I'll come." But then his voice lightened as he said, "At least I don't have to hire a private detective to find you . . ." She held her breath as he went on, "I can't come for at least a day or two. Nick's with me right now—his mother's in France—and I won't put my son at risk any more than I have already."

"I understand," she murmured shakily.

"Where? And when?"

"Can you fly to Rome next Monday? If you can't get a seat, come the next day, or the next. There's a daily British Airways flight out of Heathrow that gets to Fiumicino at five past two. You should have no problem arriving in Piazza di Spagna to be at the fountain at the foot of the Spanish Steps between four and five. Got that? The Boat Fountain. Just stand there when you arrive, and you'll hear from me."

"All right. Got it. No phone number or anything?"

"Destroy the SIM card you're using now, put a new SIM card in your phone, and don't turn it on until you arrive in Rome. Put the number for it in the Drafts folder along with the day of your flight. And David?"

"Yes?"

"I know I'm the one who needs to apologize. I'm sorry for everything. Everything now and everything then."

During the drive from Prague with Heather, Anna had realized there was one thing she still had to do before going to Rome. So after speaking to David, she picked up her suitcase at the train station, where, the day before, she had booked a single sleeping compartment on the overnight train to Paris, arriving at half past ten the following morning. She'd left the return open and just had to hope she could get a compartment for the trip back to Italy. If not, it was going to be a grueling journey propped up like a sitting duck all night in a car filled with strangers, but she didn't know how long it would take her to do what she had to do. No question—she had to make this trip to France. She was certain that at least a few answers awaited her there.

She got a panino and a pastry to eat on the train at one of the station's coffee bars, then bought bottles of water and a liter of

Coke before she boarded the train. No leaving her compartment or drinking wine tonight. She had to remain hidden and alert.

She'd planned to read the other book she'd picked up in Prague, Kurt Vonnegut's *Mother Night*, on the way. But when she opened it in her tiny sleeping compartment on the Milan–Paris express, she was unable to get past the introduction, where Vonnegut stated the moral of the story:

We are what we pretend to be, so we must be careful about what we pretend to be.

She hadn't cried much during this whole lunatic, ludicrous experience. But tears fell when she read that prescient line; they started and threatened not to stop until they'd swept her off the train and into the Lombardian countryside, a woman drowning in a sea of grief for her irretrievable past and fear for her increasingly threatened future. She had pretended to be so many things over the course of her lifetime, had let so few others know her well. How would she fare at being herself? And would she *like* the real Anna Wallingham? Finally, she climbed out of the narrow bunk and washed her face. Then she got back in, turned off the light, set her phone to wake her ninety minutes from Paris, and at last she slept.

When the alarm went off, she washed, then dressed in the most stylish clothes she currently possessed: her black jodhpurs and fake cashmere twinset and her wig. She doubted anyone was watching trains to Paris, but it made her feel safer. When she got off the train at the Gare de Lyon, she removed her wig in the ladies' room, putting it into her backpack, and softened her makeup. Then she checked her big rolling case and headed for the Metro.

She hoped she was doing the right thing. She thought back to that day in June and the doll-like little creature with her ravaged face saying, "I lunch almost every single day at Chez Jimmy. It is my tradition."

Please, please, she thought fervently, *let it still be!*

She had scribbled down the address of Chez Jimmy and found it easily. From there she just had to walk around a little until she found the apartment house. It was a snap, as Monsieur Couret was outside holding the door open for a couple who were leaving when she approached on the opposite side of the street. She kept walking, turning around a block later to double back, then crossing the street to a small café anyone walking to the restaurant from the apartment would pass.

Now she had to hope the shock of her son kicking the bucket hadn't done in the indomitable Marie Héloise and that she hadn't switched loyalties from her favorite eatery.

It was noon when Anna sat down at a table by the front window and ordered a pot of tea. It was half past twelve and she was nursing the dregs when the woman she sought walked slowly by, elegant as she had been when they'd met, in a navy-and-white suit Anna just knew was a genuine Chanel from Coco's time.

Sometimes you get lucky, she thought when she entered Chez Jimmy about fifteen minutes later, Madame Barton's table in her line of vision. She walked straight over. "Madame Barton, *bonjour.* You might not remember me—"

"*Mais oui*, I recall. I'm one of the old who pride themselves on their memory. But what brings you to Chez Jimmy, Madame Wallingham?"

"Oh, please, it's Anna. I was in Paris for a meeting and I remembered your saying how delicious the food here was."

"Did I?" The old woman gave Anna a cool look that said "balderdash!" but then smiled gently to indicate she didn't care. "Then you must join me." She motioned to the chair across from the banquette where she sat. "*S'il vous plaît.*"

Anna didn't bother with the menu, just asked Madame Barton what was good and ordered the halibut Provençal she suggested and a glass of wine. Then she cut to the chase.

"I can't tell you how sorry I am about the loss of your son," she said. "I thought he was a very kind man."

"Kind, yes." Madame Barton shook her head. "But foolish. Pierre was always foolish."

"Did you go to London for the memorial service? I wanted to, but—"

"I wouldn't cross a *cobblestone*, much less an ocean, to go to anything arranged by that woman. I rue the day Pierre met her."

"I didn't realize you weren't close," Anna lied.

"Get close to Marina?" She snorted. "That would be like cuddling a python, my dear. She's strong. Perhaps even deadly. She didn't need to physically kill Pierre; she drove him to his death from overwork and worry. But you worked for him, Anna, *non*?" she asked.

"Not for very long," she said, which was, of course, the truth. "It was just one project. I found Mrs. Barton—"

"*Très froide?*"

"*Comme glace,*" she managed to pull from her rusty French.

"More so. So cold and hard that ice could take lessons from her."

They were silent as the waiter delivered their food. Then, before reaching for her knife and fork, Anna asked, "But the boys? She'll let you see them?"

To her shock, Madame Barton snorted again, more loudly this time. "The boys! They're nothing to me and should have been nothing to Pierre. Don't look so stunned, my dear. They weren't his. Pierre's precious twins are the sons of some drug dealer who died of a heroin overdose. Luckily for them, Marina's mother is a doting *grand-mère* because Marina's maternal instincts are those of a cockroach. Pierre was so besotted, he couldn't see how common she is. You see, for all her airs, Marina's no more than the ruthless offspring of a corrupt Communist apparatchik who plotted his way into owning a chemical factory that Marina, with Pierre's help, stole out from under him."

Of course. Anna figuratively slapped her forehead: the boys weren't his. That's why the wedding date was so long after the birth of the children.

"I don't know why I'm telling you this." Madame Barton blinked away tears. "But I did love him, and I haven't been able to speak to anyone about it."

"And he loved you, I know. The whole **YOU**NGER venture was for you."

"Did he tell you that? He wanted to get rich selling the fountain of youth because of his mother?"

"Well, he did say that after your husband, um, left, you were determined to be more youthful and, um—"

"And turned myself into a monster? Don't be silly, child. Pierre's father was the one obsessed with youth." She gestured toward her face. "*He* did this. Oh, not himself; he was no surgeon. But the surgeon he hired wasn't much of one, either. Jasper told me I was too old looking for a successful man such as he'd become. I had to look younger or he'd divorce me. He hired an incompetent doctor, then he left me to live with the results."

"That's dreadful!" She was as stunned by Pierre's lies as by his father's cruelty. "How can you be so calm?"

"It was a long time ago." Madame Barton shrugged. "The past is past. I put the cream on my hands because it meant so much to Pierre. He was sure he was going to be a billionaire, and he wanted so desperately to live up to what he considered his father's genius. Then, too, Marina made him feel like a failure, spending all his money, living beyond their means, even pushing him to overpay for the company that had invented **YOU**NGER so no one else would get it first. Money is all she loves, that one." She looked enormously sad and, in Anna's eyes, no longer grotesque. "And she turned him into a liar, a man who would lie about his mother just to convince a woman to work for him."

They spoke little during the remainder of their lunch, for which Madame Barton insisted upon paying. "I'm an old woman with no one," she said matter-of-factly. "I'll stay alive as long as possible to keep that shrew from owning the whole business and in the hopes of seeing her punished." She smiled gently. "Anna, I don't know what brought you here. Perhaps one day you'll tell me. But I doubt you came here by chance, and I wish you well in finding what you're seeking." She took an old-fashioned calling card from her Chanel handbag. "Keep this. And I hope I will hear from you or see you again."

"I promise you will, Madame." She stood to go, then leaned down and gave Marie Héloise Barton an embrace with a kiss for each cheek. "I hope doing that wasn't 'common.'"

"Not at all, *chérie*. Not at all."

Anna hurried back to the station and rejoiced at getting the last single sleeping couchette on the train leaving at 7:45 p.m. Then she headed for Galeries Lafayette. She'd be seeing David in a few days. She could use some chic clothes, and where better to shop than the most fashionable city in the world, where only one elderly woman knew where Anna Wallingham was today.

Before going back to the station, she found an ATM and withdrew the daily maximum from both her Anna Wallingham account in the States and Tanya Avery's in London. She'd been avoiding ATMs to leave no digital trail, but if her hunter or hunters found out she'd been in Paris through being able to track her withdrawals, it would get them no closer to where she would be by morning. So what if someone found out she'd met with Pierre's mother? She wasn't wanted by the police—at least not yet—and she was about to make her last dash toward freedom.

She felt temporarily safe enough to eat dinner in the train's dining car, the old-fashioned, romantic kind, with starched table-cloths, uniformed waiters, haute cuisine, and prices to match. But she refused to nibble another stale sandwich, and with the withdrawals from the ATMs in France, she would more than get by.

She started *Mother Night* again, with her coffee, and kept reading afterward. It didn't upset her tonight. Lunch with Marie Héloise had lifted her spirits, not only because the other woman was an inspiration, but because what she'd learned strengthened her conviction that Marina Barton was the key. If she could figure out the connection between Marina and Martin Kelm, she might yet discover why people had died and who had killed them.

She jumped up when the alarm peeped at half past four and prepared herself to face once again the bleakness of Milan's Central Station, even less salubrious surroundings before dawn, since so many of its wee-hour denizens were the drunk and the disturbed. But she could eat a pastry and drink a cappuccino as soon as the coffee bars opened and get on the first express train to Rome, arriving while it was still morning.

She was impatient now. She had a lot of thoughts about what was going on at BarPharm and needed a sounding board, a part she was counting on David to play. After a month on the run, she wanted to make Rome her last stop. Life had turned into a bad movie; she was ready for the wrap party.

Anna had expected the Eternal City to have changed since she'd last been there, but, looking up hotels in her guidebook, she discovered there were still sensibly priced small hostelries in the middle of what had always been the stratospherically high-rent district around the Spanish Steps. Because she was afraid to use her own passport and had no credit cards for the imaginary Maria Kelm, she hadn't been able to prebook, but when she called the one closest to Piazza di Spagna from a station pay phone, she was told they had rooms.

She took a taxi there, and after looking at several rooms, decided on a twin, rather than a double for single use, because it would be the most spacious and least "bedroomy" place for her and

David to meet without leaving the hotel. The desk clerk—a gallant, mustachioed older man who introduced himself as Mario—was happy to recommend a place in the midst of this rich-tourist oasis where locals dined, and she went out again after unpacking and showering. This was what she thought of as the fool's paradise part of life on the run: she always felt safest when she first hit town, sure no one was nipping at her heels yet.

She strolled through the high-rent district. When she first caught sight of her reflection in Prada's window on Via Condotti, she didn't recognize the woman in black jodhpurs and a dark coat, black curls falling around her face, with the blood-red lips and slashes of dark rouge of a 1950s B-movie siren.

Mario's suggestion couldn't have been better. Refreshingly rustic and reasonably priced for being in the midst of Rome's designer outposts, Trattoria da Giggi was undeniably charming, but what made it most appealing to Anna were its long rows of tables filled with families, shoppers, businessmen—all manner of Italians along with the odd tourist or two—sitting cheek by jowl with strangers while eating huge plates of pasta and Roman specialties like salted codfish and sausage with beans. The people next to Anna at the table spoke English and were planning to go to the States for their next vacation. She took refuge in chatting; if anyone searching for Tanya Avery or Anna Wallingham had wandered in, they might not even have noted the hard-faced brunette dining with friends.

When she got back to the hotel, the softer pillow she'd requested from Mario was on her bed. She propped herself up and worked on adding her conversation with Madame Barton to her notes. For dinner, she ate the fresh *insalata Caprese* she'd picked up on the way back from lunch, washed down with a glass of overpriced *vino bianco* from the minibar. She fell into a deep slumber, dreaming she was on a train hurtling nonstop through the farmlands and cities of country after country, with no preordained terminus. Even asleep, she was aware that she didn't care. She just slept on, lulled by the gently rocking motion of the car on the tracks.

———————

She awaited David's arrival with anxiety and eagerness. With each passing day, she longed for human contact. Mario was off the next few days, and the woman filling in at the desk had no interest in, or pleasantries for, Anna, who scurried out briefly for lunch, her backpack loaded up for security, so the maid could tidy the room. She went out sometimes with the wig, sometimes with her hat pulled down, walking watchfully yet quickly through the streets as if she had somewhere to go.

At the closest English-language bookstore, she picked up more books—a Charles Cumming and a Sue Grafton, it seeming like the right time for mysteries. Once she went into a restaurant on her own for dinner, but she was too jumpy, practically hurling herself under the table when a waiter dropped a plate. She was more comfortable dining in her room: cold pizza, sliced prosciutto and cheese, fruit. She'd never complain about not having enough time to read again, she vowed—eat, read, sleep was all she knew now.

She thought a lot, too—and not about BarPharm for a change. This time it was her own life, and the shock of how little she'd examined it in the past years, that held her attention. How had she never realized how ashamed she'd remained of her working-class roots, how touched by the contagion of her parents' sense of inferiority? It was as if she'd been living under a spell prior to April and had now awakened to realize that, other than Allie and Richard, she didn't miss much about that old life. Yes, she'd found satisfaction in her work, but that came from the pleasure of writing and thinking creatively rather than any thrill of peddling consumer goods. And she'd thought she was empowering women! Why had it never occurred to her that so many skincare and makeup lines owed much of their success to exploiting women's vulnerabilities and self-doubts? She supposed it was because she had never even looked at her own vulnerabilities and doubts. She was Anna the strong, the independent, the loner. She'd excelled at hiding the needy and lonely Anna from even herself.

When Monday arrived, she dressed carefully to meet David, not wanting to stand out but hoping to look good. In her new gray merino sweater and flannel pants from Paris, with ballerina flats on her feet and her hair tucked into her black wig but without the harsh makeup, she looked like just another well-dressed woman of a certain age. A new pair of oversized sunglasses completed both the look and the disguise. It was warm enough to forego a coat, but she wore her black cardigan solely because it made her feel more secure, a pretend invisibility cape. She wrote a note for David on hotel stationery, then sealed it in an envelope and put it in her purse.

She ate a salad and drank fizzy water at a bar on a side street. Through its windows, she saw no one likely to have been shadowing her. Her main concern now was if anyone had been trailing David.

When she finished her lunch, she crossed Piazza di Spagna, passed the foot of the Spanish Steps, and took the elevator tucked inside the entrance to the Metropolitana up to Piazza Trinità dei Monti at the top of the most famous staircase in the world. Surely no other possessed its sensuous beauty, the wide stairs splitting into curved wings as it climbed. Standing above it provided the perfect vantage point for watching the piazza below, with its famous sunken boat fountain in the middle.

When she saw David climbing out of a taxi that had pulled up by the cabstand beyond the fountain, she made a beeline toward someone she'd been keeping an eye on, a lone, scruffy young backpacker sprawled on the stairs. *"Scusi. Parla inglese?"*

Not only did he speak English, but he was a Texan who smiled cheerfully, called her "ma'am," and asked if she needed directions. "No directions, thanks. But if you'll take this note to the man standing and paying the taxi down below, I'll pay you ten euro now and ten when you've done it. How does that sound?"

"No problem, ma'am." He glanced down at David, then back at Anna and grinned. "If it's for love, that is."

"It's for love," she assured him, blushing. "You could even say it's life or death."

"You got it."

Keeping an eye on the square below as he clambered to his feet, she said, "First, let me tell you where to go afterward. You know how to get back up here to Via Sistina, without using the stairs?"

"Yeah, you just go around by the American Express office and—"

"Good. As soon as you've handed the note to the man I point out, I want you to hurry off, okay? Run to the left and then go to the other end of Via Sistina. I'll be waiting with the other ten for you. Got it?"

"You betcha, lady."

She pointed out David, then handed him the envelope and ten-euro bill. "As soon as I see you give him the envelope, I'll head down the street, okay?"

"No problem. I trust you, ma'am." He shoved the money into a pocket of his jeans and held on to the envelope. "See you in five."

She hurried back up, then moved to the far left to watch as the boy walked up to David, gave him the envelope, then rushed off. She turned on her heel and headed down Via Sistina.

The boy actually beat her there. *Ah, the stamina of youth,* she thought as she paid him. She flagged a taxi passing by. "Thanks for your help, dude." She smiled.

He opened the car door for her, like a good Texas boy. "My pleasure, ma'am. And good luck with that love thing. Oh, and the life or death thing, too, you hear me?"

From your lips to God's ear, she thought, then she smiled and waved until he was out of sight.

Chapter 21

Her note for David gave directions for walking the few blocks to Piazza del Popolo and told him to make sure his cell phone was turned on. Anna was standing in the doorway of one of the piazza's twin churches when she saw him approaching, duffel bag over his shoulder. She turned her back and sent a text to the number he'd put in the Drafts folder. *Bar Rosati. Straight ahead. Take a seat on the terrace.* She saw him take out his phone, look at it, then put it back and peer around in search of Rosati, passing within fifty feet of her as he headed for it.

She stood guard to make sure he wasn't being followed, then crossed to the café, the terrace of which was sheltered from the square by potted bushes that provided privacy. As she entered, she spotted David at the back, pretending to study a menu. She slid into the seat across from him and pulled off her sunglasses. "Welcome to Rome."

He just stared at first. Then he raised his eyebrows. "Brunette?"

"Wig."

"I think this is the part where I say I think you have some explaining to do."

"I think you're right."

They ordered Campari and sodas. "I remember drinking these with you before," David said. "While smoking Marlboros. You quit?"

"Smoking? God, yes, years ago. I'd noticed in London that you had."

"Yeah, before Nick was born. It seems so eighties now, doesn't it?"

"In LA, no one smokes. But I guess you know that."

"I go now and then for work. Is that where you've been?"

"Sorry. I forgot you don't know. Yes, I got into advertising and PR, then moved to LA years ago. I was a consultant. Beauty, mostly."

"Was?"

She shrugged. "Well, now I'm—well, I guess now I'm on the lam."

They both laughed nervously, releasing some of the tension.

"Here." She handed him the hotel's card and a small envelope. "I didn't book a room, so they wouldn't know I knew you, but it's pretty quiet so I'm sure they'll have one. Take this flash drive, too. It's my diary covering the insane 'experiment,' files of Barton's, and my reporting of the events as best I know them. You brought a laptop? Good. When you get to the hotel, open the drive and browse my report without copying it onto your computer. Then stick the drive in the envelope, put your name on it, and ask them to lock it in the safe behind the desk. Just in case."

"The word *eager* strikes me as overly enthusiastic, but I'm certainly anxious to hear your story. When I was at the company nosing around, I found the atmosphere disconcerting. More disturbed than grieving. There was an aura of deep uneasiness, I'd say. It seems the man I worked with, Clive Madden, might be returning, by the way. Becca admitted no one's unhappy about that part. She considers Clive the real business and marketing expert. Based on my own experience, I'd say Barton micromanaged, much of it after the fact. He'd often okay something, then call the next day to say it all had to be redone. I suspected he was consulting with someone with strong if senseless opinions whom I now suppose was his wife."

"I'm sure it was. I think Marina was very much the power behind Pierre. Not a woman to take lightly." She checked her watch. "My room number's on the card I gave you. Just walk back the way you came but keep going through Piazza di Spagna and turn into Via della Vite. Knock on my door about seven-thirty. And, please, don't reach for your wallet. The least I can do is buy you a drink."

"For old times' sake?"

"And for coming all the way to Rome on a moment's notice to save my imposter ass. I just hope I haven't gotten you into something you should have stayed well out of."

"Anna, I'm here because it's you." David's clear blue eyes held her own. "Once I knew it was really you, I couldn't say no. You don't owe me anything. Except that explanation."

She nodded. "You go ahead, then, and I'll see you later. I'm going to pick up some wine and water, and I'd like to order in pizzas for dinner. I want to stay put tonight so nothing might prevent me from turning myself in tomorrow."

"Turning yourself in? Here? Now?"

"Not the Italians, no, but I can't keep running. And I'm tired. It's time to ask for help—from my government or yours."

He shook his head and exhaled sharply. "I fly from England and you tell me you're turning yourself in the next morning? That's not quite what I was expecting." He stopped, shaking his head again. "Well, I'll say more when I know more. Thanks for the drink, kid." He got up, lifting his duffel bag. "By the way, you look terrific."

She watched him until he was out of sight, then paid for the drinks. On the way back to the hotel, she bought a bottle of Rosso di Montalcino, bottled water, and clementines. The hotel could order pizza.

She hoped David wouldn't be uncomfortable dining in her room. Then she wondered if *she* would be. Just an hour or so ago, she'd told that kid on the Spanish Steps this was for love. It had been simplest to say that, but what was it that she felt? First things first, she decided, which meant the life or death part. She could think about the future after any possible murderers had been put out of commission.

Better them than her.

"Let me get this straight. The wife's Russian and warm as Siberia, the chauffeur's Russian and chummy as Putin, and the enigmatic MI6 chap is friendly but a total phony. Meanwhile, Pierre and Marina had fake UK passports calling themselves Mr. and Mrs. Kelm, which just happens to be said nonexistent MI6 agent's assumed name? You need a bloody scorecard to keep track of these clowns."

David leaned forward from the desk chair to slide another slice of pizza out of one of the boxes on the bed, where Anna sat cross-legged eating a clementine. "And who do you think has been murdered?"

"Olga for one. I haven't a clue who she really was, though I think we can confidently assume she was the actress previously appearing in my role. And Pierre—well, my money's on murder. My friend Jan? Awfully coincidental that she recognizes me and makes a scene, then gets run down. *And* that Barton's car had a smashed fender. Don't forget the mysterious Mr. and Mrs. Rusakov. It may have been chalked up as a murder-suicide, but I'll bet they were whacked."

"Whacked?" He looked momentarily horrified. "Must you Americans talk as if you all just walked out of a Martin Scorsese film?"

"Uh-uh. Just me. So, we'll say Olga, the Rusakovs, and Pierre. Probably four people"—she paused—"bumped off. Then Jan: that's one possible. Plus two potentials: that's us."

He grimaced. "So what do we potentials do?"

"The reason I'm leery of going back to London to go to the police is that, even if I made it there alive, I might be suspect number one. If Kelm's the bad guy he's shaping up to be, we have no idea what the police actually think. So I think the diplomatic route is best. Since you had me call your home phone, some thug will soon be on your trail, too, so I think you need to take that route with me. Tomorrow. The fact that I was tracked to Holland and Germany shows that no place is safe. The question is: Who gets us?"

"Us? I'm not sure how I feel about turning myself in like a criminal. Let me think a minute."

"Bad word choice on my part. You won't really be turning yourself in the way I will be. You'll just be making sure you'll be safe in London. And whomever we see might just tell us to get lost. But I do think you're at risk and we should both go and see what they say. It's not like they're going to hold you responsible for anything. They'll probably arrange police protection for you in the UK and you can fly home safer."

He turned his head to stare out the window. Finally, turning back, he said, "I see your point. The sooner this is resolved, the sooner I can rest easy about my son. That's reason enough for me. By who gets us, you mean the US or the UK embassy, right? I'd say UK, since Barton was a British citizen. And since Kelm is, or is supposed to be, MI6, they wouldn't like us going to the Americans first."

"Good point. And I was thinking the same thing because of Pierre." She stood up from the bed, closing the pizza boxes and setting them on the dresser. "Why don't we meet at eight-thirty and walk down to the square for a taxi? I'd prefer to get to the embassy as early as possible."

"Good. Good. Yes. And I'll leave that flash drive in the hotel safe for the time being, shall I?" He got up, then reached down and finished his glass of wine. "This was a nice red, by the way."

He stood but didn't move, and she realized that both she and, perhaps more awkwardly, the beds were between him and the door, so she moved in the direction of the latter. "I can't tell you how much I appreciate your coming here. I might not actually be in less danger, but I feel safer."

"As you can guess, I, on the other hand, feel a bit less safe than I did, oh, say, yesterday." His smile was rueful. "I think we'll both feel better tomorrow."

"Well . . ." She stood frozen like a teen on her first date.

He walked over, and she tensed, wondering if he'd reach for her. But he just patted her shoulder in an avuncular way. "Sleep well. I'll see you in the lobby at half past eight." As the door closed behind him, she reached to double-lock it, hoping she'd done the right thing.

───────

"Might I ask why you've come to us rather than the Americans, Ms. Wallingham?" The assistant consul peered across his desk, looking put out by the intrusion of these two troublemakers.

"It was Mr. Wainwright's suggestion."

His eyes pivoted to David, who diplomatically explained, "My opinion was that since I'm a British citizen and now at risk, and since Mr. Barton was a British citizen, and since some man who said his name was Martin Kelm seems to have been passing himself off as an agent of the Secret Intelligence Service, you would want to be in charge."

"And the passports." Anna withdrew them from her bag and handed them to the man, whose name, according to the sign on his desk, was Rupert Hyde-Bingham. *Rupert Hyde-and-Mighty,* she thought. "Sorry, I forgot to mention these. The photos are of Pierre and Marina Barton, so they're clearly forgeries."

"Hmmm." Hyde-Bingham studied them, then placed them on the little pile he was accumulating: David's passport, Anna's, and the faked Tanya one. "And you got these where?"

"They were in Mr. Barton's attaché case. When he collapsed at my house." She hesitated. "I've used the Maria Kelm passport. In Milan and here in Rome. I'm registered at my hotel as Maria Kelm."

"You knowingly used not one but two false passports, Ms. Wallingham? Not such a good idea, is that?"

"I was assured the Tanya Avery one was legitimate, and I met the MI6 agent supposedly in charge. As for the Maria Kelm passport, using it seemed a much better idea than getting killed," she said tartly. "Have someone call us a taxi and we'll go to the Americans, if you prefer."

David looked from Hyde-Bingham to Anna and back again, as if unwilling to take sides.

Hyde-Bingham blinked first under Anna's chilly gaze. He shook his head. "No need for that." He pushed a button on his desk, and the young assistant who'd escorted Anna and David into the British embassy popped his head in the door.

"Sir?"

"Malcolm, please escort Ms. Wallingham and Mr. Wainwright to waiting room 22." To all three, he said, "This will take a few minutes."

Waiting room 22 was clearly code, because there was no number on the door of the room to which they were led. "Coffee? No?

Tea?" Malcolm offered brightly. "I'll have it brought up. And the loo will be through the door there on the right. I'll come for you as soon as Mr. Hyde-Bingham is ready."

They were in a small conference room, the main features of which were a long, polished wood table and a framed photograph of some members of the royal family with the British ambassador. "Cozy, what?" David joked bleakly, flinging himself onto one of the steel-and-leather chairs. "Maybe we should have gone to the Yanks. That fool will have you locked up for using fake IDs before all's said and done."

Anna shook her head. "I can't imagine anyone would have greeted us with open arms, two idiots arriving unannounced out of the blue, bearing forged passports along with a far-fetched tale of magic potions and murder, spies and lies, and sinister stalkers."

"Well, now that you mention it . . ." He shook his head as if to clear it, then patted the chair next to his. "Have a seat. We might be here awhile."

"What if no one believes me? Or what if I got it all wrong?" Her voice rose in panic.

"There's some hard proof there. And not just the faked passports. I mean, Barton's dead, Olga's dead, your friend Jan's dead, the Rusakovs are dead. That's not nothing. Let's see what happens next."

What happened next was the arrival of a stout, plainly dressed Italian woman bearing a tray holding tea things and a plate of shortbread, which she deposited wordlessly on the table. The door, Anna noticed, was opened from the hallway by a man who seemed to be stationed there as a guard now.

What happened after that was a great deal of waiting. Silent waiting. She and David had been ignoring the elephant in the room with them, no matter what room they were in: her lying to him and asking questions about his relationship with Anna while letting him think she was Tanya. But now, Anna knew, wasn't the time to broach the subject.

David was just muttering, "Would it be rude to ask for a deck of cards?" when there was a tap at the door and Malcolm appeared.

"Come with me, please. Sorry you had to wait so long."

He led them into another office, larger and plusher. "We're moving up the ladder," David whispered.

The man seated behind the desk stood and held out his hand. "Ms. Wallingham, Mr. Wainwright. Charles Dexter, British consul's office." He indicated the two other men seated next to the desk. "Elliot Lewis from the American embassy." A short, dark-haired man shook both their hands. "And Sir Charles Etherington, SIS." A man who looked like the "aristocratic, white-haired head of intelligence" character in a movie gave both their hands a muscular shake. "Please sit down."

Dexter nodded to Etherington, who said, "As you surmised, no one named Martin Kelm is, or ever has been, a member of SIS. Someone will be arriving here shortly with photos in the hopes you can identify him. By chance, you've shown up on the embassy's doorstep the day after I arrived to meet with the ambassador on totally unrelated business. And tomorrow our agent on the case in London will be here. On *this* business, I might add. I've asked him to fly in."

"Your agent? On the case? You mean there's already a British investigation going on?"

"Oh, yes, Ms. Wallingham, for quite some time. Since before Pierre Barton's death." He tilted his head in a very small shrug. "We knew about you, and we probably should have approached you ourselves or through your own people"—he gave a nod to Mr. Lewis—"but to be perfectly honest, no one was quite sure what your role at BarPharm was, or why you were there. And then you flew the coop."

"And now?" David interjected. "What happens now?"

"Several things," said Dexter. "First, we make sure we correctly ID the mysterious Mr. Kelm. Then we get both of you out of your hotel and into more secure lodgings. You're correct in thinking you're not safe. You mentioned your son in talks with Mr. Hyde-Bingham, Mr. Wainwright? We can begin immediately to have him and his mother's house watched discreetly to make sure he's not in danger. Tomorrow, we'll meet with the agent in charge and decide how we should proceed. SIS will be in charge after that point."

"And when can we leave?"

"Leave, Ms. Wallingham?"

"Leave Rome."

It was Etherington who answered her. "That's up to us," he said mildly. "The fact is, you both have little choice in the matter at this point. You can walk out that door right now and know that, if a murderer on the loose doesn't kill you, you will be picked up very quickly by Interpol and handed over to the Metropolitan Police in London for interfering in a murder investigation. You have stolen passports from a dead body, in addition to having withheld information. You, Mr. Wainwright, have aided and abetted her. We would like your assistance and your secrecy. As a United States citizen, you can't be required to swear to anything for the UK, Ms. Wallingham. However, you will be very ill-advised indeed to make public any of the information we will need to share with you. We won't keep you here longer than we need to, but we certainly won't release you before it's safe for you to be on your own. But I'll leave that up to Barnes when he gets here."

"Anything else?" Dexter murmured, breaking the long silence that followed. "Lewis, you had something, did you not?"

The American spoke directly to Anna. "We'll be looking into the death of your friend, Mrs. Berger. It could be what it seems like, a random hit-and-run—but rest assured we're checking it out."

The phone rang and Dexter spoke briefly into it. "Photos are here, Chips. Shall we look at them someplace with better lighting?"

They all filed down the hall to another conference room, this one brightly lit. A man carrying a dispatch box arrived at the same time, handed the box to Etherington, then left.

"You sit here, Ms. Wallingham. Please go through these carefully and pull out any you think might be Mr. Kelm."

There appeared to be about forty photos in the box. The first ones were easy to reject, as they were posed identification photos or mug shots of plainly visible subjects, some of whom were blond or pointy nosed but none of whom was Martin Kelm. The candids were harder to judge, as they weren't always clear, but when she came to a snapshot of a man in a bathing suit standing and smiling on a stretch of rocky beach, she handed it to Etherington. "This one, I think. His hair's darker here, but it looks like Kelm."

He nodded. "Please continue."

She found two others: one, a passport shot in a suit and tie, and the other of poorer quality, perhaps a long-lens shot, showing him much as she'd seen him that day on the Ku'damm, dressed like a construction worker in a jacket and jeans.

Etherington beamed at her. "Excellent, my dear! Very well done. As anticipated," he announced, "it's SVR. Meet Russian Foreign Intelligence Service's man of many faces, Grigoriy Komarov. Fittingly enough, Grigoriy means 'vigilant.'"

"You're saying Martin Kelm's a Russian spy? But he's as British as—"

"As I am?" Etherington beamed more brightly. "Yes, isn't he just? Excellent actor, the esteemed Komarov. A bit embarrassing we weren't onto him sooner."

"But I thought Aleksei—"

"You thought the butler did it, did you? But, no, the butler would be the man called Mikal, wouldn't it? In any event, tomorrow is another day." He put the three photos down and stood. "It will have to wait until then. Mr. Dexter, could you keep these three photos handy for the meeting tomorrow? I'll have a car downstairs in fifteen minutes to take Ms. Wallingham and Mr. Wainwright to pick up their bags."

"We have no say in this at all?" Anna protested weakly.

While Etherington continued to beam, a steeliness came into his expression that assured her good old Sir Chips was nobody's fool.

"You came to us for safekeeping. This is how we keep you safe." He nodded and left.

Then Lewis was handing her a card, saying, "I think I'll leave you in the excellent hands of Mr. Dexter" and, as though he'd been poised at the door waiting, Malcolm was back, asking Anna and David to please come with him to waiting room 22.

"I'll return to fetch you in a few minutes when the car arrives," he said cheerfully. "You'll check out of your hotel, then come back here." His giggle was incongruous. "Free night's stay in luxury surroundings. Food, too."

"I didn't realize our embassy took captives," David said stiffly.

"Hardly captives," Malcolm reassured him breezily. "Just our guests. Have a seat. I'll be right back."

"It's just for a night or two," Anna said after he'd gone. "I'm not thrilled, either, but at least we're safe here. And they'll make sure your son is, as well."

"And at least they're taking your fears seriously."

"Did you think they wouldn't?" she asked sharply. "That they'd tell you I was just being a hysterical woman?"

"Of course not, Anna. I told you I believed you. I'm trying to help you, remember? Not making sexist judgments."

"Sorry. I was just being a hysterical woman for a moment there, wasn't I?"

"We're stuck here. No sense in fighting it. Mutual sarcasm interrupted by a spot of whining should help the time fly by."

He grinned, and her irritation evaporated. She knew he was remembering the fun they used to have being sarcastic about things that bugged them.

Just then a knock heralded the return of Malcolm, who also bowed, adding the gesture of a courtier. "Your carriage awaits."

"See?" David whispered as they followed Malcolm to the elevator. "Everyone's going in for sarcasm now."

Downstairs, a man so well muscled he lacked only a "Kiss Me, I'm a Bodyguard" T-shirt was waiting by the front door. Nor was he to be their sole companion. He led them to a black Range Rover out front and opened the rear door for them, and a second beefy escort turned in the driver's seat to nod. Hulk #1 settled himself in the passenger position. "Now we know what happens to old Chippendales dancers," David murmured.

Mario, back from his days off, looked terrified when the four of them trooped into the hotel lobby. "Mr. Wainwright and I will be checking out now, Mario," Anna told him.

"Sì, sì, Signora Kelm. I will prepare your bills now." He eyed the bodyguards.

"And Mr. Wainwright and I need the envelopes we left in your safe." In her nervousness that morning, she had forgotten the envelope of cash she'd left for safekeeping the day before.

Anna had kept so many things prepared for flight that it took just moments to gather together her belongings. She looked up at Hulk #2 after closing her suitcase, not sure which of them should be taking the bag until he politely told her, with a touch of a Scottish burr, "I need to be hands-free, ma'am."

She slung on her backpack and rolled the suitcase to the elevator. In the lobby, she paid both bills with cash and included a handsome tip for Mario. When David arrived with his duffel and Hulk #1, she told him, "The bill's covered. You can get dinner." One bodyguard stood with them while the other took a white-faced

Mario aside for a little chat, a one-sided chat in which the Hulk spoke while the desk clerk nodded emphatically in agreement.

Back at the embassy, Malcolm escorted them to a different elevator, one with a lock for each floor. As they ascended, he said, "The accommodations are quite pleasant: two-bedroom, two-bath suite, with living room and wet bar. There's a menu on the table in the dining area with an extension number on it. Just ring down and say you're ordering lunch. Then do the same for dinner. There's water and drinks in the refrigerator behind the wet bar, and you'll also find a wine rack. It's not the Hassler, but it's not a doss-house, either."

He led them down a tastefully decorated and carpeted hallway that wouldn't have been out of place at a Ritz-Carlton. "Who normally stays here?" asked David. "Do Brits often come to Rome to throw themselves on your mercy?"

"Rarely, Mr. Wainwright. Most of our good citizens come to Rome to throw coins into the Trevi Fountain," Malcolm replied smoothly, showing an aplomb that foretold a successful career in the Foreign Service. "The suites are usually for overnight diplomatic guests—a staff member from one of our services flying in for a meeting or a foreign guest needing a secure place. I can't say you're the norm." He stopped in front of a door and opened it with a key card.

The drapes were open, flooding the living area with midday sunshine. There was the requisite big wall-mounted flat-screen television, good-quality if undistinguished furnishings, and more plush carpeting.

"I'll leave you to it," said Malcolm. "My extension number is on the table with the menus. I'm here until half past six and then the night staff comes on, so if you call the extension after that, a very nice bloke named Ian will answer. I'll fill him in before I leave. Meals come from a trattoria down the street and take about thirty minutes to arrive; they'll be brought up by a staff member. You can lock the door to feel more secure if you like. But you couldn't be in a safer place: the elevator runs only with keys, and the door to the other part of the building is steel, locked and guarded. In the event of fire or any other emergency, just dial zero or pull the red alarm handle to the side of the little fridge. If you need anything, call me or Ian. The meeting tomorrow will start at half past eight, and I'll come to fetch you for that. I'll have them bring breakfast at seven forty-five, shall I?"

He turned at the door. "The telly has Sky so you can watch films. Enjoy."

Then he was gone, leaving Anna and David standing awkwardly in the middle of the room with their bags. "I think you should have first pick of the bedrooms," David said finally. "Just to play the chivalrous gent."

"Let's order some lunch first. All this cloak-and-dagger stuff has given me an appetite." The last thing she needed right now was any thought involving David and a bed. She plopped down at the table and picked up a menu, then handed him the other when he took the seat opposite. "Not a bad selection here at Death's Door Diner," she said.

"We won't die of hunger at least." David appraised the menu. "I'm doubling down on starches: spaghetti *amatriciana* followed by polenta with sausages. And apple tart after. You?"

"Yes to polenta and sausages. Grilled vegetables to start. And sliced fresh pineapple for dessert."

He picked up the phone. "I feel I should be saying, 'Room service, and make it snappy!'" Then someone answered at the other end, and he became once again the deferential Englishman. "Hello, we'd like some lunch in the suite, please. Ready?"

While he ordered, Anna checked the bedrooms. The only difference was that one bathroom had a tub-and-shower combo while the other had just a walk-in shower. Remembering that David, in true English tradition, was partial to baths, she opted for the one with the walk-in shower, which suited her American lack of patience. Well, that was settled. She checked her watch. It wasn't even two o'clock. What in the world were they going to do all day? Her emotions were a blend of feeling trapped by being unable to go outside, giddy with relief at being safe, and nervous as a teen-ager on a first date about being in such close proximity to David.

"You can have the room with the tub," she said as she came back into the living room. She grabbed her bags and bustled them into the other room. "Wonder what we can get on the TV?" she called over her shoulder.

"We can check the telly listings after we've put away our things and had lunch," David said when she came back. "Maybe a nap after lunch for me. I didn't sleep well last night."

"Me neither. And that was before knowing my own personal MI6 buddy was a lying little sneaky, stalking spyski. 'Martin Kelm'! Martin Kelm, my ass." She stomped over to the bar to survey the wine offerings. "Red or white wine?" she called after David, who was walking off with his duffel bag.

"White would be nice. Something cold and crisp."

Yeah, cold and crisp, she thought. *Like us.* Part of her accepted their being ill at ease and stiffly polite with each other. It was only natural. Still, another part wondered what his reaction would have been if she'd said, "The beds are big. Who needs two rooms?" And an even bigger part was scared that if she'd said that, he would have told her bluntly that their personal story was over, done with, deader than Olga from the Volga and that he'd preferred her as Tanya. And yet another part of her wasn't sure if she wanted to be in a bed with him, anyhow. Four parts. Drawn and quartered.

So they got through the day as people thrown together by fate usually do: small talk, lunch, a long break after lunch to nap or read or pretend they were doing both. They took a long time deciding over dinner and a longer time discussing the films on the SKY TV menu before agreeing on possibly the least romantic comedy they might choose. At long last, they chastely bumped cheeks to say good night, enough room between their bodies for someone to drive a tractor through.

———————

At precisely twenty-five minutes past eight the next morning, Malcolm arrived. "Good morning," he said brightly. "Everyone all right? Food suit you?"

"Yes, fine."

"Delicious."

"Off we go. Could you bring your laptops and memory sticks? And all your phones and whatever SIM cards you still possess? Got them? I'll take them so our tech people can have a look; you'll get them back today. All right then. We're all set."

He took them down to yet another conference room. There was a laptop set up and a wall cupboard's double doors standing open to reveal a monitor. He smiled. "Show-and-tell today. Help yourselves to the coffee on the sideboard. Sir Charles and Mr. Dexter will be right in."

"Coffee?" asked David, getting up.

"Yes, thank you. With—"

"Milk and one-and-a-half sugars, right?"

"Very good." Anna was touched he'd remembered. "Wonder if Our Man in London has hit town." There were voices outside the door. "I guess we're about to find out."

Chips Etherington and Charles Dexter bustled in. Their "Good morning" and "Sleep well?" didn't seem to require a response and neither Anna nor David bothered with one.

"Barnes is on his way from the airport now," said Etherington. "In the meantime, we can go over a few things. I'm going to go through some photos I think you might recognize. Please tell me what you know about the people."

He fiddled at the computer and, one by one, photos of some of her coaches came up, followed by headshots of Chas and Becca and Marina's brother, Dmitri. "Yes, that's Rob, the one who told me how to use the phones and computers. I hope he's not one of the baddies."

"Rest assured, none of these people are baddies," Etherington said. "Rob's a good lad."

Then the butler from the country house. Mikal. Then Mrs. McCallum. "Oh, that's the housekeeper, or fake housekeeper, at the country house, isn't it?"

"Very good. Don't worry. Most of those people have nothing to do with the BarPharm situation. We're just keeping tabs, you know. And now I think we can have coffee." His cell chirped. "Ah, yes, Malcolm's waiting for you." He put away his phone. "Andrew's taxi is pulling up now. Anyone else for coffee?" Anna didn't really want another cup—it hadn't been that long since David had poured her one—but she got up and walked over to where Sir Chips stood.

"Can you tell me if Dmitri is part of this? Sorry if I seem like Pollyanna for saying everyone's 'nice,' but I liked him. He didn't seem at all like his sister."

"I've never met him, but as far as I know, he was declared persona non grata by the old man for being homosexual, so he emerged from the family unscathed."

She felt relieved. He'd been fun, Dmitri.

She was about to ask how he knew Rob was a "good lad" when she heard the by-now recognizable tap that signaled the arrival of Malcolm. He poked his head around and said, "Mr. Barnes is here." Then he stepped out of the doorway and another man stepped into it.

Aleksei.

Chapter 22

She stared. Aleksei was the one person she'd never suspected of being anything other than he seemed to be. Well, she'd long suspected him of not being simply a chauffeur, but it had never occurred to her he might not even be a Russian.

But, sure enough, he came around the table, shook hands with her, then said in perfect upper-crust English, "Ms. Wallingham, well done. You've taught me a few tricks." He turned to David. "And Mr. Wainwright. We haven't met. I'm Andrew Barnes."

"English," she whispered. "You are actually English."

"Indeed I am." He raised his eyebrows at Sir Charles, who gestured for him to come take the seat next to him at the head of the table behind the laptop, which he assumed after sticking a flash drive into the computer. "Born and raised in Bristol, in fact."

"Mr. Barnes has—or I should be saying 'had'—been one of our top men in Moscow for quite some time."

Aleksei, now Andrew, nodded. "Russian studies major at Oxford. Recruited by SIS. After graduation, I worked in the London headquarters for several years, then I posed as an English-speaking Russian and went to Moscow as a translator for a company of interest to us. I ended up at another firm, one that sold chemicals throughout Europe and was suspected of working closely with some questionable clients in the Mideast. The company was Sybyska, and that's how I met Marina Barton.

"Now, let's see if this is ready to go." He fiddled briefly with the computer, then clicked the mouse, and a photo of a younger Marina with a slick-looking, ponytailed man filled the screen. "She wasn't married to Barton then. She was hooked up with the father of her twin boys. He's now deceased. But you both know this already, don't you? I read Anna's notes on the flight over." He paused to glare at Anna. "It would have been nice to have had them before you came to us yesterday. Yes, Marina undoubtedly would have given the children to her mother in Russia and seen them once a year except that Pierre was fond of them; he liked to pass them off as his own."

"What on earth for?"

"I don't know how well you knew him, Mr. Wainwright, but Barton had a penchant for make-believe. He rarely told the whole truth if he could embellish. His father was an inveterate fabricator, a veritable Baron Munchausen, who liked to pretend he was a tycoon. In fact, he lost a great deal of money in hopeless ventures when Pierre was a boy. After that, he just scraped by."

"But that mansion in Paris!" Anna protested.

"The apartment? It's always belonged to Marie Héloise. She comes from a wealthy family. There's not a huge fortune left, but she was too clever to let her son get his hands on much of it.

"After Pierre took over the business upon his father's death, Marina's father, who saw the possibility of using BarPharm to his own advantage, invited the son to visit Moscow. Pierre did so and ended up falling in love with Marina, whom he remembered from the old days at the Sorbonne."

"And this was?"

"Almost eleven years ago, when the boys were toddlers. At Marina's urging, Pierre signed a contract with Sybyska for

BarPharm's purchase of raw materials and pharmaceutical ingredients."

"What was in it for Marina, marrying Pierre?" Anna asked.

"Glamour, for one thing. Marina likes the high life. She loved the idea of a pampered life in London. And I think she might have loved Pierre a little at one time, when she thought he was her equal in strength. She was impressed by Pierre's dream of surpassing his father's modest accomplishments by becoming massively wealthy, a bona fide one-percenter. When he confessed his dream project, something to turn back the clock, she encouraged his devoting BarPharm's top chemists to work on it."

"And this was his dream project because of his mother?" David asked.

"Because of his father," Anna said, jumping in. "Remember? Marie Héloise told me."

"Right," said Barnes. He winked at her, and she saw that, under the bright lights and lacking Aleksei's dark glasses, he was older than she'd thought, perhaps closer to fifty than forty. "You *have* been busy. Barton *père* talked his wife into having surgery because he pictured himself as a tycoon with a young trophy wife. Unfortunately, he chose a cut-rate hack, and she didn't fight it. When she came out of it looking more pug than princess, he left her for a genuinely younger model."

"But why would Marina encourage Pierre to spend so much looking for a quick fix for aging? She's already had plastic surgery. I saw the scars."

"Marina cared about what she always cares about: herself and money. When the money seemed wasted on BarPharm's own research into a new retinol line, she nagged him, even in front of others, about giving it up. Then he found the Taiwanese company that had actually succeeded with what was then Youngskin. And at that point Marina decided rejuvenation was her destiny." Anna rolled her eyes. "Yes, she can be crazy, but like a fox. She pressured

Pierre into paying top dollar, terrified someone else would snatch it up first, and then all that mattered was getting it tested, marketed, and out in the world making money."

"That sounds straightforward," David remarked. "Not like something that would result in multiple murders."

"Yes. If only the **YOU**NGER genie had remained in the bottle and been simply skincare. Having convinced her husband that the product needed to be marketed in the largest anti-aging market in the world, the USA, Marina pushed him to acquire Coscom at the perfect time, before the introduction of Madame X, which they hoped would bring in much-needed revenues to cover BarPharm's acquisition costs. All was well." He paused. "And then she bumped into an old friend from home on the street."

"Olga?"

"No. Grigoriy Komarov. Yes, your Mr. Kelm. London University graduate, more British than Winston Churchill—on the surface, of course. He'd worked with Sybyska on a few things for his SRV bosses and knew Marina. Divorced, lives for espionage and manipulation, a dangerous man we would like very much to have out of our hair. He'd been put in place in London four years ago for use when Russian security services needed a fake Brit. Running into him, Marina had a brainstorm: Why not get even richer and help Mother Russia at the same time? She and Komarov sold Moscow on the prospect of an industrial-strength **YOU**NGER as the future choice of discerning Russian spies."

"And Barton agreed to basically commit treason?" Anna was astonished.

"Oh, he was a bit of an easy mark, poor Pierre. Marina led him to Komarov like a lamb to the slaughter. He had never met Komarov, so it was a snap for Marina and Grigoriy to cook up Martin Kelm just for him. Marina isn't a skincare chemist and Pierre was keeping the formula as his little secret, so they needed the BarPharm lab experts. Until shortly before his death, Pierre

Barton believed he was going to be a hero for working with MI6; a future knighthood didn't seem far-fetched. He never suspected Kelm was anything other than what he said he was when he made contact. We're not sure how that happened, but I suspect Mr. Kelm of SIS simply called him up and suggested a meeting, saying he'd heard through the grapevine something interesting about the Taiwan deal."

"Where did you and Olga come in, then?" Anna asked.

"Marina had to control both Barton and Kelm, neither of whom she trusted to protect her interests. She decided she needed a smart bilingual boy by her side in London. Keep in mind she thought I was nothing more than a sly bilingual Russian interpreter. Barton couldn't tell cod Russian from the real thing, so she offered me a nice salary increase and I became her cousin— available as a driver and a bodyguard."

"I saw him arguing with you one day," Anna interjected. "Then you seemed to tell him to get in the car and he just obeyed you."

"Hardly obeying *me*. I was probably reminding him that my cousin Marina didn't want him going off on his own, for his own safety, that she worried about him. He never wanted to get on her bad side." He chuckled. "You've met her. Would you? I never saw Komarov in the flesh, by the way—both Marina and Pierre kept meetings with him a secret from each other, and she never mentioned him to me. She just wanted me to keep an eye on her husband."

"Andrew's Russian is superb," interjected Etherington. "Don't fall for his false modesty."

Blushing slightly, Barnes continued as a photo flashed on-screen of a middle-aged blonde standing next to Marina. "Here's Olga, as she originally looked. Komarov insisted on someone who could be trusted for testing the safety of the industrial-strength for-your-spies-only product."

"What safety? Is it not safe?"

"No need to worry on that score, Ms. Wallingham," Etherington interjected. "It's as safe as any acid peel or laser. The sole danger would be getting yourself killed, as Olga did."

Suddenly, the meaning of her contract being "paid in full" so she could leave early sank in. Now she was sure no one had ever planned to pay her off and let her go on her merry way with her lifetime supply of **YOU**NGER. It was easy for "Martin Kelm" to offer her anything if he didn't plan on her being around to collect it. Had Pierre realized that during their last meeting when she'd told him about her conversation with Kelm at the National Portrait Gallery bar?

Barnes clicked the mouse and a smiling, younger-looking Olga replaced the original Olga, followed by a shot of the two Olgas side by side.

"You played the game for them, Anna, and while they probably would have preferred someone docile, they were satisfied enough. But Olga didn't follow their rules. And therein hangs a tale."

"And before we have that tale, I suggest we have a break for tea," said Dexter. He picked up the phone. "Malcolm, we're coming down to the sitting room now."

The reason for the break was obviously for the Englishmen to compare notes, as they quickly moved together to the far end of the room after shepherding David and Anna to wing chairs in front of the spacious, elegant room's unlit fireplace. The woman who'd brought lunch the day before arrived almost immediately to set a small tea service on the table, along with the inevitable plate of cookies.

"Ah, we British. Nothing like a spot of tea before we get to the murderous bits, eh, eh?" David put on a Monty Pythonesque voice. "After we 'ave a nice cuppa, we'll return to 'omicide most foul!"

"Weirdly cheerful, aren't they? I keep thinking how Aleksei could pass for a Brit in his flannels and blazer," Anna said, "rather than how Andrew made a believable Russian with his chilly taciturnity."

"Was he? Chilly, I mean? He seems so easygoing."

"A bit smug, no? I think he enjoyed fooling me. He was the strong, sullen type. Very believable and, I guess, all in a day's work. On the other hand, Kelm, or Komarov, tried to act all pally, but with those hard Putin eyes. Still, other than the fact that he's almost definitely a murderer, I'd call him downright warm and wonderful compared to Marina. Can you imagine luring your own husband into working for Moscow, thinking it's for queen and country?"

"Not for nothing did the Bible say money is the root of all evil."

"Dissatisfaction might be a close second," she said. "I suspect that's what lured Olga. And probably the engine behind Marina's ambitions." She shook her head reproachfully. "Perhaps mine as well. It's been a steep learning curve, but this experience has put a lot of things in perspective for me."

David was regarding her contemplatively.

"Yes?" she asked.

He shook his head. "Just thinking that it's made me reexamine my life as well. I don't—"

"I hope I'm not interrupting, Ms. Wallingham, Mr. Wainwright."

Anna could have slugged the former Aleksei. What had David been about to say? *What?* She smiled thinly. "Call me Anna, please. I was just telling David how credible you were as Aleksei."

"I had quite a few years' experience in that role. Unlike your 'trainers,' by the way. I saw in your notes that you ran into your fashion coach in a Prague mall. Small world."

"And you, were you in Prague? Was it you Fleur or Chloe or whoever saw?" She was almost disappointed when he shook his head. "So, not as small a world or as well-spun a web as I'd thought. The coaches were all very believable. What's amazing is that they thought I was playing a part as well—I mean, I was, but they thought I was an actress pretending to be an actress who was pretending to learn how to be someone else. Like an Escher drawing. Were none of them real?"

He perched on the fireplace fender. "That would depend upon your definition of *real*. Mikal's real in that he isn't an actor. Nor is he a butler. He's Komarov's man, put in the house to keep an eye on you and passed off by Kelm to Barton as an old asylum seeker who defected from the USSR."

"I hardly ever saw him."

Barnes smiled appraisingly. "Shows how good he was, doesn't it?"

"And Rob? He was good, too, wasn't he?"

Barnes had the good manners to flush. "Figured that one out, did you?"

Anna's flush was anger, not embarrassment. "Sir Charles calling Rob a 'good lad' started me thinking, and your being from Bristol convinced me."

"You were an unknown quantity set loose in London. We had to keep an eye on you, for your own safety, if nothing else."

"So who's Rob?"

"He's who he said he is. He just happens to be my cousin, as well. His father is my father's younger brother. I often drove Anezka and Lorrayne to meet their BarPharm clients. We—MI6— had installed microphones, so the privacy panel was one-way only. When I heard they were taking you to Pacha, I put Rob on it. Before you get worked up, keep in mind that we used Rob to supply you with the information that kept you safe." They saw Etherington signaling. "I think we're moving back to the other room now."

Once they were seated at the conference table, Barnes refreshed the photos of Olga on the screen. At first, Anna's thoughts were elsewhere—so Andrew's father was an earl . . . And that passionate kiss from Rob, did Barnes know about that? She felt her cheeks redden again, this time from embarrassment. Then she mentally shook herself and started to listen.

"So they needed someone to test the products—not for the retail and medical markets, which had already been done legitimately in Switzerland. They needed someone to test the so-called Formula One's efficacy for Moscow. Enter Olga."

"Where does Coscom come into this?"

"Coscom comes in only in its acquisition for retail sales, legitimacy, and, as it would turn out, Anna, for you. But let's get Olga out of the way first. And gotten out of the way she was. Chips, you have that report, yes?"

"I do, my boy. Olga Pankov, age forty-seven, employed at Sybyska as an accountant." He noted Anna's surprise. "Yes, not in marketing at all. And her name was Novrosky as much as yours was Avery. Olga was a widow and old acquaintance of Marina's. According to what the girls in the Sybyska office told 'Aleksei,' she was depressed about being middle-aged and single; she complained bitterly that rich men wouldn't look twice at a woman over thirty. Not interested in you, Andrew?" He smiled at his own jab.

Clearing his throat, he went on. "She must have had to pinch herself when Marina offered her the position of **YOUNGER** guinea pig. Younger forever: that's how they would have presented it to her, I believe. That, and the chance to be a patriot. And to live in exotic London! Nothing much required except to use the product, have frequent skin tests, and pretend to be working on that retinol project. The trick here was fooling Pierre into thinking she was legitimate—it was vital to Marina that her husband not suspect the Russian secret service was involved. Olga was presented as an old friend and coworker, eager to help and loyal to Marina."

Andrew took over. "Not loyal to anyone, as it turned out." Familiar faces filled the screen. "Enter the Rusakovs."

"The couple that followed Anna?" David asked. "I take it they were whatsisname's people . . . Komarov's."

"Yes in the first instance, no in the second," Andrew told him. "Not all Russians involved in espionage are doing it for the supposed good of their country."

"You mean either foreign spies or Russian mafia?" Anna was genuinely surprised. "They looked so normal."

Barnes shrugged. "Normal for Bratva or *russkaya mafiya*. Pavel was an ex-pimp who worked his way up to a sort of two-in-one position as assassin and spy. Galina was one of his stable of prostitutes until they married, when her role became that of his assistant. They worked for a high-level boss known mainly by his nickname, the Tracker."

"The Tracker?"

"Yes, David. His business successes are based on tracking down what the other mafiosi are working on and muscling in, as well as competing in dead earnest with the government for anything that has high monetary value."

"Like **YOU**NGER?"

"Exactly, Anna. The Tracker mixes a great deal with the gangs and triads throughout Asia. There were rumors in Taipei of a potion that could make the user look at least a decade younger, but we'd dismissed them as unimportant, erroneously writing off the product in development as mere skincare. The Tracker saw the potential just as the Russian government did. But by the time he tracked down the local inventor, the formula had already been sold to BarPharm and the inventor, who made a great deal of money and stood to earn enormous royalties as well, had moved to Switzerland. The Tracker seems to have sniffed around and learned that he was no longer in control of the formula and that there was now a more important industrial-strength formula being fine-tuned in Barton's lab. Just FYI, no single chemist has had full knowledge of or access to any formula since the first one passed to BarPharm. Pierre would tell one of them what he needed revved up on a formula and they just did it—quietly, due to stringent nondisclosure clauses. Only Barton had the industrial-strength written formula as it was improved and updated, and he kept it under lock and key. It was perhaps the only thing he wouldn't give to Marina."

"It isn't just a stronger version of the retail **YOUNGER**?" Anna asked.

"To our knowledge, no. It's a variation. And keep in mind, some of what I'm telling you is guesswork. Expert, but guesswork."

"So, Galina and Pavel were sent to London?"

Andrew continued. "Right, David. They still weren't sure there was an industrial strength, but they were interested in the product anyhow. And whom should they discover and befriend but Olga, who, now being younger looking, resented not being wealthy. She seems to have reported regularly to the Rusakovs—and might have become very wealthy once she could put the formula into their hands, though the Tracker isn't known to be the most trustworthy businessman. Still, she didn't live long enough to accomplish that. You see, Pierre never trusted Olga as he did you, Anna; she never was given the products. She was visited daily by the nurse, whom I would drive to her place before I handed over just enough of each product for a single application."

"At my apartment?"

"No, Olga rated just a tiny bedsit in Bayswater. She had nothing to offer BarPharm other than her skin and her secrecy, you see. Her working on the retinol line was just a cover; it had already been dropped, with some lame excuse given to Clive Madden and the sales VP."

"So she was a guinea pig for the Russian government while also working for their criminals?"

"Precisely. We slipped up by not seeing the potential of the product. Komarov and the Bartons all slipped up by thinking they could get away without paying Olga her due."

"It's like *Mad* magazine's *Spy vs. Spy,*" Anna murmured. "That's a comic strip," she added in response to the blank looks. "But where do I come in? Obviously, you—and they—want something from me, or you would have patted David and me on our heads, told us not to worry, and shown us the door. Yes?"

The pause that followed indicated this wasn't how briefings were properly conducted, but Anna didn't care. She was exhausted, she had been lied to and endangered by the good guys as well as the bad guys, and she didn't feel like wasting any more time on *Masterpiece Theatre* show-and-tell. "What do you want me to do?"

Barnes and Dexter both looked to Sir Charles, who smiled graciously and said benignly, "For better or for worse, you are now an integral player in this game, Ms. Wallingham. In the days before he showed up at your door in London, Pierre Barton came to the realization that his miraculous **YOU**NGER was his personal deal with the devil. How and why, we don't know. But he must have realized people had died because of the product. We do know now he went first to Switzerland, then to BarPharm's facility in Gloucestershire. At both places, he destroyed everything to do with **YOU**NGER: formulas, files, all traces of products, *everything*. So it isn't at all surprising that some people want what only you have: the last remaining traces of **YOU**NGER in the world. That's what someone is after: the key to the formula. What we're after is a murderer."

"And the chance to put bloody Komarov away for a long time," Andrew added with such force Anna wondered if this game of Spy vs. Spy was personal for him. Did he consider the Russian agent he'd never met his most formidable adversary?

"*Bait.*" She looked from Barnes to Etherington to Dexter. "That's what you're saying, isn't it?"

Etherington leaned forward and peered at her from under his shock of white hair. "Yes, Anna, we want you to be the bait."

They broke for lunch at two o'clock. Anna was amazed at how these men managed to switch to inconsequential topics as they ate their *vitello tonnato*, then she realized it was a skill that she herself had learned passably in just weeks. She grew to stop thinking of Andrew Barnes as Aleksei and she found him likable, though without particularly liking him. He was the type who had everything figured out. When the meeting resumed after lunch and she pointed out, "I don't have any YOUNGER. You know I dumped everything down the toilet," he just chuckled.

"No one outside this room knows that, including Marina and Komarov, right? As far as they're concerned, you've got the keys to heaven, Anna."

The meeting went on until six, by which point it was clear to Anna that she and David weren't really there to get any information, just to give it. "We're going to take a break until Friday morning," Sir Charles announced as Malcolm entered with Anna and David's panoply of electronics. "In the meantime we'll be sending Marina a text message from you, Anna." Before she could open her mouth to speak, he added firmly, "No reason to go into detail until we're sure the plan's working. Just trust us."

Back in the suite, David went straight to the refrigerator and removed a bottle of white wine. When he waved it at Anna inquiringly, she nodded vehemently before sinking onto the couch. "'Just trust us!'" she said acidly. "Right. Andrew must have known what was going on since before the first time I met him in Paris. He knew when he was chauffeuring me to treatments—and when he put his little cousin to work hitting on me. I could be dead by now, and they say to *trust* them? I thought it was going to be over today. Now we're *stuck* here, and I feel as if it never will end."

He handed her a glass of wine, then sat on the chair across from her and toasted. "This too shall pass."

She took a sip, then set the glass on the table. "I'm sure they can work the Master Plan, whatever it is, without you. You probably don't need to stay."

He snorted. "You think I can just call downstairs and tell Malcolm I'll be checking out? I doubt it's that easy. Look, I have my computer back, and I have work that needs doing. I'd hardly leave now anyhow. I mean, I'm the idiot who used my home phone when you told me not to. I won't rest, or stop worrying about my son, until this is resolved."

"You must be eager to get back to him."

"I am, but Nick jumped at the chance to stay at his friend's. That's how teenagers are. So I'd just be working on the computer or puttering around the house on my own, as we old men do."

"Hardly an old man. When I bumped into you that first time, I thought you hadn't changed at all. A little gray hair, glasses. But still you, very much the same you."

"You're the one who hadn't changed, except for that Day-Glo mop of hair! I like it better like this."

"In London, only rich Russians have hair like this—at least, that's what one of my coaches told me."

"Women like Marina," he said.

"Marina." She snorted. "If she weren't such a bitch, I'd feel sorry for her: her husband dead, the company in limbo, the means to unfathomable riches gone forever."

"Not that she knows it's gone."

"She'll go crazy when she finds out. A cruel trick to play on her so they can get Grigoriy for Pierre's murder. I take it that's the goal of the little *mise en scène* I'll be starring in."

"Cruel?" He shrugged. "I wouldn't waste any tears on her. Anyhow, enough of these crazy spies. Tell me about you. Do you miss LA?"

"Now, yes. But for the future? I don't know. Maybe I'd be happier somewhere else, somewhere more *real*. Funny, huh? I did all this to save my business and my house in LA, and now I'm not sure I want it all back. I might just walk away."

"Well, you're good at that, aren't you?" When she didn't answer, he added, "This might be as good a time as any to tell me why you just walked out."

She sighed. "I've been asking myself that a lot lately. I think I looked at myself through your eyes and saw someone unlovable. Your career was taking off, and what was I? A nobody, a failed actress who was never going to make it. Actress? I was a cocktail waitress with a headshot, and I was sure you saw that when you looked at me. I'd grown to dislike you, but maybe it was me I didn't like. I was unfair to you."

"Maybe not," he said after a moment. Now it was his turn to sigh. "I did look at you and see a waitress. Not that I didn't think you were a good actress—you've proven that you still are—but I knew you'd never make it, that you lacked the hunger. Me, I saw as a scrappy working-class boy prepared to claw his way to success." He snorted. "I was so fucking full of myself. I thought I deserved more than a trust-fund tray carrier. The truth is, Anna," he said, looking directly into her eyes, "that I didn't really grasp the concept of other people until my son was born."

"For what it's worth, I was a tray carrier *without* a trust fund—I'd made that up. Maybe that's why I had a soft spot for Pierre. We both liked living in our fantasies." She laughed bitterly. When David didn't respond, she quickly said, "Anyhow, my long overdue apologies for leaving the way I did. Hungry? I'm thinking grilled vegetable pizza and a green salad. You?"

"*Pizza quattro stagioni* for me," he said so quickly that she was certain he, too, was eager to escape relationship talk.

They ate at the coffee table. "Hard to beat Roman pizza," David noted. "That's the bright side of this, I guess. And we won't be here much longer. Just two more days if Marina takes whatever bait they're tossing out."

"And if she doesn't?"

"Come on, Anna, don't be so negative. These guys know what they're doing."

"Know what they're doing?" Her voice rose. "They could have gotten me—excuse me, *us*—killed. They've lied right and left. I don't believe they thought for a minute I was anything but a pawn of Pierre's. I just happened to fit in nicely with their plans. They let me continue to think I'd been chosen by Barton because I was the best person to do it; they didn't see me as someone who was in danger because I was also someone they could monitor through Rob. They didn't even try to help me when I was running for my life, David! Compared to them, Pierre Barton was thoughtful and honest. Did you even understand that stuff about Rob? They actually set me up with a young guy who pretended he was attracted to me, who hit on me. You think that shouts 'trustworthy'?" She took a big swig of wine. "Give me a break, will you? Do you still think I'm just a dumb waitress?"

His look was searing. "Excuse me, I'm going to get some more wine. You might want to give some thought to how 'trustworthy' it is to ask your ex-lover all sorts of intimate questions about how he feels about the woman he loved, when all the time the woman was you. And now you're telling *me* to give *you* a break."

She jumped up as he headed toward the bar area. "Don't you walk away from me, David Wainwright!"

He stopped and turned to face her, his face stony. "We both know which one of us walks away." He turned and kept walking.

She was hot on his heels. "Why do you always have to act so damned superior?"

"What's superior? Trying to chill you out is acting superior? You wanted me to come to Italy, I came. You wanted to turn yourself in, I came with you. These people are trying to save your life now, and you act like they're the enemy."

"And you act like I entrapped you somehow by being a sympathetic listener. Okay," she said when he rolled his eyes, "I wanted to hear how you felt about me back then. I wanted to know if you'd ever loved me. Is that so terrible?" she asked, her voice trembling. "Is that such a betrayal? Caring about you for more than twenty fucking years, is that such a crime?"

His back was to her as he reached for a bottle of wine from the refrigerator. Then he abruptly put it back and turned to face her, shaking his head. His expression relaxed. "Of course it's not a crime. Damn it, Anna, how can you still make me so mad? After all this time?"

And before she knew it, his arms were drawing her close, his lips were on hers, and all those years, like the bottle of wine, were forgotten.

———————

"You know," he said later as they lay naked on his bed, "when you came crashing into me on the street that day, I felt such joy when I thought you were—well, *you*. And devastation when I realized you couldn't be. It was as if I'd been missing you all these years, even when I hadn't been thinking of you. Does that make any sense?"

His words roused her out of her reverie. She had been luxuriating in his arms, her body weak yet fulfilled in a way it hadn't been in many years. Her self-imposed exile from sex had ended and the lovemaking itself had been extraordinary and—not only that—proof positive that not only was David still an amazing lover but also that making love was really like riding a bicycle. You didn't forget how to do it. *Oh, not at all.*

She propped herself up on her elbow to look him in the eye. "Of course it does. After that day when you came back to BarPharm and waited for me, I kept telling myself I couldn't keep seeing you, but I was like an addict. That's why I let you talk about Anna. I couldn't stop wanting to hear that longing in your voice, making me feel that you'd really cared and that I'd been wrong. I wanted to be wrong."

"It's already difficult to think of you as having been Tanya. It's as if she were some other person I met in London and now she's just, I don't know, *gone*."

"She *is* gone. I liked a lot about being her, but now I'm glad she's gone. Did you know I thought you preferred her to Anna?"

"Are you serious? I'm not into women closer to my son's age than mine. Ever. My attraction to Tanya was always to the Anna in her. What about you? You liked looking young again? You look fantastic now."

"I looked the same with my clothes off then as I do now, you know. I mean, my body's younger looking than it was six months ago because I've worked out so much, but still, I had my original body all along, which is probably all that kept Tanya from trying to seduce you. And I couldn't have done that. It's one thing when the carpets don't match the drapes, but when the upper story's been renovated while the foundation's crumbling . . ."

"Mmmm. Lovely house, though. Let's see if the door—"

His hand stopped sliding up her thigh as the phone rang. He reached for the receiver and Anna sat up, the spell broken.

"Right . . . right . . . okay. Do you want to speak to her?" He handed her the phone, mouthing the word *Barnes*.

She spoke briefly, then hung up. "My cell phone got a text back from Marina. She's arriving in Rome Saturday morning."

"Game on, eh?" David's expression was solemn.

Feeling suddenly cold, Anna reached for her clothes and swung her legs over the side of the bed. "I'm going to put on my nightgown so we can watch the news. We should catch up with the outside world, shouldn't we?"

"Everything all right?"

She nodded. "Everything's fine. Really. Just pissed off at the spooks barging into the bedroom."

"Hey," he said gently, "tomorrow's another day, and we're going to be here together all day long."

"And have I got plans for you, David Wainwright." She grabbed her pillow and threw it at his head.

He caught it, grinning. Then he said seriously, "I do still love you, you know."

"I love you, too, David. I always have."

He reached for his trousers. "Let's uncork that wine then. I think we have something to celebrate."

Chapter 23

"What exactly did Barnes say? If you can tell me that," David said a while later, as he and Anna sprawled on the sofa, not really concentrating on Sky News.

"Of course I can tell you. I doubt even they would expect me to ask their permission. Marina texted back that she's flying to Rome Saturday morning, so Barnes—as me—set up a meeting for three in the afternoon. She said she's bringing a fresh supply of **YOUNGER** and that I absolutely mustn't even touch the **YOUNGER** I have left, because the lab needs it to be sure which formula I've been using. Total BS."

"So she thinks you have the dregs and are desperate to get more," David noted. "Desperate people are easier to fool, aren't they?"

"Hey, I was, wasn't I? Barton hooked me effortlessly."

"Con artists bank on other people's insecurities," David remarked. "Komarov knew that about Pierre. And Pierre helped your age work against your judgment."

Before the meeting had broken up that afternoon, Anna had finally pressured "the guys downstairs" into showing her the text Marina had received:

Using YOUNGER only every 3 days. Down to only a teaspoon of each product! PLEASE, can you bring more to me in Rome? Sorry I've let you down, but I thought I saw Kelm following me and was scared. ASAP, PLEASE. Anna.

She told David, then remarked, "I guess if you didn't know I knew what was going on, it would seem legit."

"Obviously, they told us the truth," he replied. "Marina needs those residues or **YO**UNGER is out of her grasp, and Russia's, forever."

"Andrew must be pretty sure Komarov is hacking into Marina's phone, my phone, everybody's phone, and will be on her heels," Anna said. "Oh, God, I'll be a sitting duck."

David looked very worried but then, for her sake, she thought, he tried for humor. "Showdown at the O.K. Corral, lady."

"What a terrible American accent! And you clearly were never a cowboy movie fan: the title started with *Gunfight*. Which we are *not* going to be having."

"I grew up on ever-so-polite British espionage films, where spies said things like, 'Ever so sorry I must tie you up, Sir Roderick.'" He reached for her. "But I can tell you about that tomorrow."

"Today, darling. It's almost one in the morning."

"Say that again."

"It's almost one—"

"No, not that."

"Today, darling?"

"Just 'darling' will do." He stood up, pulling her to her feet. "Your bed or mine?"

"Oh, mine. We don't want those snoops discovering only one bed's being slept in, do we?"

———

The next morning over breakfast, Anna found **YOU**NGER and the ill-fated Pierre Barton nagging at her thoughts.

"Poor Pierre," she said suddenly. "You know, I never think of him anymore without the word *poor* in front of his name? I know he wanted things for the wrong reasons, I know he lied and that people died as a result, but I still sympathize with him. I still *like* him. He had every break in the world, yet he couldn't stop wanting to be something he wasn't."

"Which was?"

"That's what's so sad. He wanted to be a success like his father. But his father *wasn't* a success, not a real one. That's what makes him a tragic figure."

"Too lightweight for true tragedy, if you ask me. Ambition made him stupid, just as it made his wife greedy." He stretched. "And there will be tragedy ahead for me if I don't start going over that script I need to storyboard. Since we're stuck here waiting, I should get to work."

Back in her room, Anna sat at the writing desk and started going over her notes on the computer yet again. Everything was at her fingertips, yet the solution was evading her. What was she missing? If only she had more faith in Barnes and Etherington! But she feared she couldn't rely on anyone else.

When she and David broke for lunch, they were both distracted and hardly spoke, lost in their own thoughts. One of the thoughts nibbling at Anna's brain was the question of David. Were they still in love or had they just played out the drama of their reunion as romantically as possible? Did she want to be with someone who lived in another country, who had a son? And why should she take it for granted he wanted her? Could his thoughts be much the same as hers, uncertain? She pushed them away and ate with a haste springing more from her wish to be alone again than from hunger. She should worry more about keeping her life than about with whom she'd be spending it.

When she was back in her room afterward, feeling cranky, she decided a nap might reboot her brain. It was quiet outside, so she opened the shutters to let in some crisp October air and sunlight; then, when she lay on the bed, she hissed as that light shone straight into her eyes.

Irritably, she went into the bathroom to rifle through her toiletries bag. She had a sleep mask somewhere, but where was the damned thing? The last time she remembered wearing it was on the train from Paris. She hoped she hadn't left it in her couchette.

She dragged her backpack out from the armoire, and, *eureka*, there it was, in an inside pocket. She felt something else there, too, something bulky, and pulled it out. It was the sheaf of photocopies she'd gotten from Nelson Dwyer, the CCTV photos from the minutes surrounding Olga's doing a header under that incoming Underground train. She'd completely forgotten about them. Even if they did show Kelm was there, that was something they all suspected anyhow, so they hadn't seemed important.

Still, since she was wide awake now, she figured she might as well look through them again. The sleep mask dangling from her wrist, she plumped up the pillows on the bed and settled back. *Same old, same old,* she thought wearily. Here was Olga coming onto the platform; now she was rushing to the front; here were two guys in dark caps who may or may not have been together or following her; now Olga was gone and the guys weren't together anymore, as one was over there looking off to the left and one was over here, looking—

She gasped, then leaned forward into the light for a closer look. A magnifying glass would have helped, but she'd just have to trust her eyesight and her instincts.

Then she put the sheaf of papers aside.

"Tinker, tailor, murderer, spy," she murmured. Should she tell anyone what she'd just discovered? Did they know? Or, since it was her life they were putting on the line, was the wisest course to keep what she'd found to herself? Was anyone else *not* playing with a stacked deck? She'd keep her own counsel, she decided, at least until she heard what the SIS men decided to share tomorrow. If they chose to keep secrets, she could do the same.

She knew something they didn't. For the first time since she'd walked through the embassy's front door, she felt in control again. And that felt good.

She didn't tell David. When they compared notes of their day later on, she listened with unfeigned interest as he described how he went through a script with an eye toward blocking out the storyboards, but when he asked, "Come up with anything?" she shook her head. She did trust him, and him alone; still, for now it was her secret.

———————

"How do these look?" It was late Friday afternoon when Andrew, having left the conference room, returned with a bag from which he withdrew three small jars, which he set on the conference table.

Anna recognized them at once. "My Boots containers!"

"A courier was flying in from London this morning anyhow, so we had him bring these from Boots. Verisimilitude, you know. We've left about a teaspoon of product in each container: cleaner, moisturizer, and night cream."

"Could have fooled me. Now, can we go over tomorrow one more time—what's going to happen in Piazza Navona and what I'm supposed to do?"

"Certainly. You'll have these containers in a carrier small enough to fit in your shoulder bag. Marina will probably ask where you've been and if Kelm's been in touch with you. No reason to lie—I suspect Komarov knows by now you went to Prague, and what he knows, she might know. Marina's far from stupid. By now, if not before, she must have guessed how much blood he has on his hands and is probably steering clear of him, but one can't be sure. Regarding Pierre, if she asks, tell the truth: he collapsed and you panicked."

"And then?" she asked mildly, though she wanted to laugh out loud at how little these men understood Marina. As if she might take even the slightest interest in someone else's life! For super-spies, they didn't have a clue about women.

"In case she doesn't bring it up, ask if she's brought the products and what the arrangement will be to get more. Remember, you're desperate. We expect Komarov will be somewhere he can watch and wait for the handover so he can swoop in, snatch the products out of her hands, and take off, so we want you to get as much information out of Marina as you can before giving her anything." Andrew shook his head. "Marina doesn't need Komarov if she has the products, and vice versa. My educated guess is that they're now busily trying to betray each other. It's natural for Komarov to think he can get away with murder and the formula, as well."

"He'll be charged with the murders of the Rusakovs, Olga, and Pierre?" David asked the question she'd been about to pose.

Etherington had been silent. Now he spoke up. "In point of fact, no. The Russian couple? Well, spy versus spy, as you say. We'd have a hard time prosecuting even if we could prove it, so . . . no charges. The police will write it off as murder-suicide or a mob assassination. Olga, I fear, must remain among the anonymous dead. An arrest for the murder of a woman almost fifty years old when, as far as the police know, the body they have is that of some-one decades younger would raise far too many questions. A bird in the hand being worth two in the bush, Grigoriy Komarov will be charged with just one murder: the poisoning of Pierre Barton."

"Pierre was poisoned? Oh, God. How?" Though the news didn't come as a surprise, Anna was shaken.

Barnes took over. "He ingested or was injected with a lethal dose of tetrodotoxin. Difficulty breathing, thirst, sweating, immobility—you said Barton barely moved the whole time you were talking—whilst symptoms of a heart attack, are also present in tetrodotoxin poisoning. The someone he told you had almost knocked him down? Obviously, that was Komarov. You might recall the classic case of the dissident Bulgarian murdered in London? The ferrule of an umbrella was fitted up as a hypodermic to shoot the poison ricin into his system. The assassin got away; who notices a man simply walking along swinging his umbrella? The intelligence consensus was, and remains, that the killer and invention were Soviet. KGB, to be exact."

"Sorry," Anna said with some urgency, "but I'm more concerned about what I'll be doing than what was done by Soviet operatives years ago. Marina is now handing me the stuff she's brought, her version of the fake **YOU**NGER. I then take the bag out of my purse and give it to her?"

"Yes—and make sure you tell her about switching to the Boots containers in London because you were afraid of someone catching up with you if you had to flee."

"What if Komarov doesn't show up?"

Barnes laughed grimly. "The result will be the same: two more pissed-off Russians in the world. Grigoriy will be furious if he thinks Marina has the products and, with them, the reins of their deal. And she'll be beyond livid when she finds out the products are inexpensive everyday skincare. But he'll turn up. He's stayed on top of this, and he won't pass up the chance to grab the only **YOU**NGER in existence." His eyes gleamed, and again Anna was struck by his passion to see Komarov manacled and put away. "As far as we know, he's working alone, but don't let your guard down, Anna. Don't drink anything, eat anything, or touch anyone, no matter what. Got that?"

"Got it. And when Kelm shows up?"

Barnes shrugged. "Just try to stay calm. You won't see me, but I'll be there. As will David. And people with weapons. So"—he got to his feet—"that's it for today. Chips will come by at half past nine in the morning to say hello. I'll come with the sound team at half past one; they'll fix you with a wire and we'll check the transmission. Then David and I will leave you. You've got the schedule. At half past two, a taxi driven by one of our men will take you to Piazza Navona. You'll pay him, for the benefit of watchers, then sit at a table outside in the front row at Caffè Bernini. If there isn't one free, ask the waiter to put one out for you and tip him. You're a good actress, Anna; you'll know what to do."

———————

After an evening of slow and tender lovemaking that took Anna to even greater heights of ecstasy than the fiery passion of the preceding days, Anna expected to fall asleep easily. But long after she could hear David's breathing assume the measured calm of sleep, she lay wide awake, fearful and queasy. When she did doze off, she was startled awake by her dream in which a hand with a hypodermic needle came closer and closer as a voice murmured, "Just relax, Tanya. You'll be young for eternity now."

She must have groaned aloud, because David reached over in his sleep and took her hand. She unclenched her fist, lay back, and finally relaxed. With him holding her, she felt protected.

She could hear the water running in David's bathroom when she woke at eight, so she went to her own and showered, then carefully did her makeup, eschewing the deeper-hued items in favor of the softer "Anna" shades and roughing up her bob to turn it into a more youthful style. Her text had said she'd been using **YOU**NGER every three days, and, since she was begging to regain her youth, it made sense that she wouldn't have transitioned gracefully back into her old self but would be stuck between Anna and Tanya. She wore her black jodhpurs and a black jersey; she'd add her cardigan once the wire had been taped in place. She pulled on her UGGs, superstitiously telling herself that as long as she was prepared to run, she probably wouldn't be forced to.

David was seated at the table with tea and a newspaper when she entered the living room. He looked up, his face tense. "Yesterday's courier must have brought the Friday papers from London."

"Thanks. I'm not up for reading right now."

"Slow news period, anyhow."

"Let's hope it stays that way. As opposed to 'American Woman, Others Killed in Piazza Navona Shoot-Out.'"

"No one's getting killed," he said. "You look like Tanya's mum fallen on hard times, by the way. Here, have a cup of tea and ignore my anxiety. I'm used to directing thrillers, not appearing in them."

"I'm more eager to get it over with than anxious. I've been frightened for so long now, it's second nature." She was lying again, and to David this time, but she didn't want her anxiety to spread to him. Both their lives were still in danger: not only was she sure she now knew who the murderer was, but she was also positive that, while Barton had been sincere about Tanya's work schedule and pay plan, Martin Kelm had been generous with his offers of freedom whenever she wanted to quit for the simple reason that he planned, sooner or later, to kill her. A cooperative Tanya Avery would have resulted in an Anna Wallingham every bit as dead as an uncooperative Tanya Avery. She pushed away the thought and went on evenly, "I was lying awake last night thinking of how much has happened in such a short time. I can barely remember having been in Amsterdam, and that was only six weeks ago."

"And just over a week ago, I had no idea Anna Wallingham was still alive. So it's not all bad."

"I think you're actually excited today just because you get to hang out with the MI6 guys." She made her tone light.

"Well, that, too. Though it's fear as much as excitement. I can't sit back and enjoy being a spectator when you'll be smack in the middle of it."

There was a tapping, even more reticent than Malcolm's, at the door. "That must be Etherington," David said. "No, you eat. I'll get it."

Sir Charles looked carefree as ever, as though he were popping into someone's box at the races. "I won't be there this afternoon," he noted. "I leave that to the younger generation. Or generations, in my case. But I look forward to seeing you back here afterward. I'm sure you'll do us proud."

After he'd left, she turned to David. "Do you think he's forgotten I'm not a British citizen, or did he just use the first cliché that sprang to mind?"

———

There was a table free at the front of Caffè Bernini, so Anna didn't have to go through a whole pantomime with the waiter. She made a show of looking for her friend, checking out the other tables facing onto Piazza Navona and those behind. She saw a few obvious tourists, a dapper older man in a camel's hair jacket with an elegant woman in silk, a solitary man in a tweed hat with the bulbous, blue-veined nose of a serious drinker hunched over what appeared to be not his first double grappa, some suntanned Americans with Cokes and beers, but no Marina. Sitting at her front table, she scanned the piazza in an obvious way—figuring Anna the unknowing stooge would be so desperate to see Marina she wouldn't bother faking casualness. She looked at her watch; that, too, would seem natural. Still five minutes to go. Turning her head in a 270-degree arc, she saw no sign of David, Andrew, Kelm, or anyone else familiar.

Her heart lurched when she saw Barton's widow enter the square from the street on the right. She was wearing a sable jacket, even though she must have been sweltering in the mild weather. Could that be her idea of camouflage? Or was the aim to look like just another rich fashion maven on a spending spree, since she carried a couple of designer shopping bags? "Ah, Marina," she murmured as if to herself, barely loudly enough for the microphone taped to her breastbone to pick it up, waving discreetly in case she wasn't immediately recognizable as what she now thought of as Lisa/Tanya/Anna.

"Anna," Marina said when she got to the table. "I've been so worried!" she said unconvincingly while her eyes remained flinty. She sat in the chair to Anna's right, setting the bags, one large and one small, by her feet. "I am relieved now. It has been such hell for me. And the boys are, of course, distraught."

"The poor children," Anna said sympathetically. "Where are they?"

"In Russia, with my mother," came the reply, delivered with a dismissive wave of the hand. *Good old Marina,* Anna thought. "I will call you Anna, yes? What will you have? An *aperitivo,* yes? An Aperol spritz?"

"Campari soda, I think."

"Me also." She paused, staring into the square, her face unreadable. Then she got to her feet. "But not here." She picked up the bags. "Too gloomy, this place. Look at the sun shining on the other side of the piazza. Come, Anna, we must sit in the sunshine."

"Oh, but I—I got us such a good table!"

"Good for what?" Marina sniffed. "To sit and stare together at the sunny tables across from us?"

"No, but—" She felt herself melting under Marina's withering glare.

"Then why stay here? Well?"

Anna stood, slowly reaching for her bag and slinging it over her shoulder, fighting panic. Just what the day needed, she thought frantically, the wrong main actress deciding to improvise. She couldn't argue. She knew Marina; fighting her decision would strike the other woman as suspicious. And she was suspicious enough already. There was just one chance of walking away today with the entire BarPharm horror show behind her, and it didn't include refusing to indulge Her Highness.

Marina wasn't tapping her foot, but she might as well have been.

"You're right, as usual," Anna said with her warmest smile. "No wonder I was feeling chilly." She followed dutifully as Marina strode across the square and between the two famed fountains, then managed to elbow out of the way a startled young couple who'd been eyeing an outdoor table as it became free. *Oh, hell, not even in the front row. Stuck in the middle.* Anna's heart sank. Would anyone even be able to see her from across the piazza?

At least Marina was appeased, sighing in satisfaction as she set her bags down again, Anna noting that the large one bore a Gucci logo and the smaller that of Prada. "So, this is much better, yes?" Marina pronounced as she peremptorily flagged down a waiter and ordered two Campari and sodas. She plucked a pack of Benson & Hedges and a gold lighter from her Hermès handbag. "I smoke, yes?"

"I didn't know you smoked," Anna said.

"Pierre didn't like the smoking. So, no cigarettes around him. Now I smoke too much. And you? You don't look so good, Anna. The results don't last. This is good to know. You still have products, but you have not been using them, yes?"

"I cut back weeks ago to every three, four, five days at the most. You know, to stretch them out. Do I look just ancient? Did you bring me more?" She made her voice as frantic and pathetic as possible.

"No need to worry. I have them for you here, and I will provide them as long as you wish. You can even go back to the doctor again to start the full regime again if you wish." She was silent as the waiter set down their drinks, then continued in a severe tone. "But why did you leave so suddenly? I get to the hospital, and my husband is dead and Tanya gone!"

"It was because of that man, Martin Kelm," Anna said. "You know him?"

Marina nodded. "MI6 man," she lied glibly.

"Yes. Before he collapsed, Pierre was starting to tell me something—"

"And then he fell down, yes? You were thinking he wanted to warn you about Kelm?"

"I was afraid Kelm was in the street, watching. I couldn't go to the hospital; I panicked. I've been hiding ever since."

"So, Kelm is an English spy gone bad!" Marina gestured wildly with her cigarette, then tsk-tsked in irritation. "Now I have got my ashes in your drink! I must get you another." Quickly, she picked up Anna's glass in one hand and headed inside, taking the shopping bags with her. Well, trust had never been her strong suit.

As subtly as she could, Anna murmured, "Andrew, can you hear me? We're across the square now."

She took a deep breath. Was Martin Kelm in one of the apartments over this or another café, looking through a rifle scope at her blond hair shining in the sun?

Marina returned, a fresh drink in her hand, which she set unceremoniously in front of Anna. "Now, what were we saying? Ah, yes, Kelm. I must tell the police about this Kelm. Pierre trusted people too much."

Her eyes narrowed. "And your products, Anna?" she demanded. "You have them for me? What I brought is, I think, close to what you have. But I can give you something stronger next time."

"Oh, yes, that would be good. I brought what's left—not much but certainly enough to check the formula." How could she keep stalling without babbling? She opted for babbling. "I realize now more than ever how lucky I was to have participated in **YOUNGER**'s development. I hope you forgive me for leaving like that."

Marina nodded in satisfaction. "Yes. Good. So, now we are partners again, as we were fated to be. And here are your products." She reached for the small Prada paper tote at her feet and set it on the table next to her. "To our future. And to Pierre, of course." She reached for her glass.

Anna raised hers to toast, then set it down immediately to unzip her shoulder bag and fumble around in it. As she did so, she felt something jiggling inside her jersey. *The wire,* she thought. *The damned wire has pulled free from the transmitter! The others can't even hear me!* She froze in horror.

Marina took a sip, then set her glass down and sighed impatiently. "So, you have what's left of the products for me, yes?" she prompted.

"Yes, I do." Anna smiled as naturally as she could and held up the plastic Boots bag, then set it on the table next to her, opposite the Prada bag. "I transferred everything into these jars on the train out of London. The lab packaging was too obvious if someone chasing me went through my things."

"You feared Martin Kelm? Yes, of course."

"Oh, I wasn't worried solely about him," Anna said conversationally, meanwhile thinking *Okay, might as well go for broke now.* "I was more worried about you, you see." She had, as they said in the theater, just gone off-script. Now neither actress was playing her role as the director would like. Anna had gone rogue.

Marina stopped in the act of reaching for the Boots bag. "You were afraid of me? Why ever would you be afraid of me?"

"Well, you know, when I saw those CCTV photos of you on the platform at Oxford Circus the day Olga was killed—"

"Don't be ridiculous! I had nothing to do with that silly cow's suicide." She frowned. "Nor would I *ever* travel by Tube. What supposed pictures are these?"

"I got them from someone who had no doubt Olga had been given a helping hand onto the tracks," Anna replied calmly. "Good disguise. He thought you were a workman. I did, too, until I studied a photo in which you were looking down and saw your birthmark." Marina's hand went on autopilot to the back of her neck. "You must have been enraged when you realized Olga was going to ruin your plans, eh? Plus, you know," she continued in the same conversational tone, "I fibbed a little before. It wasn't something about Kelm that Pierre was about to tell me when he died; it was about you. Had he told you he'd destroyed the **YOUNGER** formula? Is that why you poisoned his cappuccino? You fooled him. He thought it was the hot coffee burning his mouth. But it was the toxin, wasn't it?"

"How dare you! You know very well Martin Kelm is a killer. Why do this, Anna? You are trying to blackmail me?" Marina shook her head and sneered. "I told Pierre you were trouble. You wish to prove me right when I'm the only one trying to help you?"

Anna reached out with both hands and ostentatiously switched her drink with Marina's. "All right. We'll drink then. To Pierre?"

"What are you doing with my drink? Have you lost your mind?"

Anna picked up the drink that had been Marina's. "Not at all. Let's toast, huh?" She had to fight now to keep her voice even. Surely, Marina had no intention of leaving her alive. Where in the hell was Andrew?

A softer tone came into Marina's voice. "Don't you want to be very rich, Anna? I can make you indescribably wealthy, you know."

"Is that what you told Pierre?"

Marina sneered as the mask fell. "Pierre was weak. Oh, you should have seen him repenting, saying he had no right to play God, sniveling that if people—even some amateur third-rate mafia spies—were going to die because of **YOUNGER**, then **YOUNGER** had to die." She snorted. "He thought I'd respect him for destroying the formulae that would make us billionaires! Did he tell you he was going to the police after he gave you the explanation he felt he 'owed' you? Can you believe that?"

"I can. Perhaps I understood him better than you did. But to *kill* him?"

"He destroyed everything without asking me! **YOU**NGER is mine, and Barton Pharmaceuticals will be, too, once that old bitch of a *maman* dies. *I* was the one waiting in the street, you idiot. I let myself into the flat with my own keys as soon as you left so I could take the products that were mine, too. I admit I underestimated you. Then I needed Mr. Kelm—to find you. But you found me instead, didn't you?" She stared impassively. "I must tell you, Anna, the hair is now too blond. You look like someone impersonating a rich Russian. But you will never be either, will you? I must also tell you I have a pistol with a silencer in my hand that's ready to fire. You will slump over like a woman who drinks too much, and I will be gone. Yes, the sable is a trifle warm and bulky but I like the inside pocket. And I am bored with your nonsense now."

"Weren't we going to drink to our reunion?" Anna said, with more bravado than she felt.

But before Marina could turn her answering hiss into words or a shot, a cheerful British voice boomed next to them, making them both jump. "Mrs. Barton! What a coincidence, running into you in Rome!"

Where in the name of God had David come from? And what did he think he was doing? She was sure she looked as shocked as Marina did.

"What—?" Fury and fear vied for prominence in Marina's widened eyes, but she regained control and looked up with cool detachment. "Mr. Wainwright, isn't it? The director? You have surprised me."

As if remembering his manners, he turned to Anna. "Sorry to interrupt, Ms . . . ?"

"Jones," she answered weakly. "Lisa Jones." She felt suddenly dizzy. Good God, was she about to get David killed, too?

"Mind if I join you?" he asked, but he was already pulling out the chair next to Marina and opposite Anna. "I hope I'm not intruding, but I don't know a soul in Rome, and this is such a coincidence!" He sounded chirpy and eager, an Englishman abroad thrilled to bump into someone from home.

"Why are you here?" Marina asked tersely. Anna could tell she was working at sounding normal, but it came out more Gestapo officer than grieving widow.

"Looking at location sites for a television series. And you?"

Marina sighed deeply, her right hand still hidden in the depths of her jacket's voluminous sleeve. "London, Moscow." She shook her head sadly. "So many memories of Pierre. When my friend Lisa called me to ask to meet in Rome for shopping, of course I said yes."

"Please"—David gestured—"drink your drinks. Don't wait for me. I'll order something when the waiter comes."

Anna raised the glass that had been Marina's and faked a sip; she'd watched the other woman drink from it, but she was taking no chances. She sat barely breathing as Marina picked up the glass that had been Anna's and raised it to her lips. Then she turned and let it slip from her grasp to shatter on the cobblestones, clear red liquid spreading in all directions. "*Ach, blyad!* Look what I've done." Marina reached down with her left hand to push the large pieces of glass out of the way.

"Don't!" Anna shouted but it was too late. Marina sat back up, her face drained of color. The hand she held up showed a trickle of red; she'd been nicked by the glass. "Oh, Anna." She sounded regretful. "*Tetrodotoxin.* So I will die, too. You'll be a murderer now. But you will die with me." Anna looked immediately to Marina's other hand and saw that the gun hadn't been an empty threat.

Anna froze. David didn't, but even as he reached out to grab Marina's arm, a man had already sprung up from behind, a man who was not Andrew Barnes but the grappa drinker Anna had noticed in the café across the square. He barked something in rapid-fire Russian as he reached smoothly around and took the gun from Marina's hand before anyone in the crowd had even noticed it. He pocketed it, then he pulled her gently but firmly back into her chair before removing his hat and nodding pleasantly to Anna and David, who were sinking shakily into their seats. The pale blond hair and icy blue eyes gave him away even if the bulbous prosthetic covered up his own distinctive nose. His other hand remained in his coat pocket.

"I was just telling Mrs. Barton I would have to shoot if she moved. I've been wanting to say that ever since I watched her push poor Olga onto the tracks." He smiled his bright fake smile at Marina's venomous look, then widened it to include Anna, drily continuing in his clipped British tones. "I couldn't help but overhear your conversation. Thank you for clearing me of Pierre Barton's murder, Ms. Wallingham. Much appreciated, I assure you. I take it you're wearing a wire now? That's what I'd have gone down for, you know: the death of poor Pierre."

"But Marina! We need an ambulance. She's dying!"

"Nonsense. She's far from dying." He shrugged. "A little cut. A little tetrodotoxin. Pffft. Our Marina is a chemist. She knows even with a normal dose, the victim has several hours to live. A speck in her bloodstream? She might feel slightly ill, but she'll survive. Unlike the husband she most probably doped with enough to kill several men."

Anna had to hand it to Marina. Her voice as she spoke to Komarov dripped with contempt, not fear. "Pierre always said, 'That Kelm is a nasty piece of work.' He knew you were rotten. But not me. I trusted you for the very reason I should have known better: I trusted you because you are Russian." She sounded almost sad. "I despair of my own people. I truly do."

Anna looked up to see Barnes emerging from inside the café, not looking especially pleased to have captured Pierre Barton's killer. "How nice to see you, Andrew," Anna said smartly. "You'll want to mop up that liquid with something. And be careful with the broken glass. It's swimming in tetrodotoxin." But Hulk #1 was already there, swabbing up the spillage with gauze held in a rubber-gloved hand and sticking that and the broken glass into the small evidence bag he held. It was all done so smoothly, no one in the café was paying attention.

"You! *Andrew?*" Only the sight of Barnes made Marina lose her cool. "Who the hell are you?" She started to get up but was held in her seat by Grigoriy Komarov.

"You're so clever you hired an MI6 agent to be your husband's keeper," Anna said, her voice trembling but triumphant. "He was the real thing, your Aleksei—only, not for your side."

"Sorry, Anna." Andrew sounded like one of those polite British film spies now. "I don't know why she suspected we were ready for her at the other café."

After a pause, Marina said, "You should know those of us genuinely from cold climates always seek the sun, fool." Her voice was diminished now, as if she was just starting to grasp the prognosis of her situation.

Andrew smiled mildly. "Be nice to me and we'll get you medical treatment." She spat on the ground next to the table, then, with head held high, she let the Hulk escort her to the black Range Rover that had materialized in the pedestrian piazza.

"And now, my friends, I, too, must be on my way," said Komarov, his voice still not betraying any accent other than well-bred English. "My role in this tiny farce has come to an end. I'll just take my bag"—he picked up the Boots bag with the hand not in his pocket—"and move along. Whatever it is that Mrs. Barton hoped to pass off as **YOU**NGER I leave with you as a souvenir."

"Not so fast," Barnes said, the ferocity of his voice assuring Anna that Komarov was the big game he'd been chasing all along with this little scenario. The Russian just chuckled.

"Sorry, Mr. Barnes, but I worked very hard to win this formula for my country. And my gun is still in my hand. Right now it's pointed at Ms. Wallingham, whom, as you heard, I just rescued from a would-be killer and who will now accompany me to the edge of the piazza. She's beautiful at any age." He smiled brightly. "It would be a shame to lose her. So this is indeed *adieu*."

He gestured to Anna with his chin. "Come along now." As she stood, David, too, started to get to his feet but sat down again when she shook her head at him.

She didn't fear Komarov. He had no reason to kill her now. If anything, she was glad for a few minutes with him as they walked slowly across the piazza. "And my friend?" she asked without preamble. "Who killed Jan Berger?"

"Ah, your California friend hit by the car, yes? Not me, Miss Wallingham. If I were you, I would ask myself, *Cui bono?* Who profits? That's most often where the answer lies." They'd reached the sidewalk, where an Alfa Romeo sedan slid up beside them. He bowed formally and smiled. "It's been a pleasure."

The car, with Grigoriy Komarov inside it, drove off. Anna turned around and headed back toward the café as David ran to meet her.

———

"That's it. He's gone," Anna told Barnes when she and David reached a different table at the café, where he sat waiting with three glasses of white wine, a uniformed technician already kneeling by the other table to clear up the last remains of the broken glass and wash away the spillage while other security types spoke to the waiters.

"You already knew he'd be able to walk away. And why not? He was just a man walking out of a piazza in Rome carrying a Boots bag." Andrew's tone was unusually bitter, telling Anna how badly he had wanted to be able to seize Komarov for Pierre's murder. Poor Pierre. At least he was the victim that counted. He gestured toward the larger shopping bag that was now by his feet. "He left us not only Marina's fake products but also the sweater and wallet she picked up at Gucci and Prada. Nothing like a wee bit of retail therapy before murder, is there? Cold-blooded as they come, the Widow Barton. And *you*? Seeing her birthmark? *Still* keeping evidence from Secret Intelligence Service? Are you insane?"

"You heard everything? The wire never came loose completely?"

"I could hear you until David here chivalrously jumped up and ran out and I had to call for reinforcements and hope not to blow the whole op or have you both killed. I can understand his impulsiveness in trying to rescue you, but I'd like to hear your explanation for the little charade you planned unbeknownst to us, Anna."

She took a long swallow of her wine. Her mouth was like cotton. What torture it had been avoiding the Campari and soda she'd been so sure Marina had poisoned. "Once I realized yesterday that she'd killed Olga, the pieces started falling into place. I figured she'd have to kill me at some point. I was a liability, wasn't I?" She shrugged.

"But I knew damned well that if I didn't do something, she might be the one waltzing out of here since you'd be in a great big hurry to grab Komarov," she said, not defiantly but not apologetically, either. "That's what you wanted, wasn't it? Getting him for Pierre's murder so you could take your nemesis out of the field? He did kill the Rusakovs, I suppose?"

Barnes frowned, but, like the pro he was, he swallowed his bitter medicine with good grace. "I'd say certain but hard to prove. In the car, I heard Pierre tell Marina you thought you'd been followed. We found Galina and Pavel and monitored their hotel room. I doubt they had a clue Marina had killed Olga, either. But she was a link to exploit, so they threatened to go to the police about Olga's death. They wanted the formula, of course. Galina called Marina to arrange a meeting for what would turn out to be the day after their deaths. Odds are Marina got her old buddy Grigoriy on it, faked murder-suicides being a Komarov specialty. Then, once Pierre had destroyed the formula and products, Grigoriy was superfluous. Marina seized the opportunity to throw him under the bus for Pierre's killing while she got the remains of your products. Or perhaps she had that in mind all along."

"Would Marina have gotten away with it if I hadn't figured out she was the killer?"

"It would depend on how sharp that CCTV photo of her birthmark is and how good an attorney she got. We slipped up by not studying the police tapes more closely before. Yes, we had them. And now we have her admissions on tape. None of which makes me look particularly good. I don't approve of the way you did it, Anna, but"—he nodded abruptly—"nice work."

"And now?" David asked. "If this were my film, I'd close with a tracking shot of Komarov walking merrily out of the piazza, then zoom in slowly on the precious Boots bag."

Barnes chuckled humorlessly. "Filled with remnants of actual Boots the Chemist skincare products. Poor Grigoriy. A black mark against one of the espionage game's top pros. He really should have known better."

This was, Anna saw, how Barnes would console himself, with the fact that his enemy had at least tarnished his reputation. "Same old story, isn't it?" she said. "Komarov's lust for **YOUNGER** blinded him to reason. Barton was right, you know. He wasn't the type to play God. He died for nothing in the long run. They all did, didn't they? There is no **YOUNGER** now, and no one will know there ever was. Those thousands upon thousands of women who would have bought it will never have a clue how close they were to their dream."

"I wouldn't worry about them," David said thoughtfully. "They're going to go on as they were before, just as you're going to go on, and Andrew is, and I am. That's life, isn't it? Getting older day by day and learning to live with it. Not so bad considering the alternative, I'd say."

She reached over and, smiling, took his hand. "Not bad at all."

Epilogue

Six Months Later

Anna Wallingham agreed to a hefty payout of £500,000 upon the dissolution of her contract with BarPharm. The payout was signed off on by her good friend Marie Héloise Barton. Madame Barton took over Barton Pharmaceuticals when her former daughter-in-law was charged with the murder of Pierre, who had died from ingesting one of several toxins British intelligence had long suspected Sybyska Chemicals of dealing in illegally. Madame Barton paid the other Mrs. Barton a fire-sale price for her shares. Moscow is in continuing negotiations with the UK as they seek extradition of their loyal citizen. Marina Sybyska Barton is awaiting the result from her cell in England. She rarely asks about her children.

A week after Marina's arrest, Becca Symonds and Chas Power received postcards from New York at their office in central London. The writer apologized for her sudden disappearance. "It's a long story," each read. "Shorter version: I was scared. I'm fine now and just wanted to say how great it was working with you. xox, Tanya." There was no return address.

Anna Wallingham currently resides in her house in Studio City, California, where, having decided it was time to live up to the fiction she'd created and falling back upon her skills as a copywriter, she is hard at work finishing the rough draft of her first novel, the one she kept telling people she was going to write. Her old friends all tell her that her long holiday took ten years off her looks; her new friends tell her they're sorry it took so long for them to get to know one another. Anna spends a great deal of her time with those she loves best, Allie Moyes and Richard Myerson. The former was recently promoted to full partner at Creativity Management while the latter is vice president and general manager of Coscom USA, where he reports to president and major stockholder Clive Madden.

After a surprise arrest, George Berger was found guilty of having hired two men whom he'd flown from Los Angeles to London for the purpose of killing his wife, Jan, in a hit-and-run. The demand for his backlisted novels increased enough for all of them to be republished; this earned his agent, Allie, a very nice bonus.

David Wainwright is directing the second season of his new television series in London. He spends most of his free time with his son, Nick, to whom he's a devoted father. He calls Anna Wallingham often, as she calls him. Neither is behaving impetuously. They have set a date to meet, in just one more month, in Paris. When they talk, Anna can tell David is as nervous as she is. Can it all work out? This time, she's sure he wants it to as much as she does. She hopes they have both changed enough and that their love is strong enough for them to find a way to be a couple. She also knows that no matter what happens, she has laid to rest her demons and will no longer confuse independence with fear of letting someone in.

A month after Berger's trial ended, Anna received a postcard of her own, this one from Moscow.

Cui bono? Who profits? He who gains is always the obvious suspect: now you know who killed your friend. And he with access is always the obvious thief: that's how I know who has the **YOU**NGER formula. And if you think about it, so shall you, clever Anna. I look forward to our meeting again. I have no doubt that we will.

The obvious thief? It struck her like lightning, and she couldn't believe that she'd missed it. In her mind's eye, the window of a big blue car smoothly slid partly down and a chauffeur's hand emerged, holding a small, plain brown kraft-paper tote bag. That hand had baited a trap not with cheese but with Anna Wallingham. Had Andrew done it from greed or for country? She might never know but had faith that patriotism was the sole motivation and that **YOU**NGER would, in the end, help those who needed it to accomplish something worthwhile.

She couldn't help but smile at the impudence of the message sent by the man who had once planned to kill her. When she turned the card over, she wasn't surprised to see Lucian Freud's self-portrait, that searing study of the dissolution of the flesh caused by time.

Acknowledgments

Writing a novel is a solitary effort enriched by the kindness of others. I'm grateful for all those who offered their time, opinions, ideas, and support. The tireless reading and astute comments of Michele Thyne, Julie Logan, Alice Jay, Paul Mungo, and Kathy Kirkland helped immeasurably, as did the suggestions and enthusiasm of Jeremy Poole, Michael Oliver, Sally O'Sullivan, Dermot Keating, Josef and Ingrid Brunner, Frank and Gaie Burnet, Brendan O'Donnell, Max Grünig, Robert Yates, Vince Cappa, Mary Atherton, Elizabeth Wholey, Cara Robin, Ivan Teobaldelli, and Ruth Allen. Special thanks to Dianna Whitley for her photography as well as her valued story suggestions.

If not for Victoria Sanders, Bernadette Baker-Baughman, and the entire staff at Victoria Sanders & Associates, who believed in this book from the moment they read it, the pages might have ended up in a drawer in Berlin, where I did most of the writing. For making it all happen, I thank both Kjersti Egerdahl at Thomas & Mercer for acquiring the manuscript and Nancy Brandwein for her diligent editing: these last steps made a dream reality.

And, finally, I want to thank the professional beauty industry in which I worked and acquired Anna's skincare and marketing

expertise, and the town of Città di Castello, Italy, repository of a
cultural and creative spirit that never ceased to inspire me in the
eight years I lived within its walls.

About the Author

Suzanne Munshower is a former waitress, short-order cook, go-go girl, movie extra, celebrity interviewer, journalist, fashion columnist, advertising copywriter, and beauty industry publicist. The author of numerous fiction and nonfiction books, she's lived in New York, Los Angeles, San Juan, St. Thomas, London, Berlin, and Città di Castello, Italy. She currently resides in Las Vegas. For more about Suzanne Munshower and *Younger*, go to www.suzannemunshower.com.